Praise for ON OCEAN BOULEVARD

"Like so many of you, I start my summer season with the enchanting novels of Mary Alice Monroe. I'm a devoted fan of her magical depictions of the Lowcountry and the charms of her characters."

—Elin Hilderbrand, #1 *New York Times* bestselling author of *28 Summers*

"An excellent addition to a popular series by a bestselling author. Readers of Mary Kay Andrews and Dorothea Benton Frank should feel at home."

—*Library Journal*

"This is a heartwarming story of Lowcountry love, loyalty, and long-standing friendships. . . . The resilience of the Rutledge family is stronger than ever. Infusing her story with respect for the local flora and fauna, Monroe continues her focus on environmental conservation in her latest multigenerational story of the Rutledge women."

—*Booklist*

"Love the characters, love the setting, love the story! Mary Alice Monroe has written another delightful addition to her immensely popular Beach House Series. Place this one on your nightstand or in your beach bag. It's a perfectly charming and comfortable escape."

—*Blue Stocking Reviews*

"Mary Alice Monroe's latest release, *On Ocean Boulevard*, checks all the boxes . . . Amid all the personal happenings, it is loggerhead nesting season, a special time for the family that goes back generations. Like these majestic creatures, the Rutledges are also going through a cycle of rebirth and returning home."

—*Grand Strand Magazine*

"*On Ocean Boulevard* is a beautiful story of love and family, new beginnings, and learning to live in the present instead of the past. As with all of Mary Alice's books, her love of the environment shines through her novel. . . . I highly recommend this book!"

—*Girl Who Reads*

Praise for THE SUMMER GUESTS

"Fast-paced and fluid . . . heartache as well as joy make this a most enjoyable read."

—*New York Journal of Books*

"Authentic, generous, and heartfelt!"

—Mary Kay Andrews, *New York Times* bestselling author

Also by Mary Alice Monroe

BEACH HOUSE SERIES
Beach House Memories
Beach House for Rent
Beach House Reunion

LOWCOUNTRY SUMMER SERIES
The Summer Girls
The Summer Wind
The Summer's End
A Lowcountry Wedding

STAND-ALONE NOVELS
The Summer Guests
A Lowcountry Christmas
The Butterfly's Daughter
Last Light over Carolina
Time Is a River

ON OCEAN BOULEVARD

Mary Alice Monroe

GALLERY BOOKS

New York   London   Toronto   Sydney   New Delhi

Gallery Books
An Imprint of Simon & Schuster, Inc.
1230 Avenue of the Americas
New York, NY 10020

First Gallery Books trade paperback edition June 2021

GALLERY BOOKS and colophon are registered trademarks of Simon & Schuster, Inc.

For information about special discounts for bulk purchases, please contact Simon & Schuster Special Sales at 1-866-506-1949 or business@simonandschuster.com.

The Simon & Schuster Speakers Bureau can bring authors to your live event. For more information or to book an event, contact the Simon & Schuster Speakers Bureau at 1-866-248-3049 or visit our website at www.simonspeakers.com.

Interior design by Davina Mock-Maniscalco

Manufactured in the United States of America

10 9 8 7 6 5 4 3 2 1

The Library of Congress has cataloged the hardcover edition as follows:

Names: Monroe, Mary Alice, author.
Title: On Ocean Boulevard / by Mary Alice Monroe.
Description: First Gallery Books hardcover edition. | New York : Gallery Books, 2020. |
    Series: The beach house series
Identifiers: LCCN 2019060271 (print) | LCCN 2019060272 (ebook) | ISBN 9781982146948
    (hardcover) | ISBN 9781982147006 (paperback) | ISBN 9781982146955 (ebook)
Subjects: LCSH: Domestic fiction.
Classification: LCC PS3563.O529 O5 2020 (print) | LCC PS3563.O529 (ebook) |
    DDC 813/.54—dc23
LC record available at https://lccn.loc.gov/2019060271
LC ebook record available at https://lccn.loc.gov/2019060272

ISBN 978-1-9821-4694-8
ISBN 978-1-9821-4700-6 (pbk)
ISBN 978-1-9821-4695-5 (ebook)

ODYSSEY

The sea is thick and murky.
Can you see me?
I am propelled forward,
swept in spiraling, swift water.

The Great Current carries me.
It writhes along the coastline,
swirls around the great gyre,
churns past vast Sargassum weed.

The current snakes from south to north.
A supernatural force
pushing me forward.
Always onward.

I am a loggerhead.
I've journeyed far in this vast ocean,
servant to my magnetic compass.
Now a voice calls to me in the current.

It is the voice of my ancestors.
An instinct that has guided mothers,
generation after generation,
for two hundred million years.

I heed the call.
I spread my beautiful flippers as
strange forces gain strength in my soul,
compelling me westward.

Light shimmers above,
then grows dark.
Aqua to indigo,
over and over on this odyssey.

Hunger gnaws at my belly
as I swim through the broth
of drifting plankton. I push past
gangly, gliding invertebrates.

Beyond the wreckfish and sea bream
that share space beneath a gilt rock
laden with pink coral
and bright anemones.

I am riding a river of current,
sliding in watery thermals
warmed by the sun,
powered by the earth's rotation.

I am soaring through liquid wind,
returning to the beach of my birth.
I am swimming . . . swimming . . .
swimming home.

Mary Alice Monroe

Chapter One

The lowcountry, also known as the low country, is, as the name implies, a low-lying area along the South Carolina Atlantic coast. This area is rich with unique culture, geography, architecture, economy, cuisine . . . and stories.

THE LOWCOUNTRY WAS spread out far below as she soared in the sky. Linnea Rutledge sighed and placed her fingertips on the plane's cool window, her eyes tracing the twisting creeks and winding rivers that snaked through the seemingly impenetrable greenery of the salt marsh. From her vantage point, the rivers looked like great arteries, and all the myriad creeks were veins. Salt water coursed through them like a bloodstream. The tides were the lowcountry's pumping heart.

As the plane descended, bringing the landscape closer and closer, Linnea felt that salt water thrumming in her own veins, as it did for all who called the lowcountry home. Her connection to the landscape—and its crown jewel, Charleston—was as vital as an umbilical cord.

She should be happy returning to her home, her family, her friends.

Instead, she felt demoralized. A failure, both professionally and personally. Two years earlier Linnea had headed west in a great show of independence. She'd won out over hundreds of applicants for a job with an environmental startup company in San Francisco. To add to her status, she was accompanied by her new beau, defying her parents, and convinced she was in love. Only to lose her job and be dumped by her boyfriend. She wasn't sure which she was more embarrassed about—losing her job, or losing her boyfriend, or just returning home with her tail between her legs.

Linnea had visited only three times during her two years away, twice for Christmas and once for the wedding of a friend. She liked San Francisco. The great city by the Pacific was a thriving, beautiful, intellectually stimulating place. But she'd been homesick for the Atlantic Ocean. For the slower pace of Charleston with its southern culture, its rich history, the narrow cobblestone streets she knew by heart, the weather-washed pastel colors of the old South, the clip-clop of horse carriages, and the smell of jasmine surprising you as you walked past a walled garden. And the food. Barbecue and sweet tea, collards and shrimp. Her empty stomach growled at the thought.

Her ex-boyfriend, John Peterson, had accompanied her home each time. A southern boy himself, he'd spent his summers on Isle of Palms and was always glad to join her and visit his childhood friends and, of course, his mother, Emmi Baker. She was her aunt Cara's best friend and neighbor. Linnea and John used to laugh that their relationship had seemed almost incestuous. But John was always antsy to head back to the West Coast. That's where he'd made his home and planned to stay. They'd still been deep in the throes of romance when attending the Charleston wedding the previous summer. Linnea had watched the bride walk down the aisle, then looked up at John dreamily. Her first clue should have been that he wasn't looking back at her.

The plane landed with a graceless thump, bounced, then glided down the runway to a stop. En masse, the sound of clicking seat belts filled the air as passengers reached for their phones. Linnea's legs felt wobbly as she dragged her carry-on suitcase into the terminal. She craved a bathroom, a face wash, and strong coffee, in that order. Her reflection in the mirror made her burst out a quick laugh. Her eyes were puffy from tears and lack of sleep, her skin chalky, and her shoulder-length blond hair was falling out of the tenuous hold of a scrunchie. The neighboring sinks were being used by women with the same idea as her. Digging into her large bag, she pulled out supplies. She splashed her face with cool water, then quickly ran a toothbrush across her teeth and a hairbrush through her hair. She applied moisturizer, a quick stroke of blush, and lip gloss, then reassessed herself.

She'd always been considered pretty in the classic southern belle style, with her small stature, blond hair, and blue eyes, a clone of her grandmother, Olivia Rutledge, a comparison that pleased her. Her Charleston accent was delicately southern, her social manners deeply ingrained. Today, however, even after her quick primp, she looked tired, a bit ragged around the edges. Her retro 1940s high-waisted capris were wrinkled from the long plane flight. At least her nautical striped top still looked fresh. She adjusted the navy bow. *Oh well*, she thought, turning away from the mirror. She didn't have anyone to impress.

Stepping outside the airport's glass sliding doors, Linnea paused and took deep breaths of the April air. It felt moist and delicious. Everything was so fresh and green here. She lifted her face to the sun, relieved and grateful to be out of the cramped, stuffy airplane and the staleness of airport terminals. She could feel her pores open under the sunlight and her cells tingle. A rush of excitement flowed through her. She was home. In a few months' time summer would descend and the scorching heat and humidity would be unbearable, the mosquitoes beastly, but now everything felt heavenly.

A shiny black Hyundai pulled up to the curb in front of her. Linnea checked the model and license plate against the order on her phone. It wasn't a fancy car, but opening the door she saw that it was roomy and obviously well-tended by the middle-aged man driving it. A bottle of chilled water had been thoughtfully placed in the back seat, as well as a *Charleston* magazine, though a few months old with curling edges. She made a mental note to leave a generous tip for the effort. She leaned back against the cushion with a weary sigh. Now all she had to do was sit and she'd be home. The car accelerated and she smiled. She was on her way to Sullivan's Island.

The address she'd given the driver had felt strange on her tongue. It was the first time she'd come home since her family had sold the house in Charleston. Linnea had been born and raised in the Rutledge House on Tradd Street. The lovely Charleston single with the two-story piazza had been purchased by her grandparents, then handed down to her father. The stately home was within walking distance of Charleston Harbor and had an impressive walled garden. The garden had been her grandmother Lovie's passion and been included in the city's garden tours for years.

Tradd Street was named for Robert Tradd, the first white child to be born in Charles Town. Names were important in Charleston, more important than the address where one lived. Linnea's father, Palmer, was a Rutledge, one of the great historic families of the old South. Even today, the names Rutledge, Middleton, Huger, Pinckney, Tradd,

Calhoun, Legare, Ball, and Pringle raised eyebrows. These great names were passed down from one generation to another, heavy with hyphens. She'd been given the name Linnea Lee Rutledge. Her brother was Cooper Pringle Rutledge. Many of her friends had some combination of these historic names. Linnea never thought of this as snobbishness; rather, it pointed to their deep connection to the city, its significant history. It revealed their roots.

So it felt odd for her to not be taking the road into the heart of the peninsula, to the renowned South of Broad, but rather to cross over the imposing Ravenel Bridge high above the Cooper River to Mount Pleasant. In truth, Linnea wouldn't miss the house, despite its beauty and the prestigious address. Maybe her bedroom, she amended, with the gabled ceiling, the carving in the doorframe that marked her growth, the elaborate dollhouse she could never let go of, and all the nooks and crannies in the old house that only a child who grew up there could know. Still, she'd always preferred living at the beach. In this, too, she was like her grandmother and her aunt Cara, who despised the Rutledge house and called it haunted.

She glanced at her watch, then made a quick call to her parents. She'd been disappointed that they had an engagement they couldn't break and didn't pick her up at the airport. The call went to the answering machine; her parents were still out. Linnea didn't want to sit in an empty house, waiting. She chewed her lip and looked out at the vista as a new thought blossomed. As much as she loved her mother and father, missed them, having to live with them in the smaller beach house would give her precious little room to hide.

She made a quick decision. "Excuse me," she called out to the driver. He turned his head a bit to hear better. "Yes, ma'am?"

"I'd like to change the address of where to drop me off."

"You don't want to go to Sullivan's Island?"

"No. I want to go to Isle of Palms. I'll give you the address."

"I'll have to change the fare," he said over his shoulder.

"No problem; it's next door to Sullivan's Island. It shouldn't be much of a difference." Pulling out a pen and paper, she wrote down the address, then handed it over to the driver.

He reached around to take hold of the paper, frowning with worry. When they stopped at a light, he punched the address into his GPS.

"I can guide you," she told him.

He either didn't hear her or ignored her. She leaned forward and kept an eye on where the car was headed, ready to call out directions. But his GPS was doing a fine job leading him down Highway 17 past the Towne Centre shopping plaza, then turning toward the Connector, an aptly named long stretch of road that rose over the marshes to reach the island. It was low tide, and Linnea smiled at the sight of the vast acres of Spartina grass, signs of bright spring-green shoots at the roots. Here and there, white egrets stood like lone sentinels in the mud.

Over the waterway, the sun was beginning its slow descent in the western sky. The sky was the color of amber, streaked with shades of purple, gold, and sienna. The last rays of the day's sun pierced the palette like an exuberant brushstroke.

"Could you slow down a minute, please?" she asked the driver as they neared the apex of the road. She scooted forward in her seat. "Look at that sunset."

He did so, almost slowing to a stop. His pinched face relaxed, and he seemed as enthralled by the sight as she was.

"It is very beautiful," the driver said in heavily accented English.

She smiled at the awe in his voice. "I don't think there is a more beautiful sunset anywhere else in the world."

"I, uh, have to speed up now, okay? The car behind me . . ." he said by way of apology.

"Of course. Thank you. It was a moment."

Linnea had seen countless sunsets in her life, yet they never failed to stun her. It was the surprise of it. They had the power to literally take her breath away. She remembered Grandmama Lovie telling her that a sunset was daily proof that God existed. As usual, her grandmother was correct. Seeing a sunset, Linnea felt connected both to the earth below and God above.

Linnea began tapping her foot in excitement as the car crossed through the light at the foot of the Connector, and they were on the island. Before she could speak, the driver had sped across the intersection, then turned onto Ocean Boulevard. She would have advised him to go a different route to avoid the traffic. As expected, they slowed to a crawl along Front Beach, where restaurants and beach shops clustered. But she was in no hurry and enjoyed the sight of vacationers on spring break strolling along the street.

There were elderly couples taking their time looking at the shop windows or checking out menus. Little children were licking ice cream cones. Lovers walked hand in hand. Cars filled every parking space, and those searching for one crept at a snail's pace. At last they broke free of the strip of shops, and the car moved at a steady pace through the residential section of Ocean Boulevard. They passed one pastel-colored mansion after another, which formed a wall bordering the ocean. Linnea remembered Lovie explaining how when she was young, there were far fewer houses on the island and one could see long stretches of sand and sea from the road.

"Turn here," she said to the driver, leaning far forward and pointing. "The road dead-ends ahead."

In a few short blocks, she spotted Primrose Cottage. It appeared shadowy in the darkening sky. No lights were on. That small, charming cottage had been Lovie's sanctuary. At the beach house, Olivia Rutledge had felt free to enjoy her own interests at her own pace. To live a simpler life. This was a gift she'd shared with her daughter, Cara. And her granddaughter, Linnea.

A jungle of shrubs and trees filled the empty lot to the house's left; Flo and Emmi's Victorian, blue with coral-colored bric-a-brac, was resplendent on the right. These two vintage homes were wedged on the block between mansions, a glimpse from a time long gone.

"This it?" the driver asked, a tone of disappointment in his voice. No doubt he'd expected to pull into one of the impressive estate houses.

"Yes, you can go right up to the porch."

He took it slow up the patchy oyster-shell driveway dotted with a few puddles from an earlier rain, and came to a stop near the front walk. *At last,* Linnea thought, and sprang from the car. Her eyes devoured the house.

In early spring, the property looked a bit shabby to the unknowing eye. But one who'd grown up on a barrier island saw the natural beauty of a place where there was more sand than soil. Lovie had taught Linnea to see the manicured lawns as abominations not meant for an island. It took pesticides to maintain them, which in turn killed important insects, like butterflies and bees. Rather, Primrose Cottage's lot was covered with tufts of unruly wildflowers, not yet blooming but sending up green shoots. Shells, sand, sweetgrass, and scrubby vegetation filled in the rest.

The driver dragged her large suitcase from the trunk, along with her carry-on. Just about everything she owned was packed into those two bags. Not a great statement at twenty-five years of age.

"Don't look like anyone's home," the driver said.

She glanced at the dark house, acknowledging the truth in his observation. "I'll be okay."

He accepted that answer, gave her a short wave, then scurried back to the car and drove off.

Linnea pulled out her phone to call her aunt Cara, but as she dialed, her battery died and the screen went black. Linnea took a deep, bracing breath of sea air and told herself that it was okay. She didn't care, because she was home.

She began dragging the giant suitcase close to the front steps, the kitten heels of her pumps digging into the sand and shells. She noted that Cara had improved the property in the past year. The walkway was now bluestone, and she had widened the front steps and front porch, adding a pergola as well, a signature touch for her. Two hunter-green rocking chairs and four hanging ferns filled the porch. Primrose Cottage had never looked better, she thought.

Struggling and cursing, Linnea at last managed to drag the suitcases to the front step. Wiping a tendril of hair from her face, she knocked several times on the front door and rang the bell for good measure. All remained silent within.

She left her luggage and walked around the house toward the ocean-side door. The shells crunched beneath her navy pumps, and from Emmi's garden she caught the scent of honeysuckle. Rounding the house, she saw the expansive deck and the glass-enclosed porch, and her heart pinged. These were the last projects completed on the house by Cara's first husband, Brett. He'd been a second father to Linnea and her brother, Cooper. Brett had been so full of life, his sudden death had been hard for them all. There was a time she wasn't sure Cara would get past losing him. Or if any of them would, for that matter. That was the lesson they'd all learned: Life was precious. Each day was a blessing. Life went on.

The porch door was unlocked, as she'd suspected. When she'd lived with her aunt, Linnea never remembered anyone locking doors. People were more trusting on the island than in the city.

"Aunt Cara?" she called out into the quiet, dark house. Only Cara's canary chirped cheerily at the sound of her voice. For a moment Linnea wondered if she should simply walk in. Did spending a lifetime inside these walls, sharing milestones, being a granddaughter, a niece, give her permission to enter Cara's house uninvited? She imagined her aunt's face, heard in her mind Cara's welcoming *Come in!*

Walking in felt natural, familiar—the aroma of coffee, the scent of jasmine perfume that was always in the air, the sound of Moutarde chirping in his cage. She flicked on a few lights, then went to plug her phone into the charger. That done, she brought her luggage inside, slipped off her pumps, and dug through the large wicker basket full of sandals. She smiled when she found a pair of her old flip-flops on the bottom. Slipping them on, she went back outdoors. She was eager to see the Atlantic Ocean again after two years of living by the Pacific.

The sky over the sea was darkening to violet, gold, and crimson. The beach house was perched high on a dune overlooking the ocean. When it was built in the 1920s, the charming cottage was oceanfront. Years later, a road had been built through the dunes to create Ocean Boulevard. Developers kept a one-foot width of the right-of-way on the ocean side of the road. Over the years, the shoreline built up more and more sand. Finally the dune was wide enough to allow new houses to be constructed, even closer to the sea. Back in that time, Russell Bennett, a great friend of her grandmother, had purchased lots directly in front of Primrose Cottage and put them into a conservation easement. It was a boon for her grandmother, who subsequently would never lose her view of the ocean. To the left of that land was the lot that Lovie had bequeathed to Cara.

Linnea's gaze swept the expanse that opened to the sea from the deck of Primrose Cottage, one of the precious few older properties left on Isle of Palms without a house blocking the view. Her gaze came to an abrupt halt and she sucked in a soft gasp of surprise. There on Cara's lot was the house her father was constructing. It was already completely framed in! Before her eyes she saw her father's dream becoming a reality.

It was going to be a beautiful house. The design was simple, with classic lowcountry features. The first floor was raised on pilings to keep out the floodwaters, mandatory now. The house was clearly built for a family that would enjoy the ocean breezes. And, she thought with a smile of approval, Palmer had kept his promise to Cara. He'd not obstructed any view of the ocean from her beach house. Not that she would let him. The new house was anchored by a two-story central structure from which a pair of one-story wings extended.

Linnea, having grown up near water, knew that everyone called the side of the house that faced the water, whether river or beach, the front. The back of the house faced the road or driveway. It was confusing for northerners, who called the street side of houses the front.

Her father loved porches. He'd included covered porches that faced the street, and without seeing it, she knew there would be another porch facing the sea.

Linnea felt a flush of pride that Palmer had built such a gracious, elegant house of lowcountry flavor. It was too bad he wouldn't live in it. He couldn't afford to. The lot belonged to Cara. It had been given to her by Grandmama Lovie, along with the beach house and all the secrets both held. Cara had confided the truth to her brother two years before, only after he'd committed to AA and begun rebuilding his life.

Palmer's intention was to sell the house and use the profit to seed his next house. In this way, he would begin his long-cherished dream of building top-quality houses. Likewise, Cara would benefit from her land. Brother and sister would share the profits, and this, Linnea knew, would have pleased Lovie immensely.

She made her way along the narrow beach-access path, her arms swinging at her sides. Seeing her father's house project left her uplifted. She remembered her father's low point before she'd left. To witness now what he'd built in the time she was gone, Linnea knew a moment of hope. An *If he can do it, so can I* feeling.

She climbed to the peak of the dunes, past the sea oats, still green and slim-stalked. The hearty ocean breeze whisked the soft hairs that had fallen around her neck. It swirled and caressed her cheeks. *Welcome home*, she heard whispered in the wind.

Linnea stood for a moment looking out over the expanse of beach and the ocean beyond. No one else walked the sand. The vast sea appeared to match her mood, reflective and shifting to deep purple. Waves rolled in gently, lapping the shoreline. She put her hands on her hips and drank in the immense vista of perpetually moving sea.

Somewhere out there, the turtles were gathering from all points of the continental shelf. Mating was a tempestuous affair as several males might try to breed with just one female, creating the seeds of a new generation. Within weeks a new sea turtle season would begin on the islands as the female turtles came ashore to lay their nests. When she'd lived on the island, their summers had revolved around the nesting season. Linnea was no stranger to the loggerheads. For as long as she could remember, she'd tended turtles with her grandmother, and later Aunt Cara and Emmi and Flo.

Grandmama Lovie had been a shining star in Linnea's life. When Lovie's feet were in the sand, she was in her element: happier, freer, expansive. Linnea could identify with that. As much as she loved the city, she too had always felt more at home by the sea. It was her grandmother who'd inspired Linnea to pursue a career in environmental science, despite her father's objections.

Linnea wasn't a child with dreams any longer. She was an adult facing adult problems. Cara was getting married again. Her father was building his dream house. Cooper was a rising junior at the University of South Carolina. It seemed everyone was moving on, except for her.

The looming cloud she'd felt when she arrived in Charleston returned, blotting out the joy she'd reveled in moments ago. Her heart physically hurt and cried out for release. Linnea missed her mother, loved her dearly. She needed to confide in someone. But her mother could sometimes ignore reality and shove problems under the rug, out of public view, with a pat phrase and a firmly hoisted smile.

She adored her father. But he'd likely bluster and blame John for breaking his daughter's heart—and worse, remind her that he'd told her that going to California was a big mistake, how she should get a real job and not waste her time with low-paying nonprofits.

Which was why she'd made the snap decision to come to the beach house and seek advice, honest and not sugar-coated, from her business-minded aunt. Cara was never one to suffer fools and wasn't afraid to speak plainly. The beach house was always a haven. A house of reason. She could get her bearings here before she confronted her parents.

From the beach she looked up at the cottage on the dune, and sighed. Cara wasn't home, and the night was falling. It was time to throw in the towel and retreat home. Linnea turned back to the sea for a final look. She crouched and picked up a handful of sand. Countless tiny particles filled her palm; clenching it tight, she brought her fist to her heart.

"Grandmama Lovie," she said aloud. "I know you're out there somewhere. Thank you for loving me, and teaching me about the turtles, the ocean. I love this beach and every particle of sand on it. It took me a while to understand, but I belong here. I came back. But I'm at square one again."

Linnea lowered her hand and let the sand slowly flow from her palm to form a small pile on the beach. Straightening up, she wiped her eyes, then wrapped her arms around her chest and looked seaward.

"Lovie, what do I do now?" she asked.

Her voice was carried away on the breeze.

Chapter Two

The loggerhead reproductive season begins when males and females mate in early spring off the coast. Males do not return ashore, but thirty days after breeding, females bravely return to their natal region under the cloak of night.

THE RED VOLVO wagon made its way at an unhurried pace through Charleston's narrow streets to the westernmost side of the peninsula. The spring rain had left dark, oily puddles in the streets, and crystalline drops glistened on the leaves of the trees. The clouds had cleared, and the sun shone brightly with comfortable warmth.

Cara Rutledge breathed in the sweet-scented air through open windows. She was nearing the Ashley River when she drove past a white stucco wall that had to be a block or more in length. Then she drew up before a pair of imposing wrought-iron gates. They were open, but she let the engine idle as she stared out the windshield. In the distance, framed by the glistening water of the river, was the last surviving plantation house on the Charleston Peninsula, Lowndes Grove. The gracious white stucco-and-wood structure with its five-bay piazza and Doric columns, curved Palladian windows, and waterfront location made up every southern girl's dream house. And this elegant venue was where Cara Rutledge was scheduled to marry David Wyatt in a late June wedding celebration.

Cara felt her heart pounding in what she thought was a mild panic attack. She leaned her head against the wheel and took a deep breath.

"You okay?" asked Emmi.

Cara turned to see her best friend leaning forward in the passenger seat, her bright-green eyes, creases deep at the corners, studying her with concern. Emmi's red hair seemed to get a deeper flaming hue every year. It was pulled back in a clasp, revealing every soft freckle on her face. She wore a floral wraparound dress and makeup, a change from her Turtle Team T-shirt, for Cara's meeting with the wedding planner. They were here to firm up final details and write a big check. Cara was pretty sure Emmi was more excited about the wedding plans than she was.

"I'm kind of panicking. The date is getting closer." Cara shook her head in doubt. "I'm feeling . . ." She took a breath. "Trapped."

"What? Why?"

"All this." She indicated the venue, then added in a rush "It's so not me."

"What's not you? You're the bride, aren't you?"

"I'm not a blushing bride," Cara snorted. "Far from it. I'm fifty-five years old."

"I know exactly how old you are. We're the same age," Emmi fired back. "You make it sound ancient. That's not old."

Cara sighed again. It wasn't about age. It was more about maturity. At this point in her life she knew what she wanted, and more, *who* she wanted in her life. Cara didn't doubt her desire to marry David. She loved him. Her love was hard-won after a long period of mourning for her first husband, Brett. She hadn't known she could feel this way again. It wasn't the act of marriage that had her quaking in her boots; it was the big, fancy wedding festivity. She didn't believe she needed a party to make that point. And she certainly didn't feel the need to waste a great deal of money on a party she didn't particularly want.

Cara had grown up a Rutledge in Charleston, the daughter of a prestigious family. Nonetheless she'd fled Charleston and the South at age eighteen for points north. She'd had no one to depend on but herself to make her way in the world. Her choice, granted, but it had been a steep learning curve requiring hard work, determination, frugality, and an edge of fear. All lessons she never forgot.

It hadn't been easy. She'd started work as a receptionist at a premier advertising firm in Chicago and gone to college for seven years at night to get her degree, all while assiduously working toward advancement during that time. She was promoted to a director of accounts by age forty. She'd been proud of that. She hadn't asked for a dime from her parents, nor did her father offer one. Yet when she'd earned that promotion, there were no hearty congratulations from her parents. They were, she remembered, silent on the subject. Other than her mother asking, hopefully, if she had a beau, and whether she'd given any thought to getting married.

When she'd told friends of her engagement to David, however, she was met with exclamations of joy and jubilee. Some grew misty-eyed, squeezed her hands and told her she "deserved" this. As if getting a husband were equivalent to bagging a Big Five game trophy. To her mind, she'd *deserved* her promotions. Finding love once, she viewed as a blessing. Twice, a miracle.

"You know what I meant," Cara said. "I didn't grow up dreaming about my wedding. You were the one who browsed through wedding magazines, circling her favorite dresses, or table settings or bouquets. I read novels, the business section of the newspapers, did crossword puzzles. If I circled anything, it was books I wanted to read from the book review."

"You were a nerd."

"Proud of it," she replied, and they both laughed.

"Look," Emmi began in earnest, "you didn't have a big wedding with Brett. This time you can do it proper."

"I thought we did do it proper," Cara replied with slight irritation. "I wore a white dress."

"You got married at a justice of the peace. You didn't even invite me." She frowned. "And we'd been friends forever."

Cara would never hear the end of that decision. Emmi had been deeply hurt. But it was what she and Brett had wanted. Cara's mother had passed, and Brett would have had to invite his whole boisterous family if he'd invited even one of them. As Brett had put it, "I'm just happy to catch this slippery fish. Now all I want to do is reel her in."

"Well, stop complaining," Cara replied. "You're invited to this one. You're even a bridesmaid."

"Yes, I am," Emmi said with pleasure. Then with a smirk, "The matron of honor." She huffed.

"But . . ." Cara felt like cringing. "Isn't it a bit frivolous, even silly, for a woman my age to be having a big wedding? Aren't we both kind of old to put on long dresses and parade down an aisle carrying flowers?"

Emmi shrugged one shoulder. "Maybe, back in the day. It used to be that if you were over forty"—she put her hand over her mouth to feign a secret—"much less fifty, you got married in a quiet little ceremony in a tasteful little suit. Preferably blue. But things have changed. You deserve whatever kind of wedding you want. Every woman does. Regardless of age." Emmi waved her hand, conceding a point. "Naturally, you want to be sensitive about things. Like your dress—which you still haven't purchased." She made a face. "I'm just saying. Ticktock."

"I know, I know."

"And for sure you don't want to show up in a Cinderella carriage or have smoke effects or switch the music from Pachelbel to 'Baby Got Back.'"

Cara burst out laughing. She could always count on Emmi to lighten her mood.

"If anyone is going to get twitters from the back row, it's me," Emmi added. "I'm the sorry old divorced woman walking down the aisle." She pointed her finger. "And there's no way I'm going to catch your bouquet."

"I won't throw one. I promise."

"Well, thank God for small mercies."

Emmi looked at her hands, a bit large, tan, and freckled. Her nails were short and polished a spring pink. She wore no rings, but her gold pendulum earrings dangled. For a moment, she grew reflective. When she turned her gaze back to Cara, her tone was serious.

"Cara, who cares how old we are? We're forever young, right? If you were one hundred years old, I'd still tell you to go for it. David wants you to have this wedding. He's so excited he's busting his buttons. If I didn't love you so much, I'd be jealous. I think it's terribly romantic."

"I think a quiet wedding with just David and me can be every bit as romantic."

"That ship has sailed, my friend. You already announced your engagement to the world. You've made the public declaration. Besides, it's all arranged." Emmi gestured toward the big house in the distance. "It's too late to back out now. Money's been put down." She paused for emphasis. "And now, we're done talking. We are going inside to finalize the food, the flowers, the wine, the timeline, the tents, the number of chandeliers. . . . And don't forget, I got *my* dress."

Emmi was thrilled with all the details of this grand wedding. Cara looked at her friend, saw the hope for love still shining in her eyes, and it moved her. She hoped Emmi would find love again someday. Tom Peterson, her childhood love, had broken her heart after years of marriage. When he'd asked for a divorce, it seemed to have come out of nowhere. Emmi had been shaken to the core. She'd lost direction, her identity. It had taken Emmi a long time to recover. But she had. Now Emmi was strong and independent . . . but lonely. Especially since Cara had found David. Emmi had not been as fortunate. She'd dated a long stream of men over the years, some of them nice, but never one who had staying power. Cara had worried that a big wedding would be shoving her happiness in Emmi's face; but quite the contrary, Emmi was all for it. Emmi was conservative in politics and loved glitter and romance. Cara was conservative in dress and freethinking. But they were sisters of the heart.

"Cara, don't be selfish. Weddings are social events. You are celebrating announcing your commitment to the world."

"That's just it. I'm not making a commitment to the world. I'm making a commitment to David. My husband-to-be. To one person."

Emmi raised a brow. "And that one person wants to invite his family and friends."

Cara tapped her fingers with budding irritation and ground out, "I just feel forced into this—this huge event." Her voice rose. "That I don't even want!"

Emmi hesitated; her brows gathered. "I didn't realize you were so angry."

"I don't know if I'm angry . . . just frustrated. Em, you've known me my whole life. I'm not into parties or big events. I'm more private. And now I'm having this enormous shindig and must walk down the aisle in a wedding gown. With all those eyes on me."

"Then why did you say yes to all this?" Emmi asked with a hint of exasperation. "You could've stopped it before we got to this point."

Cara looked down at her slim, French-manicured hand where it lay on her navy pencil skirt, over which she wore a crisp white shirt. Her only jewelry was the impressive diamond on her ring finger and small diamond studs in her ears.

There'd always been the slightest hint of competition in David's mind for her affection, because he knew how deeply she'd loved her first husband. Cara would always love Brett Beauchamps. She'd loved him with her whole being. It had been a struggle not to feel guilt at falling in love with another man, as if she were cheating somehow. Over time, she'd resolved her grief, and she did love David, with her whole heart. And since it reassured him, she'd agreed to a grand wedding: dress, cake, décor, and—she glanced up at the impressive antebellum house—this gorgeous wedding venue.

"I'm doing this for David. He wanted me to have what he thought was the wedding of my dreams, because he believed I wanted it. At least, that was what he told me. I thought about it and realized that perhaps David was the one who wanted to have a big wedding. He wanted to announce to the world that we're a couple. I don't know, it seemed miserly of feeling to deny David this joy." She shrugged. "He'd been sad for such a long time after the death of his wife. Then, of course, that brief debacle with Natalie."

"So, you're doing this for David."

Cara nodded.

"Because you love him." She waited for Cara to nod again.

"Yep. Head over heels."

"Well, then!" Emmi lifted her hands. "That settles it. 'Mahwage is what bwings us togethah today,'" she said, imitating the heavily accented line from the film *The Princess Bride*.

Cara had to laugh, captivated by her friend's incorrigible sense of romance.

"Kiddo," Emmi said with renewed seriousness, "if you're going to do this, don't be resentful."

"You're right, of course," Cara agreed, her voice decisive. "No point in hashing this out over and over. I said yes and I should stop complaining. Let's just chalk this up to last-minute wedding jitters."

"You're good?" Emmi asked, confirming.

Cara conjured up David's image in her mind: his tanned face, soulful dark-brown eyes under bushy dark brows. She smiled. If she was totally honest, there *was* a part of her—hiding deep inside—that wanted to share the joy of the day and dance with her family and friends. She was, indeed, blessed to have the occasion for joy after so many days of sadness.

"I'm nervous," Cara said with a laugh. "I still have to walk down the aisle. But, yes, I'm good."

"You still need to get your dress—"

"One thing at a time."

Emmi sat back with a huff. "Cara," she said plaintively. "I've been working in women's clothing for almost fifteen years."

"Part-time . . ."

"Even still. I've worked minimum wage to salary. I've worked weekends and holidays and more overtime than I ever got paid for. For your information," she said with a shake of her shoulders, "the women's fashion buyer consults with me about purchases. And do you know what?"

Cara shook her head.

"You've never, not once, asked me for advice. Not on a dress for a date, or if the color was right for you, or—or even anything for Hope!"

Emmi put her hand up when Cara opened her mouth to speak. "I know our tastes are different. And you wouldn't have to take my advice. But, it would've been nice to have been asked."

"I didn't know that mattered to you," Cara said, genuinely surprised. She'd never meant to hurt Emmi, but it was true. Their taste in clothes was night-and-day different. Cara couldn't imagine wearing some of the outfits Emmi put together. Not that they were bad, but they were definitely more colorful.

"It might've mattered a while ago, but not anymore." Her tone changed. "Until now. We're not talking about a dress to wear to work or on a date. We're talking about your wedding dress!" Her voice grew more impassioned. "You're my soul sister. My best friend. I'm your maid of honor." She pointed at Cara. "And don't you dare correct me and tell me I'm your matron of honor. I'm not married. I'm a maid. I don't want to be a matron. That sounds so old."

"Maid it is." Cara didn't dare smile, but her lips twitched.

Emmi nodded sharply to imply that issue was settled. "Now," she said, "I don't understand why you're dragging your feet on getting a wedding dress, but it's time. And I hope you'll ask me to be there. This is the one time it does matter to me. I love you, Cara. I want to share this with you, if you'll let me."

"Of course, I'll let you. You're my best friend too. I couldn't manage any of this without you. Let's get this menu done today, and we'll move on to the dress. Together."

"Good," Emmi said, her green eyes bright. "I've been saving bridal magazines and I've circled a lot of dresses I think will look fabulous on you."

Cara wanted to groan, but loved her friend enough to simply smile and say, "Great!"

"Okay, then." Emmi shifted in her seat to face forward. "We'd better get this show on the road."

The red Volvo wagon lurched forward as they drove past the gates along the tabby drive toward the house. Cara slid into a parking spot, rolled up the windows, and grabbed her purse. As they stepped out into the heat of late afternoon sunshine, her gaze swept across the Ashley River. A long dock stretched out from Lowndes Grove into the racing water. She envisioned it festooned with flowers and wondered if she and David could make their exit from the wedding party in David's boat. It might be fun, she thought with a smile, getting into the mood.

They turned and made their way to the redbrick patio in front of the shining white plantation house.

A slender, attractive woman in a vividly patterned J.McLaughlin dress stepped out from the glassed porch. The wedding planner had shoulder-length dark hair and a vibrant smile. Lifting her arm, she waved in a graceful arc over her head.

"Welcome!" called Elma Garcia.

Cara waved back, then linked arms with her best friend. "Are you ready to sample more cake?"

Emmi scrunched up her nose. "Cake, flowers, plates—I'm ready for it all. But let's start with the wine."

Chapter Three

Sea turtles are generally solitary creatures. They rarely interact with one another outside of courtship and mating. When it is not nesting season, sea turtles may migrate hundreds or even thousands of miles.

MUCH LATER IN the day, Cara pulled into the driveway of Primrose Cottage and turned off the car lights. Night was falling. She lazily climbed from the car and stretched. Across the car, Emmi did the same.

"I'm so stuffed, I have to loosen my dress," Emmi said with a groan.

It was true. They'd tasted and approved the four appetizers, followed by a salad of oranges, fennel, and olives served with a delicately crisp pinot grigio. The main course was filet mignon, mashed potatoes with truffle oil, and glazed carrots, accompanied by a lush cabernet. The coconut cake was as light as a feather. And, of course, a dry and delicious champagne. Cara was the designated driver and didn't swallow most of the wine. Emmi, however, was feeling delightfully giddy.

"It was fun, wasn't it?" Emmi asked her. "Come on, admit it."

"Okay," Cara replied with a reluctant smile. "It was fun. But now," she said, glancing at her wristwatch, "I must hurry to get to the ferry. David's meeting me with Hope and Rory."

"You're going back to Dewees *again*?" Emmi asked. "You practically live out there now."

The tone was slightly accusatory, and Cara knew it was because Emmi missed spending more time with her.

"You know they share a nanny, and David covers when I work late. It's easier for me to stay there on Dewees than try to catch a ferry back home. Especially when I'm going to take her back to Dewees the next morning. Or when I'm running late—like tonight."

"Okay, I get the hint," Emmi said, as she retrieved the remaining white boxes full of the food samples and leftover cake that they knew Flo would enjoy.

They chatted as they walked along the pavers to the side kitchen door. The house was dark and the two women shared a worried glance.

"Flo! I'm home!" Emmi called out as she stepped inside.

It was nearly 7:30 p.m., but the kitchen and living room were empty. Emmi balanced a box on her knee and stretched her hand along the wall to the light switch. Instantly, light filled the room.

Cara followed her into the country-style kitchen, letting the screen door slam behind her, and laid the boxes on the wooden table. She could walk through this house with her eyes closed. When they were children, she and Emmi, sisters from other mothers, had played at Flo's house. It was neutral territory, a place without as many rules. Flo's mother was an eccentric artist who'd provided art, dancing, and singing lessons. Flo was more like an aunt to both Cara and Emmi. She had acted as the buffer between the girls and their mothers when they wanted to stay up late at a nest with the turtle team.

Years later, when Emmi was grown and divorced, she'd purchased the house from an aging Flo. Though the owners were different, as before, the kitchen doors of the two neighboring houses were always open—but with Lovie passed, their turtle team gatherings had shifted from Cara's beach house to Emmi and Flo's place. Cara, Emmi, and Flo continued to spend hours talking in this kitchen. Flo's mother had decorated the Victorian house in early bohemian. After Emmi bought it, she'd promptly painted the white exterior a Caribbean blue with coral trim and tastefully decorated the house in the southern shabby-chic style that she loved. Flo never gave much mind to décor and was happy anywhere the people were kind, the food good, and the turtles nearby.

They heard Flo's voice from the stairs. "Who's there? Emmi? That you?"

"It's just us chickens!" Emmi called back, opening the white baker's box and bending near for a sniff.

Flo appeared at the kitchen entrance wrapped in a mousy-gray chenille robe, her thin white hair sticking up from her head and her blue eyes blazing. Her face was pale, and there was a look of panic in her eyes.

"Where were you?" Flo's voice rang with fear.

Emmi's hands stilled and she straightened to study Flo's stricken face. All humor fled from hers, replaced with concern. "Flo," she said in a calm voice, "I was at Lowndes Grove with Cara. The wedding venue. We went to sample the food and wine. Don't you remember?"

Flo blinked hard several times, then shook her head. Cara saw the confusion in Flo's eyes and hoped it was from being awakened, and not the Alzheimer's that had been getting worse.

"I was worried," Flo said in a scolding tone. "You left me alone. It's late!"

"I was only gone for a few hours. I'm sorry you were worried." Emmi turned her head to deliver a meaningful gaze to Cara.

Cara bit her lip, anxious at seeing further evidence of Flo's Alzheimer's disease taking hold.

Emmi walked closer to Flo and asked gently, "Did you eat?"

"No. There was nothing to eat."

"But I left you some dinner. It's wrapped in foil in the oven." She turned and went directly to the vintage O'Keefe and Merritt oven that had baked cookies and cakes for them since they were children. She grabbed a mitt from a hook and retrieved a covered plate, then carried it to the table. "See? There's chicken and a baked potato. And salad in the fridge. It's all written down on this note," she said, pointing to a sheet of paper on the kitchen table.

"A note?" Flo scoffed. "I didn't see any note."

Emmi sighed audibly and looked again at Cara for help.

Cara felt as if a bowl of ice water had just been dumped over her head. The progression of dementia seemed to be advancing more rapidly. The change in Flo was shocking. She looked more frail, older, much less able to care for herself.

"Flo, come sit down," Cara urged kindly. "Look what we've brought you. Delicious samples from the wedding menu for you to taste. I need your opinion. They're all delicious."

"What in heaven's name?" Flo asked. "The wedding menu? What wedding?"

"Cara's wedding," Emmi said as she returned to Flo's side. Gently she guided the old woman to the kitchen table. "You remember Cara and David are getting married?"

Flo did not reply.

Cara went to the cupboard and pulled out a fresh plate. Grabbing tableware on the way back, she set it all in front of Flo. "We sampled food and wine for the wedding menu," she explained again.

"Wine, you say? Just how much wine did you sample? You two are acting mighty strange. What's that?" Flo asked, pointing to a mozzarella, tomato, and basil stick. She picked it up and inspected it more carefully.

"You go on," Emmi said, shooing Cara out with her flapping hands. "You've got that ferry to catch."

"Are you sure? I can stay for a while."

"Don't be silly. We're fine, aren't we, Flo?"

Flo was chewing, her mouth full, focused on her food.

Emmi followed Cara to the door. She looked over her shoulder to check on Flo. The old woman's head was bent intently over her plate.

"Oh, Em," Cara said with dismay. "She's slipping faster now."

"Yeah, I know. She's becoming more and more dependent on me. She's afraid when I leave her alone."

"This isn't just *your* problem. When you bought the house, you didn't take on the responsibility for Flo." Cara paused, hoping to convince Emmi she wouldn't have to bear this burden alone. "Emmi, both our mothers are gone, God rest their souls. Flo is a second mother to both of us. A treasured aunt. We've always said that. I'm here to share this with you." She put her hand on Emmi's shoulder. "You won't be able to keep this up on your own much longer."

Emmi looked away but didn't reply.

Cara was aware of having to catch the ferry. "Listen, this is a big discussion. I don't want to miss the ferry. Let's arrange a time to talk about this. Soon. I'm afraid it's time. We have to make some decisions."

Emmi sighed with resignation. "I'm afraid so. But it breaks my heart."

"Emmi? You there?" called Flo. "What's this? Can't figure out if it's potatoes or cauliflower."

"Be right there, Flo!" Emmi called back. She delivered a quick kiss on Cara's cheek. "All good here. Today was fun. Thanks for including me. See you tomorrow." Then without another word, she shut the door against Cara's "Good-bye, Flo!"

Night had fallen. Cara walked along the garden path toward the white fence that separated their two properties. The reality of Flo's condition weighed heavily in her thoughts. She and Emmi both knew that eventually—someday—they'd have to make decisions regarding Flo's advancing dementia, but that day had always seemed a ways off. Tonight, Cara witnessed how quickly the disease was progressing, and how much the burden of care had fallen onto Emmi's shoulders. She'd never complained. Never uttered a word. That was like Emmi, Cara realized. Partly a saint, partly denying a reality she didn't want to face.

The gentle breeze carried the heady scent of the spring honeysuckle blooms. Cara breathed deep and exhaling, she heard in the distance the sound of a woman humming. She held her breath. There was something familiar about the song, but she couldn't place it. She swung her head toward the sound, squinting in the darkness.

In the dim light of the rising moon, Cara saw a slight woman dressed in vintage clothing coming from the beach. The woman stopped to bend and investigate a wildflower. Even in the darkening sky, Cara could see the luster of her blond hair. Straightening, the woman began humming again, strolling slowly toward her.

"Mama . . ." Cara whispered on a breath, sure she was seeing a ghost.

The woman continued to approach. Stepping into the warm yellow glow of light pouring across the path from Emmi's kitchen windows, she looked Cara's way, stopped, then waved exuberantly.

"Aunt Cara!"

Cara's breath returned in a rush, and she laughed inwardly at her own foolishness.

"Linnea? What on earth are you doing here? You should be in California!"

Linnea rushed up the beach path into Cara's outstretched arms. They were far more than mere aunt and niece. They were confidantes. Friends.

"Dear girl," Cara exclaimed, her gaze taking in the vintage clothing that Linnea preferred, "you gave me a scare. You looked so much like my mother!"

Linnea giggled. "And you thought you were seeing the ghost of Lovie?"

Cara shook her head, a bit embarrassed. "It wouldn't be the first time. But, Linnea! What brings you back? Where's John?"

"Long story. I came right from the airport. My phone died." She rolled her eyes. "I decided to see you before Mama and Daddy. They're out anyway. But of course, you weren't here. So I took a walk along the beach. It's good to see the Atlantic again. But those mosquitoes are eating me alive."

"The wretched things. I'm sorry you had to wait. I was at Lowndes Grove making wedding plans."

Linnea's eyes lit up. "Fun."

Cara sighed, letting that go. "I stopped off at Emmi's. I'd have hurried home had I known you were here. Let's get you inside. I'll rummage something up in the kitchen. You must be starved. And you might try to call your parents."

"I'd like that. They're probably camped out by the phone by now."

☆   ☆   ☆

LINNEA LOOKED AROUND dear Primrose cottage and was relieved that little had changed since she'd lived here a few years ago. It still held the same comfort of both old and new. The walls were painted white or a whitewashed blue. The polished floor was heart pine, adorned with Persian rugs in vibrant hues of red and blue. The upholstered furniture was covered in creamy linen slipcovers, and the long, matching linen drapes at the windows were open. Cara went around the room lighting the lamps on the side tables, creating pools of yellow light.

"I see you still keep the windows uncovered," Linnea said.

"Of course," Cara replied, straightening. She'd kicked off her heels and walked barefoot in her long-legged stride across the room to the kitchen. "I prefer to look out and see the ocean."

"Like Grandmama Lovie. What was it that she always used to say?"

Cara chuckled as she uncorked a bottle of wine. "She used to say she kept the drapes open because she had to check on her old friend the ocean first thing every morning." She eased the cork from the bottle. "To see what kind of mood he was in."

Linnea chuckled. "Yeah, that's it."

"Grab yourself a glass. Just one. I'm not having any."

"Oh?" Linnea said, a tad disappointed. She never liked drinking alone. Her mother said it was something a lady never did, which seemed old-fashioned and Linnea didn't believe it, but her mother's voice was still in her ear.

"I tasted wines all afternoon." Cara answered the unvoiced question. "But could you grab me a tall glass? What I need is water."

Like the china, the cottage's crystal was an assortment of favorites collected from family over the ages. Never a full dozen, usually twos and threes of a pattern. This Baccarat pattern had always been Linnea's favorite. Cara generously filled it with a Malbec. Linnea took a tentative first sip. It was delicious. Cara never served bad wine.

"Here you go," Cara said, handing her a plate of crusty, French bread topped with fresh mozzarella, a slice of tomato, and sprigs of fresh basil. "This should tide you over."

"Yum. It's perfect."

"Let's get comfy and put our legs up," Cara suggested. She led the way across the hall to the living room where lamps on the tables were lit. Outside the large window, the sky and sea were velvety black.

Linnea studied her aunt as she followed her. Cara always managed a chic look, sophisticated and subtle. Her thick, dark hair, a Rutledge trait, was a tad longer now, reaching her chin and worn in a blunt cut. Linnea admired her aunt. Despite lack of money, Cara had always exhibited excellent taste. Linnea rarely saw her disheveled and never with a fallen hem, a missing button, or a scuffed shoe. Except out on the beach. There she literally and figuratively let her hair down. In most things, her aunt was Linnea's role model.

"So, tell me," Cara said, curling up on the sofa like a contented cat. "What brings you home so suddenly? Is everything all right?"

Linnea sat on the opposite side of the sofa, setting her plate on the coffee table and bringing her wineglass near. She swirled the red liquid in her glass, considering Cara's question.

"I take it you haven't been talking to my father."

It wasn't a question. Cara's brows rose. "Palmer? We talked just last week."

Linnea thought about that. "Daddy never mentioned that I'd lost my job?"

"No!" Cara said, and from her tone, Linnea knew this was true. Cara swiveled her legs to the floor and leaned forward, her dark eyes focused. "What happened?"

She looked at Cara and shrugged lightly. "I call it the San Francisco debacle." She laughed without humor. "First the startup company I was working for closed. Too bad, really. They were smart and motivated, but they couldn't make a go of it." She shrugged. "We worried it might happen. A lot of startups fail. But still, it was crushing. We all worked so hard." She shook her head. "Then I couldn't find another job."

"Did you give it enough time?"

"No, probably not," Linnea admitted. "But I ran out of time." She was ashamed at the tears that pricked her eyes. She angrily swiped a traitorous tear from her cheek. "John and I split up." She was looking at her wine when she spoke, but she could hear Cara's heavy sigh.

"I'm sorry to hear that," Cara said with sincerity. After a pause, she asked, "What happened?"

Linnea tried to sum up all the thousands of words she and John had shared in round after round of heated discussions and fights.

"He didn't want to . . ." She paused. "Or he wouldn't commit to us being long-term."

Cara pursed her lips in thought. "How long have you been together?"

"Two years."

"You're young. That's not a long time, in the scheme of things."

"Maybe not, but there's more." Linnea took a long sip of wine. Cara waited, sitting like a cat on the sofa, her lovely dark eyes watching.

"You see," Linnea began, "I always knew that commitment was difficult for John. He had a hard time telling me he loved me and asking me to move in with him. I think he was rocked by his parents' divorce. Maybe it shook his faith in commitment or marriage, or something. . . ." Linnea shook her head. "Who knows? But he's also a Peter Pan. He likes his freedom. Hanging out with his bros. John will take off for a few days on a moment's notice. He always felt bad about leaving me behind because, you know, I had to work. I told him it was okay, but still . . . it made me feel like a drag on him. Like I was second place. That he'd rather go out with the guys than be with me."

"Watching you two together, I never got that impression. He seemed to truly enjoy your company. You hung out all the time. I used to see you on the porch, talking and talking. . . ."

"Yeah." Linnea sighed and shrugged. "It started out that way. Once we started living together, it seemed the more we were together, the more he needed to carve out his private time. He'd talk about his day to his friend on the phone, while I was sitting next to him." She shook her head in frustration.

"We were working through that issue. I thought . . ." She made a tiny movement with her hand. "I can't be sure anymore. When I lost my job, though, things really got tense. I could tell he was uncomfortable with the idea of supporting me. He kept asking if I'd applied for a job, and where. I was sensitive about it, of course. It was humiliating. I mean, who wants to be a moocher? But his questions were more concern about him supporting me than about me finding the right job. I tried to help out more—clean the house, do errands, pay for groceries, all while looking for a job. But I couldn't pay rent. I never made that much working for a nonprofit, so I had no savings." She looked at Cara. "I definitely was not going to ask my father for help."

Cara, who knew the history, huffed through her nose. "No," she agreed.

"That's when we got into heavy discussions about our future. What our relationship was all about. Some of them became arguments." She snorted. "Pretty heated. And . . . that's when it came out that John doesn't want kids."

Cara sat back against the cushions. "Oh. Well."

"Right," Linnea added with an eye roll.

Cara tilted her head. "Isn't he young to be making that kind of a decision?"

"Is he? He certainly had a lot of reasons why he didn't want them. The population. Climate change. The time dedication that having kids brings. He'd obviously given it some thought." She took another swallow of wine and stared into her glass.

"Learning to live with someone is complicated. Even when love is involved. Maybe especially then. It's not just about compromise—to succeed, one must actively try to make the other person feel comfortable. Loved. If you've lived alone for a long time, it's all the harder to even recognize when you're being selfish. I believe that's why living together before commitment often leads to a breakup. It's just too hard to stick it out."

"So, you think I shouldn't have moved in with him?"

Cara shook her head. "I'm not saying that. Your situation made sense at the time. Only you can decide that."

"We'd said we were going to try. To see how things went." She scraped her nail. "I guess we found out. I don't know if John will ever be ready."

"And you?"

"I hope so. Maybe not right now. One thing's for sure: I'm not looking for a man to save me."

"Good. Because a man can't save you. You have to save yourself."

Linnea nodded. Though that was easier said than done. "I've thought long and hard about this. John doesn't want to get married. He doesn't want kids. He doesn't want to live in Charleston." She spread out her palms, and her chin shook. "What's left?" she asked in a wavering voice. "Nothing."

Cara considered this in the silence. "You seem so decided."

"I am." Linnea wiped the wetness from her cheeks with her palms.

Cara's voice softened. "Then why the tears?"

Linnea shook her head, pinching her lips.

"You still love him?"

Linnea wiped her face again, then nodded.

"Does he love you?"

Linnea wiped her nose with her cocktail napkin. "I think so. We shared so much. But is love enough?"

"Oh, Linnea, that's a question for the ages."

Linnea took a long, shaky breath. "I made my decision."

"I am sorry. I like John. I've known him for years. He's the son of my best friend." Her expression froze. "I fear Emmi will take this harder than all of us put together. She was ready to post the banns."

"Oh, God . . ." Linnea groaned.

They shared a commiserating laugh.

Linnea was grateful to Cara for her orderly thinking, her lack of being judgmental. If she had commiserated with her misery, Linnea felt certain she'd end up a puddle of self-pity, the kind of person one pitied yet avoided. Cara's firm certitude allowed Linnea to believe that eventually her life would return to normal, albeit a life without John. Cara accepted without conjecture that Linnea had been dealt a blow and that, in time and with determination, she'd get over it. She wondered if failure was even in Cara's vocabulary.

"That's neither here nor there," Cara said by way of conclusion. "If John is holding back from a commitment, or unable to make one, better to know now than later."

"Right you are." Linnea raised her glass in a toast of agreement.

"But . . ."

Linnea's hand froze in midair.

"I can see why you're not anxious to tell your father."

Linnea's arm dropped even as she felt her blood surge. "I know! Right?"

"He's going to sit back like the cat who ate the canary. There's nothing Palmer loves more than to be in the right. I can hear what he's going to say now."

"I told you so," they said in unison.

"I'm not sure what I'm more embarrassed about," Linnea said. "Losing my job or getting dumped by my boyfriend."

"Well, my dear, you will have to go home and face them. They're eager to see you."

"They had some event they had to go to tonight. On the way here, I texted them that my flight was delayed so I could see you first," she confessed.

Cara offered a sympathetic look. "Even still. It's getting late, you look exhausted, and I have to catch the last ferry to Dewees."

"Oh, why didn't you tell me?" Linnea exclaimed, scrambling to her feet. "I'm sorry I kept you."

"No problem. I texted David and let him know I was coming on the later ferry. All's good—unless I miss it. Hope will be quite angry with me. She's getting quite opinionated." Cara rose in a graceful motion.

Linnea laughed, imagining the little girl she'd once babysat for. "I miss her. I'm sure she's changed a lot."

"You have no idea. Come back once you're settled. Hope will be thrilled to see you. David too."

"Thanks for lending an ear," Linnea said as they walked to the door. She pulled out her phone from her purse. "I just needed to get my bearings."

"Wait," Cara said, observing Linnea with her phone. "You don't have a car. Hold on, I'll grab my keys. I'll drive you."

"I can just call a car. You'll miss the ferry."

Cara glanced at her watch. "If we hurry, I can make it."

Linnea helped Cara put away the cheese and wine and after dragging the enormous suitcase into the trunk of the red Volvo, they were off to Sullivan's Island.

"One more thing," Cara said as she drove down the darkened streets. "What's going on with the job front?"

Linnea looked out the window. They were crossing the bridge at Breach Inlet. The water appeared dark and moody in the light of the moon.

"Not much," she answered truthfully. "Before I left California, I sent query letters to my contacts in town. The usual suspects—the Coastal

Conservation League, South Carolina Environmental Law Project, the Audubon Society, the Friends of Coastal South Carolina, Charleston Waterkeeper, and, of course, the South Carolina Aquarium. For starters."

"I can help you there. Any word?"

"Not a peep. I plan to follow up this week. Do you have any leads?"

"I know a lot of people. I'll put my ear to the ground. Tap a few shoulders."

"Thanks. That would be amazing."

"Don't thank me yet. Honestly, I don't think there's much out there. Environmental science is a popular major here."

"That was the same story I faced two years ago when I graduated. But hey, now I've got experience under my belt. That has to mean something, right?"

"It should," Cara agreed. "I think you're an exceptional candidate. You have all the requirements. Plus, you've been involved with coastal wildlife your whole life. I don't remember a summer you didn't volunteer for one group or another. That will pay off. Memories are long in this community."

She was glad to hear that. "I was thinking earlier, while walking the beach, that my summers here on the island with Lovie are the best memories of my childhood. Then there were the summers with you and Brett." She paused, anxiously looking at her aunt's face, but Cara appeared serene, a faint smile of memory easing her expression. "Growing up, I couldn't wait to come to the beach house. Lovie always had this big smile on her tanned face, and open arms for a hug. And there were always sugar cookies, and sweet tea in the fridge. But most of all, I remember the turtles."

"Oh yes. Always sea turtles," Cara said with a gentle laugh. "I wasn't so fond of them when I was a child. I think I was jealous of them. They were my mother's entire focus during the season. I didn't really like them till I turned forty, when I came back home."

Linnea knew Cara's history. She too had lost her job, after more than twenty years of dedicated service to her ad agency.

"I hope you don't mind my asking this. . . ."

Cara turned her head from the road briefly. "Go ahead."

"When you came home, after you'd been fired . . . were you embarrassed?"

Cara kept her eyes on the road but a look of understanding spread across her face.

"You're afraid folks here will see you as a failure."

"Well, yeah. I was feeling pretty cocky nabbing that job in San Francisco and moving across the country. With a boyfriend to boot. I had it all. And now I come home with nothing more than what is in those suitcases. How can anyone see me as anything but a failure?"

Cara reached out to take hold of Linnea's hand. Her tone shifted from sympathetic to firm. Once again, she quickly looked over to meet Linnea's gaze.

"I see a young woman who took a daring chance on an exciting new startup company. A woman who wasn't afraid to go against her family's wishes and give it a go. A woman who followed her heart. The startup failed. That's the company's failure—not yours. As for your personal relationship, that's your business and no one else's."

"But this is a small town. People talk."

Cara released Linnea. "Then control the narrative."

Linnea's attention sharpened. "What?"

"Listen to me," Cara said. "Perception is reality in the world today.

Create the narrative for your own life. Don't allow other people to do it. Linnea, people could listen to the way you just told me your story and think, *Poor Linnea Rutledge. She came slinking home from California. She lost her job and got dumped by her boyfriend.*"

Linnea put her hand to her face. "That sounds so embarrassing."

"People listen to your definition of yourself. Words are powerful tools. You learned that in communication classes. Choose your words carefully—use the truth, but spin it." She thought for a moment, then cleared her throat. "Linnea Rutledge made the decision to leave Charleston. She had a great experience in San Francisco. Now she has experience, a clearer focus, and an impressive résumé. She wouldn't change a thing."

Linnea listened, stunned by the difference in the perception. "Even *I* think I sound pretty good."

Cara lifted one hand from the wheel and pointed her finger as she spoke. "Linnea, the point is that you *chose* to return. That's a strong decision. Not a weak one." She let her hand return to the wheel and concluded, "Certainly nothing to be ashamed about."

Linnea felt her respect for her aunt redouble. No wonder she'd shot up the corporate ladder. "Brilliant," she said. "You've taken a weight off my shoulders. Thank you."

"Good," Cara said with finality as she pulled into the driveway of Palmer and Julia's house on Sullivan's Island. She put the car in park, then turned to fully face Linnea.

"The first person you can practice your narrative with is your father." She glanced up at the house, then offered a wry smile. "Good luck with that."

Chapter Four

Barrier islands are designed to protect the mainland from hurricanes, storm surge, and flooding. When we build structures on these islands, we are putting ourselves in the first line of defense against such destructive forces. The cutting back of maritime shrubs and forest leaves residents and their properties even more vulnerable to extreme weather and erosion, and destroys habitat for animals, migrating butterflies, and birds, as well.

THE RUTLEDGE HOME on Sullivan's Island was a plain, 1950s raised white clapboard house with a dark shingle roof. A single narrow staircase originated from the unremarkable front porch down to a landing from which two shorter staircases descended, one on either side. In front of this was an unadorned gravel driveway. Four tall palms stood like sentries before the façade, and beneath these were rows of forgettable shrubs of the same variety placed before so many other island houses. It was the kind of house passersby didn't notice.

The lights were on inside, but Linnea didn't see anyone beyond the windows. She set her luggage at the foot of the stairs, then climbed up and let herself in, using the keypad she'd convinced her mother to install before she'd left. She and Cooper were forever losing their keys and now that it was the family's full-time home, who knew whether previous renters might have kept the key? Back in the day, Linnea remembered how they used to leave the door unlocked, old-school. Sadly, times had changed everywhere. Even in sleepy island towns.

She closed the door quietly, then stood in the foyer and looked around, her mouth agape. While the outside of the house was woefully bland, the interior was very different, its sophisticated, bright, and utterly charming décor all the more surprising by contrast. This was all her mother's doing. Once they'd moved in, Julia had transformed the rabbit warren of rooms into a spacious, open floor plan. The creamy shiplap walls, polished heart-pine floors, and expansive, white marble and wood kitchen made one feel welcome and instantly at home. As in Lovie's beach house, a great expanse of French windows was opposite the door and, when the sun shone, allowed a breathtaking view of the maritime shrubs and a peek at the great ocean beyond. Now, the night acted as a black cloth over the windows.

Linnea's mother loved splashes of color. She'd decorated this house mostly in white, but the red oriental rugs popped, and the art, like Lovie's, was local. Over the fireplace hung a large painting, its orbs of color revealing Tradd Street in Charleston—and the family house. Linnea remembered that Julia had been ridiculously excited to see the Rutledge House in the artwork and bought it on the spot.

Julia had been a fixture in Charleston's social scene, a member of many important committees. Of course, she could stay on some if she chose, but Linnea wondered how the change of address was changing her mother's involvement with the city, and how she was coping with it.

Julia had loved the Charleston house, doted on it. The beach house had always been just the family's vacation place, one that was usually rented. Now it was home. Well, Linnea thought as she looked around the beautifully redecorated beach house, clearly her mother had put her stamp on this project. She'd brought her favorite pieces, but kept the spirit of the island rather than try to make it an annex of Charleston. But Linnea knew that decorating a house was not the same as loving it. Only a *home* spoke to you. It was a private conversation, with no reference to monetary value or importance of address. It was more intuition, even instinct. Like falling in love.

Unhurried, Linnea made her way across the living room, noting the photographs, none of them recent, housed in silver frames sitting proudly on the fireplace mantel of herself, Cooper, Palmer, Lovie, and Julia's parents. Her grandfather, Stratton Rutledge, was conspicuously absent. Fresh flowers sat on a table beside a spotless crystal bowl filled with shells, and everywhere was the gleam of polish.

Her parents' bedroom door was open. She heard the television, then saw the gray and white flickering of light in the hall. She approached the door and peeked in.

Her mother and father were propped up with pillows in bed, watching the television. Her father was wearing glasses that were slipping down his nose. He looked tan, slimmer in his madras pajamas, his hair a bit thinner at the top; she was glad to see him looking healthy.

Her mother, in a pale-blue silk nightgown with cap sleeves, was more engrossed in the magazine on her lap than the television. Her hair was in the same style she'd worn for as long as Linnea could remember, blond, curved under to just touching the shoulders. The helmet, Cooper called it. Unlike Palmer, Julia was not tan, and Linnea wondered if this was because she always wore a broad-brimmed hat in the sun, or if she was not going outdoors as she once did to work in her garden.

"Hello?" Linnea called out as she stepped into the room.

Her parents' heads swung her way and each face bore an expression of surprise mingled with delight.

"There she is!" Palmer exclaimed in a booming voice. He pushed back the blanket to rise.

"Linnea!" Julia exclaimed at the same time.

"No, don't get up," Linnea said, putting her hand out. "I just wanted to pop in and tell you I made it home. I'm sorry it's so late."

"Heavens, nothing to be sorry for. We were waiting up," Julia said.

Linnea came to her mother's side of the bed, bending to kiss her cheek. She caught the scent of her floral perfume.

"Goodness gracious, what are you wearing?"

Linnea opened her arms to show off the navy-and-white-striped shirt with a bow and her high-waisted navy pants. "Vintage nineteen-forties. You don't recognize them?"

She heard her father bark out a laugh.

"That's before my time," Julia said archly.

"Not by much, darlin'," Palmer chided.

Her mother waved the comment away and let her gaze linger on her daughter, her face soft with love. "Long trip?" When Linnea nodded, Julia tapped the side of her mattress. "You must be tired."

Linnea came to sit on the bed beside her like old times. She couldn't count the number of times she'd hopped into bed with her parents to share what had happened during her day, or even after a date.

"Yeah, I am. But don't forget we're three hours earlier in California."

"Have you eaten?"

"Yes, I'm fine," Linnea assured her mother. "I mostly want a shower."

Linnea almost added, "And a glass of wine," but remembering her father's sobriety, caught herself in time.

"Hold on now," her father said, reducing the volume on the television. "Don't go rushing off. You just got here. Tell us how you are."

Linnea sighed inwardly and felt her toes curl in a crunch. She took a breath and began to create her narrative.

"I'm great," she said with emphasis. "I had a wonderful time in San Francisco. I experienced so much, learned so much. I'm really glad I went."

Her father appeared doubtful. "Then why'd you come home? If you loved it so much."

Linnea shrugged. "It was time."

"Uh-huh," Palmer drawled. "And . . . you broke up with this John fella."

Linnea saw her mother's attention sharpen at the mention of John, could almost feel her radiating tension.

She trod carefully. Her father had been furious that she'd left town to live with a man, much less a man he didn't think worthy of her. Even after two years, the way he said "this John fella" revealed what he thought of him.

"Yes, Daddy, you know we broke up," she said with exaggeration. Then, more sincerely, "It was hard, I'm not going to lie. John's a great guy. I'll always care for him. But we decided we're better off as friends."

Her father snorted derisively. "That man was no bigger than a minnow in a fishing pond. You're better off."

"Friends?" Julia said doubtfully. "How do you remain friends with someone you lived with after you break up? Isn't that like a divorce? Aren't there hard feelings? Things to sort out?"

Linnea squelched her hurt, remembering the night John had told her that he didn't want to get married. Maybe not ever.

"Of course there are. At first we tried to work through them. She shrugged, trying to seem nonchalant when, in fact, the discussion was bruising. Most everything was his at the condo," she continued, "so there wasn't any splitting up of property or anything like that. It was a clean split, as breakups go. But the point is," she said more firmly, "that I knew it was over and I wanted to come home. I missed Charleston. I missed *you*," she told her mother and dad. She saw their worry flee, replaced by affection.

"And we missed you, honey," her father said, his eyes misting. "Come here, darlin'."

Linnea hurried around the bed to enter his open arms. She felt her daddy's arms around her, strong again and safe.

"We're glad you came to your senses and came home," he said. "Where you belong."

"Yes," her mother echoed, nodding. "I never felt good about you being clear across the country. In California . . ." She said the words as though it were Siberia.

Linnea sat back, holding on to her composure by a thin thread. "I'm here now, Mama." She looked at her father and changed the subject. "Oh, Daddy, I saw the house you're building on Isle of Palms. It's wonderful! Really beautiful."

He scrunched up his face. "You saw the house? When?"

Linnea realized she'd just put her foot in her mouth. "Oh, on the way here," she said. "The Uber driver took the Isle of Palms exit. We were driving along Palm Boulevard and I realized I was just blocks from Aunt Cara's, so I directed the driver there. I stopped in to say hello."

Julia tilted her head and asked in a wounded tone, "You stopped at Cara's before you came home?"

"Mama, you weren't even home. You were out, remember? Like I said, I was driving right by."

"How is my little sister?" asked Palmer.

Linnea smiled. "She looks great. Happy. Planning the wedding and all." She paused. Now it was her turn to look at him askance. "Seems weird you haven't seen her. I mean, you're asking *me*? I just arrived from California."

He straightened against the pillows. "We talk and all. On the phone. You know how it is. You can live right next door to someone and not see them all that often. We're all busy."

"But aren't you building that house together? I'd think you'd be seeing a lot of each other."

"Nah," he replied, shaking his head. "She put up the land. I'm doing all the construction. It's better we don't have too many cooks in the kitchen."

"I think she should be more involved," Julia said. Her glance lifted from her hands to meet Palmer's eyes. "After all, she has a lot invested in this project."

Palmer's eyes flashed at Julia before he said with condescension, "Cara's got plenty on her plate with this wedding. She doesn't need to bother with the construction."

"You better not tell her not to worry her pretty little head over business," Linnea warned. "Not if you intend to keep yours."

Palmer rubbed his jaw to hide his smile. "You're right about that. My sister can be a ballbuster." He moved his hand to point at her. "And you're growing up to be just like her."

"Why, thank you," Linnea quipped.

Palmer guffawed, shaking his head. "Rutledge women. I love 'em, but I'm not sure I can live with 'em."

"Thank you very much," Julia piped in.

"Not you, honey. You're made from a different piece of cloth," he said, patting her thigh.

Julia made a face, as though unsure if she was pleased with that comment.

"Don't you worry about Cara," Palmer said. "She's going to do good with her investment. Real good. I'll see to that. Besides, she's not going to have to worry about money, what with marrying ol' Mr. Deep Pockets."

"What?" Linnea asked, genuinely curious. "I mean, I knew he was well-to-do. . . ."

"Honey, there's rich," Palmer said with eyebrows lifted, "and then there's *rich*."

"Don't be crude," Julia said. "We don't talk about other people's money."

A low laugh rumbled in Palmer's chest. "The hell we don't."

Catching the tone of this exchange, Linnea was suddenly eager to retreat to her room. She had a strong instinct for self-preservation. "Well, what little I've seen of the house looks beautiful. I'm proud of you, Daddy. I hope you'll walk me through it."

"Course I will," Palmer said proudly. "Anytime. I'm real pleased with the way it is turning out. It's going to be a showplace."

"It'd better be," Julia said under her breath.

Palmer cast her a look of irritation.

"Well," Linnea said, rising to her feet. "It's late and I think we're all ready for sleep. Let's catch up in the morning. I just want you to know how much I love you, and how happy I am to be home."

"Good night, baby," Palmer said when Linnea bent to kiss his cheek.

She was relieved to smell the soap on his skin and the faint scent of toothpaste—no alcohol. She rose and scooted around the bed to her mother's open arms.

"Aw, good night, precious," her mother said, lifting her face to receive Linnea's kiss.

"Now, tomorrow," her father called after her, in that fatherly tone that implied he was the man of the house and going to take charge, "we can talk about what you have in mind for a job. I have a few ideas to share with you."

Linnea did not react as she had years earlier. She and her father had gone a few rounds, volleying arguments, whenever she took a stand that countered his. Most of the time, he'd won. Which had made her insistence on moving to California such an epic move. Tonight, she reminded herself, the goal was not to fight but to control the narrative.

"That's great, Daddy. I've already sent out feelers to several firms and nonprofits in the area that I'm interested in. My plan is to spend one day to unpack and catch my breath. Then I'm going to begin follow-up calls. I'm confident I'll get something soon. You'll see. I've got it all under control," she added in an upbeat tone.

Palmer stared back at her, somewhat dazed by her gung-ho bravado. "Good," he said. "Real good."

"Take some time to call your friends," her mother advised. "I'm sure they've missed you too."

"I will. Good night," Linnea sang out as she walked to the door.

She closed the door softly behind her, and paused, counting slowly to ten. She felt as if she'd just walked off a stage and was waiting for her next cue.

She crossed the living room to the front door to retrieve her bags. She put her hands on her hips and exhaled, then kicked off her heels. With her father in bed, she had no choice but to lug that damn suitcase up the long flight of stairs herself. Again.

Chapter Five

Dewees Island is a picturesque barrier island off of Charleston accessible only by boat. The island is private, consisting of just residential properties and a wildlife preserve. No cars or stores are allowed on this pristine, protected island.

CARA AWOKE TO the sound of laughing. Sunshine filtered through the linen drapes at the tall windows as she pried open her eyes. Blinking in the light, she followed the sound to the bedroom floor. Sitting on the blue Persian rug, in shafts of morning light, were David and Hope. David was stretched out, his long legs in a straight line, his head cradled in one palm. Hope was perched on her knees across from him, her palms flat on the rug as she leaned forward to better see the flash card he was holding up.

"D!" Hope said with enthusiasm.

"That's right," David replied, then turned the card. "And what's this word?"

"Dog," Hope exclaimed.

"Very good! What does the dog say?"

"Arf-arf!"

David clapped, while Hope gigged with pleasure.

"More, Daddy!"

Cara felt as though her heart would melt. This was the first time she'd heard Hope call David "Daddy." And he was her daddy. She looked forward to the day they made it legal and he adopted her. David was so good with Hope. Cara knew she was blessed to find a man who loved not only her, but her child as well.

She'd never expected to be a mother. She hadn't found love until she was forty. She'd left a corporate job in a big city to settle on Isle of Palms with a lowcountry man—Brett Beauchamps—a life change, but a welcome one. They'd joked that they'd both taken a long time to grow up, or that they'd waited for each other.

After they married, they both wanted children. They'd tried for years, spending their savings on fertility treatments. When at last they'd conceded they'd never conceive a child of their own, Cara wanted to adopt.

Brett did not. He was atypically stubborn about his decision. It had been the single largest obstacle in their marriage. Brett had been a doting uncle to Linnea and Cooper and a second father to Toy Legare's daughter, Lovie. In general, he was a warm, loving man. Cara had wrestled in agony with why this kindly man refused to adopt and love a child of their own.

Yet Cara was a realist. She couldn't pretend that he'd fall in love with an adopted child simply because she wanted him to. Her therapist had advised her to let it go. She'd explained that a man who went into a relationship with children expecting not to like fatherhood probably never would. And, an agency wouldn't place a child in a home where that child might feel his or her rejection on a daily basis—and such a child wouldn't grow to love Brett, and would likely grow angry with Cara as well.

When Brett died, Cara's dream of having a child had died with him. So, years later, Hope's arrival came all the more as a surprise. Her given name was Esperanza—Hope in Spanish—and it was appropriate. Hope had been her miracle. Cara didn't expect another.

She wasn't looking for love. As a new mother, Cara had told herself that even if she'd found a man she thought attractive, he wouldn't be interested in taking on a child who wasn't his own. Most men her age had already raised children and were ready to retire, relax, travel. The last thing they wanted to do was change diapers and babysit.

Sometimes, however, love finds you when you are not even looking for it.

David was Cara's second miracle. Not only did he love her, he loved Hope. He had only one child, Heather. He'd confessed to Cara that he'd spent most of his time as a father growing his law practice and little of it with his daughter. His first wife, Leslie, had borne that responsibility joyfully. Yet he'd always felt he'd missed out. Being a grandfather to Rory, and now to infant Leslie, was an unexpected joy late in his life. The prospect of having Hope as a daughter was his second chance.

Cara lay on the bed a moment longer, watching the two people she loved most in the world interact with each other. "Good morning," she called out. "Is that a private game or can anyone play?"

"Mommy!" Hope leaped to her feet and scrambled atop the bed into Cara's outstretched arms. Cara hugged her close and nibbled her neck, relishing the feel of her child, the smell of her.

"I'm going to eat you for breakfast!"

"No!" Hope giggled, and dug closer.

Hope's favorite thing was to wake up with the birds and climb into bed with her mother. One of the hardest parts of being an older parent was that her body was older too. Cara didn't have the same energy she did when she was younger. Exhaustion was real. She'd reached the island late last night and talked into the wee hours of the morning with David about the wedding, Florence Prescott, and Linnea's surprise arrival. Dawn had come too soon. She wanted nothing more than to lie here and lazily play with Hope all morning, but a glance at the bedside clock gave her a jolt of adrenaline.

"Okay, baby," Cara said, pulling back. "Mama's got to hurry and get dressed."

"I don't want you to go to work," Hope said, her brows gathering.

"You know I always come back. Besides, do you know what day it is?"

Hope shook her head.

"It's pizza day at school! You love pizza!"

Hope brightened.

Cara looked over to David, who had risen and stood at the side of the bed in gray sweatpants and a black T-shirt. "I'm late!"

"Not very. I played with Hope and let you sleep. We were up late last night."

"You're an angel," she said as she whipped back the blanket. "But I have to get going." She gave Hope a quick kiss. "Come on, baby. Let's see who can get dressed first. The winner gets—"

"A new toy," said Hope.

"I'll bring you a treat home from work. Hurry now!"

Hope scrambled off the bed. Cara's long pink silk nightgown skimmed the floor as she raced to the bathroom. Over her shoulder she called to David, "I'll take a quick shower. Would you mind getting her dressed for school? I've got to catch the eight o'clock ferry. I've a meeting this morning."

"On it," he called back. "Come on, sweetie pie," he said, extending his hand to Hope. "Show me what you want to wear."

Hope took his outstretched hand without a backward glance at Cara. Cara remembered the days Hope wouldn't want to leave her side for anyone, and felt a pang of regret. Then she laughed at herself for being an idiot. How lucky she was that Hope wanted to go with David! She dashed into the bathroom and closed the door.

A short time later, Cara stepped into the kitchen of David's house in tan linen slacks and a sage-green cotton shirt. A corded belt of different shades of green cinched her waist. She looked chic and professional for her meeting with the marketing team.

She stepped into mayhem. Heather was pacing the room in her pajamas carrying a crying Leslie. Her blond hair fell unkempt down her back and dark circles shadowed her eyes. David was at the stove heating a bottle. Over at the table, kneeling on the banquette, Rory was crying because he'd spilled his bowl of cereal. Milk and cereal covered the table, and his shirt and pants were drenched. Hope watched with wide eyes, a moment away from bursting into tears as well.

Cara rushed to the sink to fetch a sponge. "Here comes the cavalry," she called out in a cheery voice.

"Thank God," David called over his shoulder. He handed the bottle to Heather, then hurried to the table to begin scooping cereal from the table into the bowl. "No need to cry," he told Rory. "Accidents happen."

"That's right," Cara cooed as she wiped up the mess. "We'll get you another bowl."

"My shirt," Rory cried.

"I'll get you a clean one," David reassured him, and began removing Rory's wet clothing.

The baby's crying only exacerbated the tension in the room. At four months old, she was very colicky and was still waking up multiple times in the night.

"Where's Bo?" Cara asked David in a low voice, referring to Heather's husband.

"He got called out on an emergency." He glanced across the room at Heather, who was trying to persuade Leslie to take her bottle. "Cami missed the ferry. She's at the dock on IOP, waiting for the next one."

Cara rolled her eyes. If ever they needed the nanny! Rory had stopped crying at last and sat, sniffling, in his red and blue Spider-Man underwear, content to be dry. Cara offered him a fresh bowl of cereal. Hope, in her yellow daisy sundress, picked daintily at her berries. The two children looked at each other as they ate.

Cara checked her watch, then said to David, "If you grab fresh clothes for Rory, I'll finish cleaning the mess. Then I really must go. Cami can take them to school on a later ferry."

"No need for them to be late—I'll take them to school. I can drive us all to the dock."

"Okay. We can leave the cart there for Cami."

"Sounds like a plan. You grab a cup of coffee. We'll be ready in a few minutes."

"Aren't you going to dress?"

He looked down at his sweatpants and T-shirt. "I live on Dewees Island. Who's going to care?"

As he'd predicted, all were ready to go within five minutes' time. Heather had slipped away to take the baby upstairs. Standing alone in the kitchen, Cara thought it looked like a bomb had hit it. She was relieved to duck out and leave it to the nanny.

After buckling the children in their car seats on the oversize cart, David and Cara sat beside each other in front. Cara glanced back, watching the two children chatter amiably about silly things. She couldn't help but smile. Rory and Hope were both four and the best of friends. They'd grown up together, shared the same nanny, and went to preschool with each other. Still, living all in one house with another family was proving to be exhausting.

David started the engine and the golf cart took off. Cara held on as they jostled along the gravel-and-sand road toward the ferry. It was an overcast morning that promised rain. The humidity lay heavy in the air and mosquitoes hummed. Out on the lagoons the wading birds were hunting for breakfast. A dozen wood storks perched in one large oak tree, looking like white sails on a tall ship. In the center of the pond, preening on long legs, were her beloved roseate spoonbills. Their pink feathers were pearlescent against the gray water.

It was a short trip to the Dewees Island dock, a long wooden structure with a handsome painted sign that read DEWEES ISLAND, SC: WELCOME. No cars were allowed on the island—hence the long line of golf carts parked along the wooden walkway. David found a spot near the dock, and they unloaded. David held Rory's hand and Cara held Hope's as they walked as quickly as little feet would pace. Other passengers were already boarding the ferry.

"Good morning, Mr. Wyatt," called out the captain. "Miss Cara. How are the little kids this morning?"

"We're all fine," Cara replied with a smile as Hope clung to her leg and eyed him suspiciously.

Rory waved, more familiar with the tanned, wiry man in the captain's hat.

"Just in time!" the captain declared. "All aboard!"

No sooner had David and Cara gotten the children seated inside the air-conditioned ferry than the big engines fired up. The metal benches were nearly filled, most of them with neighbors of David's. They greeted one another warmly before settling into the morning newspapers. Rory and Hope stood on the seats and looked out the port windows as the big boat pulled away from the dock. Then, with a surge, it began its journey along the Intracoastal toward Isle of Palms.

Cara sighed with relief that they'd made it in time for the ferry. "What a morning," she said to David.

He looked her way and nodded. Cara didn't have to add *again*. They both knew that ever since Leslie had arrived, the quiet mornings had become chaotic.

David lowered his head close to hers to be heard over the churning engine. "I was thinking . . ." he began. "Once we're married, it might get a little crowded at the house. Now that Heather has two children."

Cara looked out the window at the whitewater wakes from the ferry's engines and felt awash with relief. "I've been thinking about this too, but it wasn't my place to say anything. I'm the intruder, after all. The commute to the city for work is no problem on occasion, but every day would add too much time away from Hope and you."

"I agree."

She turned to look at him. "You do? I was in a quandary. I didn't want to tell you. I know you love that house. You love Dewees."

His eyes kindled. "I love that you were willing to make the sacrifice of travel. Yes, I do love the island. I always will. But," he said in decision, "it's not working for us as a couple."

"Where do you want to live?" Cara asked him.

"Anywhere you are."

Her heart melted. "You are a smooth operator."

"So I've been told."

"I hope you know how much I love you."

David looked out the window, his hand securing Rory's back, and smiled. "I do."

She studied his profile, so handsome. He was strong enough to be gentle. "What about my beach house?"

David faced her again, his brows furrowed in thought. "We could live there. For a while. But I think not for long." Her face must have reflected her disappointment because he hurried to add, "Cara, the beach house, as charming as it is, is small. As Hope grows up and has friends over, we'll need more room."

Hope began jumping up and down, pointing out the window and squealing, "I see a dolphin! Mama, a dolphin!"

"Yes, I see it," Cara said with feigned enthusiasm. She tightened her hold on her child, but didn't look for the mammal, her attention caught instead by the conversation. She patted Hope's behind, then turned back to David.

"I never thought we'd leave the beach house. I think it could work."

"I don't think so. Aside from a playroom for the children, I need an office. And a real garage."

"I see." She too looked out the window. She couldn't say anything more.

"I'm not saying we should sell it," David said. "I wouldn't ask that. I know how much you love it. And the family history. We can rent it out."

Cara didn't respond.

David took hold of her free hand. "We both agree my house on

Dewees won't work for us. Neither will yours. Cara, you might want to consider where else we could live. Someplace that's ours and that meets both of our needs. And Hope's. Someplace we can start our lives fresh."

This was his closing argument, she thought. Calm, resolute, flawless reasoning. It was no wonder he'd been such a successful trial lawyer.

"I want to stay on the islands," she said.

"Fine with me."

The engines slowed to a low growl as the ferry approached the Isle of Palms dock. Mansions fronted with long docks lined the waterway to the left. To the right was the marina, with ocean-worthy yachts anchored beside sailboats and motorboats of all sizes.

Dewees Island had a private parking lot where residents left their cars. They disembarked from the ferry and had a brief chat with Cami, who waited for the return trip to Dewees. Then they walked at a four-year-old's pace to where two cars waited for them. Cara helped David buckle the children in their car seats. He would drive the children to preschool. She kissed David good-bye and headed to her red Volvo.

On the drive to Charleston, Cara thought more about the important conversation they'd had on the ferry. She was rational by nature and appreciated David's reasoning. If she allowed herself to be pragmatic and not emotional, she readily saw that he was right. They needed to find a new house for them as a family.

But tonight, she thought, tightening her hands on the wheel, she wouldn't go back to Dewees. She felt the need to go home to her beach house. To sleep in her own bed. No matter where they chose to live, she wouldn't give up her mama's beach house. Not now. Not ever.

Chapter Six

Loggerheads, one of seven sea turtle species, comprise nearly all the nesting South Carolina beaches. From May to August the female will lay three to six nests, approximately twelve to fourteen days apart. Each nest contains an average of 120 eggs.

LINNEA AWOKE EARLY, as usual. It had been a particularly restless night. John had invaded her dreams with his soulful green eyes, his wry smile that always made her feel he had some story to tell her—only her. Rousing, she checked her phone, sure he had texted. But he had not. Nor e-mailed. It was utter silence from San Francisco.

She propelled herself from bed. *Get up,* she told herself. *Don't wallow in self-pity.* Action, not reaction, that was the only thing that helped dispel the cloud of misery that descended on her whenever she dwelled on John. She couldn't sit and stare at the phone, hoping it would ring. She was powerless to make John want to call, and to call him would be an act of desperation. It was over, she told herself. She had to move on. She had to physically move.

She dug through her suitcase for a pair of shorts and a top. After several days at home, clothes were now unfolded and spilling onto the floor. She really had to properly unpack, she told herself. She was growing accustomed to wrinkled clothes. She knew her mother was horrified and beginning to worry. She sniffed a pair of denim shorts and a white shirt and put them on.

The coast was clear in the kitchen. After a gulp of coffee, she slipped into her old flip-flops, grabbed one of her mother's straw hats, and headed to the beach. Dawn was just breaking by the time she arrived. Looking out at the rosy horizon, she felt the warmth of a new day's promise. She slipped off her sandals, squeezing the cool, damp grains of sand between her toes, then began to walk. The outgoing tide had exposed shells along the beach. Linnea swung her arms and walked at a brisk pace, getting her heart rate up and sharpening her senses.

The water was calm this morning. No surfers lined up in the breakers. In the distance she spotted a couple walking two large dogs. One looked to be a black Labrador, leaping joyfully into the ocean in chase of a ball. Watching the dogs, Linnea wished, as she often did, that she had some furry pet to snuggle. Maybe this was the summer to do that. She could use some cuddling, she thought.

A young woman was walking her way, carrying a plastic trash bag. She was long and lean, with red hair bound in a messy bun beneath a Turtle Team baseball cap. Her sage-green T-shirt, which held the image of a sea turtle, was purposefully ragged at the edges and hung over very short denim jeans, stylishly torn. She watched as the woman bent to pick up a flimsy piece of trash from the beach and toss it into the bag. As she drew near, Linnea waved.

"Hey, that's cool what you're doing," Linnea called out.

"Someone's got to do it." She stopped next to Linnea. Her oversize aviator sunglasses covered most of her face.

Linnea pointed to the cap. "Are you on the turtle team?"

"Sure am," she said. "I joined last year. My section is just ahead, but the season hasn't started yet. Mid-May we'll start officially walking the patrol. But I like to park at Breach Inlet and walk the beach, pick up trash, see the birds, just hang. Once I start looking for tracks, I have to walk along the high-tide line and be more focused."

"I get it. I used to be on the team before I moved away. I guess I'd better go see Emmi and get back on the team."

"That might be tough. There's a long waiting list."

"I'll get on," Linnea said with confidence.

The girl tilted her head and didn't smile.

Linnea was momentarily embarrassed, realizing how conceited that sounded. She put her hand out with a friendly smile. "My name's Linnea. My grandmother was Lovie Rutledge—she started the turtle team eons ago. I guess you could say I've been on the team most of my life," she said in way of explanation.

The girl removed her sunglasses. Linnea saw finely arched brows over deep-blue eyes. After a pause, she said, "You don't remember me, do you?"

Linnea dropped her hand, scanning her memory banks. The woman seemed to be about her age. Taller, pretty, interested in turtles . . . She felt she should know her—she knew so many people around Charleston— but her mind was blank.

"Uh, you look so familiar. I'm sorry. . . ."

"I'm Annabelle. Chalmers."

Linnea still couldn't place her.

"I went to Porter-Gaud with you. I was a year behind you."

Recognition dawned. "Annabelle! Oh, of course," Linnea said in a rush. "I'm sorry I didn't recognize you right away." No wonder she couldn't recall Annabelle, a reclusive girl known for being somewhat radical, at least among the traditional students who filled the exclusive Charleston private school. Linnea remembered her keeping to herself and wearing a lot of black. She'd hung around with Marquetta, one of the few African American girls in the school. They were forever attending political rallies and putting up signs around the school. They'd never joined in school activities if they could avoid it.

"Yeah, well, you hung out in different circles," Annabelle said in summation.

There was a superior tone to the comment, but Linnea took no offense. It was true. Linnea had been popular in high school and a fixture in the school's social activities.

"It's nice to see you again. So, where'd you head after graduation?" Linnea asked.

"University of North Carolina Wilmington," Annabelle said. "How about you?"

"South Carolina. Go Gamecocks," she said lamely. She waited for Annabelle to say "Go Seahawks," but she didn't. "What about Marquetta? I heard she went to Yale?"

A smile of pride eased across Annabelle's face. "She did. She came home after graduation and right off the bat got a job in a state senator's office. Marquetta's going to kick ass."

"Good for her." Linnea thought it made sense that the politically motivated young girl was now in politics.

There was an awkward silence. Linnea rallied. "Well," she said in that tone that said good-bye, "it was nice to see you again."

"Yeah. See you around." Annabelle offered a brief wave of her fingers, then turned and headed back toward Breach Inlet.

Linnea watched her long legs and Havaianas sandals trace a parallel path to her incoming tracks. *That was such a weird exchange,* she thought. There was an undercurrent that was almost combative. As if Annabelle had some kind of chip on her shoulder. Was it because Linnea hadn't recognized her? She wouldn't recognize *anyone* behind those giant sunglasses. But in truth, even knowing who she was, she really couldn't say she remembered her. Most of Linnea's best friends in high school lived South of Broad in her neighborhood. They'd been friends since nursery school, journeyed through elementary school together. By the time they made it to high school, bonds had been set in stone. Charleston could be a small town in that way.

And yet, Linnea realized, she'd been home nearly a week and hadn't yet called any of her old friends. She knew why. She still wasn't ready to talk about the past, even if she was controlling her narrative.

She changed direction, not wanting to follow Annabelle. Not a great start to her morning, she thought, pumping her arms to get back her mojo. As she walked, she cast her gaze out over the ocean. A line of pelicans flew over the waves in formation, their broad wings almost touching the water. She counted eleven. Gulls were out in force, their raucous laughter sounding overhead. Peeps played their endless game of tag with the waves. *Dear peeps,* she thought with genuine affection.

The sand grew warmer under her feet as the sun rose higher in the sky. She slowed down her pace, not in any hurry. She had no appointment to keep, no job to get to. Linnea was lost in her thoughts when her gaze was arrested by movement farther up the beach. She stopped, squinting, trying to make out what the mounded shape was. Instinct flared. She drew closer, and her heart began pounding as the mound moved again. She stopped abruptly and held her breath.

She couldn't quite believe her eyes. It was a loggerhead! But it couldn't be. It was only the end of April—too soon for a nesting turtle, wasn't it? Her mind whirled with questions. The nesting season usually began mid-May. But staring out, there was no denying this was a loggerhead. She had to be a nesting female. In the daylight! That alone was rare. She was returning to the sea after her long trek across the sand to nest in the dunes. Linnea could readily see the telltale tracks, two feet wide, scarring the tide-swept beach. One long line led from the ocean to the dunes; the second trailed behind the turtle as she crawled back to the ocean.

Careful, she told herself. No sudden moves! She didn't want to alarm the turtle. If the turtle had been incoming, Linnea would have stayed back, out of sight, so as not to disturb her on her way to nest. It was normal for a turtle to sit in the surf under the cloak of darkness and scope out the beach. If she spotted anything threatening—a human, a strange light, an animal—the turtle would turn around at the shoreline and head back to the safety of her home, the sea. Coming ashore was dangerous business for a sea turtle. Out of the water, she had to contend with the effects of gravity on her three-hundred-plus-pound body. She was clumsy, slow. Vulnerable to attack.

Yet this turtle's work was done; she was crawling back to the sea. Linnea quickly scanned the area to see if other people were near. She didn't want to attract attention to the turtle. No one was out this far along the southern tip of the island. Again, rare for a loggerhead to nest here. Linnea moved forward again, keeping to the turtle's rear so as not to startle her. Drawing close, she marveled at her size and majesty. What a beauty! Linnea had never seen a wild turtle so close in the light of day before.

This was a full-grown female, at least three hundred pounds, probably more, in her prime. Sand covered her shell, encrusted with several barnacles. Linnea counted five large scales down the turtle's midline, bordered by five pairs of scales along the edges. The turtle lifted her blockish brown head, as though sniffing the salt air. Linnea knew the loggerhead had been given its name because of its massive head. With its incredibly powerful jaw, the loggerhead could eat any type of food it could get its mouth on, preferably mollusks and crabs, though its favorite treat was jellyfish.

The turtle heaved a heavy sigh; then, with almost exaggerated effort, her right flipper dug into the sand and she dragged her heft forward. The right, then the left, then the right, over and over. When she reached the wet sand, she lifted her head as though smelling the salt air and tasting home. The turtle sped up with palpable enthusiasm into the breach. The first wave washed over her, clearing away the sand and revealing the gorgeous deep color of her reddish-brown carapace.

Linnea put her hands to her mouth, feeling a kinship with the turtle as she struggled to reach her home. She understood what it felt like, after a long journey, to cross the threshold back into a community that was filled not with strangers but with familiar faces, smiling, and surroundings familiar and welcoming.

"You're home, sweet mama!" she called out as the turtle's powerful flippers stroked the waves, and in that miraculous moment the turtle was transformed. She lost her gangly clumsiness and with a few strokes became a beautiful swimmer, graceful and strong.

Linnea stood in the surf, tears in her eyes, her arms crossed tight across her chest, and watched the large head of the turtle move farther out in the dark water until, at last, the turtle dove and disappeared into the sea. Then she took a breath and, filled with excitement, took off running. She was an idiot to have left her phone at home. She had to call Emmi and Cara.

Turtle season was on!

✼   ✼   ✼

THERE WAS EXCITEMENT in the air as the turtle team left Emmi's garden. Emmi, Cara, Flo, and Linnea stood at the garden gate to wave farewell to their fellow team members. The Island Turtle Team had its first nest.

The team had come running when Emmi made the calls. There was an air of disbelief mixed with excitement as they'd moved the nest farther up the beach to a safer location. Sullivan's had gained a lot of land from points north, and new dunes were forming. The nest was marked with the orange SCDNR sign that declared it legally protected, and Barb had taken photos. When the nest was safely put to bed, the team had gathered at Emmi's house to hastily organize the start of a new turtle nesting season.

Flo shook her white head and said with amazement, "I've been on this team since Sally Murphy started the teams back in the eighties. The Department of Natural Resources always set May fifteenth for us to begin walking the beaches looking for tracks. But April thirtieth? Are you kidding me? I can't believe it."

"Climate change," said Linnea succinctly.

"It can't all be climate change," Flo replied dryly.

"Of course it can," Cara said. "The season is starting early for so many species. Look at the migrating birds. And this heat so early! That should be your first clue."

"Regardless of the reason," Emmi said, playing the role of team leader, "the season has begun. Michelle Pate is the boss, and she wants the volunteers across the state to start. Thank goodness we finished training the new recruits." She looked at Linnea and asked with a tease sparking in her eyes, "Do you need a refresher course?"

Linnea snorted. "No! I've been on the team almost as long as you have."

Emmi chuckled in acknowledgment. "Come on, y'all. I could use another cup of coffee."

Linnea had followed her grandmother Lovie on turtle treks for as long as she could remember. The system hadn't changed in the past thirty years, though the number of volunteers had swelled to the 140 on the team now. The volunteers walked their designated sections of beach daily at 6 a.m., then reported back to the core team. This small group was permitted by the SCDNR to make critical decisions for the nests. For Isle of Palms and Sullivan's Island, the team was led by Emmi Baker. Mary, Barb, Tee, Cindy, Bev, and Crystal made up the rest of the core. Cara and Flo were members, but more honorary than active.

As permit holders, the core members located the eggs and made the important decisions whether to leave the eggs in situ to incubate or, if the nest was in a location that could cause harm to the eggs, move it to a safer spot on the dunes. Nests were discovered early in the morning most days until mid-August. Then came the nest-hatching period, which lasted from mid-July until sometime in October. From the discovery of the first nest until the last hatchling swam off to the Gulf Stream, sea turtles were the center of the lives of the volunteers.

Linnea waved farewell to the last team member, then followed the ladies into Emmi's kitchen. Stepping back inside, she leaned against the wall and let her gaze sweep across the room. Pale-blue cabinets, creamy shiplap wood, heart-pine floors—the style was casual, comfortable, welcoming.

Linnea remembered back to when the team meetings had been held at her grandmother's beach house. Lovie and Flo had been best friends, the two of them forever traipsing between the two houses with food, gossip, and turtle news. Cara and Emmi had come to the island for the summers and grown up best friends. They too felt equally at home in both women's kitchens. Years had passed, marked by marriages, divorces, births, and deaths. But the tradition of walking freely between the two houses remained a constant. Looking at the women sitting at the table—Cara, Flo, Emmi—Linnea realized that she was the first of the next generation to roost with the other hens in these kitchens. She counted herself fortunate to have these women in her life.

She refreshed her coffee, then went to join them at the table.

"Well, that's one for the books," Emmi said, summing up the morning. "The first nest in South Carolina is put to bed. That's something."

"Yes," Cara agreed. Then, turning to smile at her, she added, "And Linnea found it. If she hadn't been out walking, I wonder how long it would've taken for anyone to notice the nest. If ever."

"It would've been a rogue nest," said Linnea.

"Another day and the tracks would've been swept away," added Emmi.

Flo stretched out her arm across the table. Her skin was so thin now that Linnea could see the veins bulge blue. "You saved the day, kiddo." Flo's eyes sparked with approval; satisfied, she leaned back in her chair.

"I was just lucky," Linnea demurred. "But I'll never forget it. Seeing that mama out there, in the daylight no less, returning to the sea . . ."

"I wished you'd called," Flo said begrudgingly. "A daytime nester is rare."

"I would've if I'd had my phone! I know, I know," Linnea said, hand up. "It won't happen again. But I wasn't planning on seeing a turtle!"

Flo said again with disbelief, "A nest in April . . ."

"I have to admit," Linnea said, "being alone made it even more special. I'd never been alone with a turtle before. It was just the two of us. It felt sacred. I followed her right up to the ocean. I walked in up to my ankles and didn't go any farther. But . . ." She hesitated. Did she dare explain what she'd felt, or would they think she was being ridiculous—even childish?

"What?" asked Cara, her voice and expression encouraging.

Linnea continued: "Watching the mother turtle, something inside me made me want to follow all the way with her. To swim out to the breakers, then dive under the water. To see where she would take me." She laughed shortly, embarrassed by the confession. "Of course, I couldn't."

Cara looked at her, her smile wistful. "I know what you mean." She paused. "Years back"—she shook her head—"goodness, it was the first time I ever saw a turtle laying her nest. I was with Mama."

Flo made a soft sound of recognition, knowing the story that was coming.

"Mama had awakened me," Cara continued. "She dragged me out of bed to watch. I was, shall we say, a bit grumpy about it. I didn't care much for turtles back then. At all. I was jealous of them when I was growing up. They took up so much of my mother's attention. Anyway, out I went. We watched the turtle lay her nest, side by side, holding hands, and for the first time, the shared experience bonded us rather than separated us. We stayed back and gave her space to throw sand and camouflage the nest, then we quietly walked the turtle back to the sea, just like you did this morning. Mama said we were her honor guard." Cara's face eased to a soft smile in memory. "We stood with our feet in the bath-warm water, and Mama talked about wanting to go with her. Just like you are now. I remember she said she wanted to dive under the sea. One breath . . . and she'd be gone." Cara paused. "That was the night she told me she was dying."

"Oh," Linnea said softly, moved. She looked around the table and saw the impact of the story on the faces of Flo and Emmi, each lost in her own thoughts.

"I don't mean to be a downer," Cara added with a short laugh. "It was just I understood what you meant."

"It was a nice story," Flo reassured her. "I hadn't remembered that in a long time. We do go to another world, you know. Someday. We all take that final breath and just . . . go," she said in her matter-of-fact manner. "Frankly, I'm ready for it."

Emmi waved her hand. "Hush now, Flo. Don't talk like that."

"Like what?" Flo asked indignantly. "It's how I feel. I lived a good life. No regrets."

Linnea looked at Flo, her blue eyes bright with confidence and assurance, and caught a glimpse of the Florence Prescott she'd not seen in years. The vivacious, funny, wise woman she'd once been.

Emmi turned to Linnea and changed the subject. "It's so nice you're back in Charleston. How long are you here for this time? Why didn't you tell us you were coming?"

Linnea felt Emmi's eyes boring into her and cast a quick glance at Cara. She returned a gaze that told her she might as well get it over with.

"I . . . I didn't tell anyone I was coming, except my parents. You see . . ." Linnea took a breath and plowed on. "This isn't a vacation." She rubbed her hands together under the table. How to tell John's mother that they'd broken up? There was no easy way. Suddenly everything seemed so complicated. She looked up and met Emmi's gaze.

Emmi's expressive green eyes, so much like John's, appeared confused. "I don't follow."

Linnea decided to be blunt and let the truth speak for itself. "I've moved back home," she said. "I left California."

"What?" Emmi said, stunned. "Why?"

"The startup I worked at failed. My job disappeared." She looked at her hands.

Across the table, Flo clucked her tongue. "Oh, honey, that's too bad."

Emmi leaned forward. "But you said you moved back home. Permanently?"

Linnea licked her lips. "Yes. John and I broke up."

It took a second for Emmi to digest this. "Oh no," she said with dismay. "You two seemed so happy together." She turned to Cara. "Didn't I just say what a great couple they were?" She swung her head back to Linnea. "I was waiting for the big announcement."

"I'm sorry," Linnea muttered.

"Nothing to be sorry about," Flo said.

"What happened?" asked Emmi.

Linnea blew out a stream of air. She was stuck in the unenviable position of having to talk about her breakup with her boyfriend's mother. She felt tongue-tied. What could she say? She didn't want to sound negative about John. Anything she said could, and likely would, be misconstrued.

"Emmi, I think you should call John and ask him about it."

"I'm asking you."

"Emmi . . ." Cara said in warning.

"No, it's okay," Emmi said, trying to sound positive. "I just want to know what happened. Maybe it's just a big misunderstanding."

Linnea didn't think John's inability to grow up and commit was a big misunderstanding. "I really don't want to go into it with you, if you don't mind. In fact"—she looked at her watch—"I must get going. It's getting late."

Emmi leaned forward and rested her hand on Linnea's arm, staying her. "I'm sorry. I didn't mean to push. Please don't feel you have to rush off."

Linnea looked into her eyes and felt a moment's relief.

Emmi smiled her enormous smile. "God, I was awful. I'm sorry. I was just caught off guard. I shouldn't have put you on the spot. But," she said reassuringly, "I can bet the fault had something to do with John."

Linnea offered her a tenuous smile. "It takes two to tango." Then, more sincerely, she added, "Just know that I'm sad. And he's sad. And we're trying very hard to remain friends."

Emmi nodded, her lips tight as though holding her thoughts in.

Linnea rose. "I really do have to go."

"Hold on," Cara said, also rising. "I've got to dash too. I took the morning off from the aquarium but must get back. Good meeting. I think everyone's got their marching orders and are gung-ho. I'll alert the aquarium when I get there. And I'll be available for turtle duty only on an ad hoc basis," she reminded Emmi.

"I know. You're doing your part for the turtles at the aquarium. But I'll call you for consults."

"You'd better." Cara leaned forward to kiss Emmi's cheek. "See ya."

Emmi walked them to the door. She said to Linnea, "We're okay, right? What happens with you and John is your business. I don't want this to come between us."

Linnea wondered if that was possible. "Let's not let it."

"I'm glad you're back on the team. We missed you."

Linnea and Cara walked along the stone path through Emmi's garden, ablaze now in red azaleas, through the white picket fence gate.

"Well, I'm glad that's over," Linnea remarked as she latched the gate.

"It went better than I'd expected. I thought she'd weep and wail and throw herself on a mock funeral pyre." When Linnea groaned, Cara said, "Take it as a compliment. You were her dream daughter-in-law. And she's dying for your grandchildren."

"She has two from James!"

"She wants John's grandchildren. He always was her favorite."

She looked at Cara. "Tell her not to hold her breath."

The memory of John telling her that he didn't want children flashed in her mind, bringing again the short stab of hurt. She didn't want to think about that now. Or about John. Emmi would have to learn to deal with John's decisions, as she had.

Linnea paused in the driveway where the vista opened to reveal the breadth of the Atlantic. Now dark clouds were moving in and the ocean reflected the gunmetal color. "Looks like a storm's coming in."

"It's due sometime tomorrow," said Cara. "I can smell the rain."

"The surfers will be happy."

"That reminds me," Cara exclaimed. "I have something that belongs to you. Follow me."

Cara led her to the storage area underneath the front porch. She flicked on the rusting overhead light. The small space was chock-full of stuff covered in dust, sand, and spiderwebs.

"It's in here," Cara said, poking her head into the cramped space. "In the far back. Yes, I see it." She turned and pointed.

Linnea's heart skipped at seeing the tall blue surfboard. It had once been Brett's. Cara had given it to Linnea a few years earlier when Linnea learned how to surf. Not only was it her first surfboard, but it meant the world that it had belonged to a man she'd loved like a second father growing up. She put her hands to her cheeks.

"Big Blue!" she exclaimed. "You kept it."

"Of course I did! It's been here, waiting for you to return."

Linnea squeezed past the old VW bug under a sand-and-dust-coated tarp.

"You really are a hoarder," Linnea said, resigned to seeing her shirt smeared with dirt. "You kept the Gold Bug too."

The VW bug was a fixture on Isle of Palms. It had originally belonged to Lovie. Everyone on the island knew that if the Gold Bug was spotted parked along Palm Boulevard, a turtle nest was involved. Lovie had passed the car on to Cara.

"Believe it or not, it works like a charm. That car will never die. Brett took such good care of it. And then . . . well, I couldn't take it with me to Chattanooga. When I adopted Hope, I bought the Volvo. The poor thing's been in hibernation all these years. I take her out on the Fourth of July, for old times' sake."

Linnea made it past the car, then climbed over a stroller and some clay pots, swiping away spiderwebs, to reach the surfboard. It was resting on a shelf Brett had built especially for it, obscured by a thick layer of grime. She brushed away the coating of muck to reveal the bright-blue color. Linnea felt the emotion of too many memories surge. She swallowed hard.

"I forgot how much I loved this board."

"Brett loved it too. I remember him waxing it. He was so methodical. He enjoyed doing it." She smiled in memory. "He used to say it was his tai chi exercise."

"It's totally a classic board. John always admired it. Told me to take good care of it. As if I wouldn't," she snorted. "It's a bit heavy for me, but Big Blue gives a good ride."

"Come on," Cara said. "Let's pull the board out. You should take it home."

"I don't have a car."

"What happened to your Mini Cooper?"

"I sold that when I moved to San Francisco. I needed the money. My parents didn't support my move, if you recall."

"I do indeed. Quite the fireworks display. I also remember being quite proud that you were brave enough to go toe-to-toe with Palmer. You went out west with just the money you had in the bank and a jar of peanut butter."

"I had a good mentor."

"Hardly," Cara said, swiping away a spiderweb as she followed Linnea through the densely crowded, makeshift garage under the porch.

Linnea could see that Cara was pleased with the compliment. "Don't forget, I also had a place to stay. . . ."

"Yes," Cara said, reaching her side. She made a face. "But I'm guessing in the end, the rent was pretty high."

Linnea felt a momentary pang. She brushed her sleeve. "Yeah. It was."

"Okay, take one end. We can carry it over our heads. It's the only way we'll get it out."

The two women squeezed back out of the storage space, then laid the board on the ground and stood a moment brushing away the dirt from themselves.

"I'll drive you home. We can stick this in the back. The tail will stick out some." She laughed. "It'll be like old times."

Linnea was awash with relief. "Thank you. I was about to call Uber."

"Well, I have some more good news for you."

"More?"

"Why don't you take the Gold Bug? It's just sitting under here, gathering dust and rust. It would be good for it to be driven again."

The offer seemed too good to pass up. She needed a car desperately. But there was no way she could afford one and her parents were no longer able to help. Everyone was pinching pennies these days. She reached up to scratch a bit of web from her hair.

"I'd love it, of course. Except I don't have any money right now. No job . . . yet. Maybe we could work out a layaway or something?"

"I'm not trying to sell it to you," Cara said with an astonished laugh. "I'm giving it to you."

"Oh no," Linnea sputtered. "I couldn't let you do that. That's too big. A surfboard is one thing. A car—"

"Don't be silly. The surfboard is yours. I just held it for you. But, Linnea, I want to give the car to you." Her voice changed to reflect her seriousness. "You're my niece, and we both know you helped me in more ways than I can count after Brett died. I'll never be able to repay you for that. You need a car, so take it. And frankly, you'd be doing me a favor. It's just sitting here taking up space, rusting away."

"But you could sell it—"

"Please," Cara scoffed. "I'd never. And I couldn't give it to just anybody. There's far too much sentimental value in that old rust bucket for that. It would give me great pleasure to see the Gold Bug buzzing around the island again. And you know Lovie would approve. It's an old car, positively ancient. It's not worth all that much." She shrugged. "Though it has surprisingly good mileage for a car its age."

Linnea smirked. "Only driven by two old ladies on the island."

Cara barked out a laugh. "Good one."

Linnea felt tears spring to her eyes. Cara's generosity seemed endless. "I don't know what to say. I've always loved this car. Did you know that?"

Cara shook her head.

"I always felt so cool when Grandmama Lovie would take me for a ride in it with the top down. When I turned sixteen, I begged Daddy to get me a VW just like it. But fickle youth . . . I saw a Mini Cooper and fell in love." She sighed with disbelief. "But now I've got the Gold Bug at last."

"Well, don't get too excited. We'll have to see if it will start up. I'll make an appointment with ol' Mr. Tut. He's retired now and his son runs the shop. But Mr. Tut still hangs around. He can't keep his hands out of the grease and motors. He knows this car better than anyone."

Linnea couldn't believe her luck. "Now all I need is a job."

"How's it going in that department?"

Linnea lifted her shoulders. "As you predicted. I've got a few leads I'm following up. Nothing solid. But, hey, I'm hopeful. In the meantime . . ." She smiled. "Surf's up!"

Chapter Seven

Oceans are the planet's lifeblood. Oceans cover more than 70 percent of the earth's surface and provide habitat for many of the planet's organisms and produce most of the world's oxygen.

A STORMY OCEAN was a siren call for the local surfers. When the wind blew and the current got rough, waves along the Isle of Palms shoreline could be measured in feet, not inches.

It was a drizzly, gray morning. Linnea woke early and slipped into her bikini and a Naish T-shirt. She packed her wet suit and a towel into her backpack, tossed in a stainless steel water bottle, then loaded Big Blue into her brother's monster truck, which she'd borrowed. As she drove along Palm Boulevard dawn was breaking, but already cars with strapped-on surfboards were on the move. She followed a rusted white truck with two surfboards poking out from the bed, fins up. It belched fumes whenever it stopped. It parked near the Twenty-Fourth Avenue beach path and she pulled in beside it.

Climbing down from the truck, she spotted two slender, ripped men emerging from the other pickup. The guys were already wearing their wet suits, which told her they likely lived on the island. No one drove too far in a steamy suit. The taller one was blond and cut a Thor-like figure with his shaggy hair and broad shoulders. She was checking him out when the second man stepped into her line of view. He was shorter, lean, and more wiry. His red hair was cut short, though the curls were beguiling in a boyish way. He glanced up and, spotting her watching, smiled and waved in a neighborly manner. Surfers shared a camaraderie on the beach.

Linnea was struck by the vivid blueness of his eyes and how his smile transformed his face from ordinary to extraordinary. Taken aback at being caught staring, she returned a brief, awkward wave.

"Nice truck," he called.

"Thanks. It's my brother's."

"And he lets you drive it?" He rested his palm against the truck bed. "He must be a nice bloke. Not sure I'd let my sister drive my truck." He laughed. "If I had a truck as nice as that one."

"It's his pride and joy," she called back. "I'm under strict orders. I can drive it once, maybe twice while he's away. He's in England. Is that where you're from?"

The man walked closer so they wouldn't have to shout. She could see that a few freckles dotted his tanned cheeks. It added to his appeal.

"Yes. Outside London." He extended his hand. "My name's Gordon."

She took his hand, felt the long fingers curl around hers, firm and tight. "Linnea."

"Linnea," he repeated. "Pretty name. Named after Linnaeus? The horticulturalist?"

"Indeed, I was." She was impressed Gordon knew who he was.

"You said your brother is across the pond?"

She smiled at the phrase. "At Oxford. For a summer abroad program."

"He'll love it. Oxford is beautiful in the summer."

"Oh. You studied there?"

"I did," he replied, nodding.

Intelligence was an aphrodisiac for her. She was liking him even more.

"But Cooper is a lowcountry boy at heart. As evidenced by this monster truck. It's a bit juiced up for me, but it carries a surfboard like a dream."

"It's a bloody nice ride."

"Yo!" his friend called from the other truck. "If you're done over there . . ."

Gordon turned and waved in acknowledgment, then faced Linnea again. His blue eyes rested on her, seemingly without hurry. "Hope to see you around, Linnea."

She was sorry to watch him turn away and trot back to his pickup to unload his board. Sorrier still that he'd not asked for her number. Was there anything sexier than a British accent? she wondered. She turned back to the massive, shiny black truck that had earned Gordon's admiration and patted it. "Thanks, you monster," she whispered.

She pulled her board out of the truck bed; then, tossing the line over her shoulder, she followed a line of surfers down the beach path. Everyone was anxious to get to the water.

Despite the stormy weather, or because of it, there were more surfers already out on the water than she'd expected. She'd heard that the sport had been growing in popularity on the South Carolina shores. She grimaced. The increased numbers of people bobbing in the water reflected what was happening everywhere in Charleston these days.

She claimed her spot on the sand, then took her time to spread an ample amount of wax on her board to help prevent her feet from sliding. As she worked, the drizzling rain dampened her clothes. When the board was waxed to her satisfaction, she stripped off her hoodie and shorts, revealing a green and navy bikini. Her figure was petite yet filled out a bikini with ample curves. She noticed a few appreciative stares from the men nearby and, annoyed, quickly stepped into her neoprene wet suit. Today she wore what was known as a shortie—a suit with short sleeves and cut at the knees. It was spring and the Atlantic waters still bore the chill of winter.

That done, she straightened and took her time surveying the ocean. The water was a muddy gray-green, like the sky, and choppy. The rip current looked fierce. She gripped her board and headed toward the sea. Sticking a toe in, she shivered. Cold water on a cool, rainy morning was not an inviting combination. But she was addicted to the high she got riding a wave and needed that in her life right now.

She held tight to Big Blue and walked through the shallows, then lay down on the board, took a breath, and began to paddle. She sucked in her breath when the first wave splashed its icy water over her.

It was tough going in the choppy water. The salt stung her eyes. But the rip current she had feared instead helped pull her farther out away from shore. She was in pretty good shape from all the surfing she and John had done in California. Still, the conditions were rough, and by the time she made it to the breakers, she was huffing and puffing.

John was always very clear that one of the major rules of surf etiquette was to be mindful of those around you, which included taking one's turn. Those with the inside position near the peak of the wave had the right-of-way. Linnea paddled to the far side of the lineup at the breakers and slowly worked her way to the inside as surfers took their turns. She pushed up to sit atop her board and looked over her shoulder, taking stock and watching how the waves were breaking. She was grateful for the moment to catch her breath.

"Hey, Linnea!"

She swung her head toward the inside where a line of surfers sat on their boards, bobbing like pelicans. She spotted Mickey Williams and lit up. Mickey was one of the old guard. In his fifties now, he was part of the hierarchy that regulated the beach. He wasn't shy about educating one of the many new surfers on how to behave on *his* beach. Beyond him, she spotted more of her old gang. She felt a rush of gladness and waved back.

"Welcome home!" called out Carson Legare, one of the first women surfers she'd met. Bobbing next to her was her husband, Blake.

"Where's John?" Blake called.

Linnea had expected the question. The guys were surfing buddies of John, who had spent summers on Isle of Palms with them growing up. Surfing had always been a big part of their lives. Out on the water, they had each other's backs. She'd come in as John's girlfriend and they'd all warmly welcomed her into the fold. She wondered how they'd feel once they found out that she and John had broken up.

"In California," she called back. It was the truth, after all.

Blake waved again, then flipped to his belly on the board. His turn was coming for takeoff on an incoming wave.

Next to Carson sat a stunning woman Linnea didn't recognize. She had light brown hair that fell in a long, wet braid down her back. She looked at ease on the board as she leaned back on one arm, watching the set of waves approaching, her body as lean and taut as steel.

A good wave was coming in. Linnea watched as those closest to the peak immediately moved to lie flat on their boards. Heads looked back, arms at the ready to take off.

"She's ripe!" she heard Mickey shout as the wave mounted.

A solid wave swept away the inside line as they rode it to shore. Linnea was pumped because she was on the inside now. It was her turn. She lay on her belly and focused on the incoming waves. She spotted the one she would ride. It was building steadily, and she felt her heart beating faster. Linnea paddled hard to maneuver her surfboard around so it pointed toward the beach. As she felt the water building beneath her, she kept her head low, attention riveted. Then she felt the lift. She was just about to pop up on her feet when from her left she glimpsed another surfer taking off, cutting in front of her. The woman blocked her ride.

Linnea quickly gripped the board, lifted her head, and aborted. Furious, she sputtered as she watched a redheaded girl with a ponytail ride what was supposed to be *her* wave to shore.

"Snake!" called someone to her left.

Snake was a derogatory term for someone who deliberately dropped in front of a surfer who had the right-of-way. She turned to see Gordon floating on his board nearby.

"Yeah!" she called back, still annoyed.

"Better one coming," he shouted, and pointed behind his back.

Linnea looked over her shoulder and saw he was right. A bigger wave was indeed building. This one she wanted . . . bad. Once again she maneuvered her board toward shore. She took deep breaths. This time when the wave lifted her, she ducked her head, gave two extra-hard strokes, arched her back, and popped up on her feet.

She was up! Grinning ear to ear, arms stretched out, Linnea rode the shoulder of the wave and felt the incredible rush of flying. This was immediately followed by an extreme amount of focus. She wasn't thinking about John, or getting a job, or about anything else. She was totally in the moment. She had to give all her concentration to every little foot movement so she didn't fall. And while doing all that, she felt utterly and completely free. Ecstasy!

It was a glorious ride to the shore. Linnea felt her fin dig into the sand and slipped from her board. Hoisting it in her arms, she carried it to the beach, smiling, still stoked from her ride.

Carson waited for her on the shore and waved her over. "Nice ride. You caught the best wave of the day."

Linnea remembered how much she liked Carson. In her mid-thirties, Carson had spent most of her summers on Sullivan's Island at her grandmother's home. She'd been one of the first female kite-surfers on these islands. She still held records in the sport. Now, however, she'd married and settled on Sullivan's Island and rode the waves purely for fun.

"It was gnarly out there in the chop, but that ride was worth it," Linnea said.

"It's why we brave the storms," Carson added with a laugh.

Thunder rumbled in the distance, drawing both women's attention as they looked out to sea. No one stayed in the water when lightning approached.

"That's it for me. I'm done for today," Linnea admitted.

"Before you go, I want you to meet someone." Carson looked around and called out, "Pandora!"

Following her gaze, Linnea saw the brown-haired woman she'd noticed on the water earlier. There were far fewer female surfers, so they were easier to remember. She was in conversation with, of all people, Gordon. He had just rolled in from his wave. They both turned toward Carson's call. Gordon spotted Linnea, and recognition flared. He waved again. She flushed, though she didn't know why, and smiled.

The woman called Pandora bid him farewell, then walked toward them in a long-legged, confident stride. She wore a full wet suit with a design at the waist that resembled a corset. Her braid was undone and she was raking her hands through her long brown hair as she walked. Linnea noticed that every man she passed had his eyes glued to her, and the woman knew it.

"Linnea, come meet Pandora," Carson said. "She's visiting from England. We're related in a very, very distant way, but decided we'd hang out simply because we like each other."

Pandora laughed at that odd introduction and held out her hand. "Linnea. Such a pretty name," she said in her clipped British accent.

"I was named after the Swedish botanist Linnaeus. My mother's mad for gardening."

"So is Granny James," Pandora said. "When she's here, she's pining for her garden in England. When in England, she pines for the ocean. So basically, all she does is complain, whichever house she lives in."

They all laughed, and Linnea felt that immediate sense that she liked Pandora. "How long will you be staying?"

"Indefinitely," Pandora replied with a blithe shrug of her shoulders.

"Pandora is in the enviable position of not having any commitments tugging at her sleeve." Carson said this with a genuine smile.

"Sounds heavenly."

"It's not as heavenly as it may sound. I'm a ship without a rudder," Pandora said. "I assume you live here?"

"On Sullivan's," Linnea replied.

"Fabulous. That's where I'm living. With Granny James. We should get together."

"I'd like that." She wondered how well Pandora knew Gordon.

"Carson has your number?" Pandora asked, looking at Carson for confirmation.

Carson nodded, then asked Linnea, "You're not staying with Cara?"

"No, I'm living with my folks. On Sullivan's. But if you call her, she'll give you my number."

Pandora laughed. "It's all very convoluted when we aren't carrying our phones. But let's get in touch. I've been here a week and I'm already getting bored. There must be a party in this city somewhere."

"I just took you to a party," Carson said with a hint of reproach.

Pandora rolled her eyes. "Oh, please. You're all married. I'm dying for a good party filled with eligible young men." She wiggled her brows. "And women. I can't very well hang out at a bar by myself." She looked pointedly at Linnea. "You're not married . . . ?"

"No!" Linnea answered with a short laugh. "Hardly."

"Excellent. I think we're going to be fast friends." Pandora flashed a winning smile. Thunder rumbled again, louder. More people were picking up their boards and heading off the beach. Pandora said, "I must get my board. Carson, are you coming?"

"See you soon, I hope," Carson said to Linnea. "Now that I know you're back, we'll invite you to dinner at Sea Breeze. Harper holds the best gatherings."

Pandora rolled her eyes again. "Marrieds . . ."

Linnea laughed, buoyed by the prospect of a new friend. She lifted her board and was heading out when she passed Mickey. He waved her over.

"I saw that shit out there," he said with a flash of annoyance in his eyes.

"No worries. It happens," Linnea said. "Great seeing you again, by the way."

"Don't be a stranger. How long are you here for this time?"

"I'm back home. Permanently."

"Really?" Mickey seemed pleased. "You left California?"

"Yeah, it was time."

❊   ❊   ❊

MICKEY SEARCHED HER face but didn't press. Then his expression changed as he spotted someone in the distance. "Hold on," he said, then trotted away. Linnea turned and saw that he was heading toward the redheaded woman who had cut her off in the ocean. Squinting, she saw it was Annabelle, the woman she'd gone to school with. A mix of emotions flashed through her—surprise, anger, then apprehension as an angry Mickey reamed her out. Annabelle stood, openmouthed and wide-eyed, as Mickey spoke to her with an angry swipe of his arm. Then he turned his back and walked away, leaving Annabelle staring after him.

"My God, what did you tell her?" Linnea asked as he returned.

His handsome face was flushed with anger. "I told her that this is a friendly beach and we don't take to kooks. Hell, she's obviously a beginner out of her depth out there. She shouldn't be out today. But if she is, she's got to learn the rules."

"And you taught her one. Appreciate it."

He snorted. "My pleasure."

The wind gusted, tossing sand into the air. They both squinted.

"Time to go!" Mickey called out and bent to pick up his board. "See ya."

Linnea picked up her backpack and followed at a smart pace as the wind whistled, shaking the sea oats and spraying cold raindrops on her face. By the time she made it to the truck, the neighboring pickup with the two surfers was already gone. She hoisted her board into the back and was turning to rush to the door when she spotted Annabelle trotting her way.

"Linnea," she called out, jogging closer. She was out of breath and water dripped from her hair down her forehead. Linnea held her breath, waiting for the onslaught of righteous anger.

Annabelle arrived and her face appeared contrite.

"Hey, I'm glad I caught you. I just wanted to tell you . . . I'm sorry. For cutting you off."

Linnea was nonplussed by the apology.

"Hey, it's okay."

"No, it wasn't. Honestly, I didn't know what I was doing. I'm not that good"—she frowned—"as you probably figured out. I didn't know I broke some rule and cut you off. I just blindly took the wave. I'm sorry," Annabelle said again.

There was none of the self-righteous attitude from earlier, only a sincere apology. Compassion came easily.

"I'm guessing Mickey explained the drop-in rule."

Annabelle sighed with embarrassment. "Oh yeah. He's like the big kahuna."

"It's *his* beach," Linnea said simply.

"I really made a great first impression." She paused, then asked with a pained expression, "I . . . Will you teach me the rules?"

Linnea didn't know what to say.

Annabelle added in a rush, "I mean, I don't want Mickey yelling at me again." She made a face, and they both laughed. "And I sure as hell don't want to be called a kook."

Thunder cracked overhead, causing both girls to startle.

"Sure. Another day," Linnea said, looking up at the nasty sky.

Annabelle smiled, and sunshine shone in her eyes. "Cool. I'd like that."

Both women squealed and ran for their cars as rain burst from the skies in a typical island soaker. Linnea scooped her keys from under the wheel, climbed into the cab of the huge truck, and slammed the door. The rain thundered on the metal roof and water streamed down her face as she reached for the towel. She fired up the mighty engine, flicked on the wipers, and slowly joined the line of traffic heading away from the beach. She was tired, wet, but ebullient.

Let it rain! She'd had a great morning out on the beach, and she'd just met two possible new friends.

Chapter Eight

The southeastern United States is one of only two large loggerhead rook-eries in the world. The second is Oman in the Arabian Sea. Loggerheads nesting in Georgia and South Carolina and North Carolina make up the Northern Recovery Unit, which is genetically distinct from loggerheads nesting in Florida and other parts of the world.

THE HOUSE THAT Palmer was building sat proudly on the more desir-able section of Ocean Boulevard, farther from popular, noisy Front Beach and close to quiet Breach Inlet. The mansions here were bigger and had larger properties, thanks in part to the accretion of sand from the north-ern end of the island.

The house location was all the more attractive because it bordered the two open lots put into conservation by Russell Bennett years earlier. Instead of manicured lawns, the dunes were bursting with wildflowers: brilliant-orange Indian blanket, pink swamp rose mallow, bright-red coral bean, tickseed Coreopsis, and Cara's favorite, the sweet yellow primrose for which her mother had named the cottage.

"It's a beautiful house," Cara said, her neck craning from left to right. "Inspired."

"Thanks, sister mine," Palmer said, tucking his fingertips into the rear pockets of his khakis. "I've had a lifetime to prepare for it. All the ideas I've had—only the good ones, mind you—are in this house."

"The turret?" she asked, raising her arms to indicate the two-story turret that housed the home's entrance and the staircase to the second floor. "Where did that inspiration come from? The Citadel?"

"Especially the turret." He chuckled, low in his chest. "Do you remember Mama used to say someday she'd build a turret porch on the beach house?"

"No," Cara said with surprise. "I never knew that. Are you sure?"

"Yep. Just because she didn't tell you doesn't mean it isn't true," he said. "I was the older child, after all. The only son with the great Rutledge name to carry on. And remember, you were gone for a very long time."

"True enough." Fascinated by this information about their mother, she pursued it. "Where was she going to put it?"

"Over on the right side of the porch," Palmer said, pointing. "She said she wanted to sit under a roof, outdoors but out of the sun. She even got some estimates. I reckon they were more than she cared to spend. So she had a pergola built instead."

Cara took a breath, remembering. "Brett built it."

"Yes," Palmer said soberly. Then with a smirk added, "A couple of times, if I recall. The hurricanes like to tear that thing down."

"Not the last two hurricanes. He built the final one to last."

Palmer nodded. "Too bad he didn't live to see it."

Cara couldn't reply, feeling the cruelty of that irony. Turning, she walked into the house's living room where light poured in from a wall of windows facing the ocean. She loved the feel of the room. It felt like hope. She wrapped her arms around herself, tightly, and blinked away the tears as she stared out into the magnificent vista of ocean, as far as she could see.

"I'm going to build a pool out there," Palmer said, coming to her side. "A raised one, right smack-dab in the middle of the deck." He put one hand on her shoulder, tenderly, the other arm stretched out against the panorama. "Can't you see it? The house will border the pool on both sides, like arms cradling a baby. That deck will connect both wings. You'll see it from every room."

"It's perfect," Cara said softly, and meant it. "I'm so proud of you." She reached up to hold tight his arm. "You did it. After all those years of dreaming . . . and scheming."

"It's not done yet," he said.

She dropped his arm and faced him.

"In fact," Palmer said, "it's coming in a bit high. Julia's choices are top-of-the-line. Of course," he added with furrowed brows. "But they're right for the house. I can't go cheap on tile and appliances. The house deserves the best."

"Don't go too high," Cara warned. "You still need to make money on this house."

"You don't have to tell me that," he said.

"You'll let me know if you run into trouble, won't you?"

"Sure, sure," he said with his typical bravado. He looked around the house, his chest expanding with pride. "I think Mama would've liked it."

"I know she would have. It's both creative and elegant. Who knows, *she* might have bought it!"

"Mama?" Palmer's eyes kindled and he shook his head. "Nah. Nothing would've pried her loose from that beach house. Besides, she was too cheap. She wouldn't have spent the money. And after all these years, I found out she was sitting on a small gold mine."

"You know she wouldn't touch that money. She would've had to tell us where it came from."

"True, true."

"All's for the best." Cara looked at her brother. He was nattily dressed in pressed slacks and a polo shirt, befitting a real estate maven. His hair was neatly trimmed, his skin tanned and close-shaven. She knew her mother would be proud of him too. "Speaking of the beach house, I could use your advice."

Palmer's head tilted and his eyes focused on her. Cara didn't often ask her brother for advice. "Shoot."

"David and I were discussing where we should live after we get married. We're agreed that we'll stay on either Isle of Palms or Sullivan's Island."

Palmer nodded in acknowledgment. "Makes sense."

"I'd always thought . . . expected . . . that we'd live in the beach house. But David thinks it's too small for us. He wants to find something bigger."

"No surprise there."

"But, Palmer, I don't want to move. You know how I feel about the beach house. I like living there. It's Mama's home. It's . . . *my* home."

"Hell, I've been telling you to sell that claptrap of a house for years. You can build another house on the same lot. Hey, I'll build it for you!"

She saw the excitement of a new job shine in his eyes and was quick to dispel it. "I've told you a million times, I'll never tear it down. I love it."

"Because of Mama," he finished for her. Then in a lower voice he leaned closer and asked, "Has she come back? Her ghost, I mean?"

Cara shook her head and felt again the pang of disappointment. "No." Then she laughed, thinking of Linnea.

"What?"

She told him about the night she'd thought Linnea coming from the beach was the ghost of their mother.

Palmer laughed and stroked his jaw. "Well, the apple didn't fall far from the tree with that one."

"In every way. One of the joys of getting older is watching how the family genes are expressed in the next generation." She studied her brother's face. "She looks more like Mama every day." Then she pointed at her brother and said, "So do you."

Palmer's brows rose as he laughed. "Thanks a lot."

"I meant that as a compliment. You've lost weight and your face is thinner." She poused, studying his clear blue eyes. "You have her eyes," she said seriously. "So does Linnea." She paused. "Cooper is all Daddy. In looks," she clarified.

"Yeah, Julia got the genes right," he chided.

Cara held back her laugh. She knew he was referring to the age-old complaint that their mother had mixed up the gene distribution: Palmer got the smaller, blond genes from their mother and Cara got the tall, dark genes from their father.

"I haven't had a visit from Mama since you were with me . . . what? Two years ago?" Cara said. Seeing her brother nod, she added, "Not even a whiff of her perfume."

"Then she's gone to heaven, God rest her soul." Neither brother nor sister spoke, each lost in their personal thoughts. Then Palmer said,

"Cara, Mama doesn't expect you to keep that house like some sort of shrine."

Cara didn't respond.

"What was that she told you?"

Cara blew out a stream of air. She could still hear her mother's voice in her ear. "The beach house is a state of mind more than a place."

"Exactly," Palmer said. "Honey, I'm done trying to get you to sell it. But at least rent it."

"That's what David suggests."

"Hey, sister, I know," he said with a light in his eyes. He spread out his arms. "Buy this place!"

Cara let her gaze float across the wide-open airy rooms. The thought of living here was tempting.

"It sure is pretty," Cara conceded. "But it's too big. And too expensive. You need to make money on this house. No family discounts."

"True, that."

"We'll find a place." She assured herself as much as a Palmer. "I'm just not in a hurry." She walked toward the front door. "Another reason I don't want to leave is Flo."

"What's that ol' battle-ax got to do with things?"

Cara took no offense. She knew that Palmer loved Flo, perhaps not as much as she did, but enough that he cared.

"It's her mental health," she confided. "Her Alzheimer's is progressing fast now. She can't be trusted to cook, she needs help with personal care. Her personality is changing too. One minute she seems herself, the next she gets so confused and angry. Emmi can't leave her alone for long. We're exploring hiring a nurse temporarily until we find a good memory-care place."

Palmer rubbed his jaw in thought. "I'm right sorry to hear that. It's hard for me to think of Florence Prescott as anything but a sharp old bird. She was the only woman I knew, other than you"—he bowed her way—"who could give Daddy what-for. I was a sniveling little coward. That alone earned my undying gratitude. I have to tell you, that woman saved me from some scrapes back in the day."

"All of us," Cara agreed.

Palmer scratched his jaw in thought. "Tell you what. I have an old college buddy whose mama had the same situation. You recall Dustin Devon?" he asked, looking at her. "One of the Summerville Devons?"

Cara shook her head. Charleston was more of a small town than a city. Folks grew up in the city and had relatives and friends spread out for miles. It was common to find out where one was from and who one knew. Discovering degrees of separation was both a pleasure and a means of connection.

Cara raked her memory and relinquished that she didn't know him.

"Anyway, his mama was in a bad way. Like Flo. Dustin seems pretty content with the place they found for her up there. She's doing real good, or so he tells me. They visit her as often as they can, though it's a shame—I don't think she recognizes them anymore. I swear, I hope you shoot me if I get to that point."

"Sure. No problem," Cara replied with a wry grin. "I'll have to get in line."

"Anywayyy," he said with exaggeration, "I'll get you some names."

"I'd appreciate it, brother dear. And thanks for showing me the house." She let her eyes travel the breadth of the windows that overlooked the ocean a last time before turning to open the front door. The warmth of the summer day descended on them. Cara looked out and saw the beach house directly across the boulevard, sitting daintily atop the dunes. The road curved, lined by one house more gorgeous than the last, widening at the dead end.

"A house on Ocean Boulevard," Cara said wistfully. "Someone is going to be very happy here."

❊　　❊　　❊

THE NEXT FEW weeks passed at a turtle's pace.

Linnea tidied her bedroom, unpacked her suitcase, ironed her shirts and skirts and dresses. She went out on two interviews, made dozens of follow-up calls, but in the end didn't score a job. Her bank account was dangerously low. Soon she'd become even more dependent on her parents than she already was. That was demoralizing for a twenty-five-year-old woman. Keeping up the brave front for her parents was becoming harder to manage and it felt more of a sham. Her father was becoming suspicious. On the occasional morning when there were decent waves and she went surfing, she'd return home to find her father in the kitchen, dressed for work, gulping coffee. He'd look at his watch and ask, "When's your vacation going to end?"

Looking at the cluttered paper by her computer, she saw the handwritten notations she'd made beside the company names: *Follow up next month* or *No openings* or just *NO*, underlined multiple times. The men and women she'd talked to were polite, even kind, when they told her there just wasn't anything available. Linnea heard the hint of pity embedded in the message.

After her last rejection on the phone, Linnea had sat at the small wooden desk in her bedroom and watched animal rescue videos. Dogs and puppies. Cats. Rabbits. Even goats. One after the other for more than an hour. It was numbing.

A polite knock on her door was followed by an immediate swoosh as the door opened. Linnea jerked her head up to see her mother carrying two glasses of wine. Linnea furtively swiped her cheeks.

"It's five o'clock somewhere!" Julia chimed out as she marched across the room and offered Linnea a glass. She was dressed in pale-blue cutoffs and a white blouse that tied at the waist. At fifty-five, her mother still had a slim figure, thanks to her rigid self-control. She ate like a bird and never missed a yoga class. Around her neck was a slender strand of her ever-present pearls. Watching her waltz into the room, Linnea knew that, for Julia, taking the time to present herself well-dressed and composed was not merely a social act, but a means of survival. Styled hair, makeup, pearls, manicured nails were a uniform that said to the world that she was in control. It sometimes seemed to Linnea that the deeper Julia's distress, the more composed she appeared.

"Mom, it's five o'clock *here*," Linnea said morosely.

"All the better."

"What do you want?" She knew the question was rude, but she didn't care.

"I don't want anything. I'm just bringing you a glass of cheer."

"I don't want it."

Julia paused, then moved closer. Her tone of voice changed. "What's the matter, honey?"

Linnea was holding on to her composure by a thin thread. Unlike her mother, she was wearing sweatpants and a torn Gamecocks T-shirt. Her hair was unbrushed, nails unpolished. Two empty coffee cups and an empty plate cluttered the small wood desk. She hadn't left the room all day except to raid the refrigerator. She was beyond chitchat.

"Nothing. I'm just tired."

Julia put the wineglass in front of Linnea's face.

Linnea sighed and took the glass. A chilled rosé just might do the trick after all.

Julia sat down on the bed beside Linnea. She took a sip of the wine, then reached out to set her glass on the desk. Then she removed the glass from Linnea's hand and put this on the desk as well. She took both her daughter's hands and, after a gentle shake, looked her in the eyes.

"Tell me," said Julia.

All the defenses she'd set up, the carefully orchestrated narrative, her straight shoulders, crumbled. Right now, Linnea was just a girl who wanted her mother. Tears filled her eyes and, at last, she let them flow.

Julia leaned forward and wrapped her arms around her daughter. "I knew something was wrong."

"I'm such a failure," Linnea choked out, resting her head on her mother's shoulder. "I'm so ashamed."

"A failure? You're not a failure," Julia said.

"Oh, Mama," Linnea cried. "I've been lying. Pretending that all was great. That I had everything under control. But I don't."

Julia patted her shoulder. "I know."

Linnea drew back and stared at her mother. "You knew?"

"Of course." Julia reached up to wipe a tendril from Linnea's face. "You forget I've known you since you were born. I know you. I've seen your moods change. Honey, lately there's been a cloud of gloom hanging over you. You're spending more and more time alone in this room. You haven't called your friends. You don't go out." She paused and said archly, "And you're getting snippy."

"Snippy? I've been trying to be upbeat."

"Uh-huh, well . . . you've fooled your father."

Linnea barked out a short laugh. "That's because he wants to believe it."

"Believe you got a job?" Julia asked suspiciously.

"Yeah."

"So, no job, I take it?"

Shamefaced, Linnea shook her head. Her voice changed to frustration. "I've been calling, interviewing, downright lobbying for a position—any job I could get—everywhere I could think of. I've looked at corporations, and endowments. . . . Anytime someone showed me a lead, I followed up." She shook her head. "The simple truth is, there's nothing out there."

"That's not entirely true," said Julia. "You can't find a job in your area of expertise. Honey, maybe it's time to start looking elsewhere."

"Out of state? But you and Daddy were all bent out of shape when I went to California."

"That's not what I meant. I mean, get *any* job," she added firmly.

"You mean, even if I ask if they want fries with that?"

"Even if."

Linnea sighed heavily in defeat. "That's harsh."

"I know you're right.

"Life can be harsh," Julia replied. "It's how you respond that builds character."

"It's time. I will." She looked up. "But I'm not working with Daddy."

"Palmer?" Julia laughed lightly and shook her head. "That ship has sailed. He can't afford to hire you."

This caught Linnea up short. "Are things bad again?"

"Again?" Julia looked at her askance. "Darling, he was a step away from bankruptcy. It's all uphill from there." She adjusted her seat, then looked at Linnea with more sternness and less sympathy. "But our finances are materially different now. Thank heaven we didn't have to endure the public embarrassment of bankruptcy. As it was, we could tell people that Palmer wanted to change gears, start a new career. We explained that our move to the island was because that's where he wanted to build houses."

Linnea said, "You were creating your own narrative."

"I'm not sure what that means."

"Spinning the story. Making the public hear the story you want them to believe." She paused, realizing it was time for honesty. "That's what I've been doing. Telling you everything is wonderful, great, perfect. When in fact, it isn't."

Julia's eyes softened, grateful, perhaps even moved by the confession.

"Then, yes," she said. "That's what we did. What people have done for years," she said. "Whatever the current jargon might be. I don't know if it worked. But we'll never really know. We moved here to the island, and our lives have dramatically changed."

Linnea saw for the first time the crack in her mother's veneer. She asked softly, "How are you doing, Mama?"

Julia adjusted her seat and collected herself. "Let's not change the subject. We're talking about you. Sweetheart, please don't ever feel you have to put on a false front for me. I'm your mother. It's that unconditional love thing."

"I won't. It was too hard to pretend."

Now Julia laughed. "I know!"

"You trained me well."

"Perhaps I did," Julia said with a hint of pride. "My darling daughter, you've never been a disappointment to me. True, I didn't always agree with your choices—"

"California."

"Yes. But when you stood up to your father, spoke your mind. I admired your strength and courage. More than I'd ever had."

"That's not true. Your claws came out when Cooper got sick. You stood up for *me*. And you stuck with Daddy and helped him back to sobriety. And then the move . . . I'd say you are the strongest woman I know."

Julia stared at her daughter; her pupils moved as she listened.

"Yes, it was a hard couple of years," she finally conceded. She reached out to take her wineglass, lifted it in a silent toast, and took a sip.

Linnea watched her mother carefully regain her composure and thought of all the years she'd observed her mother initiate this ritual.

"I admit," Julia continued, "there were days I didn't think I'd manage. Palmer has been so engrossed with the new house project that he's living in his own world. He just assumes I'll be calm and carry on. And I do," she said with pride.

"Are you happy?"

Julia smiled briefly. "Happiness is hard to measure."

"I don't think it is. You know in your heart. Mama, it's a yes-or-no answer."

"You're naïve," Julia said without malice. "Happiness means joy and pleasure. But happiness also implies contentment. Feeling satisfied that something has been done right."

"As in acceptance? Or resignation?" Linnea challenged.

"At the very least. Contentment is realizing one's good fortune. We *are* fortunate, Linnea. We hit hard times, but we had a lot to fall back on. Not everyone does." She looked around the room. "We have this house. I have a husband who loves me. Two wonderful children. A second chance. Not everyone is that lucky. And when I remember that, when I count my blessings, then yes," she said with a nod. "I am happy."

"I want more. I want that joy. Did you ever have that?"

"Of course I have! The day you were born was one of those times."

Linnea half-smiled at the tender comment. "With you, it's sometimes hard to tell if you're happy or not. You keep up a pretty good façade. That's hard work. I've learned."

"Keeping up a façade *is* hard," Julia admitted. "But necessary. I've stopped seeing most of my old Charleston friends because I don't want to betray the image that Palmer is doing well. Plus, I can't keep up financially with what I used to do. I've left all the charity committees I was on in the city. One is expected to make donations that I no longer could. We dropped our club memberships, and that was my lifeline. We're the first Rutledges in our line to leave the club. You have to remember that for all intents and purposes, we've lost everything."

Linnea watched myriad emotions flutter across her face. Her mother's life had been upended. "But, Mama, you're not gardening. That surprises me. You always loved that. That isn't expensive."

Julia shook her head. "That was the greatest heartbreak, I think. Leaving my garden in Charleston. I put all I had into that bit of land. I was so proud to keep the house on the Charleston House and Garden Tour. That was Lovie's tradition, you know. I didn't want to let her down, and later it became my pride and joy. But out here . . ." She looked out the window at the expanse of scrubby lawn that stretched out to the maritime shrubs, and the beach beyond. She tossed up her hands in frustration. "There's just no soil!"

"If anyone could create a garden here, you could."

"I'm not sure that I want to." She smirked. "And you think it's not expensive?" She laughed shortly at her daughter's naivete then shook her head. "No, my darling girl. I think, perhaps, that part of my life is over."

Whenever Linnea thought of her mother, she would be in her garden. Sensing her mother's shift in mood toward melancholy, Linnea rallied. "Well, you did an amazing makeover of this house."

"Thank you," Julia said smoothly.

"Let's be honest, it was kind of a dump before. Did you hire an architect?"

Julia laughed lightly. "No. . . ."

"You did all this?"

"Your shock is mildly insulting, my dear. Of course, it was me. I couldn't afford to hire anyone else."

"Mama, I thought the architect who designed the house that Dad is building must have had a hand in this."

"Is it so hard to believe I might have some talent?"

"Of course not. I didn't mean that. I'm proud of your aesthetics. But gutting a house is pretty major." She looked at her mother with new eyes. "Mama, you took down frigging walls!"

Julia smiled with pleasure. "*That*," she said with meaning, "I admit took courage. Linnea, I've always had a passion for design, textiles, color. And it's not my first project, you know that. You probably don't remember what the house on Tradd Street looked like when your daddy inherited it. I'm not saying Lovie didn't have good taste. Let's just say it was . . . dated, bless her heart. I also helped friends with their houses from time to time. They liked my taste and asked me to decorate their homes."

"You decorated Cara's house, right?"

"Why, yes. Did she tell you?"

"I guessed. You have a look, and that's real talent."

"I enjoyed that project," Julia said wistfully. "Oh, that poor kitchen . . ." She lifted her hands.

"Mama, you're really good. Maybe interior design can be your new passion?"

"Hardly new."

"I mean, to do it seriously. Have you ever thought about starting an interior decorating company?"

"A company? Linnea," she scoffed, "I don't have the training."

"Yes, you do," she argued, inching closer. She didn't want her mother to do her typical backstep, thinking she wasn't skilled enough, or qualified enough. "You've got your degree in art and you've been taking classes on interior design for years."

"I'd need a degree in interior design. I'd need to get a license to get in the showrooms. I'm not a professional."

"But you could be," Linnea urged. "You don't need a degree to work as an interior decorator. Honestly, Mother, the Internet has changed everything. There's access to anything you want."

"I *do* go to a lot of Instagram sites. And Pinterest." She shook her head. "I spend far too much time on the computer these days, looking at different design fabrics, furniture. . . ."

"Careful you don't slide down that rabbit hole. But that's what I mean. Seriously, all you need are clients. And, Mama, you have a lot of friends who will give you a chance. The difference now, however, is they'd have to pay you." She could see the idea taking root in her mother's mind and pressed on. "The first thing you need to do is take some pictures of projects you've done."

"Oh, I've already got those. I always love to show the before-and-after pictures."

"Look at you!" Linnea scooted forward on her seat. "I have a friend who can help you put together a portfolio. And another who can get you set up on social media." When she saw her mother's confusion she explained, "A website, Instagram, Facebook. You can start posting photos of your design work. Everyone does it. Even people who are not designers."

Julia pinched her face in worry. "I don't want to be one of those clichés of a woman down on her luck suddenly becoming a decorator."

Linnea laughed. "Forget that. There are women my age, without degrees, writing books about decorating! You've done your apprenticeship for free for years. Now it's time to be paid for your work." She could see her mother's doubt lingering in her furrowed brow. "Mama, you're a smart woman. You can get set up with a tax ID. Form an LLC. All you need to think of is a name."

Julia brushed her skirt and said nervously, "Oh, I've already got one. Sort of. I've written the name on paper a million times."

"What is it?"

Julia paused, a bit embarrassed, then said, "Rutledge House Interiors."

"I love it. It's elegant, historic—and, hey, you might as well fall back on the laurels of the Rutledge name."

Julia smiled in wonder. "I came in here to cheer you up, and you've turned the tables and cheered me up instead."

"Mission accomplished, Mama. I'm feeling much happier. It was fun to brainstorm with you about your career. And, honestly, it feels so much better to be open with you."

"No more façades. We'll only tell each other the truth. Agreed?" said Julia.

Linnea reached over to grab the two glasses of wine. She handed one to her mother, then raised hers in a toast. "To the truth!"

They clinked glasses and took a sip. Linnea smiled into her mother's eyes.

Then Julia pointed her finger at Linnea.

"But don't tell your father."

Chapter Nine

Plastic is the most prevalent type of marine debris found in our oceans and Great Lakes. Plastic debris comes in all shapes and sizes, but those that are less than five millimeters in length (or about the size of a sesame seed) are called microplastics.

MEMORIAL DAY WEEKEND was one of the year's busiest on the islands. In the morning, visitors poured onto the beach, stuck in the bumper-to-bumper traffic on the Connector to Isle of Palms and the Sullivan's Island Bridge.

Each of the islands outside of Charleston had its own unique flavor. Folly was home to the surfing community and, despite growth, maintained an aura of free-spirited fun. Sullivan's Island was Isle of Palms's older sister in terms of history. Sullivan's had been established in the seventeenth century as both a location for the pesthouses during the slave trade, and a place for Charleston's elite to have summer houses to escape to in the heat of a southern summer. Like Folly, it still maintained a vintage authenticity. Isle of Palms was a popular vacation spot in the late nineteenth century. Its northern end had been a maritime forest until it was sold for a resort in the 1970s. All the islands shared the struggle with the heavy influx of tourists and traffic during peak season.

The tourists remained in a jovial mood, however, as the sun shone in a brilliant blue sky. The public lots quickly filled, and the legal parking spaces were snatched. Cars circled, looking for an empty spot. Many would find expensive tickets on their windshields at the day's end. Still, there was little honking. In the South, honking was considered the highest form of rudeness.

Out on the beaches, colorful towels spread across the sand. Blue and red rental umbrellas and chairs lined the shoreline. On Isle of Palms, Front Beach was overflowing with tourists buying food and drinks, playing volleyball, and hanging out. On Sullivan's, there wasn't a seat to be had at any of the island restaurants.

The weekend passed without serious incident, just the few arrests for DUI and disorderly conduct. On Monday evening, the day tourists packed up and joined the long train of cars headed back to the mainland. Summer had begun on the southeastern coast.

Linnea was relieved to see the beaches quiet again, though the litter left in their wake filled her with dismay. Grabbing a large black garbage bag and donning thin reusable garden gloves, she began walking along the shoreline, picking up empty plastic cups, plastic water bottles, food containers, straws, and cigarette butts by the score, even the occasional lost sandal. There were garbage containers at the end of each beach path, she thought, exasperated. Couldn't people carry their litter that far?

Only a few die-hard sunbathers remained on the beach. By five o'clock, most people were eager to get home to dinner. She spotted one young woman under an enormous, fashionable black sun hat, her impossibly long, lean legs stretched out from a low-slung beach chair. As Linnea drew nearer, she saw the toes were painted a bright cherry red and the woman's black and white bikini bore the emblem of Chanel. She was reading a book and didn't look up until Linnea's shadow hovered over her.

The head lifted to reveal large black sunglasses. Then a slow smile eased across the woman's face.

"So now you're a garbage collector?" Pandora asked.

"Yep," Linnea replied, then laughed. "I'm just walking the beach and decided I'd pick up trash along the way. It's a small effort to help the ocean."

Pandora set the book down on the sand and lowered her sunglasses, revealing her brilliant blue eyes. "Well, good on you," she said. "Who knew you were such a do-gooder?"

"Not really. I saw another girl do it, and I was inspired." She lifted her bag higher. "Am I inspiring you?"

Pandora smirked and laughed. "Hardly."

"Come on. Make a difference, Pandora," Linnea chided.

"Please, just tell me where to send my check."

Linnea shook her head. "Hopeless."

"If you're finished with your rounds, come by my house. We can have a cuppa. It's not far."

Linnea thought that was the nicest invitation she'd had in days. "Love to."

Pandora rose in a graceful swoop. Her figure was slender, her body tamed with the polish it took money and care to create. With a few firm shakes, she shook the sand from her pink Spartina 449 towel and tucked it into her pink and green Tory Burch canvas bag. Linnea noticed that her sunglasses were Prada. She held back her smile. It was clear her new friend was a connoisseur of brand names.

"How long have you been here?" she asked Pandora.

"About a hour." Linnea laughed.

"No, I mean in the US."

"Oh," Pandora replied, hoisting her beach bag and taking a step forward. "Not long. I left England when the term was up. Came straightaway. I needed a change."

"What are you studying?"

"Engineering. I'm seeking my master's at Oxford."

Linnea almost missed her step. She glanced at the woman walking beside her. This tall, lean, sexy woman in brand clothing was studying engineering? She would have guessed perhaps fashion design. "You're an engineer?"

Pandora cast her a glance. "Don't tell me you're one of those."

"One of what?"

"Those boring people who pigeonhole women."

"No!" Linnea replied, stunned that she'd think that. "Of course not. It's just . . ."

"What?"

"You don't look like an engineer."

"I didn't realize an engineer looked like anything."

Linnea hoped her cheeks weren't flaming. "Most engineers I've met look more like Thomas Edison than Cara Delevingne."

Pandora tossed her head back and laughed. "You think I look like her?"

"Dead ringer."

"You're forgiven," Pandora said with faux haughtiness.

"What area are you studying?"

Pandora blew out a plume of air. "Good question. I need time to fig-ure out what area I want to focus on. Thus, the break. Generally, I'm in-terested in energy systems."

"Energy? As in, propulsion?"

"No. I'm more interested in natural systems, especially in this era of climate change. Particularly how science informs the societal and politi-cal aspects of energy."

Linnea was trying to understand. "So then, you're in politics?"

"No . . . and yes. I'd be more a liaison between politics and science. So in that way, yes, I'm involved in politics. But the program is designed to guide individuals who can help shape governmental positions. I be-lieve it's going to be critical at an international level in the future."

Linnea didn't respond. She was still trying to reconcile that this woman was kind of an engineer.

"But I'm still a student," Pandora continued. "And at the point where I must adjust course requirements. To be honest, I'm here for more than a break. I'm looking at programs in wind and marine energy."

This startled her. "Then you're in environmental science. Like me."

"Well, yes, but in a broad way. As I said, I'm more into energy solu-tions. I'm not as hands-on as you are. As in, I don't pick up garbage." She bumped her shoulder, jovially.

"I don't think it's all that different. You think globally, I think locally." She hoisted her bag into view. "Light one candle and all."

Pandora looked doubtfully at the garbage bag. "I suppose. . . . Except I'm definitely more global."

"So, does that make you a nerd or a power broker?"

Pandora laughed again. "Nerd. Definitely a nerd. With dreams of being a power broker. But please," she said with a groan, "don't let it get around. It's an absolute killer for any hopes for a social life. I'm dying for a good shag."

Linnea laughed, liking her more. "I'm sworn to secrecy. But I have to say, you don't look like a nerd. You had me fooled."

"That's what I hope people think. Like my favorite line in my favorite movie, *Working Girl*—'I have a head for business and a bod for sin.'"

"I never saw it."

Pandora stopped dead in her tracks. "What? It's an American film and only the most brilliant movie ever made. The ultimate women's lib film." She perused Linnea with one brow raised. "We're about the same age, I suppose. I'm twenty-eight."

"Twenty-five here."

"Then we're both millennials. This movie's about the eighties. Women were duking it out in every field." She shrugged. "We still are. This simply will not stand. I'll get it, and you and I are going to pop popcorn and watch it together."

They walked a bit farther. Linnea felt a bit intimidated by Pandora's academic prowess. She and Pandora were no longer on an even playing field. She picked up a stray plastic bottle and added it to the garbage bag.

"What about you?" Pandora asked. "What's your gig?"

There it was. The question she most hated to answer.

"I don't have one at the moment," she said, trying to sound breezy. "My degree is in environmental science. That's why I was excited by all that you're studying. At some fundamental level, we're both interested in facilitating information—you in politics, me for individuals. You may study the planet on a big scale, but me? It's all about the small and personal. Take sea turtles. I've been involved with them my whole life. My grandmother was the original turtle lady on these islands, and I was her trusty sidekick. Eventually I got my degree, but my field training was right here on these beaches. Then two years ago I got a position with a startup company in San Francisco."

"Ooh, I adore that city."

"The company had a patent on a means to eliminate plastic from the oceans. But . . ." She took a few steps. "They ran out of funding. Shut down. I was out of a job."

"Too bad. God knows we need new ideas. But funding is always critical."

"We also need government support of science and innovative ideas." Linnea paused. "Jobs are scarce in my field here. I'm looking everywhere, but the market is tight. So, that's a long-winded answer to your question. I have no gig at the moment." She laughed shortly. "At least I'm back on the turtle team."

"Those sweet little turtles. I've seen them in documentaries."

"Big turtles are on the beach now. The mature females are laying nests. The little hatchlings start to come in July."

"I've always wanted to see that. I've been to beaches all around the world yet never have."

"You'll never forget it."

"Will you let me know when a nest hatches?"

"We're not supposed to bring people to hatchings. The SCDNR doesn't even want team members there. If there are a lot of people, it might cause disruption of a boil. That's what we call it when all the turtles come out at once in a scrambling frenzy. A larger number of hatchlings emerging at the same time helps their chance of survival. They're reptiles, don't forget. Their biological model is predator glut. The more that pour out into the sea, the more chance for some survivors."

"Please, you must call me."

"I can't."

Pandora made a face. "I thought we were friends."

Linnea shook her head. "Sorry."

"Oh, rubbish."

"Unless . . ."

Pandora swung her head to look at her expectantly.

". . . you're on the turtle team and get involved."

"I can't."

"Okay."

They walked a few steps. "What would I have to do?"

Linnea was enjoying this. "Walk the beach with me in the morning to look for tracks. And pick up trash."

Pandora closed her eyes. "Must I?"

"It's up to you."

They continued walking as Pandora stewed.

"What's your problem, Pandora? It seems to me that if you're studying marine and wind energy, you might want to know a little bit about what species you're directly affecting, up close and personal. And, uh, that would include turtles."

"A sound argument . . . but hardly convincing. I'm thinking on a bigger scale. Like the planet. Climate change. Government policy. I'm not really into field work. And keep in mind, I might change my mind and go into fashion or some such." She gave Linnea a teasing glance.

But Linnea didn't want to make a joke of this. She pressed on. "Does it matter? We all share the planet. Whether you're an engineer or a fashion model, you still must breathe the air, drink the water, and exist. We all live under the same sun and moon. One either cares or doesn't. Which side are you on?"

"When you put it like that, of course I care. But do I want to get up early in the morning and look for tracks or pick up garbage?" She shook her head. "Not really. We all have to find ways to help in our own way."

"Excuses . . ."

"I'll tell you what," Pandora said. "I'll pick up trash a few times a week. Later in the morning. At a reasonable hour." When she saw Linnea's doubtful face she said, "I promise I'll do it. I really do hate to see garbage strewn about on the beach that ends up in the ocean. It shocks me how people can be such bloody pigs. That and not picking up after their dogs." She scrunched up her nose. "I've been known to shout to an offender, 'Pick that shit up!'"

"And you say you're studying politics?"

Pandora laughed loudly. "Touché! You see why I need a break. Seriously, Linnea, if I help you with trash, will you call me for a hatching? Just once?"

Linnea nodded. "Just once."

"Excellent!" She raised her arm to point. "This way. That is my beach path."

Pandora began winding her way up a narrow path, and an enormous, modern house came into view. It was the one Linnea had always thought was an eyesore on Sullivan's Island.

"Look at that house," she told Pandora. "It looks like it should be on the Jersey Shore. Or in the Hamptons. It doesn't fit in next to all the other lowcountry designs. Ugh, who would build such a thing?"

An older woman appeared on the long deck of the blocky-looking house before a long row of sliding glass doors. She leaned over the sleek metal railing and waved her arm in an arc over her head.

"Yoo-hoo! Pandora!" The woman waved her in.

Linnea looked at Pandora, wide-eyed.

"Yeah, that beast is Granny James's house."

"Uh . . . your grandmother's house?"

Now it was Pandora's chance to smirk. "She's technically my great aunt, but I call her Granny James. Come on. I'll introduce you."

☆   ☆   ☆

INSIDE THE IMPRESSIVE house, everything was white. White marble floors, white walls, white pillars, white furniture. Splashes of brilliant blue in curtains and pillows made Linnea think of pictures she'd seen of Santorini, Greece. It was stunning against the wall of plate-glass windows that revealed the bright blue of the ocean beyond.

Two elderly women were sitting at a small table in front of the windows, playing cards. Each wore a flowing caftan. One woman sat taller in her chair. Her white hair was pulled back in a chignon. The smaller woman was petite and birdlike, with red hair far too bright to be natural.

"My darling Pandora," the small woman called out in singsong. She waved her closer. "You're just in time for tea. And you brought a friend. How lovely."

Linnea knew protocol. Leaving her plastic bag and sand-crusted sandals at the door, she followed Pandora toward the table, tucking her wayward hair back behind her ears. She looked a fright next to Pandora's chic cover-up and bag.

"Granny James, this is my new friend, Linnea." She glanced at

Linnea with a troubled brow. "Well, this is bonkers. I don't know your last name."

"Rutledge," Linnea said, reaching out to accept Granny's hand with practiced grace. "It's a pleasure to meet you."

Granny James's pale-blue eyes swept over Linnea in a shrewd perusal that left Linnea feeling that she'd come out wanting. Granny James extended her arm to indicate the woman beside her, her several bangles clanging.

"And this is *my* friend, Mrs. Marietta Muir."

Mrs. Muir extended her hand. This woman's eyes were as bright and blue as the sea on a sunny day. "Rutledge . . ." Marietta said to Linnea as they shook hands. "I know several Rutledges. Which branch of the family are you connected to?"

Linnea lifted her chin a tad higher with pride. "My father is Palmer Rutledge. He's the son of Stratton and Olivia Rutledge, of Tradd Street?"

"Of course." Mrs. Muir's smile brightened with recognition. "Your father was a friend of my son, Parker. If I recall, your father was one of Parker's surfing buddies back in the day. Your daddy used to come to Sea Breeze all the time." Her smile slipped. "The islands haven't been the same since dear Olivia passed."

"Thank you. A day doesn't go by that I don't think of her, especially now that I'm back."

"Your grandmother and I spent many a summer afternoon together when we were young mothers. Olivia was involved in turtles, wasn't she?"

"Yes, ma'am. She started the first team here."

"And your father? Palmer? How is he doing?"

"My daddy just sold the house on Tradd Street and moved to Sullivan's permanently. He's building a house."

"I understand that temptation. My husband and I left the city decades ago when he retired. I have never regretted a moment of that decision. Goodness, that was a long time ago. *Tempus fugit*," Mrs. Muir said.

"Do sit down, girls," Granny James said, easing the impasse.

"I'm parched. Ladies, can I get you something?" asked Pandora. Then, glancing at the table, she smiled knowingly. "Or perhaps refresh your beverages?"

Granny James turned to her friend. "What about you, old girl," she said in a teasing tone. "Want some tea?"

Marietta wrinkled her nose. "I thought you said a beverage." She picked up her tall glass and jiggled the ice. "I wouldn't mind a bit of a fresher-upper."

"What's your poison?" asked Pandora.

"Gin and tonic, please."

Granny James said, "I'll have the same. There are cut limes in the fridge, dear."

Pandora turned to Linnea. "And you?"

"Gin and tonic sounds perfect."

"Be back in a flash," said Pandora as she turned to leave.

"Make Marietta's a double," called out Granny James. "I have to catch up."

Marietta snickered. "It will take a lot more than gin to achieve that, *old girl*," she replied, emphasizing the last words.

"What are you playing?" asked Linnea.

"Gin rummy. Do you know the game?" asked Marietta.

Linnea shook her head. "Sorry."

"Raised by wolves," Granny James said sotto voce.

Marietta laughed lightly, making a joke of it. "We'll have to teach you. It's ever so much fun. I taught my granddaughters how to play bridge, and now we have mini tournaments when we get together. They absolutely love it."

Linnea walked to the oversize white upholstered chair. She wiped the back of her pants, afraid she'd get sand on the immaculate fabric.

"Don't worry," Granny James said. "I can't seem to keep sand from the house, no matter what I do. Make yourself comfortable, my dear."

Embarrassed at being caught, Linnea slid gracefully onto the chair.

"Harper and Pandora were quite close growing up in England," Granny James told her as she played cards. "They were more like sisters than cousins, really. Pandora is such a dear. She was always at Greenfields Park. It's nice to see the two girls together again here." She discarded and called out gleefully, "Gin!"

In better spirits, she turned her attention to Linnea as Marietta shuffled the deck and dealt another round. "Pandora is my great-niece on my brother's side. But she's more like a granddaughter to me."

"Why, thank you, Granny James," Pandora called out as she walked into the room carrying a tray of tall glasses, each with a lime wedge. "I've always felt the same." She passed out the iced drinks to the two older women first. "They're both doubles. Seemed only fair play."

"Oh, how delightful," Marietta said, taking the glass. "I may have to have one of the girls pick me up after this. I won't be fit to drive the golf cart home."

"You never could hold your liquor," Granny James told her.

"I can drink you under the table any day," Marietta replied.

"You should. You're twice my size."

Marietta laughed then, a lovely trill that made Linnea smile. She watched the two women clink glasses and envied them their friendship. She glanced at Pandora, who caught Linnea's gaze as she turned.

"That'll be us someday," Pandora said as she handed her a tall glass.

Linnea liked the thought. Taking a sip, she almost purred. "Delicious."

Pandora took a sip of hers and agreed. "I was dying of thirst." She settled on the sofa and maneuvered a few of the blue pillows behind her back, stretching out her long, tanned legs, not the least concerned about sand.

"Granny, when you redo the house, you must get new sofas. These are the size of small continents. I simply cannot get comfortable."

Granny James chuckled. "You look quite comfy to me. I bought the house furnished, and come to think of it, he's a fairly large man. You met him at Harper's house. He's one of the sisters' husbands. Devlin Cassell."

"That would be Dora's husband," said Marietta.

"The very one. He sold it to me at the friends and family price."

"Granny," Pandora said with a shake of her head. "You can never resist a bargain."

"It's quite . . . grand," Linnea said, searching for a word that might compliment the house.

"Vast, you mean. Massive. Too big for one old woman alone," Granny James said. "I bought it in hopes that the house will be filled with visitors. Like you, dear Pandora. My dear, have you decided yet whether you'll take that year abroad and study here? You really must. Keep your granny company."

"It's very tempting," Pandora replied.

Granny James shifted her gaze back to Linnea. "My granddaughter Harper lives on the island too. Do you know her? Harper McClellan?"

"No, sorry," Linnea replied. "I grew up in Charleston. Most of my island friends were summer residents only."

"Well, no matter," Granny James said, adjusting her cards. "Harper grew up in New York. She only came to Sullivan's Island for summers to visit with her grandmother Marietta at Sea Breeze." She indicated Mrs. Muir. "She lives there now with her husband. Which is why I bought a house on Sullivan's myself. What's life for if not to be with our grandchildren, eh, Marietta?"

"True," Marietta agreed. "And now our great-grandchildren too." She set down a card and sang out, "Gin!"

Granny James cursed.

Linnea looked again at Marietta as connections were made. Marietta and Granny James were more than friends: they were related through marriage. *This really is a small town,* she thought.

"Carson promised Harper would invite me to dinner," said Linnea.

Marietta chirped up, "Oh, you must come. Harper is a simply marvelous cook. Farm to table, isn't that what you call it these days when you cook the food from your garden?"

Granny James lifted her brows with exaggeration. "How that happened, I'll never know. Her mother and I cannot boil water."

Linnea looked out through the vast wall of windows. The big white house was an unimaginative assemblage of square rooms that held little architectural interest. Linnea had seen many such houses built on the islands during the boom. Yet there was no disputing that the ocean views from every room were spectacular.

"The views are fabulous, aren't they?" Pandora said, noticing Linnea's wandering eyes.

"Yes," Linnea said, and took a quick sip of her drink.

Pandora took a sip, then said, her eyes twinkling, "Granny, did you know Linnea thinks the house is an eyesore?"

Linnea almost choked on her drink. She swallowed hard, unable to think of anything to say to redeem herself.

Granny James laughed, a low, throaty sound. "But it is! Just that. I bought the house for the views."

"And the price Devlin offered," Marietta chided.

Granny James picked up a card, ignoring Marietta's comment. "I'm coming to terms with the house. I thought I wouldn't mind the vast space. Especially after Greenfields Park."

"I wish you could've seen Greenfields Park," interrupted Pandora with a hearty sigh. She stirred her ice with her fingertip. "How many bedrooms were there?" she asked Granny James. "Twelve?"

"I can't remember," Granny James replied, discarding. "A lot to keep clean."

Pandora chuckled. "But it was all British charm and history."

"Sold. Gone," Granny James said without remorse.

"Oh, Granny, won't you miss it, even a little?" asked Pandora.

"After my dear Edward passed, it was all too much for me—the care of such an estate. And the memories. I miss the good times, my dear. But I was ready to say farewell to the house." Granny James gazed across the room. "I suppose I went completely in the opposite direction when I bought *this* house. I love Santorini, you know. I wanted to imitate it." She looked at Marietta. "Your sweet cottage inspired me. It worked in that small, vintage space. But here, it's all a bit overwhelming. I'll have to find someone to help me work things out."

Hearing this comment, Linnea's thoughts took flight. She slowly sipped from her drink to calm her excitement, tasting the lime at her lips. Did she dare . . . ? She decided to take the bold chance.

"I might know someone," she began.

Granny James's pale-blue eyes focused on her. "Do tell."

"My mother, Julia Rutledge, has a small, private decorating business. She doesn't advertise. She only works with a very select clientele." She let her gaze sweep the room. "I think this is exactly the kind of house she'd love to work with. She shares your color sense, and your love of light." Her lips twitched. "And white. I'm prejudiced, but I think she's very good."

"Are there houses she's done that I could see?" Granny James asked. "A portfolio?"

Linnea licked her lips and smiled. "Yes."

Marietta picked up a card and asked, "Didn't she decorate Milly's house on East Bay?"

"Yes, she did," Linnea said.

Marietta leaned across the table and said to Granny James, "Oh, she's very good."

Granny nodded, then turned to face Linnea. "Well, that's that. I'd love to meet her." Granny James beamed and lifted her glass in a toast. She turned to Marietta. "Isn't this providential?"

Marietta clinked glasses and sipped. Then she picked up a card and began to sort them. A cat's smile eased across her face. "Gin!"

"What?" Imogen brought her nose close to the cards to inspect.

Turning to the girls, Marietta said, "Come learn how to play, girls. I'm about to give this old girl a proper trouncing."

Chapter Ten

Local fishers, coastal communities, businesses, and the tourism industry are already seeing the negative effects of climate change. This means the destruction of coastal and marine ecosystems threatens the security of around 40 percent of the world population.

CHEZ NOUS WAS nestled in a Charleston single house in the heart of town. The small French restaurant had quickly become a favorite of Cara and David's. The maître d' smiled and welcomed them when they arrived and escorted them to a marble-topped bistro table in a private corner of the garden. Quickly, a wine list was provided.

David held out her seat, then sat across from her. The night was heavily scented with jasmine, creating an intoxicatingly balmy atmosphere. Candles flickered on the table, covered with the white linen. She reached up to smooth back her dark hair, letting her fingers glide to her ear to check the large pearl there. Her other hand rested on the table, the sizable oval diamond catching shards of candlelight.

"Would you like a cocktail?" David asked.

"No, just wine for me, thank you."

As though bidden, the waiter showed up, and after a brief consultation, David ordered champagne to start the evening.

"Champagne? What's the occasion?" asked Cara.

"Do I need an occasion? I celebrate every night I'm with you." He held back the smile that reached his eyes. "But, if you insist on an occasion, how about my returning home?"

"I'll drink to that. I missed you. How was England?"

"It rained." David looked up as the waiter delivered the flutes of wine.

Cara looked at the handwritten menu card, squinting in the dim light. She could hardly make out the elaborate script, yet she knew that whatever she chose, the food would be delicious. She finally settled on a melon salad, red snapper and roasted fennel with rice croquettes, and lemon mousse for dessert. David had the trout and he chose a crisp chardonnay to accompany the fish. With the food ordered, they could relax and catch up.

It was a lazy-paced evening. The food arrived as they talked. David had been in Europe for ten days checking on the business he was invested in, one of a few entrepreneurial enterprises he'd become involved in since he'd retired from his law practice. He liked to claim that he was able to squeeze a few jobs in between his babysitting work. In truth, his business abroad was expanding, and he was in Europe more often.

"Actually, speaking of England," he said, cutting his salad, "I'd like to talk to you about something." His hands stilled, and something about his tone made her look across the table into his dark-brown eyes. They were suddenly more serious. "It's becoming clear I'll need to go to London more often in the next year as we expand. I was hoping you could come with me. And Hope, of course."

Cara released a smile of relief that here was nothing ominous to discuss. "I'd love to. For how long?"

"It will vary. A week at a time. The visits will be short but more frequent for a while. But I'll have to stay a couple weeks during the merger. Maybe a month."

"*A month?* But my job . . . I can't just tell them I'm going to be gone for a month."

David picked up his glass and swirled the wine. "How long do you think you'll continue working?"

"After we're married?" She shrugged. "Indefinitely," she replied. She set down her tableware. "David, did you expect me to quit my job at the aquarium after we're married?"

He set his wineglass on the table and said carefully, "You won't have to work."

"I might want to work."

"Of course," he quickly replied, meeting her gaze. "If you wish. I just . . . You always say that you want to spend more time with Hope."

"Yes," she said, stumbling in her thoughts. "I do." She wasn't prepared for this discussion. Before Hope, there would have been no decision to make. Her job had always taken priority. But life after Hope had changed everything. Her priorities had shifted. Cara was not as definitive about her wants and goals as she had once been. Suddenly she was on a slippery slope. "I don't know," she replied at length. "I have to think about it. I love my job. But, yes . . . I do want to enjoy time with Hope."

"I would like to make that possible for you."

"David, you know I've never been the kind of southern woman my mother was, or her mother before her—for generations." She paused and looked down. "Or your first wife." She raised her gaze to see his face grow solemn. "You always described Leslie as the perfect wife. The perfect mother for Heather. She single-handedly raised your daughter. Decorated the house, had glorious gardens. Heather told me she was prominent in the Junior League. Worked for many charities."

"Cara, I never wanted you to be anything but who you are."

Cara put her fingertips to her temples. "I know, but . . . who *am* I?" she asked. She looked at David, hoping she could make him understand. "I've always been an academic. A worker bee. More inclined to carve out a path in the working world than in the social one. In truth, I was more like my father than my mother. Perhaps that's why I was such a disappointment to him. As a female, in his eyes I had failed. I had more the mind for business than his son had."

"He was a fool," David said abruptly. Then, "I'm sorry."

"You're right. He lived by the old patriarchal rules. I wasn't the only one who suffered. Poor Palmer," she said with a sorry shake of her head. "When I adopted Hope, I told myself I wouldn't raise my child to be bound by those old gender definitions. And yet, as a mother, I find myself racked with guilt for trying to be a breadwinner and a mother both. I don't know how so many women manage it alone. I rationalized my guilt at leaving Hope for work. I needed to support us." She took a sip of wine and replaced the glass on the table. "I've complained that I'm missing Hope's best years. I know that. How many times have I told you that I wished I could stay home with her?"

"Many."

Cara looked across the garden. The fairy lights had flicked on in the trees, and candles glowed on the small garden tables. What did she want now, at this point in her life? David was offering her the opportunity to make her wish of staying home with Hope a reality. The time had come for her to decide if she really *wanted* to stay home. She hated to admit, even to herself, that she didn't know if she had the temperament for it. Playing with dolls or toys sent her spiraling into boredom.

"I honestly don't know what I want to do."

"Darling, you don't have to decide now."

"But I do have to consider it now. Our marriage does change things," she said, as much to herself as to him. "More than I've given enough thought to. Why, just what you offered tonight is pretty earth-shattering." She put her hands out. "To live in Europe part-time?" She dropped her hands. "I do have to admit," she added, "that travel would be educational for Hope. And for me. I've traveled very little in my life. I'm embarrassed to say I've never been to Europe."

"I know. I'd like to be the one to show it to you."

She sighed. The man made loving him so easy. "Once Hope is in school, we'll have to stay in one place, of course. The schools don't let parents whisk their children out of school."

"More's the pity. Travel is good for children."

"So is keeping up in schoolwork."

"All the more reason for us to travel now. After she's in school," David continued, "we will work around *her* schedule. This might be our only window to live abroad. I think it could be a wonderful experience for us as a family. We'll depend on each other with no one else around. New customs, new traditions. Just think about it." He rested his hands on the table and caught her gaze. "I don't like to be separated from you for too long."

She met his gaze over the table.

The waiter appeared and discreetly removed the dishes. After he left, Cara asked David, "You realize when we move out of your house, we will need a new nanny?"

"Afraid so. I don't think Heather will let go of Cami."

"Did you tell her? About us moving out?"

David nodded. "I told Heather all about our decision not to live on Dewees."

She waited for him to elaborate, picking up her glass of wine. When he didn't, she finished the last sip with a single gulp. "David," she said placing the glass on the table. "What did she say? Was she upset?"

"Not upset as much as surprised," he replied. "But then . . ."

His reply was interrupted by the arrival of dessert. David ordered an espresso, Cara a cappuccino.

She picked up her spoon and dipped into the lemon mousse. It was sweet and tart.

"You were saying?" she prompted.

"You know I love the Dewees house," he said, digging into his apple tart. "And I love the island."

"Of course."

"You and I won't live in it after we're married," he continued. He let his fork rest. "But I've decided that I don't want to sell it."

Cara looked up from her dessert.

"As it happens," David went on, "Bo and Heather want to stay on Dewees."

"No surprise there. They love it."

"And you know they love the house, maybe more than I do. So, if you agree, I'd like to give them the house."

"Of course! It's your house to do with what you wish. I'm sure they're thrilled."

"They are," he added, obviously pleased with her reaction. "But every decision will be ours to make. Together. So, yes, if you agree, I want to give it to Heather. She's my only child, after all. Other than Hope," he hastened to add. "I don't think our girl's ready to move out yet."

Cara laughed. "No."

"Heather will be getting her inheritance early, that's all. And best of all, she'll keep a room in the house for Grandpa."

"And Grandma," she teased.

"So, we're agreed? We will give the Dewees house to Heather and Bo."

"Agreed."

Satisfied, he returned to his tart. "How's your house hunting coming along?"

She set down her dessert spoon as the cappuccino arrived. She picked up the frothy cup, took a bracing sip, then carefully returned the cup to the table. "Honestly? I haven't given it much thought. Work is crazy. It's the prime season. Then the wedding plans. Is there a hurry?"

"Well, we are getting married in a few months. It takes time to find a house, and then close on it. Furnish it . . ."

"I understand all that. But the house, work, the wedding. I'm feeling . . ." She stopped.

"Feeling what?" he asked.

"Rushed."

He thought about what she'd said, then reached out for her hand. His palm floated in the air over the table. Cara placed her palm in his, felt his strong grasp.

"We have a lifetime to discuss all this." He smiled. "Other than the wedding, of course. That date is set."

"That's a relief. David, I'd like to postpone the house hunt. At least until after the wedding. Summer will be over. Things will feel more settled. We can live in the beach house till we decide—at leisure."

David was the type of person who, once a course of action was decided upon, acted. At length, he nodded. "Sure."

"Good," she said, and it felt like a huge weight fell from her shoulders.

"Just remember, even in the beach house we need a playroom for the kids. Maybe I can put in bunk beds. I can't see Rory and Hope being separated too much. They're Mutt and Jeff."

Cara laughed. "They are that."

"By the way," he said with a wry smile, "what do you want to be called? Grandma?"

She almost choked on her coffee. "Good God, no. I'm not a grandmother."

"You will be."

She blinked in realization of that fact. "Rory calls me Cara now. That works." She pulled her cup closer. "I'm just getting used to being called Mother."

"How about Grandmother Cara?"

"That's a mouthful for any child. I like Cara. Let's leave it at that."

"But that's your name."

"Yes, I know." She stared at him with challenge.

He offered a wry grin. "Don't get mad at me if *I* call you Grandma."

"At your peril." She picked up her coffee.

He chuckled. "I'll be happy just to call you Mrs. Wyatt."

Cara did a double take. "What?" she asked softly. All mirth disappeared. When she returned her cup to the saucer it clattered. "You want me to change my name?"

David blinked, blindsided, and tilted his head. "Of course." There was a long, uncomfortable pause. "Don't you want to?"

Cara couldn't respond right away. She thought for a long moment in a tense silence.

"I've been Cara Rutledge for fifty-five years, David. I didn't change my name when I married Brett. I didn't expect you'd want me to change my name now."

David too seemed to be searching for the right words. "I . . . I suppose I simply assumed you would want to."

There followed another long silence during which Cara felt sure they were both thinking of the adage *to assume makes an ass of u and me.*

"David, it's not that I don't want to take your name." She smiled briefly. "It's a very nice name. And I'm very proud to become your wife. It's just . . . I've always been Cara Rutledge. My reputation has been built on that name. I'm not sure it's a coat I can change."

He paused in thought. "I can understand that. And I can admit I'm a little hurt that you aren't taking my name. I was looking forward to calling you Mrs. Wyatt."

She felt a pang. "That can be my nickname."

David didn't pretend humor, offering an expression of doubt.

"Well," Cara said on a sigh, "this has been a most enlightening dinner. You have given me a great deal to think about. Not to mention a few surprises."

He set his napkin on the table and lifted his hand for the waiter. "Let's finish up here. I have one more surprise."

✺   ✺   ✺

CARA FLICKED ON the lights inside the beach house and immediately felt the warm sense of familiarity. Her gaze swept around the dear little rooms of the cottage. She loved this house, and the thought of leaving it again was unsettling. David had given her much to think about over dinner. In truth, they'd skirted these issues for the past several months. It was typical of David to grab the bull by the horns and force decisions. She herself was not usually one to waffle. For Cara, procrastination was more an act of resistance. The reality of the marriage was looming large, and though she loved David and had no doubts about her decision to be his wife, the reality of losing her independence again, a hard-won freedom, was giving her cold feet.

David poured two cognacs and carried them to the long white sofa.

"I won't get up in the morning," Cara said, seeing the two snifters.

"You won't have to," David said, handing her the brandy. "I told Heather we would come by for Hope after lunch."

She met his gaze over the snifter. "Do you hope to get lucky?"

He half-smiled as his eyes kindled. "I do."

She chuckled and settled into the length of the sofa. David stretched out on the opposite side, their long legs touching between them. Cara's head rested against the big cushion, a splash of dark brown against snow white. Her heels were abandoned on the carpet. Across from her, David looked tanned and fit. He'd removed his jacket and rolled up the sleeves of his crisp white shirt. She felt his eyes on her.

"I believe," Cara began coyly, "you said something about a surprise?" She made a show of looking around the room. "I don't see any packages. A souvenir? Wait. I know! I'm getting my Big Ben tin of tea after all."

"Rats," he said. "I forgot. Next time."

"Promises, promises."

"But I do have a little something to show I've been thinking of you."

He reached over to his jacket and pulled out an envelope from the vest pocket, then handed it across the sofa to her.

Cara had half expected to see a jeweler's bag emerge from the pocket. "What's this?" she asked, her curiosity inflamed, taking the thick envelope.

"Open it."

She made a show of lifting it to test its heft. Then, all joking aside, she opened the envelope. Inside was a sheet of paper. Unfolding it, she saw it was an itinerary. She moved the pages closer to the light to read it through, then looked up, astonished.

"We're going to New York? To Kleinfeld?"

"It's supposed to be the biggest wedding dress shop in the country," he said, his eyes bright with excitement. "I consulted Heather and Emmi. They're coming along. I got us all tickets and rooms at the Plaza. Hope, too. You can choose not only your dress, but a dress for your flower girl."

Cara was speechless. Absolutely floored.

David hurried to add, "Cara, I know you've been so busy, and you haven't found your wedding dress yet. When Emmi told me how stressed you were about it, we cooked up a plan to whisk you away and make it a kind of bachelorette party all in one."

"Emmi said that, did she?" Cara was going to have words with Emmi.

"I talked to the clerk at Kleinfeld and made you an appointment. I'll babysit Hope while you girls go shopping. The saleswoman said they have many dresses in your size that can be purchased off the rack, and there's still time for alterations. Problem solved. What do you think?"

"I think . . . this is all getting a bit overwhelming," she said honestly.

"It's not meant to be. It's meant to make things easier." He paused, noting her expression and more, her lack of enthusiasm. "Is there a problem you want to tell me about?"

"Not a problem . . ."

"Then what?"

Cara felt the intimacy of the moment, and with it, the safety that came from knowing one was loved.

"I'm nervous about a big wedding," she said. "I've just never been one for parties. Put me in a boardroom and I'm at home. But at a party?" She shuddered. "I find chitchat agonizing."

"This isn't a party. It's our wedding," he said, a hint of hurt entering his voice. "Only the people we love will be there."

"Yes," she said, trying to appease him, though that did little to assuage her worry.

David looked at his snifter, swirled the amber liquid. "Is it so wrong for me to want to tell the whole world 'I got you'?" He looked up.

Cara shook her head and smiled. How could she feel anything but flattered?

He reached out to gently stroke her leg besides his. "Darling, I can see this wedding is more my dream than yours. I was hoping that by me sending you to New York, it might make it easier on you. More fun. With your girls."

Cara quietly considered this. It was typical of David to try to make her happy in a grand way. Was the gesture controlling or generous? The truth was, she'd been meaning to shop for a dress for a long while, knew she had to find one soon. She was running out of time. She looked across the sofa and saw the vulnerability in his eyes, the hope that he had pleased her.

"Mr. Wyatt, you are the sweetest man. I don't know what to say."

David laughed, relief shining in his eyes. "Say yes to the dress!"

Chapter Eleven

Thirty years after the first turtle teams were established on the south-eastern coasts of the United States, the numbers of nests are trending upward. Sea turtles reach maturity at thirty years, so the increased number of nests is believed to be, in part, a result of the work of volunteers for the past three decades.

CARA SAT ON the deck of the beach house, lazily stirring her coffee while staring out at the ocean. June was upon them, and with it the onset of the summer season. Spring blooms were past and now the red roses were showing off on the pergola. She enjoyed listening to the hum of a few bees as they hovered for nectar. *Eat up*, she thought, wishing the dear little pollinators well. Around the ocean-edge deck were big clay pots filled with annuals of showy summer colors. Three more, placed close to the porch door, held her kitchen garden: basil, thyme, sage, rosemary, and parsley.

Saturday might be her favorite day of the week, she thought. It was a day she could do whatever she liked: plant flowers, shop, go to the park with Hope, have a date night with David, or just tuck in and read a book from her tilting to-be-read pile.

Not that she didn't love her job. She was dedicated to the mission of bringing conservation awareness to the public. Loved the South Carolina Aquarium and everyone associated with it. Was proud of the sea turtle hospital. She never walked into the hospital without thinking of how her mother would've been so proud of it.

The sea turtle season was well underway too. By the end of only the first week of June, they already had seven nests on Isle of Palms and two on Sullivan's Island. An exciting start that hinted at a record-breaking season. There was always the hope at the dawn of every season that the year would be a good one. She supposed farmers thought the same, vintners, anyone looking toward a crop that would prove fruitful. Cara liked to think that the turtles coming back this season to nest were hatchlings that her mother had helped reach the sea.

Even though Cara couldn't be at the nests most mornings, she'd still been granted an SCDNR permit. Everyone understood that Cara was royalty on the Island Turtle Team. Lovie was one of the state's original "sea turtle ladies," a group of women who acted individually to help the sea turtles as they nested on their beaches long before the SCDNR teams were established. But more, Cara was working at the aquarium, helping sea turtles in a different and equally important way. The team was a family.

Thinking of family, Cara looked along the deck and saw Hope sitting in the shade of the pergola, concentrating on putting together her Legos. Her brows were knitted as she created some sort of building. Hope had a strong attention span, which Cara knew would serve her well in the future. Someday in the not-too-distant future, Cara would teach Hope, as Lovie had taught her, about the nesting saga of the sea turtles. And someday, when Cara passed on, Hope would carry the torch. Mother to daughter to granddaughter, the legacy would continue.

"Cara?"

Cara looked up from the papers on the teak patio table, following the sound of the voice. She saw Linnea walking around the house toward them.

"Hello!" Cara called out, delighted to see her niece.

Linnea climbed the few steps to the deck. "I rang and knocked, but no one came to the door. I'm sorry if I'm barging in."

"Not at all. I didn't hear. It's a perfect day, so we're taking advantage of sitting outdoors. I feel cooped up in the air-conditioning all the time." She stepped forward to place a kiss on Linnea's cheek. "It's always a treat to see you. Would you like some coffee? Or something cold to drink?"

"No, I'm good. I just had lunch. I got your message and came right over." She went over to the shaded area under the pergola and crouched down beside Hope. "What are you making?"

"I'm building a house," Hope replied matter-of-factly, not taking her eyes off the toys.

"Just like your uncle Palmer," Linnea exclaimed. When Hope didn't seem to understand, Linnea turned and pointed to the house across the road. "See that big house over there that's getting built? My daddy is building that house. It's kind of like Legos, only big. It's very important to put the pieces together in just the right way. Like you're doing."

Hope nodded and smiled. "Wanna play with me?"

"Can I watch? I want to talk to your mama."

"Okay." Hope turned back to her building, her concentration intense.

Linnea kissed the top of Hope's head, then joined Cara at the teak table.

"That was nice," Cara said as Linnea took a seat beside her. "She adores you."

"I adore her," Linnea said, slipping her sunglasses back on. "Maybe you have a future architect there."

"Maybe. Or just a child who likes to play with blocks. Time will tell."

"Speaking of the house," Linnea said, glancing at it in the distance, "it's coming along nicely."

"It is," Cara said with enthusiasm. "It's even a bit ahead of schedule. I'm so proud of my brother. I think it's going to be a beautiful house. I love the way it looks rather modest from the street and then it spreads out to this amazing surprise in the back."

"Like a mullet haircut. Business in front; party in the back."

Cara burst out with a laugh. "How do you know that? Mullets were before your time."

"They're kind of coming back. Sadly . . ."

"Well, not too much partying for your father," Cara said. "He needs to stay all business. A lot is at stake for him. I hope he does as well with the interiors."

"Mama is helping him there."

"Then I have no worries. Julia has impeccable taste. I love what she did with my house."

"Oh, a funny thing happened the other day," Linnea began. "Not funny in a ha-ha way, more . . . curious." She went on to tell Cara about meeting her new friend Pandora's grandmother. Cara had to laugh when she described the big, square house, quite the opposite of the one Palmer was building. Her smile faded when Linnea went on to tell her that she'd suggested her mother's decorating company.

"I didn't know Julia had a decorating company."

"I stretched the truth a bit. Maybe a lot. Did I do the right thing?"

"Oh, Linnea," Cara said, her fingertips tapping the table. Sometimes it was hard being the older and wiser woman. She knew how feelings could get hurt, even with the best of intentions. "You may have crossed a line there. That was your mother's decision to make. I've been burned a few times over the years trying to get Julia involved in projects. She can be headstrong. And she's been known to hold a grudge. Your mother may be very upset by this."

"She can always say no," Linnea countered, appearing suddenly nervous about her decision.

Cara pursed her lips and thought it best not to reply. Linnea was a bright girl and had already figured out her reasoning.

"You know my mother," Linnea continued, trying to explain. "She's insecure about her abilities. She's always the first to step back and let others get all the accolades. I've seen her friends accept praise for the decorating of their homes, and not even mention that it was my mother's doing. Even if she's standing right there! They all just smiled and took the credit."

"Everyone knew. . . ."

"You don't know that. And does it matter? The point is, Mama needs a little push. I believe in her talent. So do you." Linnea took a breath, moving into tender territory. "And I don't think she's doing so well out here. She misses the city. Fish out of water."

"I didn't know that," Cara said, her concern flashing. "I'm sorry. I haven't been the best friend. . . ."

"You've got a lot on your plate. We all do. And she's so very good at covering up. I don't know if you know that Mama gave up all her committees and boards.

Cara shook her head.

"She was always so busy, so involved," Linnea continued. "Now she just sits in that house and reads and watches movies. She isn't getting involved in anything. Not even her garden."

"Maybe she's enjoying the peace. My mother did when she moved out to the island."

"I thought that too. Frankly, it's easier to think that. But, Cara, it's been almost two years. And you can't compare her to Lovie. She always had her turtles—they were her passion. A woman needs to find her passion."

"A room of her own," Cara said.

"Right. In which to be creative. Mama needs to find that special something that's all her own. We talked about this the other day. Mama was actually open to the idea of creating a small decorating business."

"Was she?"

Linnea nodded. "So, my suggestion didn't come out of nowhere. In fact, the project sort of dropped in my lap. Granny James," then seeing Cara's confused look, she added, "aka Mrs. James, needs a decorator." She shrugged. "I went with my instinct. The problems she has with that big square house are exactly what I know mother can fix. She's good." Linnea released a long sigh, one that admitted her own fears. "I hope I didn't overstep my bounds, but if I did, I did it for all the right reasons."

Cara studied her niece's face and a smile eased across her own. "You have good instincts. Always did. Mama used to comment on it. I hope you're right, Linnea. If Julia does decide to go forward with starting a business, I will shout it from the rooftops. As will Palmer."

"Daddy? You think so?"

"Yes, why? Don't you?"

Linnea motioned with her hand. "He's never been very supportive of Mama doing anything but volunteer work. And you remember how freaked he was about my going to work in California."

Cara snorted. "My brother can be a chauvinist pig, just like his daddy before him. Well, his finances have changed. He'd better welcome his wife's support. He can use it."

Linnea homed in on this. "Are things that bad for him?"

Cara dodged the question. "It's really not my place to discuss it."

"Oh, come on, Aunt Cara. It's no secret he almost went bankrupt. I'm just worried that my being at home again is going to be a burden."

"It's not come to that," Cara reassured her. "You're only living in your bedroom. But I wouldn't count on your parents to bankroll you. I think it's fair to say their financial ship is on an even keel but in shallow waters. This house he's building is his best chance for the future. He needs to make a neat profit. Your mother guiding the interiors is an important means of her support. I'm very proud of them both. They've gone to hell and back."

Linnea looked down at her hands resting in her lap. "I'm not helping, am I? I've been doing what you suggested, controlling the narrative. It's working on my father, but my mother saw through me."

"I'm not surprised. That mother-daughter conection . . ." Cara paused. "It wasn't meant so much for your parents as for you. I hoped you'd see that you are not a failure."

Linnea gave a short laugh. "It's pretty hard to convince myself of that. I haven't found a job yet. If I hear one more person say, 'I'm sorry, there isn't anything open at this time,' I'll scream."

Cara leaned closer to Linnea. "That's why I called you over. There's something I'd like to talk to you about."

Linnea jerked her head up, her eyes wide with hope. "A job?"

A smile twitched at Cara's lips. "Not quite. More an internship."

Linnea straightened in attention.

Cara continued, "We got a grant for education that will allow us to expand some of our programs. I could use some help. I asked, but the program won't cover a paid assistant." She raised one brow. "But I *was* granted a position for an intern with a modest stipend." Seeing Linnea's immediate reaction of hope, she lifted her hand. "It's not much," she cautioned, "but it is something. More importantly, this is an opportunity for you to get back in the game. Especially at the aquarium. It's the best I can offer."

"Aunt Cara!" Linnea exclaimed. "Thank you. Thank you!" she repeated. "Education is what I'm most interested in. I don't know how to tell you how important this is." She was so excited she could hardly remain in her seat.

"You don't have to tell me—I know. I remember being scared and looking for a job. I didn't have anyone to help me in Chicago. Believe me, it brings me pleasure to be able to help you. But you should know," she said in a serious tone, "I need someone good, not just someone I know. There will be those who say that my choosing you smacks of nepotism. But it's not. I truly believe you're the most qualified for the position. If you'll take it."

"Of course I'll take it!"

"It's very little money," she said again.

"I'll make do. It's a chance. What are the hours?"

"Full-time."

"Okay," Linnea said, putting her fingertips to her temples as though to contain the whirl of possibilities. "I can manage. Living at home will help, of course."

"You can drive in with me to the aquarium on some days, but here's the catch. You'll need a car. There will be days you will have to go out into the community."

A cloud passed over Linnea's expression.

"So," Cara said, her eyes bright. "I heard back from the garage about Mama's VW."

"The Gold Bug?"

Cara nodded. "Good news. It *is* an old car," she began. "The tires were cracked; I had to replace those. And the oil hadn't been changed in quite a while. My bad, I'm afraid. The brakes were flushed and bled, but the brake linings are fine, and the usual suspects were replaced—the fuel and air filters. Fortunately, the Gold Bug was kept out of the sun, so the interior is in pretty good shape. All in all, that car has a lot of miles left on it." She leaned back and asked, "You do drive manual, don't you?"

Linnea laughed and wiggled her hand in the gesture that implied *a little*. "I'll get better."

"Then that's it. The Gold Bug is yours. We can go today to pick it up."

Linnea squealed with joy and leaped from her chair to embrace her aunt. Hearing the sound, Moutarde, the canary, burst into song.

Linnea stepped back, hugging herself. "I can't believe it. I'm so happy."

Cara smiled, turned her head and paused, listening. "Is that the doorbell? I can't tell with all that cacophony."

The doorbell sounded again.

"Stay put," Linnea said. "I'm already up. I'll get it."

Cara watched as Linnea stepped into the sunroom and strode to the side kitchen door, where someone was knocking rudely. She opened it and stepped back as the door whooshed open.

Flo stomped in, her spiky white hair unbrushed, still wearing her nightgown.

Cara was surprised to see Flo undressed at this hour of the day.

"There you are!" Flo called out in a snappish tone. "Don't you answer the door anymore? And when did you start locking it? I used to walk right in."

"I don't know. . . ." Linnea stammered.

Flo gazed around the room, taking stock, before letting her gaze settle on Linnea.

"Well, Lovie," she said in a satisfied huff, "it's good to see you. We've got a lot to talk about. Those young 'uns don't know what they're doing on the team. We need to set things straight."

Frowning at the sound of Flo's strident tone, Cara picked up Hope and walked into the sunroom. She was shocked to hear Flo call Linnea "Lovie." Flo's eyes were bright with confusion and she appeared frazzled as she stood in the center of the kitchen, wringing her hands and gazing around the room, searching.

"Hello," Cara called out as she entered the kitchen.

Flo saw her and headed her way, huffing like a locomotive. "Cara, you're back! When did you arrive? See?" she said to Linnea. "They don't tell me anything! That's what I'm talking about. Lovie, we don't have time for idle talk. We have a problem. They're not telling us when they find nests!" She shook her finger. "But I know. I hear them talking. They're hiding them from us. They'll listen to you. They always listen to you."

Linnea's face was ashen. She tried to smile and said softly, "Flo? I'm Linnea."

"What's that?"

Cara stepped closer to Flo. "That's Linnea," she said in a calm, even-toned voice.

Flo looked at Linnea, confusion in her eyes, followed by fear.

"I know who you are," she snapped. Then she looked around, her agitation spiking. "Where am I? I'm not home. I need to go home."

The side door swung open again and Emmi stepped into the kitchen. She was wearing her uniform of fishing pants and a Turtle Team T-shirt. Her eyes were wide with worry and relief. "There you are!" she said, approaching Flo. She put her arms around the old woman's shoulders. "You had me worried. I asked you not to run out of the house like that."

Flo took several calming breaths, then lifted her head and glared at Emmi. "I didn't run anywhere," she said shrewishly. "I walked over to see my friend Lovie. Same as I always do. Now, stop fussing at me, child. Isn't it time for you to go home? Your mother will be worried."

Emmi looked up to meet Cara's gaze, her usually cheerful countenance drawn with worry. It was clear she was reaching the breaking point. In Emmi's green eyes, red with fatigue, Cara read the message of grief that the time had come to make serious decisions about Flo's care, that Emmi had reached the end of her ability to care for her. Cara nodded in silent understanding and agreement.

"Let's go home," Emmi told Flo, slipping an arm around her shoulders. "I have some nice soup waiting for you. Chicken noodle, your favorite."

Flo appeared suddenly exhausted and subdued. "Good," she said, nodding meekly. "Chicken noodle. That's my favorite," she repeated.

Cara put Hope on the ground and tilted her chin with her hand. "I'll be right back, okay? I'm just going to walk Aunt Flo home. Linnea will stay with you." She looked up to confirm with Linnea, who nodded.

Cara moved to open wide the kitchen door. She watched as Flo took cautious steps to the ground, her frail hand holding the railing tight. In the harsh sunlight Cara saw the thin hair on Flo's head, exposing scalp.

Her skin, which had always been tanned, was pale. When had she lost so much weight? Flo looked so frail and so . . . old.

Emmi hovered, and Cara's heart went out to her friend, getting a solid glimpse of what her life had been like the past year as Flo's slide into Alzheimer's progressed. Emmi had lost weight too, and her clothes were wrinkled. Cara walked behind the pair, fully aware of what decisions would have to be made.

✳   ✳   ✳

FLO ATE HER soup, refused a salad, and went upstairs to take a nap without any fuss. Cara and Emmi looked at her asleep in her bed, and they both felt awash with love for the older woman who'd been a second mother to them both.

They returned to the kitchen for a much-needed cup of coffee and sat together, as they so often did, at the wooden table to talk. Emmi told Cara, "She's gone downhill quickly." She shook her head. "So fast. Before, it was manageable. She'd have spells of forgetfulness, confusion, then get over them and be the same ol' Flo. Which could be a pain in the ass, but not frightening."

"There was the wandering. . . ."

Emmi sighed. "Yes. Just like her mother before her. I was prepared for that. I did what Flo did for Miranda and took to locking the doors. I got her one of the alert bracelets. It worked for a while, but Flo always managed to find escape routes. In the past month, almost since the beginning of sea turtle season, she's started refusing to eat. Bathing has become a fight. And her personal care . . . She was always so careful about hygiene, like an old head nurse. Remember how she used to check our necks and behind our ears? But now . . ." Emmi shook her head. "There are days she doesn't get dressed. It's a fight to try to help her. And . . ." She looked haunted. "She's getting paranoid."

"As in suspicious?"

Emmi nodded. "She thinks I'm keeping secrets. Especially about the turtles. And"—Emmi twisted her fingers—"she's right. *I am.* I don't tell her when I get a call about a nest anymore. I can't," she exclaimed, looking at Cara with a need to be understood. "She's becoming unpredictable at the nests. She can't do anything anymore. The last few years she tagged along quite cheerfully. I'd let her do a few chores, but she got winded so easily and didn't complain. Lately, though, she's acting like she's still in charge of the team. Giving orders to the others, which confuses them. And when they don't comply, she grunts in frustration and tries to do the duties herself. When I try to stop her, she gets abusive."

"Oh no," Cara said on a sigh. "Why didn't you tell me?"

Emmi shook her head. "I don't know. It never seemed like the right time. I didn't want to admit I couldn't handle it. But her actions are interfering with the team's efforts, and spirit. I had to make the tough decision. So, now she's upset that I'm not telling her about the nests."

"I'm sorry," Cara said, knowing how hard that decision had to come.

"The irony is, I actually do tell her," Emmi said. "But not until after we've finished moving and posting them. I have to sneak out of the house to tend to the nests in the morning. Then I lock up the house behind me. I hate leaving her alone, but she can't come along, not anymore. She's just . . . acting crazy." Tears filled Emmi's eyes.

"Emmi . . ."

"I'm so damn sorry it's come to this. I know the turtles are her life. But I have a responsibility to the team. It's a vicious circle—I don't tell her we found a nest, but then she finds out we did, and she gets all agitated at not being consulted. She wants to call Lovie."

"That's what happened today," said Cara. "She saw Linnea and thought she was Lovie."

"They look a lot alike. It adds to her confusion."

"Could she come to the nests and have a volunteer be her . . . her escort?"

"We tried that. But you know Flo when she has a bee in her bonnet. She wouldn't listen to some volunteer. She became uncontrollable, pushing the volunteer away, telling her to mind her own business. Then she'd go up to the nest and try to shoo away the volunteer who was digging the nest, tell them that they were doing it wrong and she'd have to do it. It's a nightmare."

Cara thought about the problem, but it didn't take long to arrive at the answer. "I think the time has come, Emmi."

Emmi shook her head, murmuring, "I don't think I can send her to a home. This is the only home she's ever known. She grew up in it. Think how confused she'll be in some strange place."

"She's already confused. Emmi, you've taken care of her for a long time. Given her extra time in this house. In the beginning stage, there were no serious safety issues. But we have to face the facts. Her wandering is a serious problem. She's not eating well and losing weight. And it's not good for her to stay locked up in here alone. That's got to be frightening for her, and you too. Besides, she's a Houdini. She gets out."

Emmi listened quietly, then said, "I'll hire a house sitter."

"You've said you were going to do that for weeks now."

"I will. I promise."

"You have to. Or I will. This can't continue."

"I think I'm the best judge of that."

"What was that look, then? In the kitchen?"

"I was frightened. I couldn't find her. I . . ." Emmi put her hands to her face. "I don't know. I don't want to argue. Truth told, I'm too tired to decide. Between the nests coming full force during the day, my working part-time, and Flo waking up at all hours in the night, I just need a good sleep."

"You need help," Cara said. She reached out to put her hand over Emmi's.

"My giving you money isn't enough anymore. Your care isn't enough anymore. Flo needs full-time care, specialized care, so she doesn't hurt herself. Or you."

"Part of me agrees with you. Part of me also knows that once we make that decision, there's no going back. It's kind of like . . . she's dying."

"She's not. This can go on for a long time." Cara's tone was decisive, and Emmi nodded in agreement. "Let's begin by hiring a nurse. Then we can take the time to scope out the area and visit memory care centers. Palmer gave me the name of a place he heard was very nice. We can start there."

Emmi nodded, relief shining in her moist eyes. "Okay. I think that's a good idea. Let's see what our options are." She slumped in her chair, her lids half-lowered. She looked as if she was about ready to fall asleep in the chair.

"Okay. You go up and take a nap. I'll begin research," Cara said. "I know how to do that."

Emmi rose slowly. "Thank you, my friend."

Chapter Twelve

The Battery stretches along the southernmost tip of the Charleston Peninsula, where the Cooper River and Ashley River meet to form Charleston Harbor. With its scenic promenade and historic park, the Battery is one of downtown Charleston's most beloved landmarks.

THE GOLD BUG was a roadworthy car, Linnea thought as she gazed lovingly at the old VW Beetle. The old car was in prime condition. The gold shone in the sunlight, and with the black convertible top folded down, it looked nothing short of adorable. It was no wonder everyone had known the Gold Bug when Lovie drove it years ago. Cara had been generous to get the leather seats buffed and the wood console polished. All Linnea had to do was hang a cute air freshener on the rearview mirror.

The gearshift was a skinny rod sticking up from the floor, and it was a challenge to master the gearshift pattern. Well, she thought with a laugh, *master* might be an optimistic word. She'd stalled several times just driving it home from Isle of Palms to Sullivan's Island. When she'd pulled over on the bridge, a cute guy in a pickup had stopped and asked if she needed help. The car was the equivalent of a puppy as a magnet for the opposite sex.

Tonight, she was ready for a party. For the past month she'd avoided her old friends, not because she didn't like them but because she needed time to land back in town and get her bearings before facing them. With her internship and this sporty car, Linnea had gotten her groove back. She felt good about her decisions, and the *create your own narrative* plan felt truer now. Plus, with her tan from all the beach walks and surfing, she definitely was ready to face her old friends. But first, she was picking up her new friend.

She didn't stall once as she buzzed along Middle Street to Marshall Boulevard into the Jameses' expansive driveway. The monolithic white house rose up before her, as cold and uninviting as ever. She gave two quick beeps on her horn that sounded nasal, even cartoonish. A minute later the front door flung open and Pandora came rushing down the long flight of stairs, her impossibly high heels teetering on each step.

Pandora flung her arms out dramatically as she drew near the car and called out, "Darling, whatever are you driving!"

Linnea lowered her sunglasses and stared at the vision before her. Pandora had cut her long dark hair to bob length in the back and it angled longer below her chin in front; it was highlighted dramatically, so it now appeared more blond than brown. In her chic flowing pants with the wide belt and a midriff silk top she just looked cool. Edgy. But with a sweetness behind the pretty that made you want to like her.

"Who are you?" Linnea asked.

"Very funny. What do you think?" Pandora asked, twirling on her heel.

"I hardly recognize you. You look even more gorgeous, if that's possible. Very posh," Linnea said, using one of the few British words she knew.

"I decided I needed a makeover. Something more, I don't know, fun."

"Maybe a little *too*. You're not in the Hamptons, you know. This is the lowcountry. We go for Lilly Pulitzer and pearls around here." She stared pointedly at the large Lucite dangling earrings and dramatic ring.

"All the better. I like to stand out."

"You will," Linnea said softly as Pandora climbed into the car. Her legs were so long her knees drew close to her chest. "You can push the seat back."

Pandora looked on the door for a switch.

"Uh, no," Linnea said. "It's that bar under the seat. Lift it and push back."

"How . . . vintage," Pandora quipped. She found the bar, and with a whoosh the seat pushed far back, stopping with a thump. She burst out laughing. "Well, this is an adventure."

"Meet the Gold Bug. It was my grandmother's car but it has less than fifty thousand miles on it, can you believe it? It's a gem."

"The Gold Bug. As in Edgar Allan Poe?"

"High marks for you. You know I love anything vintage."

"I do indeed," Pandora said, eyeing Linnea's hunter-green shirtdress, a wide belt cinching her waist. "Is the dress your grandmother's too?"

She'd meant it as a joke, so it gave Linnea great pleasure to nod and answer, "As a matter of fact, it was. The pearls too." She lightly touched the strand around her neck.

Pandora slipped on her large sunglasses. "If I'd known there was a theme to the night, I'd have borrowed a frock from Granny James."

"You mean you didn't?" Linnea deadpanned.

Pandora burst into laughter and Linnea joined in as she pushed the gear into reverse.

"Buckle up, girlfriend. It's going to be a bumpy ride. I'm just getting used to manual transmission."

The Gold Bug purred as Linnea traveled to the Ravenel Bridge. The girls loved driving with the top down, catching the gazes of passersby and the occasional toot of a horn. Going uphill, however, the old car showed its age. Cars zoomed past them on either side.

"Won't it go any faster?" called out Pandora.

"I've got the pedal to the metal," Linnea called back. She made as if she were cracking a whip and called out, "Go, go!"

Pandora began rocking forward, joining in the chorus, "Go, go, go!" as the little car chugged at no more than fifty miles per hour. They laughed hilariously as they puttered across the bridge, the soft summer air blowing through their hair. The sun was setting over the glistening river and Charleston's spires loomed in the city. Whenever a car honked, they smiled and waved back cheerily.

Linnea knew her way around the city and took shortcuts to the Battery, where some of Charleston's greatest historic houses fronted the harbor. She circled the neighborhood until she found a place to park a few blocks away from the party's address, then put up the ragtop with Pandora's help.

"I've grown rather fond of the bug, but I fear it's been misnamed," Pandora said, pushing down one of the roof fasteners.

"Oh?" Linnea asked, locking the door.

"Yes," Pandora said, checking a fingernail. "The Gold Bug is a bit ambitious. Perhaps the Road Buzzard is better suited."

Linnea squelched a laugh. "Shhh, don't hurt her feelings," she said with a pat on the roof. "Dear old car."

"Posh neighborhood," Pandora said, looking about.

"The best," Linnea replied as they began walking along the crooked sidewalk.

Pandora grabbed Linnea's arm to steady herself in her spiky heels. Linnea walked slowly, admiring the streets she hadn't seen since she'd moved back. She knew every house in this neighborhood. She'd run along the tall walls of the gardens as a child to get to her friends' houses, climbed the large oak trees that arched graciously over the cobbled streets. The neighbors knew her name. She'd never felt lost or alone in these streets growing up. Yet, like her parents, many of the families had moved away in the past decade, the homeowners either retiring or dying or simply taking advantage of the skyrocketing home values. Linnea paused to admire one of the window boxes overflowing with flowers.

"I grew up here. I used to live a block away."

"Really? Whyever did you move?"

"I didn't," she replied. "My parents moved. Short answer, it was the right decision at the time."

"It's utterly charming. This is the Charleston I've read about. History, beautiful, important houses . . . reminds me of home." She sighed. "I could get used to living here. Maybe I'll find some handsome young man tonight who will sweep me off my feet," Pandora said with a wry smile.

"Or vice versa," Linnea said. She looked at the arching trees and the meticulous gardens. "I love it here. But honestly? I prefer the beach."

"To each her own."

They'd turned onto East Bay and immediately felt the brisk, salty breeze from the harbor. Linnea guided Pandora across the street to stand at the tall wall that bordered the harbor. From this vantage point she pointed out Fort Sumter in the distance and explained how the first shots of the Civil War were fired there.

Turning, Pandora took in the elegant, showy beauty of a row of pastel-colored houses. "This is lovely," she said.

"This area is called the Battery, named after an artillery battery during the Civil War." She smiled wryly. "Also known as the War between the States. Or the Incident of Northern Aggression. But this here is called Rainbow Row for the thirteen colorful historic houses. Come on."

As they walked, Linnea felt she was surrounded by a history lived by her ancestors. She felt again that sense of belonging that stirred her consciousness. After a brief walk she stopped in front of an antebellum house the same color as the rosy sky over the Charleston Harbor. The house enjoyed gorgeous views from the three-story bay windows, and sea breezes from the patio and piazzas.

"Here we are."

Pandora looked up at the house and smiled with contentment. "Lovely," she said. Then she turned her head to face Linnea and said, "Oh, by the way, I hope you don't mind, but I invited a plus-one."

Linnea looked sharply at her friend. "Pandora, you didn't. This isn't just some party. It's an engagement party—held in his parents' home. Very private. You're *my* plus-one; that's how I could invite you." She puffed out her cheeks. "It's really not acceptable."

"It's not a sit-down dinner, is it, darling?"

"No—"

Pandora waved her hand. "Then no worries! I promise you, my friend will fit in. He's quite dishy and well-mannered. I've been dying to connect with him. He hasn't asked me out and I've been flirting shamelessly. So rude. I simply had to use this opportunity. It's the first singles party I've been invited to since I've arrived." She made a sad face that looked bizarre with all her elaborate eye makeup. "Truly, Lin, I am sorry if I've overstepped. Forgive me?"

Linnea swallowed her frustration. "Of course. It's just . . . a bit awkward for me. Coming with another man. You see, the man who is engaged is someone I used to date. Darby Middleton. Actually, he proposed to me and I turned him down. He thinks it was because of John. It wasn't, but you can see how awkward it is now that I've broken up with John and show up with another man."

"Well, that is a juicy story. But *you* aren't showing up with a man. You're showing up with me." She tucked her arm through Linnea's. "You worry too much. Come on, let's go in. I'm dying for a drink."

The front walk was immaculately manicured with boxwood and a pair of black iron urns overflowing with summer annuals. Linnea couldn't count the number of times she'd strolled up the stairs to the Middletons' front porch. Their families had shared dinners, holidays, dances, and proms. Darby had been her date for her debut at the St. Cecelia Ball, the most coveted social event in Charleston. Only sons of members could invite a young debutante to the ball, and their parents had made the arrangements when Linnea and Darby were in middle school. Their families had planned on the two marrying, joining two historic families. It had taken a long while for Julia to forgive Linnea for breaking up with Darby. She wasn't sure Darby's parents had ever forgiven her for what must have been perceived as a slight.

Standing at the front door, Linnea looked out at the harbor. She breathed deep the salty air, smoothed her dress, and pulled her lipstick from her purse. Finished, she caught Pandora's amused glance. Linnea half-smiled and shrugged, then rang the bell. A uniformed maid opened the door and directed them to the party on the second floor. It was customary in historic houses for the ballroom to be located on the second floor where the breezes and breathtaking views of the harbor made warm evenings pleasant. Wood paneling and Tiffany-designed details caught the attention of Pandora as they made their way up the stairs.

As they entered the party, it was quickly apparent to Linnea that no one would have noticed if she came with anyone, because no one noticed her at all. All eyes immediately went to Pandora. Tall, stylish, flashy, she was a flamingo amid a flock of marsh hens. As Linnea had predicted, there was a lot of Lilly Pulitzer or some version of the same. Her friends were all pretty and fashionable, but no one had the striking, *Paris Vogue* vibe that Pandora did.

"Linnea, you came!"

Linnea turned to see Ashley Porter hurrying across the room, weaving between guests. Sweet Ashley, she thought. Ashley had been a classmate and longtime friend. Impeccably groomed with her shoulder-length blond hair, slender figure, and blue eyes, she was the perfect choice of a bride for Darby. Linnea was truly happy to see Ashley smiling with such delight.

They hugged, and when she drew back, Ashley proudly showed Linnea her engagement ring. It was a beautiful ruby with an equal-size diamond on either side.

"It's beautiful," Linnea told her.

"Isn't it amazing? It was Darby's grandmother's," Ashley said, then brought the ring close to her heart. "That makes it all the more precious." She looked from her ring to Linnea with apprehension. "I wanted to call you," she began in a rush, "to tell you about the engagement myself. But I didn't have your number in California, and it wasn't something to write in an e-mail, right? And, well . . ." She made a worried face. "I wasn't sure how you'd feel about it because . . . you know . . . you and Darby—"

"No, not at all," Linnea exclaimed, trying to put Ashley's worries at bay. "That's ancient history. Darby and I dated in high school. My God, we still had acne! We were children. We're just good friends now, and I couldn't be happier. I was just thinking how perfect you are together."

"Really?" Ashley appeared both relieved and eager to believe it. "I'm so glad. I mean, I didn't want anything to come between us."

"It couldn't."

Then Ashley gave a wide, slow smile and gently bumped shoulders. "You never had acne. You always had the best skin, but it was nice of you to say that."

"Linnea!"

Linnea turned at the familiar voice to see Darby standing behind her. He was as handsome as ever in his seersucker suit and pale-blue shirt that brought out the remarkable blue of his eyes.

"Darby."

Darby slipped an arm around Ashley and brought her closer. "Haven't I got myself the best bride?"

"Indeed. Congratulations," Linnea told him. "I couldn't be happier for you both."

"I'm a lucky man," Darby said, smiling down at his intended. Then with a wink at Linnea, he added, "Dodged a few bullets to reach her, eh? I'm kidding." He laughed and looked up, sweeping a shock of his blond hair back from his forehead.

Linnea merely smiled.

"Yes, sir, my parents are thrilled," Darby continued. "We're having a big wedding at St. Philip's. Reception at the Yacht Club."

Linnea's smile remained fixed. She'd received the invitation and remembered that it was the wedding Darby had told her he'd wanted *them* to have. Darby had his life planned out for himself. His wife was but one piece of the puzzle. She smiled at Ashley, glad it was her friend who had accepted that role, and not herself.

"They bought us a house over near Hampton Park," he continued in a tone that was boastful. "It's a beautiful house, isn't it, love?" he asked Ashley.

She nodded dreamily. "Oh, it's amazing."

"In Charleston?" Linnea asked. "What happened to moving to Columbia?"

He raised his brow. "I did a two-year stint there. Now I'm back and going to work at my father's law firm. Keep up, Linnea."

She shrugged amiably.

"So, where's your California surfer dude?" He looked around the room.

Linnea ignored the barb. "John? He's not here."

"Oh? Why not?"

"We broke up."

Darby's face stilled for a moment. "You broke up? When?" he asked sharply. Then, noticing that his reaction had drawn Ashley's attention, he added with an urbane smile, "I mean, I hadn't heard. Did you, honey?" he asked Ashley.

Ashley clearly felt uncomfortable with Darby's reaction. She shook her head. "No, I didn't. So," she asked Linnea, "if John isn't here, who is your plus one?"

Linnea looked across the living room and spotted Pandora holding court with a half dozen young men clustered around her. She almost laughed as she pointed. "That woman over there surrounded by all the men. Pandora James."

Ashley spotted her and giggled. "I wondered who she was. Look at those boys. I swear, she's like Scarlett O'Hara at the barbecue."

"She's not from around here," Darby said.

Ashley's laughter pealed. "You think?" she asked him.

"England," Linnea replied. "Don't let her looks fool you. Beneath all that beauty lurks a brain. She's an engineer."

"Amazing," Ashley said again.

"No kidding," Darby said, and took a long sip from his drink. "So," he said to Linnea. "Are you seeing anyone?"

Linnea blithely shook her head. "Nope."

Darby took another long drink.

"Hey, I'm monopolizing your time," Linnea said. "You're the celebrated couple. You need to circulate. I'm off to the bar. Congratulations again. And love to your parents," she called out as she walked away.

Darby's reaction to the news of her breakup was getting awkward. And she desperately needed that drink. There was a cluster of people around the bar and she waited her turn, greeting couples she knew, catching up. As nice as it was to see her old friends, she felt a gulf widen between herself and them. She'd gone off in a different direction while so many of them seemed to have stayed in the same place. Coming back home, she wasn't sure her square peg would fit into this round circle.

When at last it was her turn at the bar, she did a double take. "Annabelle?" she exclaimed.

Annabelle, dressed in black pants and white shirt with a black bow tie, looked startled at seeing Linnea, a bit embarrassed, but recovered quickly and smiled. "Hey, Linnea. I should've known you'd be here."

Annabelle's husky voice was always unexpected for someone so slender. "I didn't expect to see you. Behind the bar, at least."

"Yeah, well." Annabelle quickly wiped a spill on the bar. "It's tough to earn enough to live on the peninsula. A girl's got to do what a girl's got to do."

Linnea felt a slight bump against her shoulder and looked to see that Pandora had wiggled through the line to reach her side.

"God save me," she said wearily. "I need a drink!"

"Didn't one of your admirers bring you one?"

"They kept bringing me chardonnay. Ghastly stuff." She looked over to Annabelle. "A whiskey on the rocks. Please tell me it's good."

"We only have Maker's Mark, which is a bourbon whiskey made in Kentucky. In my opinion it's the best. And"—Annabelle lifted a brow—"it's stronger than most others."

"In that case, make it a double." Pandora squinted and, pointing a blue painted nail, asked, "Don't I know you?"

Annabelle merely shrugged and began fixing Pandora's drink.

"That's Annabelle," Linnea informed her. "From the beach. By the way, Pandora—you just cut in line."

"That's it!" Pandora exclaimed, eyes on Annabelle. "You cut in line. You're the one who snaked Linnea."

Annabelle's hands stilled.

Linnea intervened. "Ancient history."

"So, you're a bartender?" Pandora asked Annabelle.

The tone was mildly insulting. Seeing Annabelle's flush, Linnea jumped in. "Annabelle, I desperately need some extra money. Could you fix me up with this gig?"

Pandora looked at Linnea, mouth agape, but Annabelle's smile was grateful. "Sure thing. They're always looking for help. Do you bartend?"

"I can pour wine."

Annabelle laughed. "How about serving?"

"I can do that too."

"You never gave me your number. Here, write it down on this napkin. I'll call you." She handed a napkin and a pen to Linnea, who quickly complied.

"Thanks," Linnea said, handing the napkin to Annabelle. "And I'll skip the chardonnay and try a pinot grigio." She heard grumbling from behind and added, "Before we get trampled. The natives are getting thirsty."

"You're going to tend bar?" Pandora hissed in her ear as they walked away.

"Sure, why not? I need the money."

Pandora didn't respond. Instead, her face lit up with delight as she spotted someone in the crowd. "Gordon!" she called, and raised her hand in a quick wave. "Over here!"

Linnea swung her head and recognized the handsome redheaded surfer. Only tonight, he'd switched his wet suit for a beautifully fitted blue blazer over a crisp white shirt. He moved smoothly through the crowded room to their side.

"There you are," Pandora exclaimed when he approached. "I wondered if you'd gotten lost." She offered him her drink. "Bourbon?"

"No, thank you," he replied as he leaned forward to kiss Pandora's cheek in greeting. "That's yours. I'll find my own."

"Good luck, darling. There's a long line. And stay away from the chardonnay."

"I usually do." He turned his head and met Linnea's gaze. His eyes sparkled with mirth. "Surfer girl," he exclaimed, pleased to see her. "We meet again."

Linnea was caught in the magnetism of his dazzling blue eyes. Framed in pale lashes, they shone out from his narrow, chiseled, tanned face.

"You two know each other?" asked Pandora, not sounding pleased.

"He knows my brother's truck," Linnea teased. "I'll bet you don't even remember my name."

Gordon leaned closer and said in a seductive tone, "Linnea."

She was pleased he remembered and was sure her smile revealed that.

Pandora tugged at Gordon's arm and said, "Quick, darling, let's rush to the bar. There's a break in traffic." She wiggled her fingers in farewell to Linnea and led Gordon away.

Linnea felt a twinge of disappointment and, yes, jealousy, watching Pandora walk off with the one man she'd found attractive. Gordon was Pandora's dishy friend, she thought, watching the pair sidle up to the bar. She couldn't help but think that, as handsome as he looked tonight, he looked even more attractive in his wet suit.

Sighing with resignation, Linnea strolled through the room checking out the other guests. She knew most of the men and women. Old friends now with fiancés, husbands, or wives. She stopped to talk often, catching up. By the time she reached the guest bathroom she'd finished her wine and was dismayed to see there was a long line. Linnea set her glass on a passing tray, then detoured to the hall where an elegant winding staircase led upstairs. Her path was blocked by a man in a servant's uniform. Luckily, she recognized him.

"Andy! How are you? It's been ages."

Andy, an older man in his sixties, had been with the Middleton family for as long as she'd known them. Over the years, Andy had served as waiter, handyman, butler, and now apparently guard for the family.

His face lit up. "Miss Linnea! It sure is nice to see you back in this house again."

"Big occasion," she said.

He leaned closer and said, "Not the way we thought it'd turn out."

"No," she agreed with a wry smile. "But the way it should have, right?"

"Yes'm," he replied politely.

"Listen, there's a long line at the bathroom. Can I sneak up the stairs? I'll be quick. I promise."

Andy stepped aside gallantly. "Of course. For you, Miss Linnea."

She hurried up the elegant wood staircase and walked down the hall she knew well. Passing Darby's room, she peeked in and saw his four-poster bed strewn with a towel—his mother would be appalled—and clothing. By his bed was a photo of Ashley. She moved on, perusing the family photographs on the wall. They had one framed photo of every Christmas since Darby's birth. She smiled as she followed his growth from baby to adulthood. Linnea paused at one photograph where she spotted herself standing next to Darby, beaming happily into the camera. They looked so young, she thought. So full of dreams. She remembered that Christmas, how she'd been called into the photograph by Darby's father. Mrs. Middleton had frowned, seeing as how Linnea and Darby were not even engaged. But Mr. Middleton had insisted, and there Linnea was, forever on the family wall of portraits. It turned out Mrs. Middleton was right, she thought with chagrin. She shouldn't have been included in the picture. She was sure it had to be hard for Ashley to see this photo, and Linnea felt badly for her friend.

There was no way she could be photoshopped out of the image, since Darby's arm was around her shoulders. Linnea thought for a moment that she could steal the photo, thus sparing Ashley years of angst. Then she thought of Andy and decided she couldn't put his job in jeopardy. With a sigh, she walked on to Darby's sister's bedroom and ducked in. Gervais's bedroom was much as she remembered it, the same twin four-poster beds but bearing new linens. She used to sleep in this room when she'd spent the night. It was clear Ashley was sleeping in the room now. Linnea went to the bathroom and was careful not to snoop through Ashley's cosmetics or jewelry, trying her best to be discreet. She was quick and hurried to the stairs to escape before Andy got into trouble for letting her up.

Her fingers slid along the mahogany railing as she made her way down the stairs. Andy smiled up at her, but her gaze was caught by the man standing next to him. She thanked Andy, then turned to the handsome young man.

"Gordon," she said, smiling with surprise.

"You are difficult to track down," he said. He handed her a glass. "Chardonnay. Pandora told me this was your choice."

She took the wine, trying not to laugh at Pandora's barb. "You're a friend of the family?" he asked as they strolled toward the party.

"Very old friend. I've earned bathroom rights."

His smile was quick, yet it always struck her as a bit shy. Gordon was reserved, even bookish in manner. Not at all the flashy sort she'd have expected Pandora to go for.

"I haven't seen you on the beach," Gordon said.

Pleased he'd been looking for her, she said, "I haven't been surfing much since turtle season began."

He stopped walking to face her. "You're one of the people who monitor sea turtles?"

"I am."

"Good on you. Actually, I'm keen to study the sea turtles here."

"Really?" Linnea wondered if it was a lame pick-up line. How many men were interested in studying sea turtles? "Why turtles?"

"I work in marine science in England. It would appear we're well-met."

Gordon suddenly zoomed in her appreciation. A live band started playing in the ballroom, and with a rush, couples moved from the piazzas to the dance floor, rushing past them.

Linnea almost had to shout to be heard. "You've come to the right person. I've been on the turtle team since I was a child. My grandmother started the first teams on Isle of Palms and Sullivan's Island. How can I help?"

Gordon leaned close. "The noise is so loud I can barely hear you. Want to get out of here?"

"The veranda is just over there."

"I mean, how about we cut out?"

She looked into his eyes. The word *yes* hovered on her lips. "But we can't."

"Why not?"

"I'm with Pandora. I mean, I drove her. And . . . didn't you come with her?"

He shook his head. "She invited me to the party. Not quite the same thing."

"How do you know Pandora?"

His lips twitched. "The Pan?"

Linnea held back her laugh. "As in Peter Pan?"

177

He took a sip of his whiskey, eyes twinkling. "We call her that because she flutters about and is unpredictable. And fanciful," he added.

Yes, she could see Pandora as the child who refused to grow up.

"We're both surfers," he continued, moving to the left to make room for a couple heading for the dance floor. "We bump into each other on various beaches. The last one was in Australia."

"You're not a couple?"

He shook his head, amused. "God, no. It'd be like dating my sister."

Linnea doubted Pandora thought of them as brother and sister. Looking over his shoulder, she caught sight of Pandora walking toward them purposefully.

"Here comes Sis now."

"They're dancing," Pandora announced with enthusiasm. "I'm dying to dance. Come on, Gordon."

"I hate to dance," he told her.

"But you know how," Pandora said, determinedly grabbing hold of his arm.

He lifted his brows and smiled with resignation toward Linnea as Pandora pulled him toward the ballroom where couples were dancing.

Linnea took a sip from her wine, frowned at the taste, then caught a passing waiter to set her glass on the tray. She took a final glance at the dance floor where Pandora, of course, danced fabulously. Beside her, Gordon looked pretty good too. More couples were heading to the dance floor as the party kicked up a notch.

It was time to go. Feeling like a third wheel, Linnea quietly ducked out of the party, grabbing her purse and shawl from the attendant at the coat station. A couple was just arriving as she made her way down the porch stairs. On the sidewalk, she looked back at the grand house. Couples lingered on the piazzas, music wafted through the open doors. The party was at full tilt.

Linnea ducked her head and began walking. She'd never felt so alone.

✳   ✳   ✳

BY THE TIME Linnea drove the Gold Bug toward the aquarium two days later, she was getting the hang of the stick shift. She only stalled out twice. The ragtop was down and the breeze ruffled through her hair as she soared over the river. She was driving her own car on her way to her new internship. Reaching the apex of the bridge with the city and river sparkling in the sun beneath her, the blue sky overhead, she felt on top of the world.

She parked in the garage and walked through the park, already busy as school buses unloaded groups of uniformed children to tour the aquarium. She stopped at the security office to collect her name card and badge, then walked into the aquarium as an official employee. The gleaming surfaces and tanks on the main floor seemed to shine with even more brilliance. Groups of children clustered around a guide carrying a red-tailed hawk on her arm. Others crowded around the touch tank, a few up on tiptoes to better see the aquatic world. She held her shoulders back, proud to show off her badge that marked her as an official, someone who belonged to this lofty institution. She couldn't stop smiling.

Following the guard's directions, Linnea took the elevator to the third floor where all the offices were. Her pass card unlocked the security door, and she walked down the narrow, book-lined hall to where the floor opened to reveal the top of the Great Ocean Tank. She stared down into the edge of the three-story tank as various fish, sharks, and the resident loggerhead, Caretta, swam by.

Past the tank were the offices. Everyone who worked there shared the limited space with great camaraderie. The directors of departments, the PR and marketing team, the conservation program, and animal husbandry clustered together in the rabbit warren. It was a cheery place with high ceilings, shining with light. The halls were lined with large, framed photographs of the local marine life—release of sea turtles, dolphins in the waterways. People smiled as they passed her, most wearing blue polo shirts bearing the logo of the South Carolina Aquarium. Linnea made her way past three cubicles to the one with a window and peered in. Cara sat behind her metal desk working on her computer. Silver-framed photographs of Hope and David sat atop the desk, along with stacks of papers and files.

"Knock-knock," Linnea said, given there was no door.

Cara looked up from her computer and smiled. It was odd to see her aunt at work. Cara bristled with an aura that seemed crisper, even more self-assured than when she relaxed at home. Cara wasn't in uniform. She looked chic in her dark pencil skirt and crisp white blouse with pearls at the neck. Her dark hair fell neatly behind her ears to her chin, accentuating her long neck and early tan, and she wore little makeup. She didn't need much, her dark eyes naturally framed by thick lashes and striking brows.

Linnea had dressed carefully this morning, wanting to make a good impression. Her long blond hair was pulled back into a stylish, high ponytail. She wore a cotton green-floral sundress and white wedge heels, and her only jewelry were the gold loops at her ears and a bracelet. Next to Cara's sleek style, she felt a bit girlish, and made a mental note to ask if she should wear the uniform too. She smoothed out her dress and stepped inside.

"Welcome to the team," Cara said, smiling widely and gesturing to the two metal chairs before her desk.

Linnea sat on the cushioned seat, nervously anticipating her job description. She knew that not only was her reputation on the line, but Cara's was as well. After some brief chitchat, Cara got down to business.

"Let me bring you up to speed on the primary focus of what it is we do here in the conservation program. Then I'll narrow things down a bit to what I specifically need your help with. In time, you'll catch on to everything."

"Of course."

"We wear a lot of hats here. We are developing the Good Catch sustainable seafood program. For that, we advise and consult with restaurants and create dining events at cooperating venues. We also work with the Resilience Initiative for Coastal Education, working to arm coastal communities with information and tools to understand rising sea levels. And our big project now is to develop strategic plastics initiatives to reduce the negative environmental impacts of plastic pollution. And that," she added with emphasis, "is the area I'd like you to focus on."

Linnea nodded. The sustainable seafood program sounded like fun and she loved anything to do with education, but plastics was the hot topic in conservation today.

"One of our big pushes this season will be educating the public about plastic in the ocean and engaging public support in cleanup of the beaches and waterways. Our first big Beach Sweep takes place in a few weeks. After the Fourth of July, naturally enough. There's always a lot of litter on the beaches then." She smiled wryly. "Patriotism can be very messy. I'd like us to come up with clever ideas that will inspire the public to care. To get involved. To pick up the plastic voluntarily and, even better, to stop using single-use plastic."

"Right," Linnea said. "I, uh, I actually have an idea already."

Cara's face showed her surprise, and a touch of disbelief. "Really?" There was an awkward beat before she said, "Well, all right, let's hear it." She folded her hands on her desk.

Linnea licked her lips. "I don't know if you knew this, but the past few weeks I've been walking the beach in the morning with a garbage bag, picking up trash."

"No, I didn't know. Makes me happier in my choice for a new intern," Cara said with approval.

"It's shocking how much trash is left lying on the sand. But more to the point, it all started because I was inspired when I saw this woman doing the same. She was alone, walking the beach with a big plastic garbage bag. So I started doing it." She paused, getting to the point. "I'm wondering, if *I* was inspired, what would it take to inspire others?"

"Go on."

"I really admire the marketing of this company called 4ocean. Their purpose is to clean plastic from the world's oceans. They have those bracelets made from recycled plastic from the ocean. They pull a pound of plastic out for each bracelet sold." She lifted her arm to reveal a bracelet made up of tiny plastic balls around a green band. Cara leaned close for a better look. "They make dozens of colors, one for each animal species they select. Green is for turtles."

"I've seen the bracelets," Cara said.

"They also have bags made up from recycled ocean plastic to sell."

"Do they?" Cara's interest focused.

"Here's the thing. Often, when I'm walking the beach with my bag, someone asks me what I'm doing. So, I tell him or her. People ask if they can help. They just need to be shown what to do. How they can make a difference. I got to thinking, what if we had bags made up of recycled plastic and put the South Carolina Aquarium's logo on them? We could sell them, with all the proceeds going to the sea turtle hospital. That makes it cool. People can start walking with their aquarium bag and inspire others, and so on and so on. A ripple effect. We might not be able to go out into the oceans and clean up the plastic, but we can buy a bracelet to support those who can, and we can make picking up trash in our own neighborhoods a real, physical sign of caring—whether on the beach, at a lake, a creek, a river, wherever. Even people on vacation can join in." She finished and looked at Cara expectantly.

"I think it's brilliant!" Cara exclaimed. She leaned back in her chair, her palms on her lap. "I have to admit, I'm stunned. This is exactly what I was hoping for. It's not easy to make plastic warm and fuzzy. It's a scourge, is what it is. But your idea of putting our logo on the bag and making picking up trash a badge of support may just accomplish that." Her fingers tapped on her thighs. I'd like to think of ways we can expand this idea, to bring in the community. Sweeps for beaches, of course. But also for parks, creeks, rivers." She smiled. "Community wide."

"I'll work on it." Linnea was fired up.

"And I need to get one of those bracelets too." Cara pointed to the translucent plastic bracelet on her arm.

"I'll get you one. My treat."

"Well done, Linnea. This is what I call a great start. You always were clever. Creative. I think you're on to something. I'll talk to the promotion team here about making the bags. We could sell them here at the aquarium, in shops along the beaches, online." She clasped her hands. "Let's give your idea wings. Why don't you write it up as a proposal? I'll edit it, add my bit, and we can present it to the committee for approval. Fingers crossed, but I think it's a winner."

The day sped by as Linnea researched her idea and began work on her presentation. She was surprised how quickly five o'clock came. She was back on her game and she couldn't write fast enough. Cara had left hours earlier to attend a meeting, so Linnea was walking alone through the long, narrow hall to the elevator. She paused to look at the Great Ocean Tank and passed the food prep area for the fish and shelves of books to the waiting area.

"Linnea!"

Linnea stopped and turned to see Toy Legare walking toward her. She was dressed in the uniform of khakis and a navy polo with the insignia, her blond hair pulled into a ponytail, like Linnea's. She was a petite powerhouse. No matter whether it was starting time or quitting time, Toy's eyes were bright and her smile supercharged.

"I heard you joined us."

Linnea hugged the woman she'd known most of her life. Toy had been the companion of Grandmama Lovie when she fell ill, and later became Cara's trusted friend. Toy was considered a part of the family. She was now the director of the sea turtle hospital. But Toy was part of the project since the early days when the hospital was in the aquarium basement. Toy had begged, borrowed, and nearly stolen holding tanks for the rescued turtles. Now the Sea Turtle Care Center was the aquarium's crown jewel.

"How was your first day?" Toy asked.

"Couldn't be better. I'm really psyched to be here."

"It's getting a bit incestuous with me and Cara and now you on board."

"Don't forget Ethan."

Ethan, Toy's husband, ran the Great Ocean Tank. "Oh, him," Toy said with a giggle.

"I'm only an intern," Linnea reminded her.

"I know you'll make us proud. Let's share lunch tomorrow. Now that the weather's nice, we eat out on the deck overlooking the harbor. I'll bring dessert."

"It's a date," Linnea agreed.

Toy turned and motioned for someone farther down the hall. "I want you to meet a new member of my team."

Linnea looked up and burst into a grin. A tall redhead was striding toward them; her step faltered when she spied Linnea.

Linnea laughed first. "I don't believe it."

Annabelle shook her head with a smirk. "Are you shadowing me?"

Toy looked from one to the other. "You know each other?"

"Yeah," Annabelle replied. "We met a few times on the beach." She looked again at Linnea. "What brings you here?"

"A job," Linnea replied. "An internship, rather. I'll be working in the conservation program."

"Really?" Annabelle said.

Linnea heard a hint of either disbelief or displeasure in the comment.

"Annabelle is one of the care center team," Toy said. "She's a new hire this year." She turned to Annabelle. "You began in January, right?"

"That's right."

"She studied at the University of North Carolina Wilmington. We're lucky to have her."

"Hey," said Linnea, "I wanted to tell you thanks for inspiring me to pick up trash on the beach. I'm going to use that idea for our beach sweep."

"The more the merrier," Annabelle replied with a smile, all hint of competition gone.

"You know, I think we're meant to be friends," Linnea said. "We keep running into each other. Third time's the charm."

"Actually, this is the fourth time, but who's counting?"

Linnea smiled but inwardly considered Annabelle's response. Linnea was mildly annoyed by those people who felt compelled to correct others. A pronunciation of a name, the number of an item, some error . . . Linnea always let those small errors slide rather than make a correction in public, thus embarrassing the speaker. Most people got the mistake anyway; why point it out? Lovie used to say, "There are always people who like to put their paws on your back." Which meant they liked to display dominance. Annabelle seemed to be one of those people.

Toy glanced from one to the other, then said, "Now that you two know each other, I'll leave you to carry on. There's someone I need to talk to." She hailed someone in the hall.

Linnea and Annabelle started walking toward the elevator, where a small group was already waiting.

"There's supposed to be some good wind tomorrow," Annabelle said. "Want to catch some waves?"

"I won't have time," said Linnea. "Work day, right? I've got to make a good impression. I can't show up late."

"You won't if we get out by six. We can ride for an hour and get out in time for work. Besides, you promised me you'd teach me your beach etiquette."

"Sure, but, uh, you know you can YouTube all that."

"I want to know what the rules are for *this* beach. Before Mickey has to explain them to me again."

Linnea laughed. "I'd be a little afraid of Mickey too. Okay. Text me. We'll see if the waves hold. You still have my number?"

Annabelle frowned and shook her head. "I lost it."

When the elevator bell rang, they both hurried to catch it, punching numbers into their phones.

Chapter Thirteen

Researchers from the University of Exeter and Plymouth Marine Laboratory examined fifty animals from ten species of dolphins, seals, and whales—and found microplastics in them all.

A WEEK PASSED in a blur. Linnea worked with a feverish excitement she hadn't felt in a long time to round out her idea for the Plastic Bag/Beach Sweep campaign. Cara was focused on how to engage the community, Linnea on how to inspire the individual. Together they developed and delivered a concept that they both felt enthusiastic about.

Today would begin yet another phase of her position. She would be the representative of the aquarium's conservation program at her first meeting. Linnea took care with her appearance, wanting to put her best foot forward. She pulled out of the closet the new tan suit she'd purchased for the occasion, and a pair of open-toed bone pumps. She slipped into an ivory blouse, then the pencil skirt. Looking in the mirror, she realized it wasn't the vintage look she loved, still, she was pleased with the chic yet conservative image she presented, much like her mentor, Cara. There was something about wearing a new outfit for a special occasion that made one feel special too.

A soft knock sounded on the door and her mother poked her head in. "Good morning! Want some coffee?"

"Thank you," Linnea said, hurrying across the room to accept the mug. "That was kind of you."

"My, don't you look nice," Julia said. "New suit?"

"Thanks, Mama. Yes. I pretty much depleted my bank account with this suit and the shoes. But they're worth it, aren't they?"

"Very nice. And you'll get a lot of wear out of that outfit. One can never go wrong with a summer suit and bone shoes."

"I figure I'll wear them like a uniform this summer. Cara wants me to go out and speak to schools, companies, and community groups. I have to look the part."

"Where are you going this morning?"

"It's a meeting of local nonprofits. We're discussing solutions for problems with water quality. The focus is plastics and microplastics. Cara wants this to be my main area of work."

"I'm sure you'll impress them."

Linnea slipped into the pumps, smoothed her long hair back, and stood straight before her mother. "How do I look?"

After a perusal, Julia set down her coffee cup. "You're missing one thing. Hold on."

Linnea took another critical glance. What was missing? She thought she looked very professional. Not much makeup, polished pale nails. Cara had once told her that new clothes were like the ceremonial armor knights donned before battle.

Her mother walked in, carrying something. "Here," Julia said, handing her a pair of earrings. "Try these."

Linnea looked at the gold hoop earrings that she'd long admired when her mother wore them. Three colors of gold—yellow, white, rose—twined together. "The tricolor earrings."

"*Tricolore*," her mother corrected her, using the Italian pronunciation. She took one and began slipping it into Linnea's ear. "My favorite. Your father bought these for me on our honeymoon in Italy. They don't make earrings with that much gold anymore." She finished slipping the earrings on and stood back to look. "Much better. Now, don't lose them. They're yours."

"Mama! I can't accept these. You love them."

"Which is why I want to give them to you. You are, after all, my only daughter. It brings me pleasure to see you wear them. And"—she smiled knowingly—"I want to thank you. I got a call the other day from a woman—Imogen James—about decorating her house." Julia lifted one brow. "She told me that *you* gave her my name as a decorator."

Linnea looked up sheepishly. "Was that okay?"

"Actually," Julia replied, "yes. I'm surprised to admit this, but I'm delighted."

"I'm so glad," Linnea said. "And relieved."

"She sounds British."

"She is. That's Granny James, Pandora's great-aunt. Well, what do you know? She called." Linnea crossed her arms. "Do I get a finder's fee?"

"Happily."

"Cool. I can use the money. Once you do this house, the commissions will flow in."

"We'll see," her mother said in a worried tone. "I drove by her address, and my goodness, it's a big house. I don't know if I'm qualified to do what she wants done."

"What's that?"

"Only a transformation," she replied with a short laugh.

"Oh, is that all?" Linnea giggled. "The house is an eyesore."

"Seriously, Linnea, this is an important commission. But a huge job. Am I up to it?"

"Of course, you are. It's no bigger a house in square feet than the one Daddy's building. How did you leave it with her?"

"Mrs. James is a formidable woman. Wouldn't take no for an answer. Her friend, Mrs. Muir, apparently was very flattering about me. That has to be Marietta Muir of Sea Breeze." Julia said with a small smile of remembrance. "I haven't seen her in years." Julia shook her head in wonder. "Anyway, I explained that I would be delighted to bring my portfolio, but that I wasn't free until sometime after the Fourth of July. Linnea, I need to make a portfolio!"

"No problem. We've got this."

"Good, because I'm counting on you. You volunteered to make me one and I'm taking you up on your offer. And business cards."

"Those are easy to get done. The portfolio is going to be a push—but don't worry, I'll take care of it. And I'll get my friend to make you a website."

"Do we have time?"

"Yes, but it's crunch time. I'm so excited for you, Mama! This could be your big break."

"Or my big fall."

"Half-full!" Linnea teased.

"I've got to finish Daddy's house too."

Linnea's smile fell. "Mama, what's going on over there? It was so busy, then suddenly everything is quiet. I don't see anyone working."

"It's probably just the holiday coming. July fourth falls midweek so people are taking time off before or after. It's to be expected."

"Well, *I'm* working," Linnea, said taking a final look in the mirror. She tapped the gold hoops, thrilled to have them. "Thanks again, Mama." She kissed Julia's cheek and grabbed her purse from the dresser.

She crossed the main room to the kitchen, her heels clicking on the hardwood floors.

Palmer, hearing her, lifted his head from the *Post and Courier*. "Well, well, well! Don't you look smart."

Linnea leaned over to kiss his cheek. He smelled of aftershave and coffee. "Thanks, Daddy."

"Where you off to?"

"A meeting."

His brows rose and his eyes gleamed in, she realized with pleasure, approval.

Linnea took a final swallow of her coffee. "I'd better be going. Have a good day, Daddy."

"You too, baby," he replied as he lifted his paper again. Then he paused and called out as she crossed the room: "Linnea!"

Linnea stopped and turned. "Yes?"

A sly smile crossed his face. "Nice earrings."

⚞ ⚞ ⚞

THE MEETING WAS held in the office of Charleston Waterkeeper, which was a short walk from the South Carolina Aquarium. Linnea's arms were laden with her laptop and handouts she'd created for her new campaign, enough for the group of twenty expected participants.

The conference room overlooked the harbor, filling the space with natural light. She paused at the entrance to scope out the room. Several men and women, all of them youngish, were talking in small groups in that friendly manner that spoke of familiarity. With a sinking heart, she didn't recognize anyone. Yet everyone in the group had the natural, relaxed look of people involved with environmental work. These were her people, she told herself. Linnea strolled across the room to the table where coffee and cookies were set up and poured a cup. She didn't really want more coffee, but it kept her busy. She hoped the meeting would start soon.

From behind she heard the door open and hellos called out and returned. One of them was a familiar voice with a British accent. She turned, nervously stirring her coffee, and sucked in her breath. Across the room was Gordon. He appeared lean and fit in khakis, a braided leather belt, and a crisp white shirt, rolled up to reveal tanned forearms. His hair was neatly combed but curls managed to escape, especially around his forehead. Linnea found his rather bashful boyishness beguiling. He was speaking to one of the men, sharing a laugh, when he reached up and unconsciously ran his hand through his hair. Linnea held back a giggle when immediately more curls sprang free.

She watched him progress smoothly from one person to the next, shaking hands. People in the room sought him out, eager to talk to him, and she wondered why. When he was a few feet away he glanced her way as though aware he was being watched. She blushed and looked down to stir her coffee.

She heard his footfalls approach and her stomach clenched.

"Hello," he said in the accented voice she loved.

Linnea lifted her head, met his gaze, and forgot all about her coffee. All the pieces of his face came together nicely enough, but his blue eyes arrested her.

"Hello."

"Our paths seem destined to cross," he said, his smile encouraging.

"Yes."

"Fellow surfers, and now it appears we're colleagues as well. You told me you were a volunteer for sea turtles. But that wouldn't bring you to this meeting."

"I could say the same thing. I work at the South Carolina Aquarium. In the conservation program. And you're here because . . . ?"

"Dual role, actually," he said in mock seriousness. "Officially, I'm a representative of Surfrider International."

"Of course you are," Linnea said in gentle tease.

"But I'm also here to talk about my new research paper."

"*You're* the speaker? Dr. Carr?"

"I am. Lest you think I'm stalking you or some such."

"I was beginning to wonder," she joked.

"I really was worried. I mean, every time you turn around, there I am."

"Lucky me."

His eyes brightened and Linnea looked down at her coffee. She liked a bit too much his accent, his smile, his eyes, the way he tilted his head when he spoke.

"So," he said. "Am I meant to guess your last name? No name tags."

"Oh," she said. "I'm Linnea Rutledge."

"As in Rutledge Avenue?"

"Guilty as charged."

The meeting was beginning, and people were asked to take seats.

"Shall we?" he asked, extending his hand.

She followed him without further word to the long conference table. They found two metal chairs side by side in the center. He pulled out her chair and she settled in. Linnea set her coffee on the table, put her bag on the floor, and reached down to pull out a notepad and pen. She was very aware of the man sitting to her left and made every effort not to bump into him.

Before long, she was engrossed in the topic of the meeting. They went around the table and identified themselves and the organizations they represented. She discovered that Gordon was a postgraduate researcher from the University of Exeter and the Plymouth Marine Laboratory in England. He was here today to present his recently published paper on microplastics.

Linnea cleared her throat and introduced herself. Her voice didn't crack and she hoped she sounded professional. She hadn't realized how nervous she would be in the company of such esteemed colleagues from the College of Charleston, the University of South Carolina, Clemson University, the Coastal Conservation League, Friends of Coastal South Carolina, Ducks Unlimited, NOAA, the South Carolina Department of Natural Resources, Surfrider International, and Charleston Waterkeeper. She felt the weight of responsibility representing the aquarium.

After his introduction, Dr. Carr rose to a smattering of applause to speak. He began by bantering for a few minutes, bringing up his experiences as a surfer, his lifelong love of the oceans, and how this was his first visit to South Carolina. It worked to create a relaxed atmosphere. Linnea saw he was an experienced speaker. Confident, thoughtful, never boastful.

It was his modesty that won them over. And his British wit. Quickly enough, he dove into the meat of his subject.

"Many of you may have read our research paper printed in *Science* magazine last March. Our study revealed that a wide range of Britain's marine animals have ingested microplastics, though those results are hardly a surprise. The whole ocean is a soup of microplastics—they've been found at every level of the food chain, from tiny zooplankton to fish larvae, turtles, and now marine mammals. We examined the synthetic fibers which came from a wide variety of sources." He used his fingers to count. "Such things as clothing, fishing nets, toothbrushes. Much of the rest were fragments whose possible sources include food packaging and plastic bottles."

Gordon gestured out the window to the harbor. "Dolphins. Our sentinels in the sea. They too had ingested microplastic. The problem is widespread, and we will soon reach a tipping point. The time to act is now."

He went on, outlining his research and the findings while everyone took notes. It was an important study with worldwide ramifications. He concluded by informing them that he was in Charleston to study the physiology of sea turtles and dolphins in relation to microplastics. Linnea made the connection to his comment at the party about being interested in turtles. She listened, impressed by his intelligence. He spoke with ease not merely about marine life but on a variety of topics.

When they reached the question and answer part of the presentation, Gordon could answer any question put to him on any subject—at length—showing a wide breadth of knowledge. During the break, Gordon was surrounded by colleagues asking more questions about his work. Linnea took time to prepare for her presentation. The recycled bags she'd designed had been approved by the aquarium and she'd ordered five thousand to distribute to the community. She'd brought a few prototypes to share with the group, along with cards printed to explain the program's goals.

When they returned to the table, Gordon offered her a glass of cold water as he sat down, singling her out. She adjusted her seat and looked around the table, noting that she was getting curious looks from some of the other women at the table.

In the second half of the program, various speakers stood and shared announcements concerning their groups' plans to deal with the plastics challenge in the community. When it was her turn, Linnea rose, especially aware of the gaze of the blue eyes at her left. She enjoyed public speaking. She was good at it and relished the give-and-take with her audience. Linnea spoke about the upcoming Beach Sweep on Isle of Palms and Sullivan's Island, the first of several the aquarium would be hosting over the summer. She passed out the mesh bags made from woven recycled plastic, each bearing the aquarium's logo. She concluded with how they planned to engage the public in the sweep efforts.

"I have to say, that's a right clever idea," Gordon told her as she sat down. "Brilliant."

She picked up her glass and sipped, inordinately pleased.

The group talked on for another half hour before the follow-up meeting was scheduled and the meeting was adjourned. Linnea rose and gathered her belongings, stuffing the few remaining bags into her larger one. The meeting had gone on longer than expected and she was eager to get back to the office and share the results with Cara.

"Have you got far to carry them?" Gordon asked her, looking at her overflowing bag.

"Only to the aquarium."

"I'll carry them for you."

"It's not far. Just across the square," she objected, but Gordon had already scooped up the large bag in one hand and hoisted his briefcase in the other.

"This is heavier than it looks," he said.

"I'm used to it." She glanced up. "My surfboard isn't exactly light."

"No, but it's sweet." He lifted the bag higher, testing the weight. "What's in it? It's not just plastic bags. Bricks?"

She laughed.

He pushed open the heavy glass door with his shoulder. "Lead the way."

They left the cool of the building, bidding farewell to some of the others. It was another in a steady stream of hot and humid mornings, hinting at the record-breaking heat that was coming. The sky was clear, and the sun made the sidewalks sizzle. The only saving grace was the heady breeze that blew in from the harbor, moving the stifling air in the square as efficiently as a fan. She looked up to see his curls in complete disarray, freed by the wind. He was unable to reach up and tamp them down while holding her bags. She swallowed her smile as she slipped on her sunglasses.

"So, your work with plastics research brought you to Charleston?" she asked as an opener.

"Yes. I'm at the College of Charleston. As you heard, we're collaborating with NOAA. They've done quite a lot of impressive work with resident dolphins here and in Florida."

"And turtles?"

"Yes." He turned to face her and grinned. It lit up his face. "That brings me to the aquarium . . . and now, as it happens, you."

"I doubt you'll be working with me."

"More's the pity. No, I'll be working with Dr. Boylan. His research on the ingestion of plastic in sea turtles is important."

"Shane, yes, of course. You're in good hands."

They walked across the wide square on their way to the rear of the aquarium. With each step, Linnea felt they were moving forward into a new relationship. One she didn't yet comprehend. He'd singled her out too many times for his intention to be misread. Yet in the back of her mind, she worried how Pandora would react.

At length they reached the industrial back entrance of the aquarium. Several vans and boats were parked there, as well as a few trucks. She walked to the plain cement stairs that led to a metal door, not at all the dramatically beautiful front entrance. The heat seemed to radiate from the stark white concrete. "Here we are," she said, feeling awkward, as though being dropped off at home on a first date.

"Yes, quite." He looked around the bleak entrance.

She reached out to reclaim her bag. "Thanks. I can manage from here."

Gordon transferred the bag to her. They stood looking at each other for a long moment, as though wishing the other would say something.

Linnea said, "Well, I'd better go in."

This prompted him to speak. "Perhaps we could have a drink somewhere? Off-hours?"

She smiled, relieved that he'd asked. She was beginning to wonder if he would. "I'd love to."

"Is tonight too soon? I could come by here after work. Say after five?"

"That sounds lovely."

"Where should we go? I'm new around here."

Linnea thought for a moment. It'd been a while since she'd gone out for drinks in Charleston. "I heard about a place called the Gin Joint that serves handcrafted drinks. It's quite close."

"Let's do it. Where should we meet?"

She thought for a moment. Her car was parked in the garage across the street. "It might be easiest if you pull up at the edge of the park," she said, pointing to the far end of the long park that met up with Wharf Avenue. "I'll leave my car in the garage and wait for you there."

He looked at her, really looked at her, then smiled that almost reluctant smile she found intriguing. Slipping on his dark sunglasses, he said, "Till five, then."

Chapter Fourteen

*The temperature of the sand during incubation plays a role in deter-
mining the sex of the hatchlings. Cool sand produces males, while hotter
sand produces females. Thus the phrase, "Hot chicks and cool dudes."*

HE PICKED HER up in a Prius.

Of course, she thought as he pulled to the curb.

"Don't get out," she called as he pushed open his door. "I'll hop in."

She climbed into the passenger seat and swung the door shut. The
cool air-conditioning was welcome on a June day that had hit a record
high. Books and papers cluttered the back seat. She held back a smile at
spotting his wet suit.

"Cute car," she said, buckling up. "Good gas mileage, I hear?"

"Great mileage," he replied, and they made eye contact and smiled.
They saw in each other's gaze that they both were concerned about such
things. He pulled back onto the road. "I was surprised Hertz had a Prius
rental."

"Ah, so you don't own it."

"I'm only here for a few months."

Linnea turned her head to look at him, surprised at hearing this, swiftly followed by disappointed. His eyes were on the road and his profile revealed an elegant, straight nose. She turned her head to gaze out her window. They drove a few blocks in silence while she digested that information.

"I think I turn here," he said, taking the turn.

"Yes, it's just ahead. On the left side."

It was a miracle, but they found parking on East Bay close to the bar. Gordon locked the car and hurried to her side, offering his hand as she stepped out. On the sidewalk, he kept to the outside. Someone had taught him his manners, Linnea thought.

They stepped inside the dimly lit, long and narrow bar, relishing the coolness. The restaurant was busy at happy hour and they craned their necks, looking for a free spot. There was ample seating in the garden, but like everyone else, they opted for the cool interior. The woman at the desk had long black hair pulled high into a ponytail and the shapeless body of a child in her tight black skirt and white T-shirt. She checked the tables as they scanned the room. A long wood-slab table was filled with young people freed from work and meeting friends. They were in luck. As they paused, a booth opened up, and they were seated and handed a menu of drinks.

"Chardonnay?" he asked, tongue in cheek.

She met his gaze and laughed. "Only if it's unoaked. . . . But it seems a waste to have a glass of white wine here," she said. She scanned the menu, suddenly very thirsty. "I heard their negroni is fabulous." She looked up. "Yes, I'll have that. I'm dying for something cold and bittersweet."

The waitress came. Gordon paused a moment to scan the menu, then ordered her negroni and the *bartender special* for himself—a surprise drink concocted by the bartender.

"I feel lucky," he told her. "Are you hungry?"

"I could nibble. You pick."

Gordon looked again at the menu and made choices; that done, he folded his hands on the table and gave her his full attention.

"You grew up in Charleston?" he asked.

"Born and raised. I'm the seventh generation in Charleston. There are a lot of us. The founding family followed the Bible's directive to go, forth and propagate. I might add," she said in a teasingly superior tone. "Edward Rutledge was a signer of the Declaration of Independence against your country. We won that war, you know."

"So I heard. Nasty business. But we're friends now."

"Yes," she said with a smile.

"Then I take it your family owned slaves?"

The waitress came with their drinks. Linnea's smile fell as she stirred the ice, then took a small sip. She waited until the waitress served a charcuterie plate attractively laden with sausages and cheese and a plate of shishito peppers, asked if everything was all right, and departed. Then she answered his question.

"How much do you know about South Carolina? Or the South in general?"

"Not very much. There was the Civil War, of course. Wasn't South Carolina the first state to secede from the Union?"

"Yes, my family did own slaves. They were a prominent family, and slavery was the culture of the time. Today, no one in my family is proud that our ancestors owned slaves. It was a deplorable institution. But we can't change history. We can only try to improve what happens today and in our future."

Gordon seemed to appreciate that he'd hit a nerve. "Yes, of course," he replied with alacrity.

"Did you know that some eighty percent of African Americans can trace an ancestor through the Port of Charleston?"

"That many . . ."

"Or that in 2018, the Charleston City Council approved a two-page resolution apologizing on behalf of the city for its role in the slave trade. Or that the International African American Museum will open here in 2021 and it will tell the stories of the long journey of enslaved Africans to our shores and their histories in this country." She pushed her glass a few inches to the right. "We are not all racists."

"Point taken," he said, looking down at his drink. "I have a lot to learn."

"We all do." She sipped from her drink.

There followed a painful pause.

She glanced at him. "And your family?"

"Oh, the usual," he replied. "Mum, dad, a sister. All alive and well and living in England."

"Do you see them much?"

"We try. Not very successfully. And yours? Current, I mean. Not historical."

She laughed, a little embarrassed for her heated answer. "I see them often. I live with my parents."

He was a bit taken aback. "Really?"

She felt the warmth of a blush tinge her cheeks. "I just moved back home from California. It's temporary. Rather like your car."

"California? That's a long way off. You didn't mind living away from your family, then?"

"I missed them, of course," she replied. "Actually, I think I only realized how much I missed them when I returned home. Not just them," she corrected herself. "I missed the lowcountry. Charleston."

"Mum, dad . . ." he prodded.

"And my brother."

"Ah yes. The owner of the truck. At Oxford. I remember all. You became interested in turtles because of your grandmother."

"Yes, Lovie was a remarkable woman. She studied them simply out of love for the animal. She saw a problem and decided to help. I found that inspiring and followed in her footsteps."

"Only your area of interest is now plastics."

She picked up her glass. "It's my assigned area of interest," she clarified, and took a sip.

"I see."

"I'm passionate about this too, don't worry. Who today isn't worried that our oceans are becoming—how did you put it? A plastic soup? I just got involved with conservation through the sea turtles, but I see education as spreading the net so much further. In our conservation program, we get members in the community involved in citizen science. That's designed for individuals to give us feedback on what the problems are, so we can work on solutions. We hope that by engaging the communities to identify the problems in their own areas, we can use that data to make changes."

Linnea heard the urgency in her voice and sat back against her chair. "I'm sorry," she said in a self-deprecating tone. "I get a little passionate."

"I like that about you," he told her. "And I understand it. When you discover plastic in every marine animal off your coast, you can't help but feel passionate. That's a reason why I'm involved with Surfrider. My job is the research. My commitment to the nonprofit is action. Surfrider International's mission is to protect the oceans. So obviously we're keen on solutions to the plastic pollution."

"Pandora said that she surfed with you in Australia and South Africa and Cornwall."

He grinned. "Thus the name, Surfrider International."

"I'd love to do that someday."

"You should. The waves here are . . . well . . ."

"I know, I know," she replied. "I'm just grateful for any waves at all. California's pretty decent."

"Have you surfed Hawaii?"

Linnea sighed audibly. "No."

"Linnea Rutledge, you need to see the world."

She tilted her head and looked into his eyes. "I suppose I do."

Gordon indicated the charcuterie in invitation. They talked about surfing until they'd devoured all but a lonely piece of prosciutto and an olive.

"I'd say we did that plate justice," he said. "Would you like anything more?"

Linnea shook her head. "No, it was delicious."

"Another drink?"

She looked toward the door. "There's a long line waiting for a table. I feel guilty."

After a moment's pause, he asked, "Would you like to come to my place for a drink?"

She thought of all the reasons to say no. But none of them felt compelling tonight. They were for another Linnea—someone's daughter, friend, ex-girlfriend. The good girl. Not who she wanted to be tonight. Tonight she was simply Linnea, a young woman without entanglements, free to make any choice she wanted. Inside her body, she felt the hum of her drink in her bloodstream. Outside the bar, the sun was setting. Waiters moved from table to table, lighting candles. Across from her sat a man she was truly attracted to. They'd been playing cat and mouse since they'd met, but the chemistry between them was steadily growing. She looked into his eyes, brimming with invitation.

Linnea put her hand on her purse and replied, "Love to."

※ ※ ※

LINNEA AWOKE THE following morning confused. Sun poured in through the open blinds, creating lines across the bed. Waking further, she realized it wasn't her bed.

She blinked and brought her hand to her forehead. Turning her head, she saw Gordon lying in bed beside her, his head propped on his hand. He was smiling sleepily, his hair disheveled. He was, she realized slowly, waiting for her to awaken.

"Good morning," he said. His face held the pallor of awakening, his lids half-lowered.

Her smile was wan. "Good morning." She put her hand to her hair. "I must look a fright."

"You're lovely."

"It *was* lovely," she said, remembering all.

"Can you spend the day? I don't think we should leave this bed just yet. Maybe not all day. Maybe not ever."

She laughed, enjoying the romance of it. Then suddenly she roused further, startled by how bright the sun was. "What time is it?"

Gordon stretched over her. "Excuse me," he muttered close to her ear, then quickly kissed her neck. He reached for the bedside clock. Still lying over her, he said, "It's seven forty."

"Oh no, I've got to go."

He smiled down into her eyes, settling himself atop her. "Must you?"

"Yes," she said, and tried to wiggle away.

"That's nice."

"Stop," she said, trying not to laugh. "I really have to go. I don't want to be late for work."

Gordon slid over to his side of the bed with a groan. "Too bad."

Linnea pulled herself up to a sitting position, feeling the slosh in her head of too many drinks. Tugging the rumpled sheet up to cover her breasts, she looked around the fairly large bedroom. The queen-size bed was a platform with a modern, uninspired wood headboard. On the floor, scattered in crumpled piles, lay her clothes.

"Oh no. Damn," she muttered. "I'll be wearing yesterday's clothes. Everyone will notice. Shit. This is when I wish I wore a uniform."

"Can't you dash home and change?"

Linnea considered this and shook her head. "My parents will be up and about—my father will be drinking coffee in the kitchen. They'll see me and know I didn't come home. World War III will begin." She put her hand to her pounding forehead and wondered if she could climb to her bedroom window.

"So what if they do? You're not a child."

"You have a lot to learn about southern daughters," she told him. She looked again at her wrinkled clothing. There was nothing to do but to wear yesterday's clothes and hope no one noticed. She began to climb from the bed, tugging the sheet over her body. She paused. Gordon was still watching her amiably.

"Uh, do you mind?" she asked, waving her hand to indicate he should turn around.

"Darling, I've seen every inch of your beautiful body. Every curve is imprinted in my memory."

"That was nighttime. This is daylight. It's different."

Gordon thought about that, seemingly amused. But seeing she was serious, he pushed back the covers and rose to sit on the mattress, muttering, "Yes, of course. Forgive me. I'll leave."

"Gordon," she called, clutching the sheet higher as he turned back.

He turned his head to look over his shoulder.

"I don't think you understand. I . . . I don't do this. Usually."

He seemed confused. "Have sex?"

She laughed a bit self-consciously and shook her head. "Not on the first date."

"Oh." He moved on the bed to face her, listening.

"My first boyfriend and I dated since we were thirteen. We were practically engaged before . . . You met him, actually. He's the fellow whose engagement party you went to."

His brows rose. "That blond fellow? Daren?"

"Darby."

He considered this. "Your first love, then?"

She nodded. "We broke up in college. I had a boyfriend there. A terrible mistake. Then Darby again for a short while. Then there was . . . oh never mind him," she said with a shudder. "Then John, the man I moved to California with. We were serious. None of them were casual."

"Is that what you think we are? A one-night stand?"

Linnea looked into his eyes, boring into her like an acetylene torch. "I hope not."

"It's definitely not. And," he added in a sympathetic tone, "I understand what you're trying to tell me. Never for a moment did I think you were casual. My God, I've been chasing you down for weeks."

She laughed then, pleased.

"Now," he asked, rising from the bed, "I expect you want to hear about all my previous affairs." He faced her, utterly unconcerned with his own nakedness.

"No." She shook her head with a short laugh, then looked away. "Thank God."

Gordon walked to the closet and grabbed a robe. Slipping into it, he asked, "Can I make you a cup of tea? It's the civilized drink. Or do you insist on coffee?"

"Coffee, please."

"Cream and sugar?"

"Just milk, if you have it. Now go!" She waved him off. "I have to dress."

He put one finger in the air in the signal to wait one moment. He crossed to his dresser and pulled out a blue T-shirt. "I know you're much smaller than I am, but this is one of those stretchy shirts. It might work, if you want to try it. It's clean. . . ."

"And it's not the same color as the shirt I wore yesterday. That's important," she said, reaching out to take the shirt. "Very thoughtful. Thank you."

Their eyes met as they both held on to the shirt. She felt again the zing of neurons and for a moment she thought they might return to the bed.

"Right. Coffee," he said, and quickly turned to leave the room.

Linnea felt like laughing aloud, she was so happy. All the depression and loneliness that had been hanging over her like a dark cloud had fled like a specter at first light. She felt filled with joy and . . . dare she say it . . . love. She was absolutely head over heels falling for this man. She remembered the smell of him, the feel of his skin against hers, how he moved within her. *Oh, Lord,* she thought with a flutter. She had it bad.

She scrambled to her feet and collected her clothing strewn about the floor, chair, and bed. Her suit was terribly wrinkled, but his T-shirt actually wasn't that bad worn under her jacket. She splashed cold water over her face, ran her fingers through her hair, borrowed toothpaste and finger-brushed her teeth, then hurried out.

The main room of the house was open and sunny. Sliding glass doors lined the exterior wall, allowing a beautiful view of the ocean and spacious decks. It wasn't a particularly pretty house. The style had been popular some forty years earlier when a rash of contemporary, wood beach houses were built along the southeastern coast; this one was painted green outside with wood paneling on the inside. Most of the houses in this style had been torn down and replaced with upscale homes as the real estate values of the islands skyrocketed. It was nonetheless beachfront property on Sullivan's Island, and she imagined the rent was exorbitant during the peak beach season.

Gordon approached her, carrying two mugs of coffee. A latte. She loved him just for that.

"You know how to spoil a girl."

His smile was quick. She swallowed the coffee. She appreciated a man who could make an excellent cup of coffee.

"Delicious," she crooned over the rim of her cup.

"No credit here. I pushed a button. Thank God for Swiss engineering." Gordon leaned against the counter and his face grew more serious. "Can I see you tonight?" he asked.

"I'm sorry, I can't tonight. I have to work. I'm assisting at a sustainable seafood dinner."

"That sounds interesting. Where is that?"

"The Long Island Café."

"Right on Isle of Palms? Fabulous. Can I come?"

"Sorry. It's sold out."

"What about tomorrow night?"

"I have to sit at a turtle nest. I'm on the team." She paused. "Actually," she said as an idea came to mind, "I found it. The first of the season. Would you like to come along?"

"Of course."

"All right," she said, glad that he wanted to come. "The nest is on Sullivan's. I'll text you the details. It may not hatch tomorrow, of course. It could linger for several days. But I want to be there when it does."

"Excellent. You, the beach, turtles . . . couldn't be better."

"Oh." She pursed her lips.

"What?" he asked, taking a swallow of tea.

"I promised Pandora she could come see a nest."

"The more the merrier."

She took a breath and broached again the topic that had been plaguing her. "You don't mind? Her seeing us . . . together? As a couple?"

He looked at her over the rim of his mug, his blue eyes catching hers. "Are we a couple?"

She drew back, suddenly unsure, not answering.

He put his cup on the counter and moved closer. "I'm teasing, Linnea," he said, slipping his arms around her waist and placing his lips against the top of her head.

"But Pandora . . ."

"Strictly friends. More acquaintances. Surfing pals. I like her. But not in that way. Not like the way I feel about you."

He released her and searched her face. "I think we have something special. I'd like to continue seeing you, if that's what you're asking." He lifted a side of his mouth in a teasing smile. "If you haven't noticed, I'm trying in earnest to see you again. But you seem to always be busy. Do you think you can squeeze me into your schedule?"

"Well, I don't know," she deadpanned. "It depends on the turtles."

He laughed then and bent to kiss her. "You really are quite perfect."

Chapter Fifteen

Plastic isn't biodegradable. Depending on the type of plastic and where it lands, items can take days to hundreds of years to break down into very small pieces, which means the waste plastic is left for generations to come.

AFTER WORK WHEN she returned home, Linnea pulled several bags from the Gold Bug, then looked up at the long flight of stairs that led to the front door and groaned. When would her parents get an elevator? Taking a breath, she hoisted the many bags higher in her arms and began the climb. With each step the bags slipped lower in her arms. By the time she reached the porch, the box under her arm was about to topple out. She couldn't get the door handle and, seeing her mother reading on the sofa, she kicked the front door with her foot.

"Mom! Mama! Come open the door!" she called out.

She thought her arms would break as she watched her mother spring from the sofa and trot across the room to open the door.

"My goodness," Julia exclaimed, grabbing the slipping box and stepping aside to let Linnea pass. "What all do you have there?"

Linnea didn't have the strength to answer. She crossed the threshold and released the multiple bags onto the floor. She stayed bent for a moment, catching her breath and stretching her fingers, which were curled up as though still holding the handles of the bags.

"What is all this stuff?" Julia asked again, looking at all the brand names on the bags: Staples, the Art Shop, and local printers.

Linnea straightened, feeling bubbly with excitement. "This is the beginning of Rutledge House Interiors!" she exclaimed.

"What?"

"Grab a bag and let's look at the loot," Linnea said, lifting two of the four bags and carrying them to the dining table. She began unpacking as Julia did the same. Soon the table was littered with boxes.

Opening a long rectangular box, she revealed business cards. Pulling one out, she handed it to her mother.

Her mother looked to Linnea like a young child at Christmas as she reached out to take the small business card—all wide-eyed with wonder and expectation. Linnea held her breath, hoping her mother would approve. Julia was very particular. The pale parchment paper was simple and unadorned. On the front of the card, in an elegant black print, was the name RUTLEDGE HOUSE INTERIORS. She watched as her mother turned over the card, and at last Linnea saw the longed-for smile. There, again in simple lettering, was Julia's name and contact information.

"They're perfect," her mother said softly.

Linnea released a long sigh of relief. "I used the very best grade of paper," she said.

"How did you get them done so fast?"

"I went local. And look," she said, picking up another, bigger box. "Note cards, in the same paper and font. I didn't use a logo, given that you don't have one."

"I don't want one."

"All the better. I think the name at the top looks elegant. Strong."

Her mother's finely arched brow rose. "It's a very good name, my dear."

"Own it, baby," Linnea added with a short laugh. While her mother studied the card, Linnea walked around the table to retrieve another bag. This was the largest, from the Art Shop. From it she pulled out a large portfolio. It had cost Linnea a pretty penny. But the moment she'd seen it, she knew her mother had to have it. The brown leather was very fine, and it would give her mother confidence when she carried it with her and set it out to reveal her work to a potential client. "Now for the pièce de résistance." She held out the portfolio.

Julia took the leather folder into her hands with reverence. On the cover, her initials were embossed. She let her fingers glide over them, her breath held. Slowly she opened it, then gasped.

Linnea watched her mother flip from one page to another, her fingertips shaking. She knew what Julia was seeing, knew each page by heart, having spent hours arranging them with Dana, the art director, an old school chum. These were the photographs of her mother's years of work designing and decorating houses—her own and those of her friends. Some of the work was truly transformational. And more, Julia had her own look. Her talent was undeniable. It shone from the page. Dana had remarked on it.

When Julia lifted her face, there were tears in her luminous blue eyes. Linnea and her mother had spent endless hours together when she was very young. They were inseparable. Julia had been so thrilled to have a daughter. She wanted to share with her the things that she loved—pretty clothes, flowers, going shopping, getting her hair done, a girl's day out. She'd created in Linnea a miniature of herself. There were occasions when she'd had mother-daughter dresses made to match.

But then Linnea had grown up, and her interests changed. She still loved pretty clothes, but the opinions of her friends mattered more than her mother's. More, her focus had shifted. She spent her summers at the beach house. For her the thrill came from observation of nature, not material things. She felt challenged, stimulated, excited to learn. In this world, her mentor was her grandmother, Lovie. As Linnea entered her teens, she and her mother were not estranged exactly, but they were not close. Perhaps it was simply her age. The teenage years were a time of separation from parents. She had to discover who she was and what her own interests were. Yet her mother still clung to her expectations for her daughter. Julia wanted—demanded—that Linnea conform to the rigid social expectations of being from Charleston royalty and living South of Broad. Linnea had chafed under the burden and arguments flared. They no longer shared secrets, ideas, gossip. Rather, Linnea kept her life as private from her mother as possible. Her father had once stepped between them during a shouting match and yelled, "You two scream louder than two alley cats over a dead rat!"

Time, however, had a way of healing all wounds. That and maturity. Her mother had stood by her side when Linnea wanted to take the job in California and move in with John Peterson. Her mother had called Linnea faithfully while she lived on the opposite coast, and once came for a visit, all by herself—her first time traveling alone in a plane. What a glorious week that had been. Once again, for that brief period, they were inseparable. Linnea had taken her to the redwood forest, the Golden Gate Bridge. Her mother had taken her shopping at Gump's department store.

Looking at her mother now, Linnea felt more than love. She felt pride. She stepped forward to hug her and was enveloped in her familiar scent. The skin of her cheek was softer with age.

"I don't know what to say," Julia said, her voice quavering.

"You don't have to say anything. You'll have to pay for the stationery," Linnea admitted, "and you can start deducting it from your business expenses. The portfolio, however, is my gift."

"No, I can't let you do that."

"Mama, please. I want to."

"Thank you."

She crossed her arms. "There's nothing holding you back now. You can go into Mrs. James's house with confidence. You've got this, Mama."

Julia lifted her chin. "I think I do," she said "But I'd better put all these treasures away, so they don't get food on them. I'm about to serve dinner." She paused and looked around the room. "Oh dear, where shall I put them?"

"Mama, you need an office."

"I don't have room for an office. There are only three bedrooms in this house, and your father's taken one for his office. And you're sleeping in the other."

"I won't be here long."

"You don't know how long you'll be," her mother admonished. "And we will need a room for Cooper when he visits. I can't take a guest room."

Linnea sighed, knowing her mother wouldn't put herself ahead of her children. "Then you'll have to make a nook. You need your own space. Virginia Woolf's room of one's own and all that."

"The laundry room is spacious."

"No! No laundry, junk, no distractions allowed in your office. It's a sacred space of work and creativity."

"I was just going to set them there temporarily while I separated the paper and plastic for recycling."

"You know they'd stay there for months for want of anywhere to go."

"Well . . ."

"It doesn't have to be fancy or big. My workspace is that little wood desk in my bedroom. I've become quite fond of that desk. And Cara? She has a little cubicle in a warren of other cubicles at the aquarium. Inside there's only room for her metal desk, a file drawer, and two small metal chairs. All the directors and employees lucky enough to have a desk are squeezed onto one floor. And you know what? It works."

Linnea looked around the open floor plan room. "There's tons of space in this room since you knocked down the wall. Go forth, Mama, and claim a spot. Buy yourself a desk. A dream desk, Mama. You've earned it. Get a screen or partition, if you must. The first project of Rutledge House Interiors should be creating your office."

Julia put her fingers to her lips, seemingly enchanted with the idea. "You're right. I do deserve a space of my own." Her eyes gleamed as she looked over the room. "And I know just the desk I want."

Linnea held back her smile. If her mother loved a desk, it would set her father back a pretty penny.

"I'll do a little feng shui first," Julia said. "I have to see where the most propitious spot would be to put my office."

"What are you going for? Fame? Fortune?"

"Both," Julia replied smugly, and they both laughed.

They moved the paper stock from the dining table onto a side table, talking as they worked. Then Linnea followed her mother into the kitchen where she was preparing dinner. As Julia put a pot under the cold faucet, Linnea began washing lettuce. They discussed Cooper's latest news from Oxford, laughing at his use of a few British words and phrases, Linnea's progress at the aquarium, and her plans for the Beach Sweep. Julia had her back turned to Linnea at the stove and remarked, "You were out late last night."

Linnea leaned her hands on the counter and groaned inwardly, thinking, *This is it.* "Was I?"

Julia spun around. "You didn't come home!"

"Oh, that's right." She acted calm but in her head she was wildly groping for an excuse.

"Did you stay with Cara?"

She couldn't pretend she had. It was too easy for her mother to find out the truth. "No, I was out with a friend in the city."

"Out? On a date?"

"Sort of."

"All night?"

Linnea wanted to tell the truth. It felt ridiculous to have to lie. But seeing her mother's shocked face, she changed tactics. Shrugging nonchalantly, she began cutting the cucumber and radishes.

"It was no big deal. We were at a bar, we drank too much, and I was not fit to drive. I stayed with a friend."

"You spent the night with your friend?"

"Like I said, no big deal." Then, accepting it, Julia turned back to the stove and said, "Okay. But call next time."

Linnea dumped the cucumber and radishes into the bowl, then paused, staring at the greens. "Mama, I'm twenty-five years old."

"It's not that. I just worry."

"Okay. I will." Linnea waited, counting the seconds.

"So, who is this fellow?"

Linnea held back her laugh. It had only taken her mother ten seconds to ask. "You don't know him. His name is Gordon Carr. He's British, here for a few months doing research on plastics in the ocean. Gordon was the speaker at that meeting I went to yesterday. He's a PhD and presented his paper. It was very impressive. Published in *Science* magazine. Everyone was all over him, asking questions, wanting to get to know him."

"He must be very intelligent." Julia smiled knowingly and turned to add pasta to the boiling water.

"Brilliant." Linnea leaned against the kitchen counter, knife in one hand, a large ripe tomato in the other. "He's different from other men. I like him. A lot."

"Well, that's fast. Though you've always gone for the smart ones. Even Darby Middleton."

"Mother . . ." she warned, not wanting her to beat that dead horse again. She turned and began slicing the tomato neatly into sections, digging out the seeds. "First of all, Darby is not *that* smart. Second, lest you forget, he's engaged."

"Oh, I know, dear. I was just saying." She stirred the pot. "John is smart too."

Linnea realized that she could hear John's name and no longer feel a prick of pain. "He's a whiz-kid kind of smart." She paused and looked at the eviscerated tomato. "But he's careless."

"Yes, very."

"I heard from him, by the way."

"You didn't tell me!"

"It was no big deal. He texted."

"When?"

"Last week."

"What did he say?"

Linnea could tell her mother was getting into the topic and she found it mildly annoying. She answered tersely: "He asked how I was. Like I said, it was nothing."

"What did you say?"

"Mama, stop," Linnea said harshly. She went to the fridge and opened the doors, staring inside. "I didn't say anything. I didn't respond."

Julia drew back, wounded. "I didn't mean to pry."

Linnea immediately felt remorse. She didn't want to ruin the moment, especially not over John. "You didn't," she said, grabbing a bottle of salad dressing, then closing the fridge door. "I guess I still get a bit prickly when it comes to him. I really don't want to talk about him." She carried the dressing to the counter. Her salad was done.

"Actually, Mama, I need your advice on something."

It wasn't that often anymore that Linnea asked for her mother's advice. Julia responded promptly, turning off the heat on the stove and giving her daughter her full attention.

"I'm all ears."

"It's about Gordon, the man I was telling you about."

She saw her mother's interest peak at hearing this.

"I first saw him on the beach, surfing. We met independently. Just a wave and hello kind of thing. But I admit, I was attracted to him. Then, again at Darby's engagement party."

"At Darby's party? He knows the Middletons?"

She noticed that her mother was suddenly more interested in this man. She could almost hear the clicking of her mother's mind as it made connections. If Gordon knew the Middletons, he couldn't be all that bad.

To her credit, Julia remained quiet and waited for Linnea to continue.

"Here's the thing," Linnea said speaking honestly. "I found out at the party that Pandora had an interest in Gordon too. In fact, she invited him to it. I could tell she was after him, so I was good. Even though I had a crush on him, I figured if Pandora claimed him, then I had to step aside. Girl's code."

Her mother's nod was barely perceptible.

"Then I saw Gordon at the meeting. Total surprise." She paused. "Mama, I'm not exaggerating when I tell you he was chasing me. At the party too. He admitted it. So, when he invited me for drinks. I said yes."

"But Pandora . . ."

"I know. I asked him bluntly about Pandora, right off the bat. I asked him if they were a couple. And he told me no, that he liked Pandora as a friend. That he thought of her as a sister."

"Ah."

"Exactly," she confirmed. "There wasn't any dating going on. He said he didn't think of her in that way," she couldn't stop the slight blush on her cheeks, "that he thought of me. So . . . I went out with him."

Julia shrugged. "What's the problem?"

"Why do I feel guilty?"

Julia crossed her arms and thought for a moment. "All is fair in love and war," she said, "*only* as long as you are not breaking up a couple.

Whether they're married, engaged, or even just dating. A friend doesn't do that to a friend."

"I'd never." Then, "Are you saying you think I did?"

"It doesn't sound to me like that's what happened. You and Pandora were both interested in the same guy and he picked you."

Linnea nodded.

"But now, you have to deal with your friend. Linnea, you have to tell her. And, she's likely to be upset."

Linnea looked at her feet. "She will be. Pandora thinks she's the queen bee."

"So, you might get stung. What you have to decide is which relationship you want to keep if it comes down to it."

Linnea didn't know what to think.

"And give Pandora a chance," Julia continued. "She might surprise you. Have a heart-to-heart with her. Tell her all you told me. You don't have to ask her permission, but do let her know how much you like him. You can't control how she'll respond. In fact, who dates Gordon is not up to her or you. It's up to Gordon. Chemistry cannot be dictated. Love always wins out." She leaned forward to place a kiss on Linnea's cheek. "But do tell her before she hears it from someone else."

Linnea brought her hands to her scalp and gave it a good rubbing. The thought of telling Pandora gave her emotional hives. "I will. Thanks, Mama."

Julia smiled and went back to her dinner. She brought the pot of hot noodles to the sink. Linnea grabbed the colander and set it in the sink for her. With a gush, the hot water splattered and steam rose into the air. Efficiently, Julia returned the pasta to the pot, poured a bit of olive oil on it, gave it a quick stir and covered it.

Her pasta done, Julia smiled and asked cheerfully, "What else shall we talk about?"

"How about what's going on with Daddy's house? It's still quiet over there. Cara mentioned she didn't see anyone working."

A frown creased Julia's perfectly made-up face. "Really?" She walked across the room to the china cabinet and reached up to pull out three white dinner plates.

"I'm not eating at home tonight," Linnea reminded her. "I have that sustainable seafood dinner."

"Oh, yes," Julia said, returning one plate to the cabinet. "Be a dear and fetch some basil from the porch."

Linnea plucked leaves from the terra-cotta pots overflowing with a bounty of basil, thyme, oregano, rosemary, sage, and parsley. The scents filled the air. Even on the islands, her mother's green thumb would not be denied. She rinsed the basil and tore the leaves from the stems while her mother poured a jar of sauce into a second pot on the stove.

Julia stirred the basil and oregano into the sauce, then stopped, looking at Linnea with an intensity that was beyond curiosity. "Cara said the work stopped on the house?" she clarified. "The one your daddy is building?"

"Yes," she replied. "She thought it might be because of the Fourth of July."

Julia measured salt into her palm, then tossed it into the pot. "Possibly."

Linnea heard something odd in her mother's tone. "What are you thinking?"

"I'm just wondering," she said, wiping her hands on a towel. "The project was moving along so well, at a clipped pace. It's just odd that it would suddenly stop, even with a holiday. It's not the Fourth yet. Usually there's someone there. There's always so much to do."

"I thought the same thing."

"Your father"—she looked at her—"have you talked to him about this?"

"No. I hardly see him. I leave early if I surf, and when I get back he's already gone."

Julia stirred her sauce again, then stopped suddenly. "Something's wrong," she said. "I can't put my finger on it. But he's not himself. Or rather, he's more like the old Palmer—the one who kept secrets."

Linnea felt her stomach tighten. "Are you sure?"

Julia turned down the heat and faced Linnea. "I'm not certain, but I think he's been drinking again."

"Surely not . . ." Linnea said with a heartfelt groan.

"I smelled alcohol on him the other night. When I accused him, he denied it. He said he was at a meeting and someone spilled some bourbon on him. But his breath smelled heavily of peppermint." She shuddered. "I hate that smell. He always uses it when he's trying to cover up."

"But why?" Linnea said in a frown. "He's been doing so well."

Julia's fingers tapped the counter. "Has he? Now you tell me that the work stopped on the house?" She shook her head. "Something's not right. I can feel it."

"What should we do?"

"*You* do nothing," she said, pointing her finger in Linnea's face. "Hear? This is between Palmer and me. And Cara."

"Are you going to tell her?"

"Of course I am. I'm going to call her this very minute." She tossed her towel on the counter and walked away in search of her phone.

When Linnea began to follow, Julia turned and put out her hand. "Girl, you stay put. Go on and get ready for your dinner. This is not for you to get involved in. You'll embarrass him and it'll make things worse. Focus on your own life now. I mean it." Her gaze brooked no argument.

"Yes, ma'am."

Chapter Sixteen

Plastic debris has formed giant garbage patches in the oceans. There are five of them around the world, and the largest—the Great Pacific Garbage Patch—covers an area twice the size of Texas.

THE FOLLOWING AFTERNOON, Cara spotted Palmer sitting at the bar at Halls. It was his favorite hangout—a place where he'd spot an old chum, arrange a quick game of golf or a meeting. It was the equivalent of a locker room for some of Charleston's old guard.

The restaurant was cool and dark, a respite from the rising summer heat. Still, she closed her eyes as a sinking feeling washed through her. *Here we go again,* she thought. He was fifty-eight years old. When would she have to stop being her brother's keeper?

Never, she knew, and hoisted her resolve, put a smile in place, and, after a quick wave to Bill at the desk, walked over to the gleaming bar and took a seat beside her brother. He was neatly dressed in khakis and a polo, his blond hair trimmed, clean-shaven. But there was something off about him that she couldn't identify. A slouch, an aura of dismay that was alarming.

"Hello, Brother," she said.

He jerked his head up and turned to look at her, his surprise evident on his face. His eyes were rimmed in red, but they brightened at seeing her.

"Cara! Sister mine. What a surprise. What brings you to my neck of the woods?"

"I was searching for you," she said, and glanced at his glass. "What are you drinking?"

He grinned wryly and lifted his glass toward her. "Sweet tea. Care for a sip? Or to smell my breath, perhaps?"

She laughed and shook her head, though inwardly she was immeasurably relieved. When the bartender approached, she pointed to his glass and said, "I'll have what he's having." Cara leaned her elbows on the bar and turned to face him. He had regained his slender form in the past two years of sobriety and exercise. Julia had even signed him up for a weekly yoga session. He'd seemed on top of the world with the progress of his house. Now, suddenly, once again his shoulders slumped.

Palmer took a long sip from his tea, his thick gold wedding band catching the light. "Julia got you checking up on me?" he asked nonchalantly, but his gaze sharpened.

Though it was the truth, she sidestepped it. "Why would you ask that?"

He merely shrugged.

The waiter brought her iced tea. She took a sip of the cool sweetness and it fortified her. Setting it on the bar, she turned back to him and said, "I wanted to talk to you about the house."

Palmer's pale eyes grew hunted. "What about it?"

Cara cleared her throat, feeling the tension spike between them. "Well, you know I live right across the street from it. I can't help but notice that all the work has stopped. For more than a week. The place is deserted. What's going on?"

She saw a small muscle twitch in his jaw. "I've got it all under control."

Cara cringed and tried to cool her rising concern. Whenever Palmer said he had it all under control, the opposite was likely true. Up until now, he'd been open about the progress of the house. Boasting. Sharing news like a boy coming home from school and wanting to show off his gold-starred project. Lately, though, he'd been silent. Cara's mind had been preoccupied with the wedding plans—frankly, she was relieved not to have to think about the house. But yesterday, when Julia had confided that she thought something was bothering Palmer, and worse, that she suspected he was drinking again, Cara's razor-sharp focus had turned directly to the house. She'd walked the property. The tools were gone, the trucks nowhere to be seen, and the place deserted. Holiday or no holiday, something was off.

"Palmer, this is me. Your sister. Your business partner. Please, don't push me away. We're in the project together. My land is invested in this deal too. But more, I'm invested emotionally in *you*. What's going on? You can tell me."

Palmer's face fell, and she remembered the boy he'd been at the dining table when their father ranted about his failure to do well in school, or on the football team, or one of a hundred different things. Stratton might have been hard on Cara, but he'd doubled down on his only son. Nothing Palmer did was good enough. And God knew the boy had tried. He was smart, but he wasn't as smart as Cara. He was good in athletics, but never a star. Palmer was short, slight in build, and blond like his mother. Cara had inherited the tall, athletic, dark Rutledge looks.

Cara had always defended her brother to their father. She'd volleyed with Stratton at the dinner table, going point for point, often deflecting his drunken ire from Palmer to herself. It was Cara's nature to fight back, to defend the underdog. Palmer's nature was to draw inward, to cave under pressure. It was only with alcohol that he found his bravery. Unfortunately, Palmer, like his father, was a belligerent drunk. She'd been so proud of his sobriety these past two years. It broke her heart to think that he might've fallen off the wagon.

"What's going on?" she prodded again.

"I'm just having some problems with cash flow. Nothing to worry about. I had to let the guys off for a while." He put his hand up, seeing Cara's reaction. "Just for a while," he repeated, making as if he was dodging a blow. He chuckled.

Cara did not.

"I'll get it all sorted out."

Cara frowned. This could only mean trouble. She wasn't going to allow him to play the big brother card. She had to play this scene in the language he'd understand.

Cara's face grew stern. "Don't even try to play that *don't you worry your pretty little head* shit with me. I'm your goddamn business partner. Tell me what the hell is going on. All of it," she said in the voice that had always had her staff jumping when she was an executive in Chicago.

Palmer understood that tone, and his eyes flashed. With a set face, he said, "Fine. You want to know? Here it is. I got scammed. I was a goddamn prize fool."

Cara closed her eyes for a moment, took a breath, but didn't speak. Opening her eyes again, she waited for him to continue.

"Do you remember Simmons Pinckney?" he asked.

Cara snorted, remembering the entitled, mealy-mouthed boy who for some reason her brother had called his friend since they were in short pants. When Cara was thirteen, pock-faced Simmons had trapped her in the garage and tried to feel her up. Cara had kicked him in the family jewels and stomped off, shouting with fury that if he ever tried that again, she'd make sure he sang soprano for the rest of his life.

"That pugnacious prick," she said. "What about him?"

"You know he's in commercial real estate."

Cara shook her head, vaguely annoyed that he thought she'd know this.

"Anyway, a few months back, we were out on the golf course, and he let me in on a land deal he was involved in. Seems he knew about a piece of land that was going to be rezoned. Very inside."

Cara nearly groaned aloud. Palmer could never resist a get-rich-quick scheme. "What was it this time?"

"A new overpass was planned off Meeting Street that would bring in a lot of traffic to the area. I'm not a total idiot. I asked to see the plans. It was a prime location once that overpass was built. Just waiting to be developed as a commercial property. The property could be bought for significantly less than its value would be after the overpass was finished."

"If it was such a good deal, why was he telling you? Why didn't you buy it for himself?"

"Well, he did. Or rather, we both bought parcels."

"Let me get this straight. You bought this parcel of land," she said in a flat voice. "With the money you'd saved from the sale of your house. The money you needed to finish the construction of the island house."

Palmer closed his eyes, seeming pained, and nodded. "Yes."

Cara swore under her breath. "Go on."

Palmer wiped a bead of sweat from his brow. He had paled, and she hoped he wasn't going to have a heart attack—then wondered if he even had life insurance.

"Well, see," he began again, shifting in his seat. He seemed anxious that Cara understood. "The overpass was approved, okay? Slated to be built. I checked it out. That much was true."

"Okay . . ."

Palmer rubbed his jaw. "But not where Simmons said it was going to be built. The overpass was moved to another part of town." He spread out his hands. "The land I bought was pretty much worthless."

Cara felt her face heat up. "What happened to the land that *he* bought?"

"Turns out, he didn't buy any land. He owned the land I bought and used the money I gave him to buy a different piece of property."

"Let me guess. The property that would benefit from the new overpass."

"Bingo."

"And you call this guy your friend!"

Palmer's face colored. "Not anymore. I call him a son of a bitch."

"You were dealing with Simmons Pinckney. What did you expect?" Cara put her hand to her forehead. "Palmer, you're an idiot!"

She was furious. At Simmons, true. But also, at her brother. Her mother had always said "Palmer is on the prowl" when he was up to no good. Looking for the next deal, the way to make a fast buck. Just like their father. For years Cara had gone toe-to-toe with Palmer about the beach house property. His dream had been to buy the piece of land that sat in front of the Isle of Palms house; he'd spent years sniffing out who owned it. He'd tried to get Cara to go in with him, to sell her beach house and use the money so he could build two houses, one behind the other, thus providing both houses with valuable ocean views. Except that Cara would never sell the beach house. It had infuriated Palmer. That, and the fact that he couldn't find out who owned that adjacent piece of land.

Until two years earlier. Cara had come to the decision it was time to share with her brother the truth about that property. It was a delicate secret, one that had to be maintained, for their mother's sake. Lovie had been given that property and she'd held fast to it, quietly, never telling a soul about it until she'd left the land to Cara. Palmer had been floored to learn that all this time it was Cara who owned that undeveloped beachfront land. His frustration later turned to gratitude when Cara shared her plan of building a spec house together. Cara would put up the land for the deal; Palmer would invest the money from the sale of his house on Tradd Street in Charleston. The idea was that in the end, they'd both benefit from their mother's bequest.

But now Palmer had gone and ruined the deal. And this time, he was taking her down with him.

"I could just . . ."

"Go ahead," Palmer said. "Take that glass and pour your tea over my head. Tar and feather me. I deserve it."

"You deserve much worse," she told him. "But what you're going to do is find a way out of this mess." She fumed. "Can you sue?" she asked him. "Get your money back?"

Palmer shook his head, grimacing. "I tried. I threatened to haul his sorry ass to court. But what would I claim? He sold me a piece of property. It was all straight-up legal. When I told him I'd expose his lies, do you know what he did?"

Cara shook her head.

Tears flashed in her brother's eyes. "He laughed at me." Palmer sharply turned his head, cleared his throat, then took a long gulp of his tea. When he faced Cara again, he was more in control.

"Simmons said, 'Who are they going to believe?' Well, I told him that they'd believe me, the name Rutledge still had some influence in this town." He stopped again and rubbed his chin.

Cara waited again, giving him time. His dignity.

"He said . . ." Palmer swallowed hard. "He said, 'Your name doesn't carry the weight it once did.'"

Cara felt her fury bubble up and wished she'd kicked that sorry boy's nuts a lot harder. She exhaled, then put her forehead in her palm. She didn't know what to say. Much less what to do.

"I'm sorry," Palmer said.

She let her palm drop and saw the defeat in his eyes. Her own eyes narrowed. "Are you drinking again?"

Palmer didn't try to cover it up. He nodded with shame. "Yes."

"You'll have to go back to AA."

"I've already made plans to go to a meeting Tuesday. I feel like shit."

Cara felt a surge of relief. "And you have to tell Julia."

He shook his head, and Cara straightened, putting her hand on his arm.

"You have to," she repeated firmly.

"I can't hurt her again."

"She's not some child you have to protect. She's your wife. And she's tough. What are you thinking? She stuck by you through the last shit show. She's earned the truth. And to be honest, she already suspects. Because, brother mine, I'm warning you. If you don't tell her, and she finds out, she will leave you."

Palmer's face froze with fear at the possibility.

Cara exhaled her tension and tried to regroup. "How much money do you have left?"

"Some. Not enough to finish."

Cara sighed with frustration. There was so much left to do on the house. She rubbed her cheek in thought. "Did you pick out all the appliances yet?"

He nodded.

She let her hand slide to the bar. "I'm guessing they're not GE."

"No ma'am. Julia did the design. It's all top-of-the-line. They're ordered and delivered. Ready to install."

"Do you have enough to do a rough install? To get it ready for sale?"

Palmer shook his head. "No. That's why I called off the guys."

Cara made a quick decision, the kind she was good at. "Then we have to sell as is. We'll take a hit. But we should do better than break even." She shook her head with regret, not for herself but for her brother. "This was your big chance, Palmer. Why couldn't you wait?"

He returned a sorrowful smile. "I thought I'd found my next project. The golden ticket."

"Oh, Palmer, when are you going to learn? There is no golden ticket. The only thing that pays off is honest hard work. What's that quote? *The smallest deed is better than the greatest intention.*"

Palmer released a long sigh. "I know. I'm sorry."

"It's okay," she said, but clearly it wasn't. She felt weary, deflated, but not all that surprised. She'd chosen Palmer as her partner. Cara had been counting on the money from the sale to pay for her wedding. Now . . . well, she would think about that tomorrow.

"Go home," she told Palmer, reaching out to pick up the tab. "Talk to Julia. And a good real estate agent. You need to put the house on the market. Now."

Chapter Seventeen

Sea turtle eggs usually incubate in the nest for forty-two to sixty days, depending on environmental factors like temperature, time of year, and geographical location. Quiet during the heat of day, once the sand cools the hatchlings scrape with their flippers upward through the sand and broken shells, working together to rise to the surface like an elevator. Then they wait.

LINNEA ALWAYS FELT more herself once she was out on the beach, even on a blustery, cloudy morning such as today. Rain was in the forecast. They needed it. Still, she hoped they'd make their rounds before it fell. She stood at Breach Inlet and looked out over the ceaselessly choppy, turbulent water toward Isle of Palms. Sunny or cloudy, this confluence of the Atlantic Ocean and the Intracoastal Waterway was always wildly tempestuous.

The tide was out, revealing the large swath of shoreline that had grown with accreted sand from the north. It stretched to a narrow tip far out into the inlet, tempting tourists to stroll out, ignoring the warning signs. Locals knew how fast the tides could rush in, how they could catch you unaware if you were foolish enough to wander out. Still, the determinedness of nature, her wily ways, her unpredictability, and always her breathtaking beauty never failed to inspire Linnea.

As she stared out at the sea under the storm-ridden skies, her thoughts turned inward. Once again, memories of Gordon's face, inches from her own, invaded her thoughts. He had a way of looking at her that made her feel he was studying her, searching her mind, sorting through the files, researching who she was. His concentration was both exciting and intimidating. But that face . . . She smiled, bringing it to mind. His boyish look of innocence was always a contradiction to the intensity. She sighed and wearily shook her head. She was falling for this man.

A quick glance at her watch told her it was 6:45 a.m. She breathed out a plume of air and searched the parking lot behind her. She was meeting Pandora for their scheduled beach walk. She stuck her fingers in her windbreaker, rehearsing in her mind what she might say to her about Gordon. Her emotions were as tempestuous as the inlet.

At last, Pandora's golf cart pulled into the parking lot. Linnea watched her climb from the cart and grab her gear; spotting Linnea, she waved and began the trek to the beach. Her long legs quickly crossed the lot. Pandora wore a green Turtle Team T-shirt that matched her own. Linnea felt a burst of admiration when she saw Pandora bend to pick up a plastic bottle from the parking lot. She made a show of waving it high in the air, then tossing it into her South Carolina Aquarium recycled plastic bag.

Linnea applauded as she approached. "Good morning! Well done!"

"Just doing my part." She looked up at the sky. "Looks like rain to me."

"We need the rain. If we hurry, we might just beat it."

"You realize," Pandora said, "that I only awakened at this ungodly hour for you."

Linnea said. "It's for the turtles."

"Whatever," Pandora said with a loud yawn.

"Look at that sea. This beach. No one is out here. Come on. You love it."

Pandora slanted her a glance. "You owe me. Besides. I haven't found any tracks yet."

"Patience. There's no guarantee you'll find a nest. Some volunteers have walked for years and not found one. It's a matter of luck."

"Coming from a girl who takes a stroll and finds the first nest *and* the turtle."

"Some people are born with the knack, I suppose." When Pandora gave her a fist bump she laughed. "Honestly, Pan, you know there aren't that many nests on Sullivan's Island."

"I don't care. I'm only doing this so I can see a nest emerge."

Linnea knew this was her opening. "Well, you're in luck. Tonight we're going out to check the first nest."

Pandora swung her head around, eyes wide. "Really?" Then her smile fell. "Wait. *Tonight?* Bollocks. I have a dinner date tonight." She frowned. "But the nest doesn't hatch until late, right?"

"No guarantees. Usually, that's true. If it rains, however, the sand will cool and it likely will be earlier."

They walked farther. "Well," Pandora said at length, "I suppose I could try to reschedule dinner. What are the odds it will emerge tonight?"

"Let's take a look. The nest is right on the dune coming up. We have to check it anyway."

They angled from the high tide line at the beach to the nest sitting on the small dune. Orange tape on wooden stakes encircled the nest, marking it as protected by federal law. This was Linnea's nest, the one she'd observed being laid by that glorious mother on that fateful morning. She felt territorial about it, as a mother might. When they were near, Linnea instructed Pandora on what to look for.

"We search to see if there's any disturbance. Sometimes the roots of plants encroach on the nest. And, of course, we must be on the lookout for ghost crabs. If ever you see a ghost crab hole in the nest, call the team number and they'll come check it out. Don't ever poke your fingers in it or do anything inside the orange triangle of space. Our role is to observe and report only."

"What's the fun in that?"

"It's the thrill of the hunt. But let's remember, our job is to protect the turtles, not to have a good time," she chided her.

"Oh, I know. I just love to tease you when you get into your professorial role."

"Sorry. I get a bit excited about all this. Especially this nest."

"It's your baby. I get it."

Linnea crouched low to investigate the sand over the nest. The blustery wind swept the beach, but she saw a small crater in the center of the nest "Look here," she said to Pandora, excited now. She waited for Pandora to bend low. "See this?"

Pandora peered down. "You mean that little crater?"

"Yes. That is a sign that the nest is getting ready to emerge."

"Tonight?" Pandora exclaimed, her eyes wide.

Linnea smiled at Pandora's excitement. "We can't be sure when, but certainly in the next few days. This rainy weather makes it more unpredictable. But I'll be here tonight, regardless."

"I don't want to miss it. I'll see what I can do. Dumping him might be awkward. Could I bring him?"

"We aren't allowed to have crowds at the nest, but in this case, I suppose." She paused. *Speaking of awkward . . .* she thought. Linnea rose and brushed the sand from her knees. Pandora straightened beside her and adjusted her backpack.

"Uh, Pandora, Gordon will be coming to the nest tonight."

"Gordon? Brilliant!" She smiled in understanding. "Of course he is. This is right up his alley." Then, "How did he know about it?"

"I told him."

Pandora looked confused. "You?"

"We ran into each other at a meeting earlier this week. He was the main speaker. The topic was microplastics in the ocean."

Pandora nodded, putting the pieces together. "He's a star in that world."

"He told me he's doing research here on plastics ingested by sea turtles. So of course I invited him. Because of his research, he's a VIP with SCDNR."

"Well, this puts a spin on things," Pandora said. "I suppose I really do have to extricate myself from this date. Too bad. He's rather a dish. But, oh well."

"Pandora, there's something I need to tell you."

Pandora waited.

Linnea took a breath. "Gordon and I went for drinks . . . after the meeting."

"Colleagues do that."

"It was more than colleagues having drinks."

"You went out with him?" Pandora's eyes flashed. "But you knew I liked him."

"Yes, but honestly, I like him too. Please, let me explain." She took a breath, aware that Pandora was hanging on every word. Her face was expressionless, but her eyes burned in interest. "I met Gordon before I met you. Out on the beach. There was a spark. But once I knew you'd invited him as your plus-one to the party, that you were interested, I steered clear. You know I did."

Pandora didn't respond. Linnea couldn't read her straight face.

"Then we met again at the meeting. He invited me for drinks, and . . ." She sighed. "Pandora, we really hit it off."

Pandora's cheeks flamed. "You slept with him!"

It wasn't a question. Linnea said softly, "Yes."

Pandora's eyes flashed with rage. "I can't believe you'd do that! There are rules about such things. Codes of conduct. You don't sleep with another girl's boyfriend!" She thrust the aquarium bag into Linnea's stomach and began walking away. "This is bollocks. I quit."

Linnea hurried after her. Her heels dug deep into the soft sand.

"But he wasn't your boyfriend," she called out after her.

Pandora stopped and spun around. "You knew I was interested in him."

Linnea caught up. "Yes, I did. And I asked him about that. To make it clear I wasn't going to interfere. But he said—" She stopped.

Pandora's voice went cold. "What did he say?"

"He said you were friends."

She considered this. "We are. So far. You knew I wanted more."

"He said you were good friends. Surfing buddies. Like . . ." Linnea took a breath. "Like brother and sister."

Pandora blanched. She didn't speak for a moment. "Well," she huffed out.

"It all happened so fast. I'm sorry, Pan. I didn't do it to hurt you. I would never. When I heard there wasn't a relationship between you, and there was no chance for one, I let it happen. I don't know if I could've stopped it. We both felt it."

"There's still the code," Pandora said coolly. "And you broke it. That tears it with us."

"Pandora . . ."

"Save it." Pandora turned her back on Linnea and began walking away.

Linnea felt crushed, but there was nothing left for her to say. There was no argument that would persuade Pandora to turn around. She watched Pandora stride back toward Breach Inlet without a farewell or a backward glance.

✳   ✳   ✳

THE RAIN HAD rolled off the island and out to sea by early evening, leaving the air fresh and void of the menacing mosquitoes and no-see-ums that could plague the beach during periods of humidity. There were puddles here and there along the beach path, but for the most part the water had been absorbed by the beach. Linnea wore her rain slicker, just in case, and carried her turtle team supplies should the nest emerge. She had taken extra care with her appearance, knowing Gordon was coming.

When Linnea arrived at the nest at 8 p.m., she found Mary Pringle and Barb Bergwerf already there. Companionably ensconced in beach chairs, they waved her over. She glanced around the beach for Gordon;

not seeing him, she detoured to check the nest before joining her friends. The dime-size depression was now the size of a half dollar. This meant the hatchlings were sitting at the top, waiting for some cue that it was time to emerge. Linnea felt the excitement she always did at an impending emergence. She'd seen hundreds in her life, and it never got old.

Walking back to join the others, she spotted Emmi approaching with her backpack. She carried a large beacon lamp that they sometimes used to help the hatchlings find their way to the sea. In nature, hatchlings were guided by the brightest light. For millennia, that light had been the moon and stars on the sea. But with the advance of electricity, the moon couldn't compete with lights shining from houses and the city. The sun was lowering, and in the twilight Linnea searched for any beachfront houses that might have exterior lights burning. She wasn't shy about knocking on the doors and letting the owners or guests know that the islands had established light ordinances they called Lights Out for Turtles. All beachfront properties were required to have beachside exterior lights turned off. The most mindful of renters knew to close the shutters and curtains too. She was pleased to see that all lights were out.

Behind Emmi were Tee and Cindy, lugging beach chairs and bags. Cara followed, carrying the fabled red bucket. The bucket had once belonged to Lovie and was treasured by the team. They used the bucket whenever they needed to transport turtles closer to the sea. Linnea looked up to scan the sky. Faint early stars were beginning to appear in the pearlescent sky. Tonight, she thought, nature's light might yet prevail to guide the hatchlings to the sea without human assistance. Like Lovie, Linnea always preferred nature to win out.

She felt the joy of the team bubble beneath the discussion as they gathered for this first nest. They laughed and shared experiences of the first fifty days of the season. There was always the story of the crazy tourist, the sad turtle stranding, a discussion of the DNA study. But most of all, they talked about how this season they were already above previous nest records. And not just them: all along the southeastern coast, reports of a high number of nests brought the hope that this would be a banner year for the sea turtles. While she listened, Linnea kept an eye out for Gordon, checking her watch from time to time, wondering where he could be.

At long last, after darkness had descended and a bright moon rose higher in the sky, Linnea spotted a single figure approaching, tall and lean. She recognized the sway of his shoulders as he moved. A smile curved her lips, and she rose from her chair.

"Gordon, you came."

"Of course I came," he replied, kissing her lips lightly.

Linnea cast a surreptitious glance at the team nearby. As she feared, they were all watching her, witnessing the kiss. She turned and introduced him to the group as Dr. Carr, a visiting biologist from England here to study plastics in turtles. This news won the team over and they were eager to meet him. When she introduced Emmi, however, her tone was cool and she cast Linnea a curious look. Linnea smiled stiffly and ignored it. She didn't feel the need to explain herself to her ex-boyfriend's mother. The group chatted for several minutes, eager to learn about Gordon's research. The Island Turtle Team was nothing if not passionate about the ocean and all the marine animals living in it.

When the conversation flagged, Linnea led Gordon to a quiet section of a beach a bit away from the group and they settled on towels on the sand. Linnea glanced back to see Cara's and Emmi's heads bent in conversation. She could guess who they were talking about.

"Any action?" Gordon asked, oblivious to the friction his appearance was causing.

"It's all systems go. There's a crater in the sand over the nest, but it could stay like that for hours. Even days."

"I'm feeling lucky," he said, and his eyes sparkled in mirth.

Linnea drew circles in the sand. "I had words with Pandora," she said.

He cocked his head. "About what?"

How could men be so obtuse? she wondered. "You."

"Me?"

"She's not pleased that you and I are seeing each other."

His face grew troubled.

Linnea clarified: "She doesn't see you as her brother. . . ."

"Ah," Gordon said in understanding. "I didn't know."

"And she feels I've betrayed her, knowing how she felt about you. And I suppose I did."

"Linnea," Gordon said in a serious tone, "I like Pandora. A lot. But as I told you, my feelings for her are entirely separate from my feelings for you. You shouldn't feel badly."

"But I do."

He skipped a beat. "I'll talk to her."

"Don't. It will only make things worse."

"One of us must, and since she's not talking to you . . . Really, I want to clear the air." He reached out to take her hand. "It will be fine. Trust me."

"She was supposed to join us tonight. She really wanted to see this."

"You never know with the Pan. She might show up." Linnea wanted to believe him, and sitting on the beach beside him, under a rising moon, with a gentle breeze, it was easy to do just that.

As predicted, the hatchlings were taking their time, waiting for some ancient instinct to trigger their emergence. As the hours waned, Linnea and Gordon talked about anything and everything. She found him vastly interesting when he discussed his work. He was involved in her field and a natural teacher. Plus, she loved his accent, his voice, melodious and rich. He was careful with his word choices and brought his subject to life with a turn of a phrase or a bit of humor that was as funny as it was surprising. A southerner, Linnea appreciated the art of storytelling and found Gordon a master.

After several hours passed, their conversation was interrupted by farewells from the team members who, one by one, gave up waiting, packed up their gear, and headed for home.

"It's after eleven. You don't have to wait," Emmi told Linnea. Her voice was matter of fact and she offered none of her usual joking and friendly banter. "With the moon up, there's plenty of light. They'll make it on their own."

"I'll wait a bit longer," Linnea replied. "Do you want me to call if there's any action?"

Emmi shook her head. "No. Only call if you have a problem. But don't hang around. Go home. They'll be fine."

Cara came up beside them. "It's her nest. She wants to wait," she prodded. "Good-bye, then," she said to Linnea and Gordon, then glanced at Emmi with a meaningful look. "Ready to go?"

Linnea wanted to kiss Cara. Emmi relinquished, turned and followed Cara to the beach path. Cara glanced back at Linnea with a wink.

Alone, Linnea and Gordon moved their towels closer to the nest.

The night was dark and balmy. Closer to the dunes they could smell the lemony scent of the blooming primroses and hear the gentle scraping of the sea oat panicles as they shook with each breeze. She felt her eyelids lower and yawned.

Gordon stretched out and patted the spot on the towel beside him. Linnea lay beside him, her head against his shoulder. She enjoyed the feel of his chest moving up and down slowly as he breathed.

He reached up and pointed. "There," he said. "The brightest star is Sirius, also known as the Dog Star, for its position in the constellation Canis Major."

"I see the Big Dipper," Linnea said. "And the Little Dipper. That's all I can name. Oh, and Venus when she deigns to appear."

"Ursa Minor," he said. "The Little Bear. Ursa Minor is home to the Little Dipper and Polaris, the North Star."

"So you love the sea *and* the stars, I take it?" she asked.

"True. Back home, I have a telescope. My father used to spend time with me, pointing out the constellations. I suppose I find the night sky comforting."

"Are you close to your father?"

Gordon hesitated. "I try to be."

He began pointing out other constellations.

Linnea listened, trying to find all the constellations he described. The sky was littered with brilliant stars tonight, twinkling against the velvety blackness seductively. She turned her head and instead watched his face as he talked, his enthusiasm for the subject palpable. Again she was struck by the force of his intelligence. His was different from John's. Gordon was modest about his breadth of knowledge. It slipped out as he spoke, surprising her. He was a constellation of knowledge. In contrast,

John's brilliance shone like the North Star. He was quick-witted, sharp, avant-garde. Both surfers, both bright, but that was all the two men had in common. John was a hip techie from California. Gordon was a well-mannered British professor.

Gordon turned his head to find her watching him. His smile was barely visible in the moonlight and his eyes shone in the dim light. "Am I talking too much?"

"No," she said softly. "I could listen to you talk forever."

He moved his arm to brace her shoulders, then shifted her closer to him.

"How did you get interested in all this?" she asked. "Stars, sea, turtles . . . Was your family interested in animals and conservation?"

He snorted and shook his head. "My family's only interest in animals is to shoot them," he replied.

"What?" she said with a laugh.

"The Carrs are big game hunters. Or were. Ages ago. The only shooting we do now is with a camera."

"So, the answer is no."

"I suppose they do as much for conservation as some, not as much as others. We all can do better."

"If they weren't involved, how did you get hooked?"

"Surfing."

"Of course," she said.

"Like you, I got started young. Being in the ocean—oceans all around the world—I felt connected to the beings that swam in the water with me. I was always drawn to the natural world. I loved the oceans, excelled in science at school, and eventually it all caught up with me. And here I am."

"Did you do more academic or field research?"

"Both."

She envied him his experiences. "You love it. I can see it in your eyes."

"I do. Research is the great hunt. But I don't have to be in the wild. I have to admit, I'm enchanted by the lowcountry. The marshes and all the creeks that snake through them. Dolphins, turtles, alligators, wading birds, bald eagles, white tail deer—so much wildlife. I go out in a johnboat and it's paradise."

Linnea sighed, grateful that he appreciated the wonder of the local landscape, as she did.

"But," he added, "I confess that I might love teaching as much."

"You're a *teacher*?" she asked, genuinely surprised.

"Professor, if you don't mind," he teased.

"Professor Carr. You never mentioned that choice bit of information. Where do you teach?"

"Oxford. Only part-time. I do research as well."

"No . . ." Linnea was genuinely surprised. "You mean you might teach Cooper?"

"Is he studying environmental science?"

"Cooper?" She snorted. "The closest he'd come to science is engineering, as in motors."

She heard the laugh rumble in Gordon's chest. "Ah, yes. Trucks. Then, no. I won't be your brother's teacher. More's the pity."

"Count your blessings." She listened to the gentle lapping of the waves against the shore, felt the rise and fall of his chest. "You said your parents could do better about conservation. Do you feel *you're* doing enough?"

He sighed and drew her closer against him. "That's hard to answer. What is enough?"

"I don't know. That's why I'm asking."

"All I know is that I'd like for my children to enjoy the same animals, fresh air, and water—the same natural beauty—that I have."

"Me too. All this . . . It's priceless, isn't it? And heartbreaking to think that all this beauty could disappear. Species going extinct. Climate change wreaking havoc. What kind of a world are we leaving behind for the next generation? What wouldn't we pay to preserve beauty for our children and grandchildren?"

"Thus, we fight the good fight."

She sighed. "Yes, we do."

He slid her body closer to his on the sand. Comforting. Yet, again, so close she felt her body come alive. The air thickened between them. He leaned over her so that his hips pressed against hers. He smoothed the hair from her face. Brushed a few grains of sand from her cheek. She saw his eyes over her like two brilliant stars. Staring into them, she moved her hand up to cup the side of his face. Turning his head, he kissed the tender skin of her palm. Then he lowered his head to her neck and his breath came hot along her throat. She felt her cells tingle as he lazily trailed kisses to her mouth. Then, with a breath, his lips were on hers.

She moaned deep in her throat and stretched her arms to wrap around his back, drawing him tight. Kissing him, she was lost in the stars. One of his arms moved to cradle her head, the other was free to stroke the length of her body.

The kiss was interrupted by the feeling of something weird climbing across her leg. Something small and spiny. With a start she jerked away her leg, bolted upward, and began swatting at her ankle.

"What is it?" Gordon asked, sitting up.

"I don't know." She jumped to her feet. "A ghost crab, I think." She shuddered. "I hate those things."

Gordon reached behind him for his flashlight and flicked it on. The red light flooded the sand around them, revealing one three-inch hatchling scrambling off toward the ocean.

"Gordon!" she yelped. "It's a turtle!"

He sprang to his feet.

"Careful where you step!" she exclaimed. She also flicked on her red flashlight and spread the cone of light around her. Then she shone it at the nest. There was an opening, but it was small. No other turtles were out.

"That must be the scout. That's the single turtle that heads out first. It sometimes happens, though we don't know why." She looked around the sand. "We should pick up our towels. The entire nest could hatch at any moment." She gathered her wits. It was happening!

"Why don't you follow that hatchling to the sea?" she told Gordon. "The tide is out and he's got a long way to go. Don't let a ghost crab get him."

"I'm on it."

Linnea smiled, watching as his beam of red light swept the beach in search of the small turtle. Then, he walked at a snail's pace beside it until all she could see was the beam of his red light in the darkness. Sharing this with Gordon was bonding.

She shook out their towels and moved to sit beside the nest. The wind had quieted and overhead, the thin, wispy clouds were moving fast. The stars were playing peekaboo.

She waited at the nest, eyes peeled for any flippers moving in the sand. She stretched out to grab her backpack and retrieved her phone. Scanning through her messages, she didn't see anything from Pandora.

"Darn you, Pan," she muttered. "You're just hurting yourself." She texted her for the tenth time, alerting her that an emergence was imminent.

COME NOW! she wrote, all in capitals. Then clicking off her phone, she decided there was nothing more she could do.

The tide was coming in, swallowing the beach in gulps. The hatchlings would have a shorter trip to the sea, she thought, pleased. Overhead, the moon rose higher in the sky, its light shimmering over the ocean. Only a few thin clouds trailed the storm and soon those would be gone too. All was in readiness for the hatchlings to race to the sea.

A lone figure was striding slowly back up the beach. When Gordon drew near, she saw his grin stretched from ear to ear.

"I'm guessing the turtle made it to the sea," she said.

"It did," he exclaimed and sat next to her on the sand. His excitement was palpable. "I saw the dive instinct. It was just as I'd read about. One minute it's a clumsy little turtle, and the next, bam! It's swimming." He peered over her shoulder to scan the nest. "Anything?"

"Not yet," she replied. "They're down there, just sitting under the sand. They rest in an air-filled cavity beneath the surface. They've unfolded and their carapaces straighten. At the same time, the yolk sac is being pulled inside the body, giving the hatchling nutrients for the journey ahead. I can just imagine them under there. Waiting. But for what signal? No one knows."

"Temperature of the sand? Sense of time?"

"Whatever it is, when they're ready, they boil out," she said, rising to her feet. "And hold on," she said, shining her red light on the nest. "'Cause here they come!"

Before their eyes the sand began to cave in and ten or more flippers broke through, waving wildly in the air. Out they scrambled, one over the other, pushing and shoving in a comical frenzy to escape. Behind them, an army of tiny, three-inch hatchlings moved en masse, pouring out of the nest.

"It's a boil!" Linnea exclaimed.

"Look at them all."

"They look healthy. Good-sized and lots of energy," Linnea said. Looking at the nest, she saw more turtles climbing out, flippers waving, one over the other. She bent over the nest, trying to get a rough count on the turtles.

The night sky had brightened and as Emmi had predicted, the hatchlings were on the right course for the ocean. The tide was coming in. She could hear the gentle roar of the waves lapping the shore and wagered the hatchlings could too.

"There has to be over one hundred," he said, and she heard his excitement.

"At least. I'm guessing more."

"We almost missed them. You, Miss Rutledge, are proving to be a distraction."

The last sea turtle waved its flippers in the air as it struggled to climb out of the hole. Without its comrades, the turtle was having a hard time scrambling out.

"Can you help him?" he asked.

"He has to do it on his own. But . . ." Linnea bent to smooth out the edge of the hole, careful not to touch the turtle. After a few tries, the turtle got purchase on the sand and climbed out. The hatchling began its race to the sea.

"Well done," Gordon exclaimed, and rose to a stand. He helped Linnea up, and together they followed the sea turtles down to the shoreline on the lookout for ghost crabs.

Linnea was happy that everyone else had left and it was just Gordon and herself. She didn't want to be selfish, but alone, the experience felt more personal.

They reached the edge of the shoreline and stood watching as one turtle after another reached the water's edge and eagerly pushed forward into the sea, their home.

"There's the diving instinct," Gordon said, pleased to see it again.

"Millions of years of instinct," she said. "It guides them to the sea. In that one miraculous moment their comical crawl becomes a determined dive. They'll swim for three days along the surface to reach the Gulf Stream and the huge flats of Sargassum weed. Birds will pluck them from above, and fish will gobble them from below. It's a miracle any of them survive to adulthood. Only one in a thousand will."

"Predator glut," Gordon said, citing the biological model the reptiles followed.

"But if they make it, they'll tuck in the Sargassum to hide and have a chance for survival. And in thirty years, she'll come back here to nest again." She looked up at him. "I find that very inspiring."

"And rather hopeful."

They stood hand in hand at the shore's edge and watched the last of the hatchlings reach the water.

Linnea leaned against him, feeling the late hour mingle with the satisfaction of watching her nest safely escorted to the sea.

"They're on their own now," she said softly, staring at the dark sea. It was a bittersweet moment.

"Thank you," Gordon said, slipping an arm over her shoulders as they stared out. "For inviting me to share this with you. You made it truly special. I'll always remember it."

"I can see you someday, an old man, telling your grandchildren, 'I remember one night . . . where was it, oh, yes. South Carolina. I was with this girl. I can't remember her name, but she was nice. I saw my first turtle nest hatch.'"

He chuckled softly. "That's not quite how I'll tell the story."

"Oh?"

"I'd say, 'One magical night on an island in South Carolina, I watched a hundred hatchlings run home to the sea under the light of a half moon. And I was holding the hand of a woman with starlight in her eyes.'"

She turned to look up at his face and smiled, thinking how she'd thought the same about his eyes.

"Your story is much better."

He looked down into her face. "And you know how I love the stars."

She only smiled.

"Let's go home."

She turned in his arm to tilt her head, feeling his breath mingle with hers. "I can't think of a more perfect ending to this perfect night."

Chapter Eighteen

Research has found perceiving nature's beauty to be a significant predictor of life satisfaction. In other words, the more one perceived nature's beauty, the more one reported life satisfaction.

"I LOVE NEW YORK!" Emmi shouted.

Cara stood, arm in arm with her best friend, staring up at the Empire State Building. Toy, Linnea, Julia, and Heather clustered near, all giggling and remembering scenes from the classic romantic film *An Affair to Remember*. They were all dressed in their chic best as they walked down Fifth Avenue toward Kleinfeld Bridal, gawking at the windows, the historic buildings, and the people. It was a breezy morning and the city seemed to be exulting in the sunshine and warmth. Attractive women strolled by in colorful dresses, abandoning blacks and browns for a lighter palette. Men carried their suit coats over their arms as they stood in line for a hot dog or bagel, and tourists lifted phones into the air.

Cara didn't care if they looked like tourists. They were tourists! She was one of many women on her wedding-dress trip to the Big Apple with her best friends. She had every intention of buying corny souvenirs, cheap scarves and bags, pretzels from a street cart, and just maybe a gyro. She looked at Emmi, glad to see her signature wide smile on her face again. They'd hired a nurse to stay with Flo. Already the difference in Emmi was palpable. She squeezed Emmi's arm and said, "I love New York too."

A few blocks' walk and they arrived at their destination. The monolithic stone and glass entrance of the Kleinfeld salon was before them. They pushed through the impressive doors into a bridal wonderland, entering the lush store with hushed reverence. The large waiting room had arched entryways and pillars with a regal red carpet. Cara was surprised by how many groups of women were clustered there, waiting for their names to be called with an air of excited expectancy. The sharply dressed sales force, all in black and high heels, moved quickly with wide smiles as they escorted troops of wide-eyed brides and fawning entourages.

Cara checked in at the sleek front desk, framed by potted orchids. She was anxious because she was a few minutes late for her appointment, her friends having stopped too many times to admire the shop windows on Fifth Avenue. It was like herding cats. The receptionist greeted her warmly nonetheless, and within minutes her sales consultant came to greet them.

"Is this the Rutledge group?" A woman about Cara's age with creamy skin and stylishly cut salt-and-pepper hair approached carrying a clipboard.

A chorus of yesses chimed out.

"Welcome to Kleinfeld. My name is Anita and I'll be your consultant. Who is my bride?" she asked the group. Her voice was cultured and very pleasant. Her gaze lingered expectantly on the younger Linnea and Heather.

Cara met Emmi's gaze, and her lips twitched. "I am," she said, and lifted her hand.

"Oh!" Anita recovered quickly and hurried to take her hand. "Welcome."

"I'm sorry we're a bit late," Cara told her.

"Don't worry about a thing," Anita said. "This is your appointment. We want you to enjoy every moment. You have one of the first appointments of the day. Enjoy the peace—before too long, there will be mayhem. Please, follow me."

She led them into the main bridal salon, a single grand room decorated all in white, with high atelier ceilings and ionic pillars. It was brightly lit, largely thanks to the camera lighting affixed to the ceiling for the popular television show *Say Yes to the Dress*, which was filmed there. The room was divided into five areas, each with a large gilt mirror and a small podium for the bride to stand upon, surrounded by velvet cushioned seats. And everywhere there were dresses—on mannequins, hanging in brightly lit closets, and on brides. Cara felt adrift in a sea of taffeta, lace, tulle, and silk in all shades and hues of white. It was all like some great, luscious wedding cake. The ornate gowns, the gleaming floors and carpets, the sparkling displays of headpieces and jewelry—Cara was bedazzled. Looking at her friends, she saw the same openmouthed, wide-eyed wonder on their faces.

They all took a seat before a gleaming platform that Cara knew she'd be posing on before long. What she needed, despite the early hour, was a glass of champagne.

Cara introduced her guests, amused to see her friends, young and old, perched on the edges of their seats in excitement.

"Tell me about the wedding plans," Anita began in rote fashion.

Cara said, "It's a smallish wedding, maybe one hundred people. We're having a sit-down dinner, so I will need something formal but also lightweight. No long sleeves. The wedding is being held at a beautiful plantation house in Charleston. It can get hot."

"Oh, I love Charleston. How lucky you are to live there."

Cara smiled. She heard this a lot.

"Do you have any idea what kind of style you're interested in seeing?" Anita asked. "Any designer in particular?"

"I don't have a designer in mind, but I prefer something simple in design, more sleek than fluffy. Nothing with too much lace or sequins or—"

Emmi piped in, "More Meghan Markle than Diana."

Anita perused Cara's classic pink linen shift dress and bone heels, pearls at the neck, and nodded. "I understand. Is there a price you feel comfortable with?"

"It's not the price as much as the time frame I'm worried about," said Cara. "The wedding is only a couple months away. Won't that limit me to ready-to-wear?"

Anita nodded. "I'm afraid so. But don't worry, Kleinfeld has a large inventory. You've come to the right place. I'm sure we'll find something you love."

"I'm not a young bride," Cara told her, feeling the need to say this. "I'm apprehensive about looking too, well, girlish."

"You're not old," Anita said with a light laugh.

But Cara didn't want her meaning brushed aside by polite banter. "Mature?" she offered.

A smile of understanding eased across Anita's face. "I understand. Come with me and let's get started." She directed Cara out of the main room to a private section.

Anita was, Cara soon learned, a patient woman. The first armload of dresses she brought into the dressing room offered samples of several different styles of gowns from assorted designers. Cara dismissed them all without trying them on.

"I'll be back," Anita said as she carried the dresses back out.

As Cara sat in the dressing room waiting for Anita to return, a thin robe wrapped around her, her mind wandered back to when she was preparing for her first wedding to Brett. It had been a completely different approach to getting married. Once Cara had agreed to stay in South Carolina and marry him, Brett was hotfooted to tie her down. He didn't want to wait. In a rush, Cara had gone to a boutique in Charleston to search for a suitable dress or suit that she could purchase that day—no entourage like today, just herself. She'd pulled a few white and ivory dresses from the rack, found a white-lace, knee-length dress that was on sale, and bought that. She remembered it had cost a little over one hundred dollars. The least expensive of the dresses Anita had brought in was over a thousand dollars.

Anita returned, pink-faced from rushing and carrying a second load of heavy gowns. There was nary a sparkly, sequined, or bling-laden dress among them. The quality of the fabric and the construction was much finer. And, Cara noticed, the prices were much higher. Cara liked this batch better. Anita assisted as she tried on one gown after another, quickly deciding on what was in the right direction, and dispensing with those that were not.

There was a knock on the door. Anita opened it and Emmi's face poked into the room. "We were wondering if you got lost."

Anita quickly took charge, shooing Emmi out of the room. "We're making progress. Cara knows what she wants. She'll be out shortly."

"We found a few dresses you might want to try."

"No," Anita and Cara said simultaneously.

Anita turned to smile at Cara. "Be patient," she told Emmi. "I think we have a few to show you."

A few minutes later, Cara strolled out into the main room wearing a bow-backed strapless gown. She stood on the podium and waited for the response. Her friends were silent. Their eyes were narrowed as they stared.

"What do you think?"

"It's . . . pretty," Heather offered halfheartedly.

"You look beautiful," exclaimed Toy.

Linnea smiled but said nothing.

"You look like you're about to take flight!" Emmi exclaimed.

Immediately the other women started to giggle.

"What?" Cara asked.

"That bow is so big it looks like wings," Emmi said.

"The front is simple enough," Julia offered kindly. "It has great style."

Linnea shook her head. "Next!"

Cara laughed lightly, agreeing with them, and headed back to the dressing room, her long bow train trailing behind her.

"I think I need that glass of champagne," she said to Anita on entering the dressing room.

When Cara came out in the second gown, the women were in a jovial mood, chatting, drinking champagne. In the surrounding areas, two other women were trying on gowns in front of their groups. Cara stepped up to the podium. This gown was better received.

Again simple in design, the form-fitting silk and taffeta dress had a V neckline that plunged to the waist.

"I love it," Heather said. "It's so striking."

"You look beautiful in that one too," Toy said, ever encouraging.

"You'll make David a very proud man," said Emmi, tongue in cheek.

"Don't you think it's a bit . . . daring?" asked Julia.

"If I had Cara's figure, I'd dare to wear it," Emmi remarked.

"I don't know," Linnea said. "It's so form-fitting and dramatic, I think the dress is wearing you. Do you know what I mean?"

Not seeing the enthusiasm she was hoping for, Cara said, "It's nice, but it's not the one."

"This is good. We're narrowing it down," Anita said. "Are you willing to bump up your price a bit? There's one gown I have in mind that would look beautiful on you."

"I'd love to see it."

"Sip your wine. I'll be right back."

From this final selection, Cara slipped on a bateau-necked, A-line gown of pure silk. It slid over her body like cool water. Cara loved the creamy feel of the fabric. Anita did the long row of back buttons, handed her a pair of heels, then guided her across the dressing room to turn to the full-length mirror.

Cara hadn't known what to expect when she tried on gowns today. Honestly, she hadn't expected to feel much at all and was prepared to purchase the one dress that was the least disappointing. So she was caught by surprise by her reflection in the mirror. Her mouth slipped open in a quick gasp that soon became a wide grin. The elegant silk complemented her skin tone and flowed from her shoulders, fitted at the waist, then flowed loose and full to the floor like a waterfall. Without any embellishment, her body was highlighted.

Cara wanted her friends to love this dress as much as she did. In her heart, she knew this was *her* dress. She sucked in her tummy, held back her shoulders, and walked out into the salon to the group she knew would be her harshest and most honest critics. The silk swished around her legs as she walked. She heard a great sucking in of breaths as she stepped up on the podium.

To her great relief, this time they all oohed and ahhed and exclaimed how beautiful she looked in that dress. The store manager, Dorothy, stopped by their station and told Cara that she simply had to see her in this gown.

"It's my favorite gown. But only someone with your long, lean figure could carry it off with such a style," Dorothy said.

"And that silk," added Anita. "It's the highest quality."

Cara searched out the one person whose opinion mattered most. Across the short space that separated them, Cara met Emmi's gaze. The expression on Emmi's face told her everything. Tears had flooded Emmi's green eyes. She brought her hands to her mouth and nodded.

In that moment, Cara felt ageless. Anita approached to place a long, unembellished veil on her head that swirled around her shoulders to fall to the floor. It was the coup de grâce. The squad gushed. Cara twirled around, basking in their praise and feeling, for the first time, as giddy as a bride-to-be should.

✄　　✄　　✄

LA GRENOUILLE WAS the French restaurant Cara most wanted to visit. The ambience was as romantic as if they were in Paris, with heavy white linen, red upholstery, a gilt ceiling, and small, shaded lights on the table. And flowers, everywhere were brilliantly colored fresh flowers.

David ordered champagne to begin their dinner, and the women clapped when the cork popped.

"My favorite sound in the world," exclaimed Julia.

"More champagne?" Toy asked with awe. "There was champagne in our hotel room when we arrived, champagne at the bridal salon, and now more! I could get used to this."

"It's my bachelorette party," Cara exclaimed. "We want you to feel special, because every one of you women here is very special to me. You've been there for me for the ups and downs, when I needed a shoulder to cry on, or someone to kick up my heels with. You've walked the beaches with me, and ran into the waves by my side." She raised her glass. "To friends!"

Glasses clinked and a few tears were wiped away from cheeks.

"I feel special, all right," Emmi exclaimed. "I'm staying at the Plaza! I've wanted to sleep in that hotel ever since I was a little girl and read *Eloise*."

"I love that book," said Heather with a quick hiccup. "When I was little, Daddy and Mama took me to the Plaza to stay in the Eloise Suite. Do you remember? It's all pink. Daddy, you'll have to take Hope there when she's older."

David smiled at Cara.

Cara's thoughts raced to Hope, staying with a babysitter in the hotel. At her last sight of her daughter, Hope was sitting in bed against a pile of pillows eating mac and cheese from room service.

Her friends were giggling and getting a little loud, comparing notes about how they could see Central Park from their rooms. Toy began talking about their adventures in the bridal salon, but Emmi shushed her and pointed to David.

"There's a fox in the henhouse," Emmi told her. "No spoilers."

Picking up the menu, Cara thought it might be time to order. She met David's eye. He signaled, and immediately the waiter appeared.

Cara looked at the impressive menu, and ordered escargot for the table.

"Snails?" asked Julia, with doubt ringing in her voice.

"You love oysters, don't you?" asked Cara.

"Yes," Julia said.

"These are better. Just wait."

"You're a coastal girl," said Toy with a hint of admonishment. "Snails are shellfish. Enough said."

David was quickly absorbed in conversation with the sommelier about the wine list.

Cara watched her friends study the elaborate menu. "Now, girls," she said, drawing their attention. "This is my party. I want you to order whatever you like. Don't look at the cost. This is once in a lifetime." She looked again at the menu, then ordered chilled foie gras with figs, salad, and the grilled Dover sole. David smiled his approval. One by one the ladies ordered. It was such fun for Cara to hear what items from the fabulous menu tempted her friends. To order without thought about cost was, she knew, a true extravagance, one she was happy to share with them.

It was a dinner of stories and laughter, one she'd never forget. They all ordered desserts and coffee, and then fully sated, the troop enjoyed a summer night's walk back to the Plaza.

Back in their room, David paid the babysitter while Cara checked on Hope. She was sleeping soundly in the middle of the bed. Cara slipped off her shoes and leaned far over to kiss her cheek. She smelled of fresh soap.

"I couldn't eat another bite. I'm utterly stuffed and exhausted," she said, and collapsed onto the ornate king bed.

"Did you have a good time?"

"David, I had the best time. Thank you. It really was such a good idea to come here. You know, I've only stayed once before at the Plaza."

"When was that?" David asked, walking closer to the bed as he unbuttoned his shirt.

Cara stretched out her arms with a lusty yawn, then let them fall to the mattress. "Oh, a long time ago. I was seven years old and it was a rare trip with my parents. My father's business was booming, so he was in good spirits. My mother was too." She laughed at a memory. "One night when my parents went out to the theater, Palmer and I ordered room service. We got hot fudge sundaes. They were the biggest and best we'd ever had. I don't want to think about what it must've cost my parents, but they never mentioned it. Not once on that trip did my father lose his temper," she said thoughtfully. "Not with me, or Palmer. Nor did he berate us. Or worse, Mama. It was a rare oasis of time when everyone seemed simply happy."

David sat on the mattress beside her, listening.

She turned her head and looked into his dark eyes, so intuitive. She felt she could tell David anything.

"Stepping into this hotel this weekend, after all those years . . . it's hard to explain. But I was filled with the same awe and childlike wonder I felt when I was seven. Looking up at that fabulous chandelier and the elegant, irreplaceable, old-world craftsmanship of the great lobby." Her smile was bittersweet. She reached out and took his hand. "And you. You were such an angel to babysit all morning so we could go to Kleinfeld's."

"We had a blast in Eloise's tearoom," he replied. "Besides, getting your dress was the point of the whole trip."

Cara smiled, knowing that even so, not every man would have spent the morning sitting in a pink tearoom with a four-year-old. In the afternoon, they'd walked through Central Park with Hope while the others dashed about the city fulfilling their own bucket lists.

"It went by fast."

"Tomorrow we're home in Charleston, mission accomplished."

Looking around the room, seeing that their clothes had been picked up and hung in the closet, fresh flowers and chocolates delivered with the turndown, Cara reveled in a moment of luxury. Then she reluctantly rose to change into her nightgown while David gently moved Hope to the twin bed in the suite.

At last they lay side by side in the big bed, the sounds of the city serenading them from below. Cara turned her head on the pillow to gaze at the man beside her.

"Happy?" David asked, his voice rumbling in his chest.

"I had a perfect day," she told him.

"I hoped you would."

"I can't stop thinking about that trip here with my family," she said. "It might have been our only real family vacation. My mother always took us to the beach house in summer. I never thought of that as a vacation, not like a trip to someplace new. My father went to Europe every year on business trips. He took my mother with him at first, but after

Palmer was born, her trips ended. I don't know if she decided she couldn't leave her child for weeks at a time, or whether he never invited her. A woman's place, as it were." She paused and decided not to voice her thought that it was possible, even likely, given the unhappiness of her parents' marriage, that he'd had an affair in Europe. There had been rumors enough of another woman in Charleston.

"Don't you think it coldhearted that he never took his children to Europe? Like you did with Heather. I'm both impressed and envious of all the countries you showed her. What an experience for a child."

"She was a very shy child, if you recall. We were just becoming aware of her anxiety disorder."

"Even still, high points for you and Leslie."

"I'd like to do the same with Hope."

She understood that he was reopening the discussion of them living in London part of the year. But she didn't want to go down that path in their discussion. Not tonight. She had something else in her heart to share.

"I don't believe the family trip has to be grand, like going to Europe or Asia. Any trip with one's parents that involves going somewhere different, having to solve problems together as a family, make choices, have fun, talk, laugh, creates memories. A different city. A hotel in one's own city. It doesn't matter." She sighed. "You know, my whole life I've wanted to take a trip on a houseboat."

"Really?" he said, amused.

She knew by his expression that he was tucking away that bit of information for the future. "Especially on the Mississippi," she continued. "Like Mark Twain. Anyway, the most memorable trip I ever had with my family was here to New York City. I'm sure it was because my parents were happy. That means so much to a child. A meal with McDonald's hamburgers can be as memorable as the four-course meal we had tonight if the mood is joyful." She patted his hand. "I'm speaking metaphorically, of course."

He laughed. "I'm glad you don't equate tonight's dinner with fast food."

"You do get what I'm saying, though, don't you? I want those experiences with Hope. You and I together, with her. The three of us."

"And we will." David turned on his side and she felt his dark eyes studying her. "What are you trying to say?"

Cara turned toward him and propped her head on her pillow. The light was dim and sounds from the street echoed in the room.

"I'm thinking of my father."

"I don't think I've ever heard you talk about him. Only in passing, and not very kindly."

"I know," she said softly. "He wasn't a kind man. But I have happy memories of being with him here. More than anywhere else. Here, he was the father I wanted him to be." She felt her throat thicken and she swallowed hard.

She was grateful David didn't press. He remained silent. Giving her time.

"I'll never forget that time. It was the way I'd always wanted us to be—my mother, my father, Palmer, and me." She fell silent, then said, "I was wondering . . ."

"Yes?"

"Do you think, I mean, I know it's a lot of trouble, but would it be possible . . ." She took a breath. "For us to stay another day? Just you and me and Hope."

"Yes. Of course. I'll call the front desk. What do you want to do?"

"I'd like the three of us to go to Coney Island."

"Coney Island?"

His expression made her laugh, and she scrambled to sit up. "Yes. It's where my father took me and Palmer. Mama stayed at the hotel or went shopping, I don't remember. But he took us on the train out to the park. We had the best day. I remember him laughing." She paused. "There weren't many occasions I can recall that. And he didn't yell at us. Not even once." She looked earnestly into David's eyes. "I'd love to go back to Coney Island with Hope and you. Let her experience all that. With you. I want her to have the memories."

David scratched his jaw. "We can do that. Except, Hope is only four."

"That's old enough to create memories. And, I don't know," she said softly, "I may need this trip more than she does. Before we get married, I'd like us to do something as a family. Just for us."

David reached out and gently, without haste, drew Cara down into his arms. "Done," he said softly against her ear.

"I love you, Mr. Wyatt."

"I love you too, Ms. Rutledge."

Outside the terrace window, laughter sounded from the street. Traffic still bustled and horns honked. The breeze lifted the curtain and wafted around their bodies. Another siren screamed in the night.

✳   ✳   ✳

THE FOLLOWING AFTERNOON, a tired Cara sat on the F train beside David. Hope was fast asleep in her lap. David carried a bag full of souvenirs, a stuffed animal, and bottled water. They jiggled and swerved as the train took the curves and made stops on the trip from Coney Island to Manhattan.

Cara let her lips rest on the soft hairs of Hope's head and smiled, remembering the highlights of the special day. Coney Island was a bit shabbier than she remembered; then again, most places were when compared to the idealistic dreams of children. Yet the magic remained. The Cyclone, the carousel, the carnival atmosphere brought the memories back.

When Hope was desperate to ride the Cyclone roller coaster, Cara tried not to laugh, remembering how agonized she had been when told she was too young and too small. She'd fumed as she had to stand outside and watch her brother snicker as he boarded the ride. Cara and David had decided not to spend an entire day, hoping to avoid a meltdown from Hope. They'd spent just enough time at Luna Park for her to enjoy a few kid-friendly rides. Predictably, Hope was wild for a boat ride. She'd stared warily at the street performers but was in awe of the enormous pile of pink confection and her first taste of cotton candy. For lunch, they'd skipped the long lines at Nathan's hot dogs and gone instead to Little Odessa for some Russian food.

The highlight of the day was watching Hope ride the carousel with David. They'd lucked out on the weather, sunny and with the temperature in the low eighties. A breeze blew in from the Atlantic, replete with the scents of cotton candy, hot dogs, and the sea. Hope was clinging to the pole of the carousel horse, kicking her legs and yelling, "Giddyup!" Cara stood outside the carousel and snapped pictures from her phone. Finally she'd lowered it and just stood watching the carousel go round and round, Hope and David going into and out of view.

Remembering it now, Cara knew that the image of David standing beside the carousel horse, his protective grasp on Hope's waist, the smile on his face, would stay with her forever. Cara had loved him more in that moment than she thought possible.

Memories of the day she'd spent with her father, riding that same carousel, had fluttered through her mind all afternoon. Stratton had smiled at her in that same way, held her hand tightly. She'd felt safe and loved. In a wisdom forged from time and experience, Cara found she could, at last, remember the good times with her father. She couldn't change the past, but she could look at it with less emotion and more compassion. In doing so, Cara set herself free from the tiresome burden of anger and hate. As her body swayed with the movement of the train, left to right to center, with her cheek resting against the head of her sleeping child, she realized it was so much easier to just let go of the past. To forgive and move on.

She sighed and glanced at David sitting beside her. He met her gaze and held it.

"Thank you," she said softly.

"For what?"

"For the day. For the trip. For everything."

He reached out and put his hand over hers, cradling Hope. She felt a gentle squeeze and thought that, yes, that was answer enough.

Chapter Nineteen

Hatchlings emerge either en masse or sputter out in small groups. Emerging together increases the chance of survival as many hatchlings can overwhelm would-be predators. A single, vulnerable hatchling would be an easy target.

IT WAS THE summer solstice, a perfect night for a party. Emmi had lit the garden with fairy lights and set tables out under the stars. The weather was cooperating for the wedding shower. Balmy breezes kept the mosquitoes at bay, assisted by citronella candles on spikes encircling the tables.

Cara wore a pale-blue dress that swirled with each movement, low gold sandals, and sizable blue topazes sparkling at her ears. A sprig of jasmine was tucked in her hair, piled high atop her head. Every time she caught a whiff of its delightful fragrance, she thought of her mother. It had been Lovie's signature scent.

As the maid of honor, Emmi had left no detail unattended. A gorgeous cake in the shape of a turtle dominated the table. She'd made a delicious champagne punch served in her grandmother's crystal punch bowl. Cara, who usually despised punch, loved it; she could swear it was really a big bowl of French 75 cocktails. Emmi also had a keg of ale on tap for the men. The side table groaned under the weight of food made by the wedding party—Emmi, Julia, Heather, Toy, and Linnea. All the southern favorites were there: deviled eggs, fried chicken, pimento cheese sandwiches, bean salad, potato salad, green salad, a big bowl of pickled shrimp. Homemade corn bread and biscuits sat beside bowls of creamy butter and honey. The garden was redolent with the scent of Carolina pork. There was nothing better than a good southern barbecue.

Cara had requested, firmly, that all gifts be donations to local charities. She was moved by the amount contributed in her and David's name to the institutions they were involved with. At this point in her life, she didn't need more towels or lamps. She wanted a future for Hope and Rory and Leslie.

The children were ensconced in the beach house with a babysitter. Cara had wanted to bring Hope to the party, had bought her a pretty blue dress for the occasion. But she'd come down with a summer cold and was out of sorts. Flo was present, but her nurse was not far away. Flo seemed in excellent spirits tonight, however. She was having one of her good days.

The evening proved to be a delight. Cara stood on the porch, leaning against a pillar, and looked out over the garden. She didn't know what time it was. The moon shone high in the sky; the food was devoured; the laughter pierced the night, loud and hearty. These people were nearest and dearest. She looked around at her friends and family and counted herself very lucky. Her wedding was less than a month away, she realized, and felt a swirl of true bride-like anticipation.

Cara's phone vibrated in her pocket; it was her sitter. She quickly answered it. "Yes?"

"I sure hate to bother you during your party," said Kate, "but I think you might want to come take a look at Hope. She's spiking a fever. I just took it and it was a hundred and one degrees."

Cara felt her heart beat harder in her chest. "You were right to call. I'll be right there." She tucked her phone in her pocket and craned her neck to find David.

"You okay?" asked Flo, coming to her side.

"No, not really. Hope isn't well. I need to find David."

"I saw him over by the bar. He's talking with Ethan and Bo."

Cara was grateful Flo was lucid tonight. "Thanks," she said with a gentle squeeze of Flo's arm, then went to get David.

Flo was right. David, the tallest, was easy to spot amid a group of men rocking on their heels and laughing, each with a cup of beer in his hand, save for Palmer, who had a soft drink. David's green gingham shirt under his blue blazer still looked crisp and fresh. He was clearly enjoying himself in the role of the groom.

Cara stepped close to him and leaned near his ear. "Hope is sick."

His head swung around, and his eyes bored into hers. "We should go. Emmi can make our apologies." He set down his drink, took her hand.

They walked with purpose, heads tilted downward so as not to make eye contact and be stopped, through the garden, out the gate, and across the driveway to their kitchen door. The overhead light was on, guiding them up the stairs. David pushed open the door.

"Hello?" Cara called out as she and David walked through the house to Hope's bedroom. Kate stepped out of the bedroom as they approached, eyes wide with worry. She was in her twenties with waist-length hair. A student at the College of Charleston, she had babysat many times.

"I'm glad you're here," said Kate. "I can't settle her down."

Cara murmured something and pushed past her to Hope's bed. Her daughter looked so small in the wrought iron twin bed. It was her "big girl" bed that she'd received on her fourth birthday. The pink peony blanket was kicked off and the pink sheet barely reached her belly. Her pink and white ruffled nightgown appeared damp with sweat. Her face was flushed, and she moaned softly. Then her little body contorted as she coughed, doubling over with the effort.

Cara put her hand to Hope's head. "She's hot. How long has she been like this?" Her tone was harsh, critical.

"She was sleeping for most of the time since I arrived," Kate answered. "Then she cried a little bit, saying she was thirsty. I gave her cool water and that's when I noticed how hot she was. I took her temperature, under her armpit. If that says a hundred one, I think it might be higher. Her coughing seems to be getting worse too. I've been putting cool compresses on her head, but she's calling for you."

"You were right to call me. Thank you," Cara told Kate, not wanting the young woman to think there was any blame on her part. Hope began coughing again. It sounded as if she were coughing up her lungs.

Cara looked at David, conveying a message of worry. "It wasn't this bad when we left."

"Where's Rory?" David asked Kate.

"He's asleep in the other room. I kept them separate, on account of the cold. He's fine. No fever or cough."

"Good decision," David said. Then, turning to Cara, "I think Heather should take him home. There's no point in him getting sick too. Thank God she left Leslie at home with Cami."

"Yes, good idea," said Cara. "You'll stay here?"

"I'll text her. I'll stay here," he confirmed.

Cara felt a bit embarrassed for asking him to stay, but she didn't like the way Hope looked. "I'm going to call the doctor."

David settled into the seat by the bed that Cara vacated while she stood in the hall and hunted for the number of her pediatrician. Her fingers were shaking. At last she found it and tapped the number in her phone. Promptly, she heard the voice of the answering service. Cara quickly explained what was happening and asked the doctor to please call her back as soon as possible. She tucked the phone in her pocket and put her fingers to her temples, assessing the situation. Cara could usually garner her wits and act decisively when others flailed in panic. She re-entered Hope's bedroom. Kate stood with her arms clenched around her waist, staring at the moaning Hope.

"Kate, did you give her any Tylenol?"

Kate shook her head. "You didn't give me permission to do that."

"Follow me," she told Kate, and took off for the kitchen. "We need to bring down her temperature." Thankfully, Cara kept an organized kitchen. "I want you to know where I keep all medications. Next time if this happens, call me right away to ask if you should give medication. Don't give it on your own—but I do want you to give it before it reaches this point. You need to know where I keep it."

She pulled out a stepstool and climbed up to the shelf over the refrigerator. This was where her mother had always kept medicines and emergency kits. Lovie had said such things needed to be kept out of the reach of children who might see the pretty pink pills or the grape-flavored syrup and think it was candy. Cara pulled out a sealed plastic bin and brought it down to the counter.

"I keep my emergency supplies, like bandages and antibiotic ointment, here. And the medicines." She dug through the bin, then pulled out a small red bottle. "This is it." She brought the bottle to the light to try to read the tiny lettering. She couldn't. "Damn, can you read this?" she asked Kate.

Kate took the bottle, lifted it to the light, and read aloud the designated amount for a four-year-old.

"Okay," Cara said, and took off for the bedroom with Kate at her heels, just as Heather came rushing into the hall, her heels clicking on the hardwood floors. Her blond hair was pulled into a twist and her floral summer dress swished as she walked.

"Is everything okay?" she asked Cara with concern ringing in her voice.

"Hope is sick. She has a fever."

"Oh no, I hope she'll be all right."

"We thought it best if you took Rory home. You don't want him exposed to whatever virus she's caught."

Heather's blue eyes flickered with worry. "Yes, of course. Thanks for calling. Where is he?"

Cara pointed to the bedroom across the hall from Hope's. "He's asleep."

Heather nodded, spun on her heel, and hurried in that direction.

Stepping into Hope's room, Cara was stunned to see Flo there, bent over Hope's bed.

"Flo! What are you doing here?" Cara knew she sounded angry, but she was too worried to care.

"I came when I heard Hope was sick."

"Cara," David said with a tone of caution. "She thinks—"

"I have to give Hope Tylenol," Cara said, approaching the bed. "We need to bring down the fever."

"Cara," Flo said sharply.

Cara looked up. It was automatic. Flo had the authority back in her voice, like her old self.

"Listen to me," Flo said, her eyes intent, her voice calm. "This child has measles."

"Measles?" Frustration and confusion bubbled, putting her on pins and needles. "Of course she doesn't have measles," Cara said. "She's been vaccinated."

Flo gripped her arm tightly, forcing Cara to look back at her. "I know what I'm seeing," Flo said. "I've worked with children all my life. You know this. Back in the day, I saw a lot of cases of measles. And I'm telling you, this child has measles. Look for yourself. She's got the rash—look at her neck, by her ears. It will get worse, creeping up her face and trunk in a few hours. And that fever, that hacking cough, she's got all the symptoms. Cara, you've got to get this child to the hospital."

"Really, Flo? Are you sure?"

"Yes, dear girl. Trust me, I know."

Cara saw the old certitude in Flo's eyes. She nodded. "I will."

※ ※ ※

THE MEDICAL UNIVERSITY hospital was immaculate, the doctors who tended the pediatric care unit attentive and knowledgeable, the nurses friendly and helpful.

Cara had never been more terrified.

Arriving at the hospital, Cara had immediately told the receptionist at the emergency room that they were worried it could be measles. The intake nurse hurried over, took one look at Hope, and called for a quarantine. Masks donned, the team rushed Hope to an isolation room, leaving Cara and David to sign papers at the desk. A squad of doctors and nurses hurried in and wouldn't allow Cara and David into the room until they both confirmed they'd been vaccinated for measles. Cara held Hope's hand as the team worked quickly and efficiently. The nurses did their best to put Hope at ease, explaining what they were doing to minimize her fears as they swabbed her mouth, took blood samples, and offered fluids. Hope clung to Cara, afraid of all the strange people poking and prodding. David stood by Cara's side. She knew he had to feel as helpless as she did. She leaned against his strength. His hand on her shoulder felt like a lifeline.

After what felt like hours but was in fact much less, Hope was once again asleep. The medicine she'd been given was helping. She wasn't coughing as frequently and her fever had gone down. But the rash had already spread across her face. Flo had been right. Hope was still very sick.

The head doctor approached and asked Cara and David to follow him. David gently squeezed her shoulder, and they joined the doctor in the hall. He was a middle-aged, balding man with kind eyes behind wire-rimmed eyeglasses. His white coat bore the name *Dr. Manigault* in script.

Cara expected warmth and perhaps a soothing bedside manner. She didn't expect the doctor to be so terse.

"It's measles," Dr. Manigault said.

"But . . ." Cara stammered. "I don't understand. How did she get measles?"

His eyes flashed with annoyance. "That's what happens when a child is not vaccinated."

"But Hope *was* vaccinated!"

Dr. Manigault looked doubtful. "That's not possible. She has the disease."

"I gave her pediatrician her records when I moved back to Charleston. We went over them together. He said all was in order. I'm sure she was vaccinated."

"Ms. Rutledge," he said with authority, "your child definitely has contracted measles. You must know it is one of the most highly contagious of all infectious diseases. And it remains one of the leading causes of death among young children. It's beyond me how parents can put their child at risk when vaccinations are so easy and inexpensive."

Cara brought her hand to her throat. This doctor was sparing her nothing.

He continued in his matter-of-fact manner: "At four years of age, your daughter is at high risk. She's mildly dehydrated. We're focused on fluids and hope she doesn't develop vomiting or diarrhea. Unfortunately, she's developed an ear infection, a common complication."

"I'm telling you. She was vaccinated."

He lowered his head, as though containing his frustration. "We cannot accept verbal statements that she's received the vaccine. We will need to see her records. And we will have to quarantine her. Furthermore, we will need to know the names of everyone she's been in contact with for the past fourteen to eighteen days. A person with measles can spread the virus to others for about eight days, starting four days before the rash appears. Especially to other children."

David stiffened with alarm, and she knew he was thinking of Rory and Leslie.

"How is the disease transmitted?" David asked.

The doctor shifted his gaze to him. "Direct contact with infectious droplets, of course. But most likely through airborne causes—a cough or a sneeze. Do you have other children?"

"I have two grandchildren who have been exposed," David replied.

"Are they vaccinated?"

"The four-year-old is. My granddaughter is an infant."

Dr. Manigault frowned with concern. "The MMR vaccine is given when the child is at least twelve months old, so the risk is highest for that child. You will need to be in touch with their pediatrician immediately," he advised. "Anyone who had contact with Hope should review their inoculations."

The doctor turned to include Cara. "She most likely caught the disease ten to fourteen days ago. The measles virus incubates. You likely didn't see any symptoms during that time."

"She developed a cold this week, maybe three days ago," Cara said. "Coughing, runny nose. The temperature was low-grade, typical for a cold. I wasn't alarmed—until tonight, when it spiked. That's when we saw the rash and brought her in."

"Classic pattern," Dr. Manigault said. "Has she traveled during that time? Where do you think she may have contracted the disease?"

Cara looked at David as she replied. "We went to New York."

The doctor pursed his lips. "Where in New York?"

David replied soberly, "Manhattan. Coney Island."

The doctor inhaled deeply and nodded, as though to say, *I understand*. "There have been several outbreaks of measles in that community."

Cara felt a chill spread through her body as a cloud of doom descended over her. "What should we do?" she asked.

"Hope will need to stay in the hospital. We can make accommodations for the mother to stay with the child. The nurse will help you with that. We've given her medication and fluids." He paused. "Now, we wait."

Chapter Twenty

After the sea turtle lays her eggs, she pats the disturbed sand down with her shell, then uses her flippers to toss sand in order to camouflage her nest. Her work done, she lumbers down the beach back to the sea, never to return to her nest. Back in the ocean, she is a lone swimmer.

CARA HAD HARDLY slept a wink in the wobbly and hard makeshift bed that was provided, but she was experiencing a nightmare nonetheless. Every noise Hope made had her jumping up to make sure she was all right. The small hospital room was institutional with a want of comfort. Metal bed frames, tables, and chairs with thin, nubby cushions were shadows in the dimly lit room. She shivered, feeling the chill in the air. Going to Hope's bedside, she tucked the blanket higher up under her chin. Letting her fingertips graze her forehead, she felt the heat still radiating from her skin. She let her palm rest there, hoping its coolness brought some comfort.

She stood like that until the first gray fingers of light broke the blackness beyond the windows. When the nurse entered, that was her cue to leave for a few minutes. Cara straightened, feeling the stiffness in her joints, and went to the coffee shop in the lobby, relieved that she finally was freed from the pretense of sleep. She drank two cups of coffee, then went to the bathroom, where she brushed her teeth with supplies from the hospital. Returning to the lounge of the pediatric ward, she set to work assembling the information Dr. Manigault had requested.

First, she contacted her pediatrician's office to e-mail Hope's vaccination records to the hospital ASAP. Then she painstakingly went through her calendar to figure out who Hope had been in contact with during the past few weeks. She called Rory and Leslie's nanny and, after bringing her up to date on Hope's situation, got more contact information for children Hope had associated with.

Then she had to notify them.

She was nervous that the parents of Hope's friends would react with fear and blame. Most, however, received the news well. Their first reaction was shock and then, with a few exceptions, compassion. These were the women who knew Hope—and Cara—well. Women who arranged playdates and birthday parties, who paraded around the schoolyard with Cara and Hope at Halloween and May Day. Most of the mothers reassured Cara that their children were vaccinated, so they were not fearful. But a brazen few felt the need to ask arrogantly how Cara could choose not to have Hope vaccinated and thus risk not only her daughter's health but that of all the children in the school.

Once that was done, Cara, shaken, had to notify the nursery school. Having been an executive in Chicago years before, Cara was accustomed to making tough phone calls. But this was personal, not business. The emotions took their toll.

The principal at the school received the news somberly.

"Ms. Rutledge, we take this news very, very seriously," the principal informed her. "We will immediately initiate appropriate procedures to alert all the parents of the school. Measles is highly contagious." Cara held back her comment that of course she knew the disease was contagious. That was why she was calling.

"We don't allow anyone in our school who hasn't had the MMR vaccination," the principal continued in a tight voice. Then with a hint of criticism, "Your records indicated Hope was vaccinated. I don't understand how this happened."

Cara tried to explain what had transpired. She could hear the shift in the woman's tone from annoyance to concern and at last, sympathy. Still, the issue was serious, and the school had its work cut out for it. Cara promised to keep her updated.

The afternoon was shifting into evening. Cara laid her head in her hands, exhausted and utterly drained.

✠ ✠ ✠

LINNEA DOUBLE-CHECKED THE beach house before locking up. The bright sun lit up the rooms. Seeing the cream sofas and Heather's painting over the fireplace, Linnea felt soothed by the cocoon of happy memories.

She and her mother had come to the house to feed the canary and pack up clothing and toiletries for Cara. While there, they tidied the bedroom, washed up the few dishes in the sink, and gave the house a good sweeping and dusting. It was nothing Cara wouldn't do for them. As they stood by the front door, all seemed in order. Moutarde was chirping in his cage, pleased with the fresh greens they'd offered.

"I think we have everything," Julia said, taking a final sweep of the house.

"Poor Cara," Linnea said. "I can't imagine what she must be going through."

"Whoever thought Hope could catch measles in New York?" said Julia. "It certainly puts a pall on the trip."

"Don't say that! The trip was perfect. This was one of those weird accidents that happens that makes us shake our heads in wonder."

"But it happened because we went to New York," Julia pointed out. "See what happens when you take a southern girl out of the South?"

Linnea rolled her eyes, hoping her mother was kidding. She could never be entirely sure.

"Let's go," Julia said. "I'm sure Cara is dying for a change of clothes." Then, realizing her poor choice of words, she frowned and led the way out of the house.

✳   ✳   ✳

THEY STEPPED OUT of the elevator onto the main floor of the pediatrics unit. After checking in with the desk, they walked through the brightly lit, pleasantly decorated halls to the waiting room of the isolation unit. There, Linnea saw Cara sitting at a table, her head bent and eyes closed. She was still wearing her party dress, though now the linen was woefully wrinkled. Linnea approached carefully, in case she was asleep.

"Cara?"

Cara jerked her head up and her eyes sprang open. "Linnea," she said as a smile of recognition eased across her face. "Julia."

Julia stepped forward, pulling the roller bag. "We brought you a change of clothes, some toiletries, a few bottles of water."

"And your computer," added Linnea.

"Bless you," Cara said gratefully.

Linnea thought Cara looked exhausted. Her face was chalky despite the tan, and shadows encircled her red-rimmed eyes. "How's Hope?" she asked.

Cara shook her head wearily. "It's measles."

"Oh no," said Julia with some alarm.

Linnea held her breath. She'd been expecting Cara to say Hope was much improved, ready to go home.

"I'm waiting for an update. She's breathing well, but . . ." Cara's lips trembled and, pinching them tight, she looked away.

Linnea couldn't remember seeing Cara cry since Brett's funeral. Cara was always the staunch one, the woman who stood strong when everyone else was caving. To see her on the verge of collapse shook Linnea.

"Is there anything else we can get you?"

Cara looked at them, shook her head. Then suddenly, she broke down and began to weep. Julia immediately stepped closer to wrap her arms around her sister-in-law.

"She'll be all right," Julia murmured as she patted Cara's shoulders.

Linnea knew pat phrases were always expressed at such times. Though spoken in rote fashion, they nonetheless expressed all one's sympathy, concern, and hope. The few chosen words were exactly right.

Cara collected herself and wiped her eyes with a napkin from the table. "Thank you," she said. "For being here. I was feeling so alone."

"You're not alone," said Julia. "Your family is here."

"We're always here," Linnea echoed.

Cara reached out her hand and Linnea took it. "Thank you," she said, her voice more under control. "Moutarde is well? I was worried about him."

"He's fine," Linnea replied. "Chirping away. Is there anything else you need?"

Cara nodded. "There is something I need to ask you."

"Anything."

"I feel badly having to dump all the ongoing work projects at the aquarium on you, but I have no choice. You are in charge now. Do you feel up to it?"

"Absolutely."

Cara returned a brief smile of relief. "I thought you'd be. The Fourth of July Beach Sweep is a lot to handle, but it's your baby. When you need help, go to Toy. She's been at the aquarium for long enough to know everyone and can steer you in the right direction for help."

"I've got everything under control," Linnea assured Cara. "You don't have to worry about a thing other than your precious daughter."

"I'll call you to check in."

"You can if it makes you feel better doing so, but you don't have to," Linnea said.

Julia handed Cara the suitcase. "Just take care of Hope. And yourself." She leaned forward to kiss Cara's cheek. "We'll leave you now. But call if you need anything."

※　　※　　※

CARA WAS GRATEFUL for their kindness. She brought the suitcase to the bathroom to clean up and change clothes. She felt much more collected and refreshed when she emerged. She picked up her phone and checked her messages. There were dozens, most of them from friends and family concerned about Hope and wishing her well. As she scrolled through e-mails, then texts, she was concerned that the only person she hadn't heard from was David.

He'd rushed off the night before to see Heather and Bo. He was dreadfully worried about the children, as well he should be. He'd texted that Heather was having a full-blown anxiety attack about the baby. Cara had texted back that he was in the right place, and that she'd see him in the morning.

But morning came, and she didn't.

Cara waited in the lounge while the doctors were in with Hope. She bent over her computer, sipping terrible coffee and researching measles. She'd read about the outbreak of measles in the country a while back. There had been that false claim that the measles vaccine caused autism, now thoroughly debunked; still, some people refused to get their children vaccinated. She'd thought the issue had died down, but she'd been wrong. The number of measles cases was still increasing across the world. The virus was deadly, causing hundreds of thousands of deaths, especially among children. Just in the United States, almost fifteen hundred cases had been reported in thirty-one states already that year. She continued scrolling until she read one statistic that struck her cold. *More than 75 percent of those cases were linked to outbreaks in New York.* Cara's hands lay still on the keyboard as she reread that statistic, her breath quickening.

"Miss Rutledge?"

Cara swung her head over to see Dr. Friedman, Hope's pediatrician, standing near. She was a stately looking woman with thick white hair neatly trimmed around her pale face, her heavy dark eyeglasses a dramatic contrast to all that white. She had a kindly manner, even old-worldly.

"I'm sorry to interrupt, but I want to discuss Hope."

"No, heavens, no. I was just reading about measles. In fact, I'm waiting for you." She closed her computer and was about to rise when Dr. Friedman gestured for her to stay seated. She came closer and sat beside her. Although she smiled, her face remained solemn.

"We've looked into Hope's medical records," she began.

Cara swallowed and clenched her hands together.

"Hope was adopted, isn't that right?"

"Yes."

"And her mother was an undocumented immigrant?"

"It's complicated," Cara replied. "Elena, Hope's mother, was here on a student visa, all perfectly legal. She was a bright girl. I was her mentor in a program with the college. Then one day she just disappeared. I didn't hear anything for months, not until I received word that she'd been killed in an automobile accident. It was horribly sad. Such a loss. A woman from Social Services came to tell me about Elena's death and informed me that I was named next of kin. It seems that, unfortunately, she got pregnant and her American boyfriend dumped her." Cara paused. "I was Hope's legal guardian. When I adopted Hope, I received her medical records. They stated that Hope had received her measles vaccination. I gave those records to you."

She nodded. "Yes. In retrospect, I should have done tests to confirm that Hope had received the vaccine, or the right amount. Believe me, I would never take measles lightly. But I haven't ever seen a case in my practice, thanks to the high vaccination rates. True, in recent years we've seen the number of cases increasing in our country, though not in South Carolina. Most of those cases originate from outside the country, from people who were unvaccinated or didn't know whether they were vaccinated." She paused. "Or, as in your case, when the vaccination report was falsified."

Cara's mouth went dry. "Falsified?"

She nodded. "Yes. We were able to track down the source. And now, of course, we know she was never vaccinated."

"My God. I never thought—I mean, why would they falsify that? What difference would it have made?" She put her hand to her head. "I should have checked."

"I assure you, we will go over her immunization record with a fine-tooth comb. But for now, there's no point in looking back. We have enough to deal with for the present."

Cara felt her knees weaken when he took her hand.

"Hope is a very sick little girl," she began, her voice kind but full of concern.

Cara remained quiet, grateful for her bedside manner.

"As we said, measles can be dangerous, especially for young children. One in five will be hospitalized. I'm afraid she has developed complications."

Cara froze. The complications included ear infections, pneumonia, deafness, brain damage, even death. "You said she had an ear infection," Cara said with hope.

"Yes. We have that under control," she replied. "However, her body is in a weakened condition. This leaves her open to more complications. Cara," she said, "Hope has developed pneumonia. We're monitoring her closely," she hastened to add. "But this is serious. She will have to stay in the hospital for a while longer."

"Of course." She licked her lips, trying to get hold of her racing thoughts. "What dangers are there?"

"There's always a risk it could worsen, of course."

"Worsen?" she asked. "How? What does that mean?"

"Let's not go beyond where we are right now," she replied, patting her hand.

Suddenly her bedside manner felt more like condescension. "Dr. Friedman, I'd like to know the possible prognosis. What if her pneumonia worsens?"

Dr. Friedman pursed her lips. When she spoke, she used that doctor voice that was oddly calming. "Hope was a strong, healthy child before the measles. Severe complications usually come in children who were malnourished or had a compromised immune system at the onset. But . . . Hope's immune system is compromised now. She's on antibiotics and we expect her to recover." She paused to let that statement sink in. "However, if the infection causes the air sacs to fill up with fluid . . ."

She didn't finish. Cara finished for her.

"She could die."

Her eyes softened with pity. "It's a possibility. We're not going to let that happen."

Cara felt cold. She couldn't speak.

"We are doing everything in our power to prevent any further complications. I've consulted with the CDC and we are observing the most up-to-date practices. Be assured. Hope is in good care."

Cara nodded and tried to smile but couldn't manage it. When Dr. Friedman rose, she rose as well.

"Thank you, Doctor."

"I'm going now. But I'm on call and we will be monitoring Hope very closely. Don't hesitate to let me know if you need me."

"Thank you," she said again in a rote manner.

She watched her walk away in a smooth stride. A nurse hurried up to her with a chart, which she perfunctorily signed. Cara wondered if her husband or partner was at home waiting for her to return and have dinner. If she had children. Grandchildren. How many children had she seen die?

Cara went directly to Hope's room and stood, staring down at her child. She thought of Elena. Odd that she hadn't thought of her in quite a while. She used to think of her often, especially right after she'd adopted Hope. She had searched for Elena in the baby. Elena's dark eyes had been so full of life. Hope had her mother's eyes.

"I'm sorry, Elena," she whispered. "You entrusted me with your daughter. And I let you down." She felt her voice waver and took a deep breath. "I'm so sorry. But . . . I'm upset, too. Angry. Did you even know Hope's records were a lie? This could've been avoided. So simple. One vaccine."

Cara bent closer and let her gaze sweep over Hope's face. She was sleeping soundly, hooked up to an IV. Her face was still aflame with the hated rash—and her breathing was labored. Her little chest moved up and down in the struggle.

Cara slumped into the chair beside the bed. She felt helpless. Alone. Where was David? She needed him, his strength. He'd promised to be right back. She looked at Hope and remembered how happy she was on the carousel, holding on to the mechanical horse, laughing, waving and calling out, *Look at me, Mama!*

Cara looked down and took Hope's hand. All those germs on that horse. The doctor said it was likely she'd caught the measles on the trip, possibly Coney Island. The area had a high incidence of measles. She brought Hope's small hand to her lips, felt the heat of it, and felt her frustration building in her chest. Why had David insisted they go to New York? Why did he always have to have his way? She'd never wanted to shop for a fancy wedding dress. She didn't want a large wedding. Why? Feeling her frustration fuel her anger, Cara began to cry.

"Excuse me," came a voice from behind her.

Cara sniffed and wiped her eyes.

"I'm sorry to interrupt," said the nurse. "We have tests we must do. Now would be a good time for you to get something to eat."

"Yes," Cara said, "of course. How long will you be?"

"Not more than twenty minutes."

Cara kissed her daughter's hand, then left the room. She stood in the hall feeling adrift. She didn't know where to go, what to do. She couldn't eat a thing. Perhaps coffee, but she didn't think she could drink another cup of the hospital brew. There was a coffee shop a block or two away.

Cara pulled her phone out of her purse and checked for messages. Lots of junk. Nothing from David. She stuck the phone back in her purse, feeling a flush of resentment. Where was he? Wasn't he worried about Hope? She could barely breathe, her anger grew so hot. All the worry and frustration that had simmered in her gut all day found a target.

She went to the elevator, needing to get out of the hospital, to get some fresh air. The bell rang and the metal doors slid open onto the lobby. The outside was just a few steps away.

Suddenly, standing in front of her was David. He looked ragged, chalky-faced, his eyes rimmed with dark circles. But he was shaven and neatly dressed. His eyes lit up at seeing her.

"Cara!"

She stepped back, pinching her lips tight, not trusting herself to speak.

"Were you going out?"

"Yes." Her voice was frigid.

He moved aside to make room.

She stepped out of the elevator and turned toward the front doors.

"Where are you going? How is Hope?" He followed her outside the building. "How's Hope?" he asked again when they reached the sidewalk.

"Nice of you to ask."

He stopped and grabbed her arm. His voice was gruff. "What's that about?"

She jerked her arm from his grasp. "Where were you?"

"I'm sorry. I was with Heather and the children, sorting things out. I knew you had Hope under control."

"Did you? And you finally decided to show up."

His face went cold. "What do you mean?"

"Where. Have. You. Been?" she snapped, her eyes blazing.

"With Heather. I told you. I was very worried."

"So was I. About *our* daughter."

He put his hands on his hips. "Cara, you know what happens when Heather shuts down. She hasn't had a panic episode in years. It's hormonal after the baby, the doctor said. That plus the stress and worry about the measles. I had to get her settled."

"She has a husband."

"He's never dealt with this, and certainly not with two children."

"And a nanny."

"Cara . . ." he said, but his voice had hardened.

Good, she thought. She wanted him to know how angry she was. How hurt she felt at being abandoned.

"Heather's anxiety spiked into a full-blown panic attack. And with good reason. We're not talking about the flu. Measles can kill an infant."

"Measles can kill Hope too!" Cara shouted at him.

He stared back at her, openmouthed. "What are you saying?"

"She has pneumonia! She could die," she cried, her voice breaking.

David gently took her arm and steered her to a pocket park outside the hospital. She let him lead her to a park bench and slumped down onto it.

"What's happened?" His voice was low.

"I told you what happened," Cara said, wiping her eyes. "You would have known if you'd bothered to call."

"I'm sorry. I knew I was coming back, and I guess I felt everything was okay once Hope was in the hospital. I was trying to get back, but . . ."

"It's been a disaster," Cara interrupted. "Hope's medical records were sent. It turns out they were falsified. Hope never was vaccinated."

"*What?*"

Cara continued. "I had to notify the school, the parents. . . . You were there when I got my marching orders from Dr. Manigault. Did you help me? No! You said you were coming right back. You didn't. You left me alone to deal with it all by myself. Heather has a husband. And a nanny. Why couldn't they have taken care of her? Why do you always have to treat her like she is some child?"

"She is my child."

"She's thirty-two years old! Hope is our child. Is it always going to be like this? Heather comes first. Then Rory, then Leslie. Then Hope?"

"Cara, stop. You know that's not true."

"Do I? Then why weren't you with us when we most needed you?" She took a deep breath and ground out, "I am so angry."

"Worried I can understand. Even upset. But why are you angry?"

She clenched her hands in fists at her sides. She told herself not to say it, that she would regret it, but she couldn't hold it in.

"Because you made me go to New York!" she screamed.

David leaned back as though slapped. "I thought you wanted to go."

"Did you ask me?"

"Yes."

"No. You announced we were going. You'd already bought tickets."

"Because Emmi said you hadn't bought a dress. The wedding was coming up. We wanted to surprise you."

"Well, you did. And once again, I caved. I went along." She took a breath. "You always get your way. I was fine getting a dress off the rack in some store, but no." She shook her head. "That wasn't good enough for you. Not for David Wyatt. You had to make a big production of it. Your constant need to make everything an event. Buy airplane tickets and take the whole entourage to New York. To the biggest bridal salon in the country. You orchestrated it just like you orchestrated having a big wedding. But you know what? I never wanted a big wedding!"

She was shouting now. David's face grew mottled, but he remained silent.

Cara pointed at him. "You push and you push in your nice way, but you always get what you want. Well, guess what? Do you know what you got this time? This time you got measles. Did you know that seventy-five percent of the cases of measles reported this year came from New York?" She saw his eyes widen. "That's right. New York. That's where Hope caught it. Probably at Coney Island."

"You were the one who asked me to take you to Coney Island."

"I know. Because we were in New York." She put her palms to her cheeks. "Why did you make us go to New York? It's your fault Hope is sick!"

Cara turned away. She knew she was being unfair, but she couldn't stop. Her heart was beating fast and she felt broken.

David didn't speak. He sat beside her, staring out at the street. Traffic rolled by. A few cars honked. Pedestrians passed, unaware of the scene unfolding on the park bench. When at last he spoke, his voice was low and lifeless.

"I didn't realize I was *making* you do anything," he said. "I thought you wanted a big wedding. I thought you wanted to go to New York. I just wanted to make you happy."

She suddenly felt drained.

"Then why did you go through all of this?" he asked.

"Because I wanted to make *you* happy."

He didn't reply.

"You left me alone today," she said to him, her voice calmer now but deathly cold. "Alone to deal with the doctors and the nurses. Alone to find out that Hope's records were falsified. Alone to learn that my daughter has pneumonia. That she could die."

"I'm so sorry."

Cara couldn't bear to hear David say *I'm sorry* one more time. "I can't do this," she said, standing up. She looked at David, saw the hurt in his eyes, and felt the pain in her own heart. "I'm going to see my daughter. I don't want you to come with me." She emphasized the word *my*. She knew it would hurt him. She wanted it to.

"I thought she was our daughter."

"I thought so too."

Cara turned on her heel and walked out of the park, back into the hospital. Alone.

Chapter Twenty-One

Sea turtles are ancient mariners that have survived on Earth for more than 100 million years. Today, their future is jeopardized. Sea turtle species face extinction due to human impacts including fisheries by-catch, coastal development and loss of nesting beaches, plastic ingestion, and the consumption of sea turtles and their eggs.

CARA SAT HUDDLED in a chair in the waiting lounge, her heart broken. She had not felt so lost, so utterly bereft since Brett's death years earlier. Was she cursed to love and lose love? Did love always end so harshly? she wondered.

The elevator doors swished open. Looking up, she was startled to see her brother step through the sliding doors. He was neatly dressed but his face looked somber. When their eyes met, he extended his arms as he quickened his pace to her side. Cara rose and walked into them. She put her head on her brother's shoulder, relishing the comfort she found there.

"Sister mine," Palmer said. "I'm so sorry."

Cara was too choked up to reply.

"Come sit down," he said gently, guiding her back to her chair. "Have you eaten? You're skin and bones."

"I'm not hungry."

"You have to eat. You're no use to Hope if you end up sick in this hospital as well. I'll go get you something."

Cara lurched out her hand to hold his arm. "Don't go. I just want to sit here awhile with my big brother."

"Don't fret. I'll stay."

"I'm waiting for word from the doctor. And truly, I couldn't eat a bite now."

Palmer sat in the chair beside hers, adjusting his seat. "You'd think they'd make more comfortable seating, knowing people would be putting their asses down in them for hours."

"My body aches so badly it doesn't notice any longer."

"What's the word?"

"She has pneumonia. She's on antibiotics and we're waiting to see how she responds." She spoke without emotion.

"They know what they're doing here. Don't you worry."

Cara didn't respond. Telling a mother not to worry about her sick child was like telling her not to breathe.

"I saw a friend of yours downstairs."

"Who?"

"Your fiancé."

Cara startled. "David? He's downstairs?"

"Yeah. Apparently you told him not to come upstairs with you."

"Not exactly. We . . . had words."

"So I understand." Palmer gave her a knowing look. "Did you break it off?"

She took a breath. "I may have."

"Did you mean to?"

"I honestly don't know," she said wearily. "I was just so angry at him."

"Well, he thinks you did. And he's hurt. And maybe a little angry too."

Cara reached up to scratch her skull with a soft moan. "I can't worry about him now. I just can't."

Palmer said, "Cara, I know you're in a state and all, and I'm sorry if I hurt your feelings, but I feel I ought to tell you something."

Cara looked at him warily.

"I don't think you fully appreciate the power of your personality," he began.

"My what?"

"Hear me out. When we were young, even though I was older, I was always a little afraid of you."

She scoffed. "Oh, come on."

"I'm serious. I don't mean you weren't loving and all. I can't think of a better sister. But when you got mad, or someone got in your way, you could cut them off at the knees. Why do you think I let you do battle with Daddy? You were better at it than I was! Hell, I'll wager *he* was a little afraid of you too . . . the ol' son of a bitch. Reckon that's why you were so good at being an executive. You're smart, you think fast, and you don't suffer fools."

Cara took a deep breath. She'd vaguely known, as one is aware of one's own strengths and weaknesses, that she was strong-minded. But to hear her brother describe her in such a way was sobering. "What are you trying to tell me?"

"Only this. You gave David both barrels. He's reeling. I don't know if you can come back from this."

Cara felt stung. "I don't know if I want to."

Palmer put his palms up. "Fair enough. But be sure, Sister. Because if you have doubts, you might still have time to rectify the situation."

Cara mulled this over, leaning back in her chair. "I thought you didn't like David," she said morosely.

"It's not that I don't like him. Truth be told, I was jealous of him. He's rich, successful, and as if that wasn't enough, he's goddamn good-looking too. That's a lot to take when your own ship is going down." He leaned back in his chair and crossed a leg over the other knee.

Cara let out a short laugh, more from emotional release than humor.

"Cara, he's a good man," Palmer said. "And as Flannery O'Connor wrote, a good man is hard to find." He paused, then slapped his hands on his knees and rose to his feet. A man on a mission. "I'm going to get you something to eat. Maybe cheese and crackers. A candy bar. Want coffee?" When she shook her head, he said, "I'll be back." He turned and began walking toward the elevator.

"Palmer!" Cara called out.

Palmer stopped to look back over his shoulder. The elevator rang.

"Thank you."

⚓ ⚓ ⚓

IT WAS THE longest night of her life. Cara sat in the chair beside Hope's bed. Her backache was a constant. Her mind plagued her with worries about Hope and questions about her feelings for David. Palmer's words had shaken her. Cara didn't pretend to try to sleep. She wrapped her shoulders in the thin hospital blanket, but her feet were as cold as ice. Still, she must've dozed off because she roused when the night nurse came in to check on her patient.

Cara's head darted up from Hope's mattress when she felt a hand gently shake her shoulder. "What?" she gasped.

"Sorry to waken you," the nurse whispered. "I have to check on your daughter."

Cara's gaze darted to her daughter. Hope lay sleeping on the bed, and it appeared she was breathing steadily.

"Yes, all right," Cara said, mopping her face with her palms.

She stood and moved away, then watched the nurse check the IV and the instruments. She took Hope's temperature. Hope moaned but didn't awaken.

"How is she?" Cara asked.

"She's stable and that's good." The nurse smiled kindly. "She's a fighter."

"But not out of danger . . ."

"You'll have to ask the doctor about that."

Cara felt another chill. She reached for her purse. "Where's the chapel?"

The nurse looked at her with compassion. "On the third floor. Turn left when you step off the elevator."

"Thank you."

One foot in front of another, Cara walked across the horrid pattern of the green and blue carpeting. The hall and lounge were deserted. Not a soul was in sight. She didn't even see a nurse at the station. The dim lights and isolation made the place seem ghostly. She quickened her step and punched the elevator button.

The chapel was easy to find. She pushed open the wood doors and entered a dimly lit room heavy with scent. No doubt, many candles were lit in this room over the course of time. Cara had had all night to think about the things she'd said to David. Palmer was right—she'd been deliberately cruel. She didn't know what had come over her. She'd felt a rage bellow out, unstoppable. She'd kept her feelings bottled up for so long that when she was traumatized and lost control, they exploded, like a shaken can of soda. Still, she was ashamed of having hurt him. True feelings or not, she should have been honest with him long before about the wedding. It was wrong to yell at him when she could have talked to him. Should have . . . *Oh God,* she thought, covering her face. It seemed her life was a litany of things she should have done.

The small chapel had a pretty window of stained glass above the altar, and a crucifix of brass, handsome and not too big. She let the door close silently behind her. The dozen wooden pews, six on each side, were empty except for one man on the left.

David. Even in the dim light, she could recognize him. His head and shoulders were bent. Cara walked up the center aisle and moved into David's pew. He jerked his head up at the noise. Seeing it was her, he went still, watching her with his dark eyes. His face looked tired.

Cara sat beside him and looked straight ahead at the altar.

For a long while, neither of them spoke. In time, however, the stiffness she felt in her spine softened. She didn't feel anger any longer. Or hurt. She felt afraid. Helpless. She hadn't been in a church in years. She'd never even christened Hope. She'd never been much of a churchgoer. She believed in God and prayed in her own way, in her own time and place. Usually out on the beach when she saw the dawn rise over the ocean in a show of hope and blessings. Or at night during a sunset, when the sky was aflame with the royal colors of gold and purple. Her mama used to tell her that sunsets were proof that God existed. And she believed it was true.

But now, sitting in an actual chapel, she felt compelled to speak directly to the Lord. To plead for his mercy, even if she didn't deserve it. Cara lowered her head, clasped her hands and began to pray.

Dear God, she began silently. *I know it's been a long time since I've prayed in a church like this, but I've always known you're there. I'm praying to you tonight, in your house, because I've been brought low. I don't know what to do. I'm not here for myself. I'm praying for my daughter. Hope. Please, Lord, let me have the measles,* she prayed, clutching her hands fervently. *Let me have the pneumonia. If someone must die, let it be me. Please. Don't take Hope. She's so young. She has her whole life ahead of her. I've had a good life. You've tossed me a few things I didn't think I'd ever forgive you for. But I kept going, and you blessed me with a child I never thought I'd have, and a second love I never dreamed possible. I thank you for those miracles. You're known for miracles. I believe in them. So I'm praying for one now. Grant me this one. Let me bear this for Hope. Please, God.*

Next, she prayed to her mother. She hoped this wasn't sacrilegious. But she felt certain her mother was up in heaven and that if anyone had connections with the Almighty, it would be her.

Mama, take care of my baby, she prayed. *Please, don't let anything happen to her. It's not her fault. I'll take the punishment. Please, she's all I've got. Put in a good word for her, will you? Hope is your grandchild. I wish she could have known you. She would have loved you, and you her. But don't you call her now. I need her more. I don't ask for much. But . . . Mama . . . I'm begging for this.*

Cara felt the tears flow down her cheeks and she couldn't stop the sobs anymore than she could stop the fury hours earlier. She felt David's arm slide around her shoulders and draw her closer to him. She leaned against him, felt his strength, and let her sorrow flow from her in a great release. His hand kept patting her shoulder, a steady reminder that he was there. That she wasn't alone.

The tears subsided as quickly as a summer storm. She wiped her eyes but kept her head on his shoulder awhile longer, relishing the comfort she felt there. She wasn't sure she had the strength to lift it.

"I'm sorry," she said at last.

"I'm sorry too."

"I said some terrible things."

There was a long pause before he said, "Yes, you did."

She took a breath and straightened to look him in the face. He returned her gaze unflinchingly.

"Cara, if you were so angry, I wish you would have told me."

"I know. I should have."

"You really didn't want a big wedding?"

"At this point, I don't really care anymore. I can't even think about it. Hope is so sick. All I can think about is her."

"I understand. But here, in God's house, please tell me the truth. Do you feel that I'm controlling? That I'm pushing you to do things you don't want to do? Because, Cara, I hope you know that's not what I'm trying to do. I just . . . I love you. I know you've been hurt so many times in your life. I simply wanted to make you happy."

"I know. And because I know that, I tried to make you happy by going along."

"Going along? With what?"

"A big wedding. A fancy dress. The whole shebang."

He offered a sad smile. "I did want it. I just never realized how much you didn't want it."

She reached out to take his hand. "David, I hope you know I didn't mean those things I said."

"I think you did."

She winced. "Partly, perhaps. But I was speaking about how I felt, and I blamed you for it. Yes, I was mad. But I was angrier at myself than you. I tried to put my feelings aside. Now I know that's not a good idea because the anger just builds and builds until I can't hold it in anymore. But, for what it's worth, I did it because I love you too."

"So, you don't think I'm pushy."

"You're determined," she amended. "But you're also very generous, and kind, and your motives are always pure."

He shrugged, but she could see he was mollified. "What hurt the most was that you called Hope *your* daughter."

She tucked her hair behind her ear, registering what he'd told her. Determined to be honest, she said, "It hurt me quite a bit that you put Heather ahead of Hope."

She heard the sigh rumble in his chest. He looked older in that moment, weary with worry. At a breaking point himself.

"Cara," he said, then paused. "I'm a father. I don't put any child in front of the other. If I'm guilty of anything, it was not putting you first. I'll try to do better communicating with you. I rely on your strength. I haven't had someone to lean on in a long time. But I didn't stay away because I love Heather more than Hope. I simply thought she needed me more. And I was wrong. I'm sorry."

Cara nodded, accepting his apology. "David . . ."

"Yes?"

"I'm not that strong." She spoke so softly he had to lean closer to hear. "I'm afraid."

"I am too."

"If she doesn't . . ." Her voice cracked.

"Shh . . . she will. She has the very best care. And she's a fighter. She has a lot of her mother in her."

In the dim light of the chapel, enveloped in incense, Cara thought of Elena, the courageous young woman who'd fought to keep her daughter, to give her life. Who'd given up her family, her country, all that was safe and secure, for her child. Even though Cara knew David had meant her, the strong mother had been Elena. Yes, she thought, Hope was a lot like her mother. And her mother had named her daughter Esperanza. *Hope.* She had been Cara's gift when she most needed it. Her answer to her prayer. Hope would be what she clung to now.

"When she gets out of the hospital," Cara said on an optimistic note, "she will need time to recover. Weeks. Maybe longer." She was quiet a moment, then looked up at David. "We have to cancel the wedding."

He looked momentarily stunned. "But we will still get married . . . ?"

"Yes! Of course." She smiled. "I love you. I want to marry you. But I can't—" she began, then amended: "I don't want to deal with a big wedding while my daughter is recovering."

"Our daughter," he corrected.

"Our daughter." She looked into his eyes and waited.

"I agree," he said promptly. "We'll postpone the wedding."

She had to speak her mind now, she told herself. "When we do get married, I don't want a big wedding. Just family and friends. At home."

He understood all. "Fine with me."

She smiled and felt the weight of the world slide from her shoulders. This was about so much more than a big wedding. They both knew the wedding was merely a symbol for communication, making amends, putting the other person's wants and needs first. What they were saying now was about what was at the heart of being married.

Cara conceded, "Though I could still wear my dress."

He chuckled. David took her hands and his smile fled, replaced by a look of such earnestness, even devotion, it took her breath away.

"Cara Rutledge, here, in this house of God, I promise I will seek out your opinion, your wishes, before I rush into making arrangements. I will take your feelings into consideration."

"David Wyatt, here, in this house of God, I promise I will share my feelings with you and not bottle them up inside. I will strive to be honest and fair. And kind."

"I vow to love you, care for you. And cherish your independence."

"I vow to love you, care for you. And cherish your generosity."

"I will be your husband. And love you forever."

Cara felt her throat thicken. These were the vows she'd wanted to make all along. Meaningful promises made to each other, just to each other, him and her.

"I will be your wife. And love you and only you, forever."

Then they both smiled and said at the same time, "And Hope."

Chapter Twenty-Two

Every year, millions of tons of plastic enter the oceans, of which the majority spills out from rivers. A portion of this plastic travels to ocean garbage patches, getting caught in a vortex of circulating currents. If no action is taken, the plastic will increasingly impact our ecosystems, health, and economies.

THE FOURTH OF July was the busiest holiday on the islands. The sun shone in a brilliant sky, bringing a flood of visitors onto the beach. The beach was littered with colorful towels. Unfortunately, after the sun went down and the fireworks celebrations were over, the visitors left and the beaches were littered with garbage, castaway chairs, tents, toys, cigarette butts, and plastic.

The fifth of July marked Linnea's first Beach Sweep for the South Carolina Aquarium. She arrived in the aquarium van with Annabelle and Toy, who'd volunteered to be her assistants in the sweep. She was anxious that the event be a success. It could make or break her reputation at the aquarium.

It was late afternoon and the day-trippers to the island were queuing up along the Connector to get back to the mainland after a day of sun. She parked in a reserved spot and looked at her friends in the front seat. Everyone was dressed in khaki shorts and a bright yellow aquarium T-shirt.

"Ready?" she asked.

"Let's do this," Annabelle said, and pushed open the door.

They stepped out of the van into a wall of heat.

"It feels like an oven," Toy said with a gasp, fanning herself with her hand.

"You could cook the proverbial egg on the pavement," agreed Annabelle.

"Just our luck. I hope the volunteers still show up," said Linnea. She looked up at the sky. It was 4:30 p.m. and the sun was still bright. "It'll cool down . . . eventually." She slammed the van door shut. "It's showtime. We might as well get set up."

July was the hottest month for the islands, and today was on course to become another record breaker. She went to open the back of the van. The metal was hot to the touch. There weren't the crowds of yesterday, but plenty of people were still hanging out at the beach. The local restaurants were offering discounted drinks and food for all the sweep volunteers, which Linnea hoped would keep everyone hydrated. She pulled her hair into a ponytail, and brushing back her hair from her forehead, she felt a sheen of sweat. She slipped on her SC Aquarium ball cap.

The three women worked together to pull out the Beach Sweep kits, the tent, the table, and bags of supplies. In short order, the sign-up station was set near the Front Beach entrance. They had nearly one hundred people signed up for the sweep, which would go on for three hours. Not everyone would come for the full time. All they asked was a minimum of thirty minutes. By five o'clock, Linnea counted more than fifty people gathering at the station. She gave Toy and Annabelle a thumbs-up.

Linnea called together her support team from the aquarium and their partners, the Isle of Palms Cleanup Crew. Annabelle handed out the Beach Sweep kits to the leaders. Linnea was proud of them. The kits included reusable sweep bags and gloves, clipboards, data sheets and pens for data collection, hand sanitizer, and first aid kits.

While organizing teams, she spotted Gordon approaching from the Front Beach path, where a steady stream of beachgoers made their way between the beach and the shops. He was dressed for the heat in a Surf-rider cap over dark sunglasses, his navy swimsuit, and a white, long-sleeved UV shirt of the type surfers wore to protect their skin. He waved when he spotted her. Behind him walked the tall blond man she'd seen with him the first morning she'd met him. His hair was salt-stiff, his tan golden. Women who passed him on the path looked back again to gawk. Linnea began to chuckle, but her smile froze when she spotted the tall, leggy woman following him under a large, black floppy hat. Pandora.

She hadn't seen her erstwhile friend since they'd had words. Pandora had not responded to Linnea's calls or texts, and she hadn't shown up at the last turtle walk. She'd thought Pandora had cut her off and certainly didn't expect to see her here today. With an effort, she dragged her gaze away and returned her attention to her job. She smiled at her waiting support staff.

"Good afternoon, y'all," Linnea began, mustering enthusiasm. "I don't have to tell you how excited we all are about this event. Our first Beach Sweep! Thank you for your help. Today the volunteers are here to collect trash, but we're also interested in the data we collect. This is a critical aspect to our research efforts. Picking up litter without data collection barely scratches the surface of the issues facing our communities."

As she spoke, she was aware of Gordon and Pandora joining the crowd to listen.

"This is our first sweep, but we hope to spread out across the state—to rivers, creeks, parks, anywhere crowds gather. Our collection of data is critical to identifying the most problematic debris hotspots and the kind of trash being tossed in order to develop solutions that benefit the communities. So, while the volunteers are out there collecting trash, we collect the data. Okay? Let's make it a good one!"

Everyone clapped their hands and moved out to gather their volunteers. The Beach Sweep was underway. There was a flurry of activity as more kits were handed out. More than sixty volunteers had shown up, a good start. She anticipated another forty to come later.

Annabelle sidled closer and said in a low voice, "Look who showed up."

Linnea at last had a free moment to look up. She saw Pandora waiting in the shade of the tent. She glanced around but didn't see Gordon.

"Yeah, I saw her earlier."

"What do you think she wants?"

"To help?" Linnea offered.

Annabelle scoffed. "Want me to find out?"

"No. Man the table, okay? I'll be right back."

Annabelle turned to another staff member. "Cole, would you man the ship a minute?" She smiled innocently at Linnea and followed her to Pandora's side.

Pandora offered a short wave as she approached. Linnea couldn't see her eyes behind the large dark sunglasses, so it was hard to gauge her expression. Then again, Pandora was hard to figure out in any situation.

She could be mercurial and one never really knew if she was being amusing, catty, or serious.

"I didn't expect to see you here," Linnea said. She skipped a beat. "But I'm glad you came."

Pandora faced Annabelle. "Oh, it's the bartender."

Annabelle smiled stiffly. "Oh, it's the bitch."

Pandora barked out a laugh. "Touché. I like her." Then, lifting her chin, she said, "Blimey, could you have picked a hotter day?" She began fanning herself with the beach sweep instruction paper.

"We have cold water available in the Windjammer," Linnea said in a professional tone.

Pandora shook her head. "I'm fine."

There was an awkward silence.

Pandora said to Annabelle, "Would you mind? I'd like a word with Linnea."

Annabelle looked at Linnea. When she nodded, Annabelle said, "I'll be at the table."

As she walked away, Pandora said, "I didn't think you needed a bodyguard."

"Of course not. We're here working. Speaking of which, I have to get back."

"Wait. Please."

Linnea crossed her arms and waited.

Pandora looked out at the ocean. "The other day . . ." She sighed. "I may have overreacted."

Linnea was surprised by the admission but said nothing.

"I was hurt," Pandora said, turning to face her. "You knew I liked Gordon. There are rules. . . . You shouldn't have gone after him."

"I didn't. He went after me."

"No matter," she said in a huff of frustration. "You went *with* him. *Sisters before misters.*"

Linnea's defense crumbled. "I'm sorry."

Pandora took off her sunglasses. Her large eyes revealed that she was sincere. "So am I. It was childish of me to walk off like that. I was miffed."

"What changed your mind?"

"Gordon came to see me."

Linnea opened her mouth to say something, but closed it again.

"He can be quite persistent, you know," Pandora said. "Besides, it was clear from the moment he started talking that he's mad for you. Poor man. He seemed quite anxious that I understood you'd never meant to cross me." She lifted her shoulders. "Never saw him like this before." She made a face. "I should hate you, but it was clear I never had a chance." She looked appraisingly at Linnea. "Do you like him?"

Linnea nodded. "A lot."

"Good." Pandora replaced her sunglasses. "I'd be put out if you didn't. He's a nice chap. I'd hate to see him hurt."

"I hardly think there's any worry about that. We've only started seeing each other and he's leaving soon."

"You don't know Gordon. He's not a player," Pandora said in all seriousness. "He doesn't gad about, if you understand what I mean. He's always so into his work. Traveling for work." She sighed. "I'm happy to see him with someone. I'd begun to wonder if he was destined to spend his whole life alone."

Linnea wondered about this revelation. She was unprepared to consider how deep Gordon might be getting into the relationship. She was only just recovering from John.

"But he's leaving in a few months. . . ."

"So am I. Supposedly. But that doesn't mean we won't come back, does it?"

Linnea stood awkwardly silent, considering the implications of all this.

"It all turned out for the best anyway," Pandora said in that lilting voice Linnea was relieved to hear again. It signaled the serious talk was over and Pandora intended to have a good time. "He introduced me to his roommate. He's quite a dish."

"I haven't met his roommate." Then she thought again. "Do you mean that big Viking?"

Pandora almost purred as she smiled. "Lars. From Sweden. He's a colleague of Gordon's here to study dolphins. And he surfs."

"You mean the Viking?" she repeated, incredulous. "My God, he's gorgeous."

Pandora narrowed her eyes and pointed her finger at her in faux anger. "You stay away from him. If you lure this one away, I swear, I'd have to feed you to the sharks."

Linnea smiled, relieved to have passed this hurdle with her friend. "Promise."

Pandora rose and looked toward the teams spreading out across the beach. "Well," she said and pulled out her SC Aquarium bag. "I guess I better get busy. What's that saying? No rest for the wicked?"

"You've come for the beach sweep?" Linnea asked, genuinely surprised. "I thought this wasn't your thing?"

Pandora slipped on her sunglasses, masking her face, but her emotion rang through her words. "One thing you should know about me, Linnea. I may put on a show, but I care. I'd have to be a fool not to see what's going on with plastic and climate change. I love Australia and it's burning up. Breaks my heart. If picking up plastic and litter will help, then I'm walking the walk. You saw Annabelle pick up trash and started doing it. I saw you, and now I'm doing it. It's a ripple effect. I may aspire to work with governments, but I don't underestimate the power of the individual. You showed me that. And I needed to understand it. So listen carefully because I'm only going to say this once." She paused, then said with feeling, "Thank you."

Chapter Twenty-Three

It is widely believed that hatchlings imprint the unique qualities of their natal beach either in the nest or during their trek across the sand. These could include smell, low-frequency sound, magnetic fields, the characteristics of seasonal offshore currents, and celestial cues. Studies have also shown that sea turtles have the ability to detect magnetic fields to help them navigate.

THE NEXT FEW weeks rolled in and out like the tide, steady and calm, and in a predictable manner. After all the emotional turmoil of June, Cara was grateful for the lull in July. Nothing remarkable happened. The sun rose and set each day. The routine was comforting, even healing.

She stood at the shoreline, her feet in the sea. The water was as warm as a bath and swirled around her ankles in a caressing manner. She remembered how her mother had always called the ocean her old friend. Standing here now, in the pink rays of the early morning, Cara at long last understood.

Mornings were her favorite time at the beach. Especially early, when the sand was cool and the sun was not yet hot. Then there was dusk, when the crowds had dispersed and only the peeps played tag with the waves.

These quiet, cooler moments were the only times she brought Hope out on the beach these days. Her daughter had been medically cleared from the measles and seemed her old self, frolicking in the waves with David. She didn't care if David accused her of hovering; after that scare, she wasn't taking any chances.

She smiled as she watched David lift a squealing Hope high into the air. Cara had learned the beauty of a peaceful life in the past few weeks. She'd always been goal-oriented, rising in the morning with a purpose, working hard and determinedly, and relaxing only when those goals were met. She liked being in control. Oh, how naïve she'd been.

Hope's illness had been a humbling lesson that no one, or no thing, controlled life. One could only take each day as it came, accepting whatever fate put in one's path. She should have learned that lesson when Brett was taken from her so suddenly. Yet instead of searching within, she'd become all the more focused on outward changes—moving to Chattanooga and starting fresh. Then Hope came into her life, and once again, her life changed. She'd opened her heart again, which in turn opened her up to accept the possibility of love. She'd loosened her tight-fisted grip on her rigid plans and goals and, with David, set out on a new course. But once again, the wily fates intervened. This last time, she'd been lost in a wave of uncertainty, tumbling, unable to breathe, not knowing which way was up or down. The more she struggled, the more she neared collapse.

Once again, it was love that had saved her. By letting loose of her anger and opening her heart to love—and forgiveness—she'd found the strength to survive. To persevere. And this time, she had the courage and determination—and perhaps the wisdom—to change her life once again. She had finally learned the hard-won lesson that life was like swimming in rip current. It was a strong moving current, rife with hazards. If one struggled against it, panicked and struck out blindly, that person could perish from exhaustion. If, on the other hand, one kept one's wits and continued swimming, letting go of fear and keeping afloat, eventually she would make it back to shore.

She'd spent the past several weeks on leave essentially floating. She wanted to stay home with Hope. She'd thought she was indispensable at the aquarium; that the conservation program would fall apart without her. She'd been wrong. Linnea was doing just fine. The aquarium was carrying on in her absence.

As she'd promised, Cara and Emmi had visited memory care centers and decided on one that was close to them and had a lovely view of a large pond that held several land turtles. At summer's end, they would introduce Flo to the home and gradually get her settled.

Cara had also begun scanning real estate advertisements and brochures. She hadn't yet contacted a real estate agent, but she'd accepted the inevitable that she was going to move from Primrose Cottage. This was a major step in letting go, she realized. Her mother had been right, as usual. The beach house was not so much a place as a state of mind.

Cara heard another squeal and laughed, watching Hope jump over a small wave at the shoreline. With her knees out, she looked like a jumping frog. She caught David's eyes and he waved. He stood tanned and tall. Was it her imagination or had his hair whitened more in the past few weeks? Men only looked more distinguished with white hair, she thought, with a twinge of resentment.

Squinting, she caught sight of Linnea walking along the shoreline toward them. Cara waved her arm in an arc over her head. She'd invited Linnea over to discuss the ongoing projects at the aquarium. Linnea had been doing a fabulous job in her absence, and it had been noticed by

Kevin Mills, the CEO, as well as the marketing department. Cara had received glowing letters praising the success of the Beach Sweep and her bag idea. As a result, seven other communities had signed up for the sweeps.

Linnea was wearing khaki shorts and the T-shirt from the aquarium. Her blond hair was pulled back in a braid under her aquarium ball cap. In her hand, she carried the aquarium's recycled trash bag; it was half-full. Cara was so proud of her niece, the way she'd taken charge and made the program her own. Cara knew that she was ready for the offer she was about to make her.

"Did you walk here from your house?" Cara asked, seeing her easy stride. "That has to be over five miles."

"Yep. I'm getting in shape. Wanted to get a good walk in." She turned and waved at David and Hope. "Hey, you two!" she called out. Turning back to Cara, she added, "She's like a little fish."

"I can't keep her out of the ocean. You were like that."

"Was I?" Linnea smiled. "Kindred spirits."

"Let's sit," Cara said, indicating the towels higher up on the sand. "I've got water."

"Love some, thanks."

They strolled up to where a scattering of towels was strewn under a large blue umbrella. Near a bag spilling out beach toys and a half-built sandcastle sat a small cooler. Cara opened this and retrieved a stainless-steel thermos. She poured water into reusable glasses, and handed one to Linnea, who drank thirstily. Once settled, the two women stretched out their legs.

Linnea looked out at David and Hope cavorting in the ocean. "You'd never know how sick she was a month ago."

"The resilience of children is amazing. As for me, I think I aged ten years."

Linnea looked at her closely, lowering her sunglasses. "You never age. It's not fair. But you have lost some weight."

"I know. It'll come back in time. I can't remember eating much when she was sick." It was her turn now to study her niece. Linnea sipped water and looked at the sea. Her profile was so much like Lovie's, Cara sometimes stared at her, remembering her mother. Linnea appeared more serene. She'd lost the cloud of sorrow that had hovered over her when she'd arrived home in April. Still slender, she looked more fit, even robust, from all the walking. Her skin was tanned, and she was bubbling with energy.

"You, on the other hand, are simply glowing."

Linnea smiled. "It's called happiness."

"Does this have to do with Gordon?"

Linnea nodded. "He's really wonderful. Kind."

"That's a good quality."

"The best," she agreed. "And yet . . . I can't quite put my finger on it. But somehow, he remains elusive. Like he's holding back."

Cara frowned; she didn't like the sound of that. "Holding back what? His affection?"

"Or some secret he's not telling me."

"Good God, he's not married?"

"He says he's not."

"Engaged?"

Linnea shook her head. "No, unless he's lying, of course. But it seems against type. Besides, Pandora says he's not attached and I trust she'd know."

"Then what?"

Linnea shook her head. "That's just it. I don't know. It's more a feeling. An intuition."

"Well, follow that. It never fails me." Cara tossed a bit of sand. "Too bad. I liked him."

"I like him too. Please, don't misunderstand. He's not devious or anything. Just the opposite. He's just . . . reserved. Maybe it's just his being British. But Pandora told me something I can't quite get out of my mind."

"What was that?"

"She said she'd wondered if he was destined to live out his life alone. That he didn't have many relationships because he was so dedicated to his work."

Cara considered that. She'd known many such men. And women. Women like her who had put all they had into their careers, only to find out at forty or fifty that their youth was spent, and they'd forgotten or not allowed time for relationships or children.

"That could be a phase. I was like that. How old is he?"

"Thirty-two."

"The same age as John."

Linnea's lips twitched. "Yes."

"By the way, any word from him?"

Linnea's face clouded. "Actually . . . he's been texting. And calling."

Cara was surprised that Linnea hadn't mentioned this. "What's he saying?"

Linnea reached into her pocket, pulled out her phone, and searched her text messages. Finding John's, she handed the phone to Cara. She wiped the sand from her palms, took it, and began to read the series of unanswered messages.

How are you? You okay?

Hey Miss Priss. Thinking of you. Call.

No response? I'm sorry the way things ended. Would like to talk.

Lin, place feels empty without you. Miss you.

I tried to call. You don't answer????

I get that you're mad. I was a fool. I hope you can forgive me. I always thought that, no matter what, we'd remain friends.

Hello???

What? You're ghosting me now?

Okay. Got it.

Cara lowered the phone and handed it back to Linnea. "That's a lot of texts. And you say he also tried to call?"

Linnea nodded. "Several times."

"Linnea, honey," began Cara. "You're avoiding him, obviously. But why? Because you don't like him any longer? Or . . . because you do?"

"I don't know," she said plaintively. "I'm confused. I was in love with John. I thought he was the one. We lived together. And then, we didn't." She shrugged. "That's not easy to get over. Or forget."

"And now there's Gordon."

"Gordon," Linnea repeated. "I didn't expect to feel so strongly so quickly. Not after John. But I do."

"You don't have to decide, you know. John's in California. Gordon is here. See what happens."

"That's what I'm trying to do. But every time I get a message from John, it's like this little arrow of doubt pricks me. I can't reply. Not yet. I don't know what to say."

"Well," Cara said, moving her legs, "it sounds to me like you won't have to worry about any more messages coming too soon."

Linnea huffed. "No. I guess not. I hope he doesn't just pop home for a surprise visit. To his mother."

"If he does, you'll deal with it. If there's one thing I've learned in the past month, it's that you can't control what life will bring. You can only deal with each issue with equanimity and an open heart."

"And how does one do that?"

Cara smiled. "Look at the ocean a lot."

Linnea chuckled. "Thanks. I can do that."

"There's something else I'd like to talk with you about," she began, moving the discussion in a new direction. "Along the lines of accepting life as it comes, I want you to know that I'm stepping down. I'm leaving the aquarium."

Linnea's mouth slipped open. "What? B-but . . ." she stammered. "Why? You love your job!"

"I should think that's obvious," Cara replied kindly. Then, in all seriousness, she tried to explain what had been a life-changing decision. "The moment when Hope turned the corner and opened her eyes, I stared into them and realized fully how close I'd come to losing the most important person in the world to me. And how quickly the last few years had passed, and how quickly the next several would as well. I swore I'd enjoy every moment I could with my daughter." She smiled. "The decision came easily."

Linnea didn't speak. She appeared to be trying to understand.

"I've decided to be a full-time mother to Hope. And wife to David. At least until Hope is in elementary school. After that, who knows? Again, life changes. The best-laid plans, and all that. Don't look so shocked," she said with a light laugh at Linnea's expression. "I've worked all my life, since I was eighteen. I've never taken a year off. I want this time. I need it. I'm enjoying waking up in the morning and just . . . being. Not having a to-do list in my head, a timetable to follow, someone to call, something to arrange. It's transforming."

Linnea removed her sunglasses and looked at Cara, her blue eyes searching. "You do seem calmer."

Cara laughed. "I don't know if it's working *that* fast," she chided. "But I am happy. And yes, I do feel calmer. Which brings me to why I called you over. I wanted to tell you personally about my decision. You've been doing such a great job holding down the fort while I've been gone. I can't thank you enough. I never worried a moment, and that's saying a lot from me. Anyway, I had a long talk with Kevin, told him my decision, and . . ." She paused. "We'd like to offer the position of director of the conservation program to you."

Linnea gasped and brought her hand to her mouth. "I can't believe this."

"Believe it," Cara said with a laugh. "You earned it. And you're practically running the show on your own now anyway."

"Perhaps, but there's a lot I don't know."

Cara heard the panic edging Linnea's voice and was sympathetic. Summer was the busy season, and they'd been overworked even with the two of them. The prospect of handling it all alone while on a learning curve would be overwhelming.

"I'll come in once a week starting Monday and continue through the fall. We'll work out the date. After that, I can stay on as a consultant when needed, or join in for special projects. As you request it," she emphasized. She didn't want Linnea to think that she would be running the department from satellite. "I'll work out those consultant details with Kevin. But I'm not abandoning you. Next summer, you can get your own assistant for the Beach Sweeps." She put her hand on Linnea's. "You'll be great. Honestly, you're the most qualified for the job. I started the position, but now it's yours. Make it your own."

Linnea leaned back on her arms and stared out at the sea. She turned. "Aunt Cara, can you believe how pathetic I was when I got here last April? And now, thanks to you, I've got my dream job."

"I merely facilitated. You did the work. And trust me," Cara added with a sympathetic pat, "the work is just beginning. It's your baby now. You'll bring work home with you, dream about it, wake with ideas in your head. But don't forget to enjoy life along the way. It's the little moments that count."

She turned to look at Cara. "I won't. And I *do* thank you, Aunt Cara. For the job, the car. For your love and your support when I needed it. For everything."

Cara smiled, feeling the torch passed. "You're welcome."

Linnea lifted her arms high into the air and shouted a loud "Woot!" "I can't believe it!" she said again. Lowering her arms she added, "And to think I was worried about the men in my life. Well," she said, sitting straighter, jutting out her chin, and crossing her legs. "Not anymore. Look out, world. Now it's my turn."

❀   ❀   ❀

NIGHT WAS FALLING. Linnea sat on the deck of Gordon's beach house looking out at the sky darkening over the sea. Cumulous clouds, thick and menacing, were gathered like a great squadron, promising rain. A gust of wind stirred her hair, rustling the panicles of the nearby sea oats on the dunes, chasing away the bugs. She loved sitting outdoors awaiting an impending storm. She could feel the drop in barometric pressure, the moisture in the air, almost taste the sweetness of the rain. Thunder rumbled in the distance like the warning growl of an approaching beast.

The ocean was turbulent. Whitecaps formed on the waves. Linnea tucked her legs up on the wicker settee.

Gordon stepped out onto the deck, two snifters in his hand. He paused to close the door behind him.

"Sounds like it's getting closer." He bent to hand her a snifter, then settled beside her.

She lowered her feet to make room for him on the small settee, enjoying the feel of his shoulder against hers.

"They've left, then?" she asked. Pandora and Lars had shared a dinner of curry with them. Pandora was mad for curry and had spent hours preparing the dinner. It was delicious, hot and spicy. Linnea had drunk several glasses of wine to cool her mouth.

"They have," Gordon said, stretching out his legs. "Pandora's left a terrible mess in the kitchen."

Linnea chuckled to herself. Pandora might be a great cook, but she never considered cleaning up. She and Lars had tickets for a show in the city. Gordon and she had declined, preferring to spend the evening alone. There were not that many days left of Gordon's stay, and they were very much alike in that way.

"Well, she cooked. It's only fair we clean." She put her nose to the snifter and inhaled the heady scent. "They get along, don't they?"

Gordon just lifted his shoulders.

"What?" she asked. "You don't think it will last?"

"Pandora and Lars?" he scoffed, and shook his head. "Hardly. They're both too footloose and fancy-free. As brilliant as they are, each of them has the attention span of a flea when it comes to the opposite sex. Always flitting to the next."

"Okay, I know Pandora is a terrible flirt, but I've only seen her with Lars. She's not dating anyone else." She paused. "That I know of."

Gordon only shrugged and took a sip of his cognac.

She wondered about all the men who'd encircled Pandora at Darby's party. "Have you and she ever . . ."

He shook his head. "No," he said with gusto. "Like I said. Brother and sister."

"What about Lars?"

"Uh, my darling, you do know that they're sleeping together . . ."

"Stop," she said, bumping her shoulder with his. "I meant, what's he like with women?"

"Lars?" He snorted. "I can't count the women I've seen him with. Bees to honey, that one."

Linnea wasn't surprised. She'd seen for herself his effect on women. Pandora's nickname for Lars was Thor. Linnea was never attracted to men who were attractive in the ultra-sexy manner. For her, it was all about the muscle between the ears, not the arms or chest. Brains before brawn.

She turned to study Gordon. His good looks were quiet more than flashy. He was not handsome as much as attractive, with the seemingly shy boyishness that women often fell for. For being so smart, he was not wise in the way of women. She thought of what Pandora had said about him not seeing anyone.

"And you?"

He turned to look into her eyes. His eyes had a way of capturing her gaze as his face grew solemn. "I don't like the game of chase. The thrill of the hunt. The trophies on the wall."

"Yes, I remember. You don't hunt."

"Well, I wouldn't say that exactly. For my research I'm always hunting. But as concerns the fair sex, let's say I am more choosy. I wait. Take my time. And when I'm ready"—he lifted a finger and tapped her nose—"I take careful aim."

She smiled. "Do you always bag your game?"

"I don't know yet."

She took his meaning and looked away, taking another sip of the cognac.

"Why don't you move in here, with me?" he asked.

She looked at her drink. "Why change things?"

"You're here most of the time anyway."

She shook her head. "I've tried that before and it didn't work out."

"I'm not John."

She looked at him, saw the hurt. "No, you're not. But still . . . You're leaving in a few weeks. I don't want to be chased out of a place again, have to retreat to my parents' house."

"Does that mean"—he paused to swirl his drink—"if I ask you to come back to England with me, you wouldn't consider it?"

Her breath caught in her throat. She wasn't prepared for this question. Hadn't seen it coming. And yet, the answer came easily.

"First, what a wonderful invitation. I'm honored that you asked, thrilled that you want me to come."

"But . . ."

"But no. Not now. I can't."

"I see." He took a long sip of his drink. "Has this got anything to do with John?"

Linnea turned slightly so she could fully see his face. A faint color flamed on his cheeks, and she saw the hurt he was trying hard to conceal. "Gordon," she said gently, "this has to do with *me*. I'm finally on my path," she told him. "I have a job I love and I'm good at what I do. People depend on me. And I still have so much to learn. I can't just give it all up. You asked if it has anything to do with John. Only in that, because of him, I learned that I'm not going to drop everything just to be with a man. Not to California." She waited until he looked at her. "Not to England. This is my turn. I have to work on me now."

He was silent for a while as they sat and looked out at the sea. She felt the static in the air, full of unuttered statements and declarations.

At last he spoke again. "I did try to extend my stay."

"You did?"

He shook his head. "Couldn't be done. I'm scheduled to teach at the college back in England. That couldn't be changed, I'm afraid."

"Professor Carr," she said, trying to imagine him in his robes. It was surprisingly easy. "So I guess it's *Goodbye, Mr. Chips*."

He laughed. "Hardly. Good movie, though."

"Classic."

They sat in silence a moment.

"But," he added with a hint of enthusiasm, "I did manage to arrange to return in April. I've got the funding for another season at the College of Charleston."

Linnea felt a surge of adrenaline and leaned closer. "For how long?"

"For the summer. Like this year."

"You'll be back," she exclaimed, and kissed him soundly.

"I hoped you'd be pleased," he said, smiling.

"I am. But come to think of it," she said with suspicion, "you had to be more than just hopeful. You had to be pretty sure I'd be thrilled. I mean, to go ahead and arrange it all. Cheeky," she added, using a British word.

"Well," he said, "it *is* my grant, regardless."

She made a face and playfully punched his arm. "Well, we'll see if I'm still available."

He slipped an arm around her and grew more serious. "I don't want to wait till April. Can you come to England for a visit?"

The thought stilled her breath. "I don't know. I suppose so. It depends on when. I'm working."

"We can work out the dates, but I was thinking around the Christmas holidays. London is always so festive, and I have a long break." He moved a strand of hair from her forehead. "I could introduce you to my family."

Linnea licked her lips. "You want me to meet your family?"

He nodded. "I do. I know they'll love you." His smile came slowly. "Almost as much as I do."

She looked into his eyes, to be certain he wasn't teasing her or being flippant. She saw a vulnerability there. He was waiting for her to say something.

"You love me?" she asked in a near whisper.

He cupped her face. "I love you."

She couldn't speak. She knew what he wanted her to say. But she couldn't say the words. Not yet. Not to anyone.

So, instead of words, she moved to put her lips against his. Gently at first, then she leaned into him letting their bodies mold together.

Pulling back, he said to her in a low voice, "I know it's only been the summer. And I know you're still getting over your last relationship. I'm not rushing you. But I'm not letting go of you either. Please say you'll come. I'll send you tickets. Just board the plane."

"I'll come," she said softly. "This winter. During your holiday. I promise. I don't want to be separated too long, either."

He released a satisfied smile, like someone who had just been handed a lifeline in a turbulent ocean. Then, tilting his head toward the house door, he lifted his brow in question.

She nodded.

Gordon shifted to take hold of their drinks and set them on the small table. Then he took her hand and helped her to her feet, encircling her waist as she rose.

"Lead the way," she murmured. And took a step forward.

Chapter Twenty-Four

The Endangered Species Act, passed in 1973, was enacted to halt the rapid loss of plant and animal life. A species is considered endangered if it is in danger of extinction. A species is considered threatened if it is likely to become endangered. Once a species is declared threatened or endangered, the ESA ensures that it will be protected, and all efforts will be made to assist in its recovery. Four of the seven species of sea turtles are deemed endangered; three are threatened.

IN THE SOUTH, August marked the end of summer. By the middle of the month the school bells called reluctant children into the classrooms as relieved parents packed lunches and settled into another year of routine. Labor Day marked the beginning of fall for the South more surely than the autumnal equinox.

Summer had always been Cara's favorite season. She loved the sun and the beach. Waking early for a walk by the surf, watching people cavort on the sand, barbecues, ice-cold drinks, fresh fruit, licking ice cream cones on long walks, boat rides and dolphins, listening to beach music while sitting under the stars. A time to swim, laugh, take vacations. And, of course, turtle season.

Yet it was in summer that she'd also experienced her greatest losses.

Brett had died in the beginning of a summer. Her mother at summer's end. This past summer she'd almost lost her daughter.

She leaned against the pergola on her back porch. And still, life went on. She'd made the right decision giving up her job at the aquarium to stay home with Hope. She was learning to slow down, to not set such lofty goals, to appreciate that these were precious days that she didn't want to miss.

The wedding had been canceled at Lowndes Grove. Deposits were lost. There were no regrets. As far as she was concerned, she and David had said their vows in the hospital chapel. Anything else would be a formality. They'd talked about having a ceremony, some smallish party that they could celebrate with their family and friends. Perhaps in the fall, she thought. Or at Christmas. Hope could wear red.

She smiled at the thought; she wasn't quite ready for winter. Autumn was an introspective season. Perhaps fall would become her new favorite season. Then she thought of hurricanes, and banished the thought. The worst part of August, September, and October was that they marked the peak of hurricane season. She shuddered and looked over the lowcountry landscape she called home. The roses of her pergola were aflame, the panicles of the sea oats were fat and golden, and wildflowers dotted the dunes again, now that the blistering heat of summer had passed. Soon flocks of birds would begin their migration and monarch butterflies their perilous journey south.

"Good-bye, summer," she said aloud.

Cara looked at her watch, then glanced again over her shoulder toward the beach house. She and David were expected at an open house for the home that Palmer had built. He'd found funding and finished it, great news indeed. They were going to be late, she thought, seeing it was already 2 p.m. David was inside on the phone; a business call he said he couldn't miss. Hope was inside with him, playing with dolls. Cara was ready to go, dressed in her tried-and-true petal-pink, boat-necked shift. She sipped her iced tea and resolved not to be annoyed. She wouldn't live by the clock anymore, she reminded herself. Besides, how could they be late for an open house that went from two to four o'clock?

Across the road, cars were already beginning to slow down as they passed the house, and some pulled into the driveway. She watched some man putting a bunch of balloons on the OPEN HOUSE sign. *Idiot,* she thought. Didn't he know that balloons could escape their hold and be carried out to the sea by the wind? Once deflated, they would fall into the ocean, adding to the plastic problem—and worse, underwater the balloons looked like jellyfish, a favorite food of sea turtles. They'd eat them, and eventually, the plastic could kill them. She resolved to take the darn things down when she got there, and she'd give the realtor an education.

But it certainly was a beautiful house, she thought, admiring the long white porches, the redbrick trim, the turret that she was especially fond of. She hadn't been through the house since Hope's illness and was curious, even eager, to see the finished product. She hoped someone nice would buy it—the house deserved a good owner. Palmer had risen to the occasion once again. He'd found a builder who would buy the house and finish it, for a good price too. Cara had made a small profit from the sale, but Palmer had earned more than money: he'd regained his self-respect. Once again, he'd joined AA, and with Julia by his side, he was building another house, smaller this time, in Mount Pleasant. But it was a start.

Lessons learned, she thought again. Knowledge was acquired. Wisdom earned.

"Cara?" called David. "Are you ready to go?"

She turned and felt her heart flutter at the sight of him. He stood in the door of the beach house, Hope in his arms. His hair had more white strands mingled in the dark. His face was not as tanned as it had been early in the summer. But he never failed to take her breath away. She thought he looked particularly stunning today in his navy blazer, tan pants, and crisp white shirt.

"Isn't an Hermès tie a bit much for an open house?" she asked as she drew near.

"I thought I might take my girls out for dinner after," he replied.

"Lovely. But I'm not dressed up," she said, looking down at her pale-pink shift, one she'd worn so many times over the summer it was beginning to look a bit tired.

"You look beautiful."

"No matter about me—look at our girl!" she exclaimed. "She changed to a fancy dress."

"You know Hope. Once she makes her mind up . . ." He held out Cara's bag, which was more carryall than purse, holding all manner of must-have items for Hope when they left the house.

"Shall we go?" He moved to the back stairs.

"We're walking?"

David laughed. "Cara, it's across the street."

"Okay." She looked down at her heels. "One minute." She hurried to the porch to grab her flip-flops, tossed them on the floor, and stepped into them. She picked up her heels. "I'll stick the sandals in my purse when we get there." She looked at his navy jacket. "You won't be too hot? It's eighty-nine degrees."

"I'll be fine. Mind your step," he said as he guided them down the porch stairs.

They made their way along the beach path to Ocean Boulevard. The row of mansions created a pastel wall in front of the ocean. Only the remaining lot that Russell Bennett had long ago put into conservancy remained open, covered in wildflowers, providing sanctuary not only to the sea turtles but to the wandering eye of every passerby who hoped for a glimpse of the great sea. The brilliant blue sky was reflected in the water. It seemed to sparkle in the surf like shards of diamonds.

When they arrived, the driveway was full of cars.

"Hold on," Cara said, her gaze focused on the real estate sign in front of the house. She took off across the fresh sod straight for the sign and tugged at the strings of the balloons attached there. Cursing, she tried to untie them.

"Mama, I want a balloon!" exclaimed Hope.

"I'm trying to take them down," she called back. She swore under her breath. They were all knotted tight. In frustration, she gave up and walked across the grass to join David and Hope on the driveway. "I'll have to come back with a pair of scissors. I'm going to give that agent a piece of my mind. I don't think balloons are even allowed on the island."

"Come on, dear," David said, prodding her along. "You'll get them taken down. But it is a bit warm out here."

Still fuming about the balloons, Cara accompanied him toward the house. Palmer had created a lovely walk covered with a pergola in the Italian style, similar to the one Brett had created for Primrose Cottage. The red roses, so much like the variety at her own beach house, were blooming.

"Isn't that charming," Cara said, moved almost to tears as they walked underneath. "What a nice touch."

"It's a handsome house, don't you think?" David asked.

"Yes. I've always loved it. The design is exquisite. I haven't seen the finished inside yet."

They walked a few more steps. "Is this something in line with what you'd like for us?" he asked.

"Oh, yes," she replied. "It's lovely. Perfect." Then, always practical, "And off the beach, we should find better prices."

They reached the door, and Cara slipped on her heels as David tried to open it. "It's locked." He rang the doorbell.

"I don't think you need to ring the bell," Cara told him. "It's an open house. Unless perhaps it's by appointment only?" She glanced over her shoulder at the sign. "But it says OPEN HOUSE." She looked at the driveway. "And it's full of cars."

The front door swung open with a swish. Cara was stunned to see Palmer standing there. He too wore a blue blazer over his pale-pink silk polo shirt. He was spit-polished and beaming.

"Welcome!" he exclaimed.

"Look at you!" Cara said. "Are you an agent now, too?"

"It's a bit more complicated," he replied with a grin. "Come on in. I want to show you the house." He stepped back, swinging the door open wide.

Cara took a step inside. She first saw the long, large spread of windows and a burst of sunlight coming from the ocean vista. She always loved walking into a house and seeing the vista first. It took her breath away. Then, as though in a fog, she became aware of people in the living room. Lots of people. Men and women. Children. As the faces came into focus, she froze. Not just people, she realized. People she knew.

"Surprise!" The room roared as one with the shout.

Cara stood rock-still, her mouth agape, unsure of what was happening. She looked behind her to see if anyone else had walked in. Confused, she turned to David. He looked as stunned as she did. Hope was kicking her legs in his arms, excited, begging to get down. Rory had run up to his grandfather's legs and wrapped his arms around them. Cara turned to Palmer, eyes wide as the crowd gathered closer, laughing, sipping champagne, celebratory.

"Surprise, little sister," Palmer said, laughing now.

"Will someone tell me what's going on?" she exclaimed.

"Welcome to your wedding." Palmer's arms were extended.

"My what?" Cara looked again to David. "Did you know about this?"

David shook his head, his face revealing as much confusion as she was certain hers did.

Palmer kissed her cheek, beaming. "It's time to celebrate, little sister! You've put this wedding off long enough. And now that our little lady Hope is back to her old mischievous self, it was high time this man made an honest woman of you."

Cara gazed again at David. He was surrounded by well-wishers, kissing and hugging him.

"But . . . how?" she stammered, overcome.

"We knew you'd get around to a ceremony," Palmer continued. "Someday."

Julia stepped close to place a kiss on her cheek. Cara's were flushed with excitement. "We just helped things along."

Palmer stepped closer and spoke sotto voce. "What better place to do it than here, in this house, your gift to me?" he said. His face filled with emotion. "A gift I'll never forget. One that was from our beloved mother." He paused as tears flashed. "It's the least I could do." Then, stepping back, he flung out his arms again exuberantly and indicated the room filled with flowers and smiling people. "It's just your friends and family. Exactly what you said you wanted."

"I'm speechless!" Cara exclaimed.

"No time for talk anyway," Emmi said, linking arms. "Let's get this party started."

Cara realized Emmi was wearing the green maid of honor dress she'd selected and a circlet of flowers in her hair. "You knew!"

"Of course I did," Emmi said, giving her a quick kiss. "Everyone knew. Except you and David, of course. That's why it's called a surprise party." She laughed again as Linnea and Heather drew close.

Suddenly Cara was surrounded by her girlfriends, laughing and giggling and herding her to another room. Emmi held her around the shoulders. Linnea had taken her arm. Julia ushered her from behind. They guided her through a room of smiling faces. She caught a glimpse of a wooden arch in the center of the living room bedecked with white flowers. Flowers were everywhere—lilies and hydrangeas, freesia and stock, in gorgeous arrangements. They entered a large bedroom that overlooked the ocean. Given the size and magnificence, it had to be the master. A mahogany four-poster king bed dominated one wall and faced the windows. Lying on it were delicate undergarments, all lace and ribbons.

Heather handed her a glass of pink champagne. When all the women had a glass, Emmi raised hers and made a toast.

"To Cara, the best friend, sister, aunt, mother, and soon-to-be wife."

They raised their flutes in unison. "To Cara!"

Cara sipped the wine, feeling the bubbles in her brain.

"This can't really be happening."

"Why not?" asked Linnea. "You've done things for us all your life, gone out of your way to help us. Why not let us do something for you for once?"

Cara looked at Emmi. "Be honest. Did David arrange this?"

Emmi laughed. "For once, no. He didn't. We thought it was his turn to be surprised. Palmer arranged everything. With Julia."

Cara turned to her sister-in-law. "You shouldn't have."

"Oh, but it was so much fun!"

"Who all is out there?" Cara asked.

"The usual suspects." Julia replied with a wink.

"Family and friends. Just like you requested," Emmi said. "Enough questions. Now, hurry up, dear. You really must dress. Your wedding awaits you."

Cara heard a sound to her right and, turning, saw Linnea coming forward, carrying her wedding dress. The beautiful sheath of silk, the gorgeous creamy color, was as lovely as she remembered. Beside her, Heather carried the veil, a long swath of fairy-light gossamer. Tears sprang to her eyes, and putting her hands to her face, Cara let down her guard and began to cry. Her girls encircled her, holding her tight, laughing, crying.

"Oh. My. God," she stammered, wiping the tears from her face. "Where's that glass of champagne?"

Emmi thrust the tall flute with the delightfully bubbling pinkness into her hand.

Cara raised her glass in the air. "You girls . . . you wonderful, beautiful, strong, powerful, bighearted women. My best friends, my family. I could not have reached this moment without all of you at my side. You've helped me each step of the way. I love y'all so much." The sentiment became overwhelming. Cara felt the tears begin to stream. "I'm getting married!"

�   ✻   ✻

CARA LOOKED AT the diamond eternity band on her left finger. It caught the last rays of sunlight at the end of this perfect day.

She was a married woman. Again. She'd woken up this morning Cara Rutledge and would go to sleep Cara Rutledge-Wyatt. She'd signed her name with a hyphen. A compromise, she thought. Wasn't that what marriage was all about?

She looked around the house. The sun was setting somewhere off in the west. The ocean was deepening in color, while the sky blazed with streaks of deep blue and gold. All was quiet now. The guests had left, calling out their good-byes and congratulations and leaving a tower of unfinished cake, empty champagne bottles, glasses on every surface, and a pile of gaily wrapped gifts in the corner. Two to four, the invitation to the open house had said. The party had lasted until eight. She laughed. Her wedding had been a smash. One for the books. Who knew?

The front door opened, and looking up, she saw David walking in, a bit unsteady on his feet. She opened her arms and he stepped into them.

"They're gone," he said in a low voice. His kiss was deep and amorous, far too much for a house full of people. "Heather has Hope for the night."

He lifted her hand and gazed at the diamond band that sat beneath the stunning diamond engagement ring. "So, we did it, eh, Mrs. Rutledge-Wyatt?"

She groaned. "Lord, that's a mouthful. What have I done?"

He laughed, a sonorous sound deep in his chest that she always found both sexy and comforting. "You can always change it to Wyatt."

She looked into his eyes. "I can, can't I?" She released herself from his arms and went to gather three glasses sitting on the hall table.

Nightfall was settling in fast. Cara and David walked from room to room, picking up glasses and plates, moving at a leisurely pace. She couldn't bear to talk anymore. Her cheeks hurt from smiling. She simply wanted to walk the house, empty now, so she could see the details of the woodwork, the heart-pine floors, the built-in bookshelves.

There was a lot of square footage to the house, but it didn't feel *big*. Curves, interesting nooks, surprise gardens, walkways to different wings, made the house feel cozy in the European manner. Yet it was distinctly southern lowcountry. She readily saw why it appealed to David. He appreciated good architectural design, and like his house on Dewees, this one made her feel connected to the outdoors.

She took her time, especially in the kitchen.

"This is the crown jewel of a home," David said. "Where the lady of the house reigns."

"You mean the cook, the baker, the chief bottle washer?" She looked at all the top-of-the-line appliances, the well-built cabinets, the Viking stove. "I can hardly boil water. But I must say, if ever I wanted to, I would want to in this kitchen. It's perfect." She pointed at the brick pizza oven. "You'd have fun with that."

"I would." He laughed. "I make a mean pizza dough."

They moved on to the other wing of the house, where three bedrooms nestled. She paused in one with gables. "This would be perfect for Hope," she said.

As she walked through the rooms, Cara let her fingertips graze the woodwork, the counters, the stair railing. The house was a *tabula rasa*, a blank paper on which a buyer could create anything she wanted.

"What do you think of the place?" he asked her. "Now that you've spent a day in it?"

"What's not to love? It's a perfect house." She turned to face him. "We should find a house like this, I think."

He went to the bar and found a chilled bottle of champagne. He opened it, releasing the loud signature pop. Cara walked across the room to join him. She found two clean glasses and set them on the counter. He poured the wine to the top, waited for the bubbles to subside, then topped it off.

"To my wife," he said, raising his glass.

"To my husband," Cara said, clinking his. Their eyes met over the rims of their glasses.

"I'm exhausted," she confessed, kicking off her heels. She looked at her wedding gown, still as gorgeous as when she'd first put it on. "It *is* a pretty dress. I hate to take it off."

"Then don't," he said. "Yet." He took her hand. "Let's catch the last view of the day."

He led her to the deck and helped her to sit in a cushy chair. The last rays of the sun streaked over the blackened sea. She leaned back into the cushion and sipped her wine, reflecting on the day.

"Hope looked precious sprinkling the flower petals, didn't she? So serious."

David nodded. "I think she felt as special in her fancy dress as Emmi did."

Cara laughed, remembering. Someday, she hoped, Emmi would find love again too.

"I have to admit," he said, "while I thought I wanted the grand wedding, I don't think any wedding could have surpassed this one. Palmer did us up proud."

"And think, no one could have jumped in the pool at Lowndes Grove," she said, thinking how Bo had jumped in, fully dressed, on a dare.

"At least he waited until after the ceremony," David quipped.

Images of the wedding played through her mind like a movie—the simple ceremony under the arch of flowers officiated by their friend Captain Robert . . . a trio of musicians playing as Palmer walked her down the makeshift aisle . . . her bouquet of white roses, the tiered wedding cake, a house full of white and blue hydrangeas. Julia had quietly informed her that all the hydrangeas were going into the garden after the wedding.

"Are you hungry?" he asked.

Cara shook her head. "Not really. Tired . . ."

David rose. "I'll be right back."

Hearing the porch door open a moment later, Cara turned her head to see David cross the deck. In his hand he carried a small blue Tiffany box. She caught her breath. She had no gift for him. David stood before her, looking at the box thoughtfully, then handed it to her.

"This is my wedding gift to you," he said with some import. "I didn't know I'd be giving it to you today. . . . The wedding was truly a surprise. But I had this gift, well, arranged. Anyway, this is the right moment to give it to you."

She took the box in her hand, saw the pretty white Tiffany bow, and looked up into his eyes. "I don't have a gift for you."

He shook his head. "No matter. Open it," he told her, his eyes full of anticipation. "I'll explain."

Cara gingerly tugged at the ribbon and watched the soft bow slide apart and fall to the ground. The box was bigger than a ring box, too small for a necklace. A bracelet, perhaps? A brooch? She couldn't imagine what it could be. She lifted off the top and handed it to David. Then, with her fingertips, she lifted the crisp white tissue paper. Nestled inside was a single key. Not a fancy golden facsimile of a key that she would wear around her neck. But a real key. The kind she'd get at any hardware store. Picking it up, she saw that it had the name *Schlage* on it.

"What's this?" she asked.

"It's the key to my heart," David said.

She chuckled and closed her fingers around it. "David, you old romantic!"

His eyes kindled and he took her hand. "Come with me."

"Where are we going?"

"You'll see."

He led her back into the house. They crossed the living room, past the large fireplace, to the entrance hall that was the turret. It had a high ceiling with wood gables that arched dramatically overhead. He went to the front door and opened it. Night had fallen and the sky outside was as dark as black velvet.

"Where are we going?" she repeated.

"I think that depends on you," he said. Reaching to the wall, he flicked on the porch lights. She saw the six rocking chairs of hunter green, the hanging pots of fern, and her favorite red geraniums in big black iron urns by the front door.

"Do you have the key?" he asked.

"Yes." She opened her palm, revealing the metal key.

"See if it fits."

She gave him a questioning glance.

He didn't reply.

Cara bent closer to the door handle and slipped the key into it. The key fit perfectly. When she turned it to the right, the dead bolt came forth.

"This is the key to the house," she said, feeling a bit dazed.

"Yes."

She slowly straightened and stared at him, unsure what to say.

David stood at the open door, his face solemn, his expression hopeful. "I bought this house for you, with no strings attached. It's yours to do with as you wish. If you want to live here, we will. If you want to sell it, you can. It's your gift. It's your choice."

"*You* bought the house?" she asked.

He nodded. "Last month, Palmer called me. He wasn't trying to sell me the house," he hastened to add. "He was in a jam and was asking my advice, friend to friend. He had to put the house on the market, as you well know. We talked about the market, the economy, stocks. He wanted to make the right decision at the right time."

Cara listened quietly.

David reached up to scratch his head. "Now, I knew you liked this house. A lot. You'd said so every time you looked at it—how pretty it was, how much you liked the design."

Cara couldn't deny it. She felt her heart beat faster in anticipation.

"So, I came to see it with an inspector I know. One of the best in the business. We took a good, hard look. For me, it had to be a solid investment. I have to say, this house is built like a rock. Palmer knows what he's doing. He was careful, made good choices. And what really sold me, he installed up-to-date hurricane protection." He looked at her. Neither of them had to remark that, for Cara, who was terrified of hurricanes, that was a salient point. "In my mind, this house was a good investment. There aren't many lots left on Isle of Palms, and some of the houses have been built so flimsily, the first hard storm will blow them down."

"You were the buyer?" Cara asked again, breathless.

"Yes. But, Cara, I don't want you to think that I was doing it solely to be Mr. Fix-It again. I'm not forcing the decision on you. If you don't want it, just say so and we will sell it." He stepped closer and slipped his arm around her waist. "But frankly, I admit I am hoping you'd like to live here. I fell in love with it the first time I walked through it. I can see living here with you. Raising Hope here. Having family parties. Growing old together. And look," he added, turning to point to the beach house across the road. "Your beach house is right there. You don't have to sell it. You shouldn't. I know that cottage means everything to you. And Emmi is right across the street too. And Flo. You can be near them."

She swallowed hard. It was all too perfect.

"Keep the beach house. Or rent it. Whatever you want. And maybe, when Hope grows up, she'd like to live there."

He was warming to the topic. If only he knew she was already swooning.

"Just think," he continued, "we can sit on this front porch here and maybe someday watch our children living across the street. And when we get very old and want to downsize, we'll switch houses, and we can live in the beach house and sit on the porch and watch our grandchildren in this house." He stretched out his hand, pointing. "I thought I'd extend the pergola to go all the way to the road. Then continue it to the beach house porch. We'd be connected. Two houses, the beach house and this one, side by side on Ocean Boulevard."

She was utterly and completely beguiled. She raised her fingers to his lips. "Stop! Yes! I want to live here. You had me at the key."

He stood blinking, unsure of his victory. "You want the house?"

"I do." She smiled. "Seems I'm saying that a lot today."

He took her hand and kissed the ring. "There are still a lot of decisions to make. It's only a shell. The colors, the drapes, the furniture, of course. All the furniture in here now is rented for staging. It disappears in the morning." He glanced toward the bedroom. "Except for the bed."

She followed his gaze to the hall leading to the master bedroom. "The four-poster?"

"I bought that. For us."

She laughed and shook her head in amazement. "Husband, are we spending the night in this house?"

"We can."

"How did you know I'd say yes?"

"I didn't. I hoped."

She brought his hand to her mouth and gently kissed his knuckles. "Yes."

He took her hand. "Shall we try out our new bed, Mrs. Rutledge-Wyatt?"

Chapter Twenty-Five

Loggerhead nests are trending upward, with 2019 being a record year. The nesting females are believed to have been born in the 1980s when stringent nest protection was underway. The number of females suggests even more nests for the future. Obstacles remain, but hope springs eternal.

CARA LAY IN the big four-poster and watched the morning sun create a prism of color in her diamond. She heard the thump of the plumbing and gush of water as the shower turned on. She sighed, thinking how from this morning forward, listening to her husband dressing would become part of her morning routine.

She rose and walked to the closet. Her friends had thought of everything. Last night she'd found a lovely white negligee, toiletries, and a change of clothes waiting for her. She slipped on the silk robe and walked at a leisurely pace from the bedroom into the great entrance hall. Sun poured into the house and she looked about as one in a dream. This was her new home, she realized, and felt a giddiness like a child.

Hurrying to the kitchen, she found fresh ground coffee and orange juice in the fridge. Blessing her friends, she started a pot of drip coffee and poured two glasses of juice. She thought of adding champagne for mimosas, but decided against it. Neither she nor David was a heavy drinker, and she'd had so much champagne the night before.

Carrying her coffee into the living room, she stood at the breadth of windows and looked out at the brilliance of a morning sky over the ocean. To think she could wake up to this every morning! Suddenly, she spotted a large truck pulling into the driveway bearing the name of the equipment rental company. Behind it was another truck, this one the caterer. She returned to the bedroom to find David drying his hair with a towel.

"Good morning, wife!"

"Good morning, husband," she exclaimed. "There's coffee in the kitchen. And orange juice." She gave him a quick kiss but escaped from his grasp. She went to her closet and began stepping into white shorts.

"What's your hurry?"

"The caterers are pulling in."

He leaned over to peer out the window. "So they are."

Cara slipped a shirt over her head, stepped into her sandals, and went out into the hall, raking her hair with her fingertips. She opened the door to the crew. They filed in and David stepped out of the bedroom, freshly shaven and dressed. He took over directing them.

"Honey, I'm going to run over to the beach house and grab a few things."

"Don't be long," he said. He reeled her in for a quick kiss and said sotto voce, "We're on our honeymoon."

The sky was crystalline, and she felt the freshness in the morning air that she'd missed during the beastly days of July and August. It was a quick walk across Ocean Boulevard to the beach house. Seeing it with new eyes, she recognized that regardless of how precious it was, the house was small. David would be happier in their new home. But she wouldn't have sold the beach house. She never could, never would. This sweet cottage was the heart of her mother's legacy. It carried in its walls the memories of the past, and with them, lessons for the future for all who lived here.

She climbed up the deck steps, catching the scent of the roses as she approached the door. Opening it a crack, she called out, "Hello?"

There was no response, save for the immediate chirping of her canary.

"Hello, sweet boy," she called to Moutarde on the porch. She spent a few minutes changing his seed and water, talking to him as she did so.

"Wait till you see your new house," she told the bird. "You are going to love it. So much sunshine I might have to get you a friend."

Feathers floated to the floor as Moutarde jumped from perch to perch, chirping. The canary was in the final days of his molt. He looked silly with his tail feathers missing. She'd have to find the perfect spot for him in the new house.

She walked toward her bedroom and stopped short. In the air, she caught the scent of jasmine. Her mother's perfume.

Cara sucked in her breath. It had been years since she'd felt her mother's presence. Not since that night two years ago, when she'd reconciled with Palmer. Her mother had never returned, though Cara had waited. Hoped. She thought perhaps her mother rested easy now, and had at last gone to the other side, knowing her children were at peace.

But now . . . She inhaled again. The scent was unmistakable. It was her mother's perfume.

She stepped into the bedroom doorway and peered in. Hearing a noise, she turned, then put her hand to her throat. From the dim light of the bathroom she saw a figure approach—a woman, small and delicate. As Cara stared, she saw the woman stop.

Suddenly the lights went on. Cara saw Linnea standing, frozen, her arm outstretched and her hand over the light switch.

"Oh, my God, you scared me!" Linnea exclaimed, bringing her hands to cover her mouth.

"Linnea!" Cara put her hand to her heart and began laughing. "I called out. . . ."

"I was in the shower. I didn't hear you."

"You gave *me* a scare too."

Linnea giggled. "Let me guess. You thought I was Lovie. . . ."

Cara shrugged, her cheeks coloring. "In my defense, the scent of jasmine was overpowering."

Linnea came forward to kiss Cara's cheek. "I hope you don't mind my staying here last night. You told me I could, anytime . . . I wanted to give my parents some space. Plus"—she looked around—"I love it here."

"You're always welcome."

"What a night!" Linnea said. "A surprise wedding. I can't believe my parents pulled it off. There were so many times I thought for sure you'd guess. It may have been the best wedding I've ever been to. I suppose it's the first of many coming up."

"Are you in the running?"

"Me?" Linnea shook her head. "No. Not yet. Besides," she said smugly, "I love my job." She shrugged impishly. "Who knows? I may never get married."

"Stranger things have happened. Look at me. Married twice!" Cara made a face that sent Linnea giggling. "A piece of advice, my dear. Never say never."

"I won't." Linnea hoisted her towel. "I'd better get dressed. Gordon's coming by."

"Before you rush off," Cara said, "I should tell you. David and I have bought the new house."

Linnea's face lit up. "Daddy's house?"

"The very one. I mean, we have to, right? It's the site of our wedding. The scene of the crime."

Linnea lurched forward to hug her in a girlish squeeze. "I'm so happy for you. It's perfect! I'm glad we're keeping the house in the family." She stepped back, grabbing hold of her towel as it loosened.

"Speaking of keeping houses in the family . . ." Cara began. "I'm keeping the beach house. I want to rent it. You wouldn't know of anyone who'd be interested? I think we can arrange for a very reasonable rent."

Linnea's face went still. "You're not serious. You mean . . . I can rent it?"

"I understand you're gainfully employed now?"

Linnea squealed like a little girl, jumping up and down, saying, "Yes, yes, yes!"

Cara had to laugh. "Get dressed before that towel falls off again," she chided Linnea. "I'm going to grab a few things from the kitchen and duck out. My husband is waiting for me." She turned, and then said, "I couldn't be happier you want to live here. It's perfect."

Linnea placed another kiss on her cheek. "I love you, Aunt Cara."

"I know, sweet girl."

Cara filled a bag with eggs, cheese, and bread, then quickly exited before Gordon arrived. As she crossed Ocean Boulevard, she was filled with a sense of satisfaction at seeing all the pieces of a puzzle fall neatly into place. She walked up the drive of what was now her new home. David was right, it was so convenient. She imagined in the years to come family running from one house to the other, an open-door policy.

She looked with a sense of ownership at the imposing house as she approached. It would be, she hoped, the last house she'd move into. She wanted to settle down. To watch her daughter grow up in this house. To mark the doorframe with notches of her height. Maybe they'd get a dog. Or two. A swing set.

She climbed the flight of stairs to the front porch, then turned to look out at Ocean Boulevard. From this vantage point, she could see Emmi's house, the beach path that led along Russell's property, the dune where her mother and Russell's love story began. So many memories, so much history. She let her gaze settle on Primrose Cottage. It was partially obscured by the waving golden sea oats at full height. The glass sparkled in the sunlight and the riot of red roses over the pergola contrasted sharply with the blue sky.

She spotted Gordon and Linnea stepping out on the back porch. Linnea was wearing one of Lovie's vintage dresses, a lovely creamy shirt-waist dress with floral embroidery and a red patent belt that showed off her tiny waist. It had been one of her mother's favorites. The resemblance to her mother was uncanny, Cara thought, and laughed at her folly in thinking—once again—that Linnea was her mother's ghost. In fact, she realized, Linnea was her mother's clone: bright, eager, graceful, creative, interested in turtles, and most of all, she had a good heart. Cara wasn't worried about her niece's future. Linnea would find her way. It was the right thing to do to offer her the beach house to live in. There were few times in one's life when things dovetailed. One could almost hear the click of all the pieces coming together. This was one of those moments.

And Gordon . . . There was something about him that had tugged at her memory from the first time she'd met him. She couldn't put her finger on it—she was certain she'd never met him before. But there was something so familiar. . . . And now, seeing him at the beach house, walking hand in hand with Linnea, suddenly she saw it clearly.

Russell Bennett. Not so much in his features or his coloring—Russell Bennett had been blond; Gordon Carr was a redhead. But the similarities were there in his lean, taut build, his thoughtful eyes, the high cheekbones, the shape of his head. And the quiet elegance of manner. She had looked at Russell Bennett's photograph so many times in the past, wondering about the man who was the great love of her mother's life. Trying to imagine how her mother had endured all those lonely years, keeping her secret with nothing but his memory to hold close. Could a love like that ever die? And how ironic that Gordon researched marine animals, just as Russell Bennett had. The only thing Gordon didn't do was fly a plane. Thank heavens.

"Mama, you old matchmaker," she said aloud. "You must have had a hand in this."

She stood on the porch a moment longer, watching the two lovers talk in a casual, comfortable manner. No ghosts, she knew. Just Linnea and Gordon, two young people with their lives ahead of them. But she couldn't deny, there was something about seeing the two of them together. She couldn't help but wonder about kismet and second chances.

Cara reached into her pocket and pulled out the key that David had given her. It sat in her palm, a plain silver key, but one that held so much promise. She stared at it a moment.

"Mama? What do you think?" she whispered, feeling her mother's spirit. No vision, no perfume, just a subtle knowing. "This house is pretty special too. Isn't it? Plus, the fact that Palmer built it . . . You must be having the last laugh now. You called me home all those years ago and I came running. And here I still am. My feet are firmly entrenched in lowcountry sand." She shook her head in disbelief. "Me. Caretta. The lone swimmer. The daughter who never wanted to get married. Who wanted a career. Who ran as far from Charleston as she could. Here I am," she said again, this time feeling the words deeply. "Married again. A wife. A mother. A sister. A friend." She paused. "A daughter," she added, feeling her love for her mother pulse. "Always your daughter."

A breeze floated by, carrying the sweet lemony scent of the yellow primroses for which the beach house was named.

"Well, Mama, you got your wish. I daresay, your family is doing pretty well. I think you'd be proud. There's a whole new generation coming up."

Cara thought how the torch had been passed. She was no longer the young woman seeking her path. She felt sure-footed. Now it was *her* turn to aid and assist the young ones coming up. To give a nudge when they needed it, a helping hand. Sweet tea and sugar cookies.

"My Lord, Mama," Cara exclaimed with a sudden realization. "That makes *me* the matriarch!"

She shook her head, amused.

Another summer was over. Another generation of sea turtles had emerged and were swimming in the sea. A new season was just beginning. And so it all began again in the circle of life.

Cara wondered if it was her advancing years that made her more sensitive to the passing of time. She chuckled. Time certainly seemed to be passing more quickly.

She closed her eyes and listened to the sounds of the island settle around her. Overhead she heard first the raucous laughter of the gulls, and from farther off, the unmistakable, piercing cry of the osprey. She smelled the sweet scent of wildflowers returning to the island in the fall after the scorching heat of the summer dispersed. And as always, the ocean. That great, unpredictable, beloved, living body, rolling in and out like a metronome.

Opening her eyes, Cara looked again at the key in her palm. Taking a breath, she stepped forward to place the key into the lock. She heard the click, turned the handle, and opened the door. Cara Rutledge-Wyatt entered her new home. Her new world.

Acknowledgments

A BOOK DOES not write itself. I'm inspired as a writer by my experiences, by the people I meet, and by those dear to me who help me persevere through the journey of a novel. In this brief section I have the opportunity to thank those very special people, in but a few words, for the enormity of what I feel.

In *On Ocean Boulevard* I return again to my beloved sea turtles. This has been an extraordinary year for nesting sea turtles along the southeastern shore. Record numbers of nests were laid in all the states. We celebrate this year's success, which I attribute to the dedication and efforts of all the turtle teams who monitor the nests on the beach; the dedication of the members of the Department of Natural Resources and the US Fish and Wildlife Service who guide the teams; and the sea turtle hospitals that rescue, rehabilitate, and release the precious adult sea turtles. All of us working together are contributing to the trend of increasing turtle nests. I humbly thank you all for what you do. Yet we are witnessing the effects of climate change on the nesting cycle, as well as on the heat-determined sex of the turtles. This new development prompted me to write once again on this species.

On a personal level, I have those near and dear to me I want to thank.

Heartfelt thanks to Sally Murphy, DNR sea turtle coordinator, retired. Mentor and friend for twenty years and counting, thank you for reading my manuscript and confirming that all details were accurate.

You're great with grammar too! Sincere thanks to Kelly Thorvalson, conservation programs manager at the South Carolina Aquarium, for twenty years of inspiration with the sea turtles, and this year, for the recycled mesh plastic bags. To Kevin Mills, president/CEO of the South Carolina Aquarium, thank you for your leadership, your vision, and your friendship. Finally, thanks to Michelle Pate and the team at the South Carolina Department of Natural Resources Sea Turtle Conservation Program.

In this novel I raise the question of how individuals can help make a difference in the seemingly overwhelming problem of plastic pollution. I want to thank Goffinet McLaren and the Chirping Bird Society for their support and for spreading the word about the devastating effects of plastic.

I don't have the words to thank my dear friend Barbara Neimer Bergwerf for her endless support for my work, both with sea turtles and in life. Photographer of my children's picture book, *Turtle Summer*, Barb is also the photographer for most of the sea turtle/Isle of Palms photographs you see on my post! Thanks, Barb, for all that, and for coming up with the title of this book, *On Ocean Boulevard*.

I am blessed to be a member of a sea turtle team made up of women I count as my dearest friends. I love y'all: Mary Pringle, Barbara Bergwerf, Tee Johannes, Bev Ballow, Barb Gobien, Cindy Moore, Jo Durham, and Christal Cothran.

In my publishing world, I'm also fortunate indeed to have so many wonderful, talented people on my team.

My editor, Lauren McKenna, has worked with me for eight books, four of which are in my Beach House series. We get excited as we brainstorm and edit each book in a series we love so much. Thank you, Lauren, for your superb creative editing and storytelling. It's been a meaningful journey. I'll always treasure this book, especially for our time working together at Windover.

This year I celebrate the tenth anniversary at Gallery Books. In the past decade we've built a body of work I'm proud of, and I am truly grateful for your enthusiasm, support, and affection. The Beach House series is an especially important series to us all, and I'm profoundly grateful for your continuing faith in me and in the power of story to effect change. Thank you, Jennifer Bergstrom, for being at the helm, as well as Aimee Bell, Jennifer Long, Eliza Hanson, Sally Marvin, Abby Zidle, Bianca Salvant, Anabel Jimenez, Lisa Litwack, and Maggie Loughran. A shout-out to the incomparable Joal Hetherington for understanding my books and making magic with copyediting. I especially want to single out Michelle Podberezniak for going above and beyond to help me at any hour of day or night with her calm, confident competence. A heartfelt thank-you to Rick Pascocello and the excitement he brings to the house. Finally, to John Karp and the entire S&S sales force, thank you sincerely for your faith in my words and for tirelessly bringing them out into the world.

Agents have the dual task of guiding a career while also holding a hand. I'm blessed to have an agent that excels at both. Thank you, Faye Bender, for your perspicacity, brilliance, and serenity. We travel this journey together.

I am forever grateful to my dear friend and manager, Kathie Bennett, founder of Magic Time Literary Publicity, for being a relentless champion of my body of work and for her staunch faith in the why of my writing. And big thanks to the fabulous team—Roy Bennett, Susan Zurenda, and Patricia Denkler—for your kind, ever-loving care.

I am so grateful to all the booksellers who hand sell my books. This year I'd like to say a special thank-you to Polly Buxton of Buxton Books; Aaron Howard of Barnes & Noble, Mt. Pleasant; Vickie Crafton at Litchfield Books; Debi Horton at M. Judson in Greenville; the girls at Pelican Books; and the Foxy Ladies (and Gary) at FoxTale Book Shoppe.

Locally on Isle of Palms, I love singling out my friends and family Christiana Harsch and Ravi Sher for making The Long Island Café my second home, and for your endless support. I'm proud of my close affiliation with Wild Dunes Resort and our efforts to bring great ideas and authors to our community while supporting literacy. Thank you especially to Anna Maginn and Samantha Martin and Amy Gay.

I have so many friends whom I treasure, but in this small space I want to thank those who stepped up to help with this particular book. First, I'm forever grateful to my pal Cindy Boyle for believing so strongly in The Beach House series, for being my muse, for encouraging me with relentless tweets. Thanks for always being my fearless cheerleader.

To my dearest tribe—my heart kindles with love for you for always being there with your words of advice, creative ideas, walks on the beach, cover and title ideas, a cup of coffee or a glass of wine, and that je ne sais quoi when I need it most—Patti Callahan Henry, Signe Pike, Cassandra King, Marjory Wentworth, Patti Morrison, Katherine Kaneb, Linda Plunkett, Mary Edna Fraser, Barbara Hagerty, Nathalie Dupree, and Wendy Ellis. And great love to my ARTists who never fail to support and encourage me. And to my family tribe who always calls me to check on how I'm doing: Marguerite, Ruth, Maureen, Nuola, and James. My heart is captured and held tight by my children and grandchildren, who are a continuing source of joy, pride, and support—Claire, John, Jack, Teddy, Delancey; Gretta, Patrick, Henry; Zack, Caitlin, Wesley, and Penelope.

A special thanks to Elin Hildebrand for the beautiful quote.

I'd like to bow my head in memory of missing members of our tribe: Dorothea Benton Frank—Dottie, and Anne Rivers Siddons. You live on in your books and in our hearts. You are missed.

No acknowledgments would be complete without stating my profound gratitude to my literary and PR assistant, Angela May. She is my right hand, my left brain. Thank you, darling friend, for your cheerful support, your insightful observations, and your creative talent.

I always end with the man who comes first in my life—Markus. You are the wind beneath my sails, my sun and my stars, my steady rock. Thank you with my whole heart.

Keep reading for a sneak peek of the next book in Mary Alice Monroe's
New York Times bestselling Beach House series

THE SUMMER OF
LOST AND FOUND

Coming May 2021 from Gallery Books!

Chapter One

Beware the Ides of March.
William Shakespeare, *Julius Caesar*

March 2020

HOW COULD THIS happen to her? Again?

Linnea Rutledge drove her vintage gold VW bug across the vast expanse of marshlands on the arching roadway known as the Connector. It was the main route from the mainland to the small island she called home. Below, the tide was low, revealing marsh grass that was just beginning to green at the bottom—one of the lowcountry's first signs of spring. When Linnea reached the apex of the roadway, she caught her first glimpse of the Atlantic Ocean. Today she didn't feel her usual euphoria. Rather, she felt numb.

She crossed onto Isle of Palms and drove the short distance seaward to Ocean Boulevard. Less than a mile more until she reached the quaint house she called home. Primrose Cottage was one of the few remaining 1930s houses on the island. It sat now dwarfed by the luxury mansions that dominated the boulevard.

Pulling into the gravel driveway, hearing the crunch of stone under tires, Linnea climbed from her car and walked swiftly to the front door, struggling with tumultuous thoughts of the injustices of fate. She didn't take in the first signs of wildflowers dotting the dunes or stop to enjoy the heady scent of honeysuckle along the fence. Linnea climbed the stairs with savage purpose, seeking safety. She pushed open the door, then closed it behind her and leaned against it, as one holding back a storm.

Closing her eyes, she panted, mouth open. She'd held herself together by sheer force of will while she gathered her personal photographs and belongings and carried them out in a cardboard box from her cubicle office at the South Carolina Aquarium. Her face muscles ached from hoisting a smile and bidding teary farewells to her fellows. It was a mass exodus of nonessential personnel. The aquarium was closing its doors to the public because of the pandemic.

She collected her breath and opened her eyes. Looking around the dimly lit house, Linnea felt the quiet familiarity embrace her. This was her aunt Cara's beach house, left to Cara by her mother, Linnea's beloved grandmother, Lovie. Linnea had grown up visiting here, becoming part of the group of women who loved the beach, sea turtles, and each other with an abiding devotion. This little beach house had been their sanctuary from whatever buffeted them outside the clapboard walls.

It was her house now, albeit by rental from Aunt Cara. She let her eyes glide across the creamy-white and ocean-blue walls of the small rooms, along the fireplace mantel where sat silver-framed photographs of the Rutledge family that went back generations in Charleston, across the shabby-chic white slipcovered furniture.

Linnea feared she wouldn't be able to stay here any longer. She dug through her purse and pulled her phone to her ear. Within moments, the familiar voice of Cara answered.

"Hello, Sweet-tea. You're home early today."

Linnea loved the nickname her aunt had called her since she was little. "I, uh . . . was let off early. Can you come over? I have to talk to you."

A pause. Then in a more cautious tone, "Of course. I have to get Hope gathered. She has a doctor's appointment. I'll be there in ten."

Linnea tucked her phone away and strode directly to her bedroom. Sunlight poured in across the pine floors and oriental rugs. Her gaze swept the view of the ocean beyond; seeing it, she felt an immediate connection. Bolstered, she unzipped her pencil skirt and laid it on the mahogany four-poster bed that dominated the small bedroom. A simple skirt and crisp blouse constituted her uniform at the South Carolina Aquarium where she worked as the conservation education director. It was a style adopted from Cara.

Linnea had been Cara's assistant at the aquarium. After Cara resigned, the position as education director was offered to her. It was her dream job. Linnea loved teaching and inspiring others, as she had been taught and inspired by the women in her life. Though Linnea emulated Cara's sleek dress at work, at home she changed into her favored vintage look.

She went to the bathroom and, with efficient movements, washed the makeup from her face, then unpinned her blond hair, letting it fall to her shoulders. Scratching her head vigorously, she tried to shake off the tension that had held her taut since the news. Feeling a bit better, she put on cuffed jeans and a worn pink sweater, finally stepping into blush Capezio ballet slippers, a favorite since she'd taken ballet lessons as a girl.

Feeling more comfortable, she went out onto the porch from her bedroom and took in the view of sea and sky. The power of the vista had a calming effect. Then, hearing the crunch of tires on the driveway, Linnea hurried down the deck stairs and rounded the house to the driveway to see Cara's car parked there.

"Thank you for coming!" Linnea called out.

Cara's long legs, encased in black jeans, slid out from the car. She offered a quick wave. "I can only stay a moment. I was on my way out for Hope's physical."

Linnea waited while Cara removed her precocious six-year-old from her car seat. Hope's dark hair was tied in two braids and she wore a blue-gingham smocked dress.

"You look like Dorothy in *The Wizard of Oz*," Linnea said, placing a kiss on Hope's cheek.

"Who's that?" asked Hope.

Linnea looked at Cara with mock indignity. "She doesn't know *The Wizard of Oz*?"

Cara lifted her shoulders. "She's only six. Those evil trees and monkeys . . . I think Baum had older children in mind."

"Oh, please. Let me read it to her. It's a classic." Linnea lowered to meet Hope's eyes. "You're not afraid of witches or scary trees, are you?"

Hope's eyes were round, but she shook her head. "No," she said with a hint of doubt.

Cara laughed. "If she wakes up in the middle of the night, it's on you."

"Oh, she won't," Linnea said, then turned to Hope. "It has a happy ending. Let's read it." Then looking back at Cara, she added, "Even if the Wicked Witch of the West tells me not to."

"Who's that?" asked Hope.

"Later," Linnea answered with a wink. Straightening, she asked Cara, "Want to go to the deck? I have wine? Coffee? Water?"

"Nothing. Thanks. I have to leave in a few minutes." As they began walking to the oceanside deck, Cara's dark eyes focused on Linnea. "So, tell me, what's up?"

Linnea gestured to the patio chairs under the pergola. They sat while Hope hurried through the porch doors into the house to the toy bin that was filled with Hope's playthings. Linnea pulled her hair back into her hands, then let it go with an exhale.

"The aquarium is closed until further notice. I'm furloughed."

Cara's face reflected her shock. "My God. But of course they had to. The coronavirus is shutting down everything. They can't allow people to gather. Still, it's sobering." Always practical, she asked, "How are you fixed financially?"

Linnea shook her head. "You know what my salary is. I'm in trouble."

"Savings?"

"None to speak of. Even with you helping with rent, I'm not sure how long I can keep afloat."

Cara waved her hand. "Forget the rent for now."

Linnea was awash with relief. "Seriously? Are you sure?"

"Don't be silly. These are hard times." She put her hands on Linnea's shoulders. "Back when I was in financial"—she lifted her shoulders and her lips in an ironic smile—"and emotional trouble, my mother welcomed me into this little house, knowing I'd find my way. And I did. And now, it is my turn to offer the same to you. This is what we Rutledge women do. We take care of each other. And other women as well. It's a tough world out there for women, as you've just experienced." She let her hands drop. "So, darling girl, no thanks necessary. This is your legacy. And the purpose of this dear house. With so many blessings, we pay it forward."

Linnea felt the responsibility of her aunt's mandate profoundly. This was a passing of the torch. There were no words, so she remained silent.

Cara said, "Frankly, I'm more worried about the aquarium. How long will they be able to survive with their doors closed? They still have all those animals to feed and house."

"They've kept on a skeleton crew. I know it was a hard decision for Kevin to furlough us."

"He had no choice. Bosses have to make the tough decisions and do what's best for the institution." She sighed then shook her head and said wryly, "Beware the Ides of March."

Linnea looked at her aunt sitting across from her. Always cool and practical, she had a long history in management. She'd left Chicago almost two decades ago to settle in the lowcountry, but even on the island, she maintained her city chic. In jeans and a crisp chambray shirt, she looked elegant. Her hair was cropped short again and framed her face in a style that flattered her cheekbones and dark eyes.

Cara had the dark Rutledge looks of her father, Stratton. Linnea, like her father—Cara's older brother, Palmer—had the softer, petite, blond genes from Grandmother Lovie. As always, Linnea was taken by the way her aunt casually waved her hand in the air as she spoke or raised her fingers to tuck a wayward lock of hair behind her ear. Linnea studied the subtle and refined gestures, wanting to emulate this woman she admired. Cara was not merely elegant or in possession of a razor-sharp intellect, she was generous. Family came first with her. Cara might look like her father, but in this, she was most like her mother, Lovie.

Cara glanced at her watch. "I really must go," she said, rising. "Don't worry, Sweet-tea. Keep the faith. We always pull through somehow, don't we?" She looked over toward the house. "Hope! Time to go, honey."

From inside they heard a wail: "I don't wanna go to the doctor."

Cara met Linnea's eye, smirked, and went to fetch her daughter. Linnea heard a brief complaint before Cara walked out of the house with her daughter's hand firmly in hers.

"Come for dinner Sunday?" Cara asked Linnea as they walked together down the gravel driveway to Cara's car. "I'm hoping David will be home."

"I thought he was back."

Cara's lips tightened as she shook her head. "Not yet. The coronavirus is hitting London hard and he's been trying to get out for days. Flights are packed and there's talk of shutting down the airports."

Linnea heard the worry in her voice. "If anyone can get home, David will." She smiled. "He's like a homing pigeon."

Cara met her eyes with a grateful smile. "He's pretty resourceful." Then she said in a more upbeat tone, "Shrimp and grits sound good?"

"I'll be—" Linnea broke off. Catching a movement from the second-floor window of the carriage house next door, she stopped short, gripping Cara's arm.

"What?"

"There's someone in the carriage house," Linnea said sotto voce.

Cara looked up to the window and broke into a wide grin as she waved. "That's John."

Linnea felt her throat grow dry. "John Peterson?"

Cara laughed and looked at her with amusement. "Of course, John Peterson."

Myriad emotions flooded Linnea. This shock threatened to break the dam of her emotions, already brimming over with worry over being laid off.

"What's *he* doing here?" she demanded, her cry sounding petulant to her own ears.

"He had a conference in the area and stopped to visit his mother. Emmi, of course, was over the moon. She dotes on that boy. While he was here, he got word one of his colleagues in San Francisco tested positive for coronavirus. So, rather than take a chance of infecting others, he put himself into quarantine in his old apartment. He's worried not only about his mother, but about Flo. In her eighties, she's vulnerable. I admire him for that decision."

Linnea's brain was stuck on the fact that John was back. Living next door. She hadn't seen him since their breakup a year earlier. She'd thought he was the love of her life. And then he wasn't.

"Why didn't Emmi tell me he was back?" she asked.

Cara's brows rose. "Why would she? You've made no secret of the fact that you don't want anything to do with John. He is her son. That put her in a tough position."

Linnea crossed her arms. "She could have at least given me fair warning." Her gaze shot up to Cara along with her temper. "Wait. *You* knew. Why didn't you tell me?"

She felt the tension flare and saw the spark of indignation in Cara's eyes, the slight lifting of the chin.

Cara waited to speak, considering her words. "I suppose I could have told you. And might have if I wasn't so preoccupied." She paused. "Excuse me if I'm worried about my husband. The fact is, I just didn't give John's being here much thought."

Linnea swallowed, awash with shame for her show of pique. "I'm sorry. I shouldn't have jumped at you like that. I'm all off-balance, thinking only of myself." She reached out to place a hand on Cara's arm encircling her daughter. "Is there anything I can do for you? Watch Hope for a while? Make you a casserole?"

Cara's shoulders lowered and she quickly shook her head. "Please, no casseroles!" She smiled. "You know what I really need?"

Linnea shook her head.

"A nanny."

Linnea's heart sank. "Oh?"

"I have to get the house ready for David's arrival and Hope is cranky. She hasn't been able to play with anyone since they've closed the school. Not even her cousin Rory. Heather is under lockdown with him and Leslie." She sighed dramatically. "Hope is clinging to me. Honestly, I could use a break to get something done. I'll pay you, of course. And"—she raised a brow—"don't you need a job?"

"I do. And of course I'll be your nanny."

Cara looked skyward. "Thank heaven. I'll take her to the doctor's for her checkup, then could you watch her for a few hours? I want to spread plastic in the hallway, spray things down, get everything ready."

"Just drop her off."

"Thanks. Better go." Cara looked meaningfully at the carriage house window. "Be nice," she said cajolingly, then leaned forward to kiss her.

"How long is John going to be here? Gordon is coming from England in April. I don't think I can bear the battle of the beaux."

Cara raised a brow. "I didn't think John was still in the beau category."

"He's not," Linnea said firmly. "At least not in my mind. But I haven't seen Gordon since he returned to England, what . . . Linnea did a quick count on her fingers. "Over six months ago. That's a long time to be apart. I don't want my ex hanging around when he finally gets here."

"You and Gordon are still together, right?"

Linnea nodded.

"Then it's only a problem if you still care about John."

Linnea felt a prick of uneasiness. "Right."

Cara looked at her watch. "Really must go. Thanks so much for being Hope's nanny. It's only temporary."

"I'm her aunt. 'Nuff said."

Cara smiled and climbed into the car.

Linnea waved, then stepped back from the Range Rover as it backed out of the driveway. Then, because she couldn't stop herself, she glanced up at the large arched window of the carriage house. In the light of midday, she saw John clearly. His dark auburn hair caught the light but his face was shadowed. In her mind's eye, she could see him smiling his crooked smile.

John lifted his hand in a wave.

Linnea reluctantly raised her hand and gave a halfhearted wiggle of her fingers. Then she turned heel, rolling her eyes, and walked resolutely to the rear deck. Once out of his sight she grabbed her phone and texted her friend Annabelle. She was on the staff of the sea turtle hospital and was also a victim of this morning's layoffs at the aquarium.

Can you come over? Must commiserate. I have wine.

She went indoors to pull out two wineglasses. As she set them on the counter, her phone pinged with a return text.

On my way.

LINNEA SETTLED BACK into the wicker chair, tucked her feet up, and crossed her arms. The large wood deck extended seaward from the house over the wild dunes of the Rutledge property. Most of the yards on Ocean Boulevard had been manicured with grass and plantings to resemble mainland lawns. Her grandmother had adamantly refused to alter the natural landscape so their property was a riotous collection of wild grasses, plants and flowers. Across the road, a large lot was held in conservation, allowing the sand dunes to roll on unimpeded to the beach. It was a rare view on the developed island.

Looking at the sea, Linnea realized how grateful she was for the friends in her life. She remembered what her Grandmother Lovie had told her: *In life you'll have many acquaintances. But consider yourself lucky to have one or two true friends.*

Linnea had always been popular in school. She'd had a dozen girls she'd called friends. But none of them had gone in the same direction she had after graduation. Some were married with children; some had moved elsewhere. Linnea had been part of the latter group. When she'd returned home from California last year, she found she had less in common with her old friends. It had been hard to realize how friendships shifted over the years. She'd made new friends—Pandora James and Annabelle Chalmers. No two women could be more different. They were like oil and water and didn't get along. Still, a tenuous, new friendship had developed.

Pandora was high style, gorgeous, fun, and flamboyant. She was in graduate school for engineering in England and, Covid permitting, planned to fly back to her grandmother's beach house on Sullivan's Island for the summer.

Annabelle was a local girl. She and Linnea had attended the same private high school in Charleston but had never been friends. Linnea was part of the South of Broad elite society of old Charleston. She and her friends had hung in the same circles since the nursery and seemed destined to continue throughout their lifetimes. In contrast, Anna was a scholarship student who lived with her mother in a poorer part of the city. She'd never blended in with the popular group at Porter-Gaud. Though she and Linnea had had a rocky start last summer, over the past year working together at the aquarium they'd experienced a tidal shift in their relationship. Annabelle's habitual resentment of Linnea's privilege had ebbed, and in turn, Linnea's ability to open up, as a true friend must do, began to flow.

Linnea heard the crunch of Annabelle's car pulling up in the driveway. She got up to go greet her but hesitated at the edge of the deck. She sighed with annoyance. She didn't want to get tangled up with John again. Once burned/twice shy and all that. Instead of walking out on the driveway where John could see her from his window, Linnea crossed her arms as she waited for her friend to arrive. *This could make for an annoying few weeks,* she thought. When was John to hightail it back to his beloved California?

"Just go," she muttered. Then lifted her frown to a smile as Annabelle's face appeared from around the corner.

"I come bearing wine!" Annabelle called out as she climbed the deck stairs, a bottle of red in one hand, a bottle of white in the other. Her long red hair hung straight past her shoulders and on her ears she wore large gold loop earrings. She was dressed, as usual, in jeans and a black T-shirt that read Save the Seabirds.

"Bless your heart!" Linnea called back, grinning. They walked together into the house in search of wineglasses and a corkscrew.

"Red or white?" Annabelle asked, corkscrew in hand.

"Today we're going to need both."

Annabelle chuckled in her low-throated fashion. "I hear you."

Linnea watched with awe as Annabelle twisted off the capsule around the neck of the bottle. She made it look so easy.

"How do you do that?" Linnea asked. "I'm pitiful trying to scrape that wrapper off."

"Comes with practice," Annabelle replied smugly. "Perks of being a bartender. Interesting fact: the original capsule was wax. Each bottle had to be dipped in wax to seal the end to prevent mold growth. The next innovation was lead. No surprise, that didn't work out, for obvious reasons, but it took them till the 1980s to switch to these polylam ones."

"So, if you collect old wines . . ." she said, thinking of her father.

"Yep. They still have those lead capsules."

"That explains a lot," Linnea said with a laugh. She gratefully took the offered glass of white wine. "I'm sorry, but I'm going to be tacky and add ice cubes. I can't drink warm chardonnay."

Annabelle shuddered. "I'll put this bottle in the fridge—and pour myself a Malbec." She worked on opening the new bottle as Linnea plopped ice cubes in her wineglass. "So, let me guess—you got laid off too?"

Linnea said with a groan, "*Again*. I can't believe I'm back here."

"At least we weren't fired."

"We're not getting paid. . . ."

Annabelle frowned while pouring out her wine. "Jeez, I hope it's not for too long."

"No one knows. That's the scariest part. It could be a while." Linnea brought her glass to her lips. "If the aquarium gets in trouble, people will have to be let go permanently."

Annabelle's finely arched brows narrowed deeper and she took a long sip of wine.

"Let's sit outside," Linnea suggested, hoping the fresh air would lift the sudden drop in mood.

Annabelle grabbed the bottle of wine and followed her. "How are you holding up?"

"Same as you, I expect."

Annabelle settled in the chair recently vacated by Cara. She crossed her long legs. "Not quite the same." Leaning back in her chair she tossed out, "I'm guessing your family will help you out."

Linnea paused to sip rather than rise to the bait, recognizing Annabelle's knee-jerk reaction to the wealth difference between their families. "They'll try, I'm sure," she replied in an even tone, then side-stepped. "Seriously, are you okay, money-wise?"

Annabelle's shoulders lowered as she stared into her glass. She exhaled loudly and shook her head. "No. I'm worried."

"I am too. I have zero savings."

"Savings?" Annabelle snorted. "What's that? I was barely making rent with my extra bartending job. Thank God for catering gigs. That's how I ate most weekends. It's so damn expensive living in the city—hell, even *near* the city—that there's no hope of putting money away. I don't know how I'm going to make next month's rent."

"I'm guessing you won't be bartending much, will you?"

"Nada. Zip. Restaurants are closed. No one is having events."

Linnea looked at her friend's face. Annabelle's normally serious expression had a deeper edge bordering on desperation.

"Can you move home?" she asked.

"Good God, no. My mother's remarried to this creep," she said with a hint of disgust. "Who knows how long this one will last?" She rolled her eyes. "I can't go there."

Linnea licked her lips as a thought played in her mind. Part of her balked at the idea. But the other part, the one that made her think of Aunt Cara as inspiration, won out. In a rush, the words came pouring out.

"I have an extra room here, and Cara is giving me a break on the rent until this virus thing blows over. Seems only right to pay it forward." She paused. "You can move in here with me if you want. You wouldn't have to pay rent. But we'd split utilities and food. That way we'd help each other out. What do you think?"

Annabelle's eyes went wide. "Are you serious?"

"Never more serious."

Annabelle put her glass down on the table, resting her hand there as though to steady herself. Relief flooded her face and she replied, "Yes."

Linnea smiled and felt that gush of joy born of one woman helping another. She lifted her glass. "Well, then . . . here's to being roommates."

Anabelle's face lit up. She lifted her glass, and they clinked in the air. "Roommates!"

Linnea sipped her chardonnay, then settled back in her chair. As she swirled the glass in her hand the ice cubes clinked, and she wondered if this was the best of ideas . . . or the worst.